MARISA JONES

# A Dangerous Land - A Novel

*A gripping story of love and belonging set in the wilds of World War Two New Guinea.*

*First published by Jonesing for Books 2023*



*Photo Credits:*

*Mountains: JAT Photography*

*WW2 Planes © Ivan Cholakov | Dreamstime.com Photo 43566141*

*Clouds: Photo by ARTHUR YAO on Unsplash*

*Couple: Arcangel Images*

*First edition*

*ISBN: 978-0-6458005-3-1*

*Editing by Jane Smith*
*Cover art by Nada Backovic*
*Cover art by Johannes Terra - JAT Photography - Cover photo*

*This book was professionally typeset on Reedsy.*
*Find out more at reedsy.com*

*For Richard,*

*thank you for sharing your home with me.*

# Contents

# Acknowledgement

Thank you to the Papuan and Niuginian people for allowing me to share in your land.

I

# Part One

*December 1941*

# 1

# Amelia

Amelia pulled the throttle, fingers tingling as the wheels of her Gipsy Moth took flight. The dials sputtered while the wind whipped her cheeks. It'd been nearly a year since she last flew, but it all came back in an instant. She peered over the side and smiled. Her flaming red aeroplane made a stark contrast to the verdant hills below, the untouched blanket of jungle that was screaming to be explored ... exploited. It was unique, this land — her home. She was lucky to be back. Not even the threat of war would keep her away from her beloved New Guinea.

She turned the plane west, and the gold-speckled beaches of Logui village coasted past, bare black bodies washing in the waves; she could almost hear their laughs, feel their infectious warmth. She waved wildly from the rear cockpit, a trail of pikininis chasing after her. She gazed ahead at the township of Salamaua – a narrow isthmus that joined the mainland to a peninsula of more rolling green hills – except, when she looked ahead again, the peninsula was closer than she had realised. Clenching the throttle, she pulled harder, trying to gain height, but it wasn't enough; the plane coursed towards the hills. It was too late to turn; the adjoining mountains were so close that she'd fly straight into them.

Amelia racked her brain for the various skills her father had taught her over the years. When the correct one finally came, muscle memory took over and she thrust the plane into the wind at full throttle. The nose shot up, the plane turning vertically towards the heavens, its tail brushing the treetops. The clouds swallowed her up, and the dials on the dashboard spiralled as she surged further into the white-out, the abyss mirroring her thoughts, until finally she pushed through into a pale-blue expanse. Levelling the plane off, she loosened her grip, and the blood rushed back to her knuckles, her breath releasing as she sucked in the cool air.

*I really need to be more careful, to not take so many risks.*

Sailing over the sea, her heart rate slowed; a breadth of ocean was laid out below – water like glass as the pillowy clouds reflected off its surface.

*Time for a few tricks!*

Her pulse shot up again as she looped the plane around, thrusting it into the wind, climbing higher and higher, before diving back down, stomach lurching with each curve. Rolling the plane onto its back, she laughed. Belly full of freedom. Blood rushed to her head in the brief moment she hung upside down, before twirling in a spiralling free-fall action, screaming as she fell, voice lost in the howling wind. When she'd had enough playing, she cruised along, gazing at the rising sun, the heat of the impending day warming her cheeks.

She looked ahead to Lae, where her father's company was based — the tiny town with the busiest aerodrome in the world. The mouth of the Markham River swelled as it released a rush of water into the Huon Gulf, the body of water gushing more than a hundred miles inland through the plains that opened up to the Markham Valley. She was tempted to fly up the valley, but she didn't have much time; the morning tea her mother was hosting would start in a few hours. She groaned and looped the plane back towards the direction she'd come from, that feeling of freedom already fading.

* * *

Amelia ran up the isthmus towards the house, the intoxicating smell of frangipani lingering in the air, and pushed through the front door. She keeled over to catch her breath, chest heaving, watching the houseboys scurrying about. Dressed in their finest lap-laps – stark white below their hardened bare chests – they busied themselves with polishing the silver, pressing linens, rolling pastry. All the things her mother, Ruth, had taught them when their family first arrived in the Mandated Territory in 1930.

Amelia detested these morning teas. They were never simple affairs. Even in the tropics, where a shipment of Twinings had to be flown in for the occasion. Tea was even more of an ordeal when her mother was hosting Administration wives — only ever the best for the likes of Lady McNicoll. Amelia entered the kitchen and stuck her finger in a pot of jam. She licked it and cried out in pleasure, reacquainted with the sweet taste of pineapple. She dipped her finger in again, the cook boys not daring to look.

"Get your dirty fingers out of there," her mother said as she walked into the kitchen.

Amelia wiped her hand on her trousers. "Just having a taste."

Her mother pressed her hand to her chest. "Good heavens, Amelia! What are you wearing?"

Amelia looked down – her standard dress of khaki trousers and a sleeveless white-button up blouse clearly a bad choice, especially compared to the brown swing dress with embroidered burnt-orange flowers her mother was wearing, complemented by a short-brimmed felt hat that was pinned perfectly against her mother's sleek waves. She shrugged and said, "Sorry. I got back from ..." but stopped short, knowing it wasn't wise to mention flying. Luckily her mother was too busy harassing the staff to notice.

"Ephraim," she said, addressing one of the cooks.

He stepped forward, gazing at the ground. "Yes, missus?"

"I thought I said to use the asparagus in the quiche?"

"Nogat asparagus, missus," he replied. "Balus i no kam."

Her mother pursed her lips. "That's unlikely seeing as we own the aeroplane it arrives on." Her eyebrows darted upwards while Ephraim glanced at the other cooks, before looking to the ground. Clearly unhappy with his response, Amelia's mother picked up the quiche and tipped it onto Ephraim's head. Bits of congealed egg and runny tomato dripped down his bare chest. He flinched but didn't speak. "Now clean up this mess and prepare a new quiche. This time with asparagus."

"Yes, missus." He stepped back in line with the other cooks, all eyes on the ground.

Amelia's mouth fell open, and her mother turned to her and said, "Are you trying to catch flies?" Amelia snapped it shut, wanting to reprimand her mother but not sure how. "Why are you still standing there? Surely you must understand the need to change?"

"Mum, you know I'm much more comfortable in trousers—"

Her mother waved her away. "Nonsense. Just because you're back in the tropics doesn't mean you can let your standards drop."

"I wear trousers in Sydney, Mum."

"Well, you shouldn't! We're not paying for you to attend nursing school so you can sully yourself in menswear. Imagine what Lady McNicoll would say. Now hurry, the women will be here any minute."

Amelia retreated to her bedroom and reluctantly changed into a green polka-dotted collared shirt dress, fidgeting with the buttons so her décolletage wasn't exposed. She smoothed back her hair, conscious her fringe was sticky with sweat, but since she didn't have time to wash it and didn't think it'd make much of a difference anyway, she let it sit awkwardly halfway across her forehead instead. She was never going to be as beautiful as her sisters. The eldest, Evelyn, had inherited their mother's dark brown hair and pale complexion, while Sofia, the youngest, was lucky enough to be blessed with their father's Scottish heritage, with blonde curls and rosy cheeks. Amelia was an odd mix of both, with wispy, short dark hair and a freckled face.

She returned to the back verandah, where her mother was inspecting the tables and examining the linens to ensure there wasn't a wrinkle in sight. Ruth fiddled with the floral arrangements – vases filled with the brightest shades of pink, orange and red, fresh-picked zinnias and marigolds that flourished in their front garden – confirming each flower was perfectly placed, and that each arrangement sat twelve inches apart, using a ruler to measure. She lifted the stemware against the bright morning light that shone from the bay, ensuring each glass was smudge free, and examined each spoon, looking for her reflection in the gleaming silver piece.

Amelia yawned.

"Let me take a look at you," her mother said as she turned to face Amelia, lips pursed as she eyed her up and down. "Hmm. Not as nice as Sofia would've managed, but it'll do." Amelia's shoulders drooped as her mother continued, "Now, you will help me serve the tea."

"What about Evelyn and Sofia?" Amelia replied. *At least they look the part.*

Her mother moved along each place setting. "Evelyn's at the hospital ... working, and Sofia is unwell after the trip."

"Of course she is," Amelia muttered under her breath. Her little sister always got away with everything.

"Now you must ensure you follow me carefully as we pour. The women must be served in a strict order, starting, of course, with Lady McNicoll."

"What about Alice or Gladys?" *Your actual friends?*

"*Mrs* Middleton, and *Mrs* Jacobsen, as you should refer to them, will be served last. They are planters' wives, well below the Administration women."

Amelia pursed her lips. "And what about you, Mum? What order would you be served in?"

"Well, as the wife of the man who owns one of the biggest airlines in New Guinea, I'd come after Lady McNicoll, of course." Her mother picked a piece of lint off her dress. "But that is of little consequence to you, dear, as we will be doing the serving."

"Shouldn't Silas do the serving?" Amelia asked, wondering where her favourite member of the staff was.

"Absolutely not. He's bound to muck it up." Her mother fiddled with the cutlery. "Speaking of that halfwit, can you please find him and make sure he's looking after the tea, as I instructed him this morning."

Amelia ground her teeth. "Yes, ma'am."

"And Amelia ... look out for Tiger Lil. You know what she's like, bound to turn up uninvited."

"I thought all the women were invited?"

"Please ... not *that* piece of work!"

* * *

"Silas!" Amelia yelled when she saw him tending to the orchids in the front garden.

He looked up and smiled, eyes crinkling into narrow slits. "Melia!"

She raced across the lawn – the strappy sandals her mother had forced her to wear sinking into the sandy grass – and opened her arms to hug him, but he stepped back, extending his hand instead. He shook hers vigorously and beamed.

"Mi lukim yu," he said, asking to look at her. He was dressed in a white lap-lap like the other houseboys, even though he was considered the boss boy.

"Silas, yu orait?" Amelia asked how he was in Tok Pidgin, even though she knew her mother would be horrified to hear her speak the local language. She didn't care; Silas had helped look after her and her sisters when they were little, and they were comfortable speaking his language together.

"Mi orait, missus Melia." He was still smiling as he switched to English, something he had learned from the girls over the years. "But missus Ruth cut the orchids for the party."

Amelia looked over his shoulder, smiling at the branches of bright purple flowers that were hanging behind him. Their front garden at Salamaua was a thing to behold, a colourful collection of fragrant frangipanis and bright pink bougainvilleas, with hibiscus, zinnias, marigolds and gerberas adding pops of colour, while delicate orchids clung to tree trunks. It was Silas's greatest joy, even though Amelia's mother took all the credit.

"Not to worry, Silas. They'll grow back." Amelia turned towards the house and noticed Tiger Lil walking up the main street as if she was dressed for a royal garden party, with a wide-brimmed sun hat and white lace dress. She loved how free-spirited the woman was, but remembered her mother's words and quickly gestured for Silas to follow her inside. "Now, I believe Mum thinks you are attending to the tea?"

"Aiyo!" He stopped, eyes bulging. "I forgot."

"Not to worry. I'll help you."

They hurried to prepare the tea, the floral aroma of Darjeeling wafting through the steamy air. Silas set out the silver teapots and gave them a final polish as her mother walked into the kitchen.

"There you are," she said, eyeing the teapots. "All set? The ladies have arrived."

"Yes, missus," Silas replied with his head down.

"Good." Her mother turned towards Amelia. "Shall we?"

Amelia took the tray from Silas and whispered, "Tenk yu," on her mother's behalf, before following her out.

"Now, remember the order, starting with Lady McNicoll," her mother said, face already stitched with a tight smile, but Amelia saw it falter when she discovered who was sitting at the head of the table. Tiger Lil.

"Lilian!" her mother said. "How ... how are you?"

Tiger Lil offered a wicked smile. "Positively parched." She leaned back in her chair and eyed her cup. "Surely we don't have to wait all day?"

Ruth twitched, while Amelia did her best to stifle a laugh. Her mother would never confront Tiger Lil publicly; that would go against her rules of decorum. She glowered instead as she poured Tiger Lil a cup, before stitching her smile back on as she shifted towards Lady McNicoll. "Hildur, you remember my daughter Amelia, don't you?"

"Why, of course," Lady McNicoll replied, her Norwegian accent barely noticeable. "Amelia, dear, how do you do?"

Amelia forced a smile. "Very well, Lady McNicoll. I returned from Sydney last night."

"Heavens!" Lady McNicoll pressed a hand to her chest. "You're doing well to be joining us after such an arduous journey."

Amelia shrugged. "Oh, it's nothing. We get used to the travel, as you know."

"How could I forget? I've travelled from Rabaul to Sydney several times over the years, and now from Salamaua ... though with everything happening in Europe, I really thought I'd be south by now. I'm surprised you came back."

Amelia glanced at her mother. She'd wanted Amelia to remain in Sydney to finish her nursing exams, but Amelia's father – and Amelia, for that matter – wouldn't hear of it. "Well, Lae ... Salamaua ... they're my home."

Lady McNicoll eyed her curiously. "That's very admirable of you, dear. I wish my boys could return home. They're all serving at the moment—"

"Such bravery," her mother interjected. "To leave their wives and children like that."

"Well, only the older two," Lady McNicoll replied. "The younger ones aren't married."

Her mother's lips crept up. "Well, perhaps when they return? There are many young women in need of husbands." She glanced at Amelia, who stiffened.

Lady McNicoll offered a hesitant smile, before saying, "Could I get a spot of tea, dear?"

"Of course, ma'am," Amelia replied. Her hands shook as she poured Lady McNicoll's tea, and a small amount splashed into the saucer. Her mother sucked air through her teeth, and she gestured for Amelia to move down the line as they served more than twenty ladies. They started with the wives of the district officers, before moving along to the assistant district officers' wives and finally the few planters' wives who'd travelled to Salamaua for the occasion. Amelia's smile never wavered, even though her cheeks were aching.

Once they had moved through the line of women again, ensuring everyone was adequately refreshed, Amelia took her seat and gulped down her tea, which had turned cold. Her foot was tapping idly on the kwila floors as she listened to her mother discuss her upcoming debut with Lady McNicoll, when her father walked in. A couple of men were hovering behind him, but Amelia couldn't make out who they were behind her father's large frame. He was trying to get her mother's attention, but she was deep in conversation with Lady McNicoll. Her father wasn't one to be kept waiting, nor to be quiet, and he cleared his throat so loudly the ladies couldn't help but look up.

"Lasses," he said, his Scottish accent still thick even after fifteen years in New Guinea. "Terribly sorry to interrupt. I forgot you were meeting today. I'm leaving for Lae and wanted to say goodbye to my wife."

Her mother smiled at the table of women, before rising to greet her husband. "George, darling. How nice of you to join us. And you brought company ..."

Her father stepped back so the men were now visible. Amelia tensed, her pulse quickening when she realised who it was. *Daniel.* She fidgeted with her hair, hoping her fringe wasn't sticking to her forehead. *If only I looked more like Sofia.*

It'd been nearly a year since she'd seen him, since she returned to Sydney last January. He looked different. Taller, more built, lean muscles creeping out from under his short-sleeve shirt. He'd officially grown into a man, no longer that gangly boy she once knew. Amelia sipped her tea, letting the cup linger at her lips as she tried to hide her smile. It was only Daniel. The boy she grew up with. She glanced at her parents, who were having a private conversation – her mother's face still wearing a tight smile – and glanced back at Daniel, who was staring at her, face lit up and both of his dimples showing. He gestured a small hello with his hand.

The skin on the back of Amelia's neck tingled, and before she knew it, she was walking towards him – but she tripped on her own feet along the way and tumbled to the ground.

Daniel bent down to help her. "Meels," he said, dimples pressing further into his cheeks.

She could feel herself blush but returned his gaze anyway. "Hello, Daniel." She wanted to embrace him – give him a peck, feel his skin against hers – but knew she'd better not. Not with all these women watching.

"Meely, lass," her father said as Daniel pulled her up, Amelia's hand tingling as he let go. Her father kissed her on the head, and Amelia blinked; she'd forgotten her parents were even there. She returned her father's affection with a hug. "Enjoying the party?" he added.

"Of course," Amelia replied, trying to hide the truth from her voice.

"Do you have everything you need now, George?" her mother asked, lip curling upwards at the sight of Daniel.

Her father chuckled. "Aye. We'll get out of your hair but shall see you at the Cecil tonight? I'll be there with the lads."

"Good heavens, George," her mother replied as she raised her hand to her chest. "You know I won't be able to make it back to Lae tonight."

"I'll be there!" Amelia interjected, glancing at Daniel.

"Course you will!" Her father pulled her into another embrace. "The Moth is waiting for you in the hangar. Do you need a refresher before you fly?"

"Don't be silly, Dad. You know I'm better at flying than any of these lads here." A chill ran down her spine as she remembered what had nearly happened that morning, but her mother quickly squashed the feeling by resting her hand on Amelia's arm and saying, "You know how I feel about you flying, dear."

"It's only the Moth, Mum. I've been flying it since I was twelve."

Her mother squeezed her arm. "I thought you would've grown out of those childish antics by now."

Amelia sucked in air.

"It's only to Lae," her father said.

Amelia's mother tensed. "Surely it's time she gave it up. She's going to be debuted in a few months; we can't have her flying."

Her father pressed a hand to her mother's shoulder. "Let her have her fun while she still can." He kissed Amelia on the cheek and left.

Amelia caught Daniel's eye as he walked past, wondering if he'd be there tonight. It'd be nice to catch up with him away from her mother's prying eyes.

* * *

Later that day, the stifling heat seared Amelia's skin, the surrounding shoreline offering little respite, not even a breath of breeze on the cloudless December afternoon. Rainy season was officially over, Lae's air steamy with stillness. Amelia fanned herself as tiny beads of sweat dripped down her spine. Nearly twelve years living in the tropics – since she was eight – and she still wasn't used to the weather. But the discomfort was a small sacrifice to be in the place she called home, the only real home she'd known.

Cold bubbles cascaded down her throat as she sipped her G & T. She glanced at the entrance again.

"I dare say ..." her father continued, "if America doesn't join soon, the Allies will be done for."

Amelia looked around the table, trying to guess which one of her father's underlings would respond first.

"The Yanks won't want to get involved in Europe's mess," Tom Carmichael replied. *Tom. Of course. Always trying to be heard.* He relaxed back into the wicker chair and in a matter-of-fact sort of way, said, "It's not like Hitler will make his way across the Atlantic anyway."

"I thought you of all people would be over there, Tom," Amelia interjected as she stared across at him, "... helping out with the *mess*."

Tom coughed and looked away. "You know I'd be there in a heartbeat if I could, Meels, but someone has to look after my father's business now he's gone."

Her father slapped Tom on the back. "Good on you, lad." Amelia took another sip of gin, watching their exchange over the rim of her glass. Her father had always had a soft spot for Tom. He was his best mate's son, after all. "Your old man would be proud," her father added.

Tom sat a little taller in his chair. "I don't think we have anything to worry about. Who cares about a tiny island in the middle of the Pacific?"

Her father took a large drink of his beer. "Well, they never thought Hitler would take the Soviets, and now he's nearly to Moscow ..."

Amelia glanced at the door, wondering if Daniel was still coming. It'd be dark soon – the afternoons quickly turned to dusk in the tropics, making for impossible landing conditions.

"But surely we're safe here in New Guinea," Tom said.

Her father scoffed. "Who knows for how much longer? The last of the German missionaries have sailed ... don't you think that's a sign? I swear one of them hailed Hitler as the ship took off, the dirty bastard."

"Hitler will never make it this far," Tom replied.

"Christ, lad!" George slammed his beer on the table. Amelia tensed, hating how easily her father was set off. "I'm not talking about Hitler," he continued. "Look at the Japanese, how aggressive they're getting. This is war! Anything could happen."

The room went silent, no one daring to challenge her father.

"Excuse me," Amelia said, and the men rose as she walked away to the bar.

"Don't know why she doesn't call for one of the Kanakas," her father said. He hissed at one of the locals to come.

She bit the inside of her cheek. *Because I'm perfectly capable of ordering a drink myself.* She placed her hands on the bar – the rosewood smooth against her delicate skin – and smiled at the bartender, who hurried over.

"Yu laikim wanpela moa, gin?" he asked without meeting her eye.

Amelia shook her head. If she had any more gin, she'd be on the floor of the Hotel Cecil. Not a good look for a lady of her standing. "A glass of water ... plis."

She leaned against the bar and pressed the glass to her cheek, the cold condensation cooling her skin as she admired the work "Ma", the hotel proprietor, had put into Lae's only establishment – its plantation shutters and wrap-around verandah, with views out to the surrounding Huon Gulf and across to Salamaua. She walked outside to the verandah, fingers tapping on the rail as she peered across the tall grass that surrounded the hotel to the bay. Salamaua sat idly in the distance, lights twinkling on the horizon as the sky faded into amber rays of dusk. The aerodrome was towards the right, but it was too dark to tell if his plane had landed.

Had she missed his arrival? She'd been distracted by her father and the talk of war on New Guinea's doorstep. She would've heard the Junker coming in, the propellers whirring as they descended into Lae. But with the number of planes landing every hour – Lae being one of the busiest aerodromes in the world, with more air traffic than all of Australia – she could've easily missed it. Daniel had been flying a few years, her father having given him a job after his father died. Amelia had wanted to become a pilot herself after she'd met world circumnavigator Amelia Earhart a few years earlier – right here in the last place Earhart had been seen before her plane went missing over the Pacific – but her mother had insisted she go to nursing school instead, like Evelyn. Nursing was a much more practical pursuit for young ladies.

She sighed, and was wondering if women would ever be able to do what they wished, when she heard yelling in the distance. It sounded as if a fight had broken out amongst the locals, random bits of Pidgin flying through the air.

"No Kanakas!"

"Mi no wanpela Kanaka. Mi Scotsman."

*Daniel?* She looked towards the entrance of the hotel and caught a glimpse of him. He was being dragged away by two locals, his white-collared shirt torn.

"No ken holim mi!" Daniel yelled. "Get your hands off me!"

"Tom, I need your help," Amelia called out. "Daniel is being accosted by the staff."

Tom waved her away. "Not now, Meels. I'm in the middle of a conversation."

Amelia jerked her head back. "Don't be daft! He's your brother and needs your help."

"Half ..." Tom loosened his tie. "And of course he needs my help, but I'm otherwise engaged."

Amelia wanted to scream, to shake Tom for his indifference, for his ill-treatment of his younger brother. But there was no point. As a lady, she must keep her cool. She ran towards the entrance, arriving as the two locals were throwing Daniel onto the dirt road.

"Wantok!" Amelia said to the local man, who was kicking Daniel in his side.

"Missus ..." he replied, looking down.

"Don't 'Missus' me," Amelia spat back at the shirtless man, who stank of sweat and bully beef. "I saw what you did to him."

Daniel held onto his side as he pushed himself up. "Don't worry about it, Meels. I'll go."

"Absolutely not! You have as much right to be here as I do."

He shifted on his feet and dusted the dirt off his trousers. "Maybe. But I don't feel like arguing with these two about it."

Amelia pressed a hand on her hip and glared at the men. "You won't have to, because my wantoks here know it was all a misunderstanding …"

The men scratched their beards. "Missus … wanpela Kanaka tambu."

"I understand that *locals* are not permitted within the hotel, but my friend here is a Scotsman."

The men wrinkled their brows. "Nogat waitskin."

Amelia huffed. "Mi save nogat waitskin … wanpela New Guinea mama, Scottish papa." The men looked at each other but didn't speak. "So let him in!"

"Meels, forget about it—"

"Let the boy in," her father's voice interrupted. He was standing at the top of the steps to the entrance, his tall, burly figure overshadowing them. The men stared up at him with bulging eyes. Amelia wondered how long he'd been there. "Yu no ken harim?" he added. "Let him in!"

"Yes, masta," the men said in unison and hurried to usher Daniel inside.

Daniel dragged his feet up the stairs and muttered "Thank you, sir," as he walked past. Amelia followed, catching her father's indecipherable eye as she went.

* * *

Daniel stood at the bar and took a long sip of beer, beads of condensation dripping down as he stared over the edge of his bottle. When he finally put it down, he was silent, gaze focused on the twilight sky.

Amelia bit her lip. "I didn't think you were coming."

"I wished I hadn't …"

"It was an honest mistake. You know Ma's dumb rule about locals. Those two must be new and don't know who your father was." Daniel and Amelia's fathers were best friends from Scotland who had travelled to New Guinea after the Great War in search of gold. Daniel's father, Harry, had made it big at Edie Creek in '26, while Amelia's father had looked to the sky, being one of the first to pioneer air travel in New Guinea.

Daniel looked to his feet. "Must've …"

"Danny *boi*," Tom said as he walked towards them, shaking the strands of loose blond hair out of his eyes. "I see you've managed to weasel your way in again." He slapped his brother on the back, causing Daniel to flinch.

"He's never had to weasel his way in anywhere," Amelia replied.

"Whatever you say, Meels." Tom put an arm around each of them and pulled them into a tight squeeze. Daniel immediately shoved him away, while Amelia stiffened under his embrace.

Tom dropped his arms and stepped back. "Woah ... easy there, Danny *boi*. Wouldn't want them to kick you out again." He laughed as Daniel bunched his hands into tight fists, body rigid and jaw tight.

"Why don't we go outside?" Amelia said as she grabbed Daniel's arm and pulled him towards the verandah.

Daniel gripped onto the rail and steadied his breath.

Amelia looked up towards the star-studded night sky, where in the distance, towards Salamaua, heavy clouds lingered. "It's going to rain," she said as she breathed in the cooler air. A slight breeze had picked up, the tree branches rustling. She listened as the jungle came alive, the rhythmic croaking of the tree frogs – or rokroks, as the locals called them – soothing her nerves.

"I don't need you to defend me all the time," Daniel said, interrupting the cacophony of night noises.

"I wasn't defending you," she said quietly. "I was merely explaining the situation."

"I'm well aware of the situation, Amelia. I live with it every day."

"I know, but it makes my blood boil when they treat you poorly."

He turned to look at her, his dark eyes penetrating. "And how do you think it makes *me* feel?"

Amelia didn't say anything, looking out towards the water instead. She couldn't imagine how Daniel felt being mixed-race, never really belonging to either world. He bore the brunt of it as best he could, holding his head high anytime the white men spoke down to him. She knew he didn't like to dwell on it, that getting on with it was easier than making a thing about it, but it must've eaten away at him. The constant belittling enraged her.

But she let it go, resting her hand on the rail next to Daniel's, their fingers brushing. She felt him stiffen, but he didn't move, the air between them perfectly still. They stood there for what felt like hours, Amelia convinced her heart was going to give her away, but the only sound was the repetitive croak of the rokroks. Time had expanded into this moment – a moment that might never happen again … and then, like glass shattering into a thousand pieces, was broken.

"Time to leave, Amelia," her father's voice loomed from behind.

She stiffened and turned to see him standing at the door of the verandah. How long had he been there? This time she thought her heart would burst right out of her chest, and she snatched her hand away from Daniel's, not daring to meet his eye. Daniel ran his hand through his hair as he turned towards her father, posture stiff as he met him face on.

"It's getting late," her father added, flicking his head for Amelia to come. Amelia nodded and scurried towards him, hoping her father couldn't hear her racing heart.

# 2

# Daniel

Daniel tinkered beneath the belly of his Junker, sweat trickling down his bare arms. Arms that were streaked with grease much darker than his own skin. He ducked out from under the plane and scrubbed at his skin, the white cloth now streaked with black. He eyed a group of pilots having a smoke and wandered over to join them. Their Aussie accents were as thick as Lae's humidity, another thing that made him stand out like a leper – his own imperfect English and lack of private boys' school education made him sound like he didn't belong. He searched his trousers for a cigarette, moaning silently to himself when he came up with nothing, before plastering on a smile that'd make Ruth McKenzie proud.

"Mind if I bum a smoke?" he asked the pilot named Kevin, one of the friendlier ones. The man happily obliged and even offered to light it for him; a flame flickered in front of Daniel's nose before he could say no.

He nodded a thanks and turned to look out at the Huon Gulf towards Salamaua. The airport sat at the edge of Lae, and a stream of planes were flying low over the water as they descended from the mountains behind Salamaua. He wondered if Amelia had flown back after last night. It was hard to ignore how beautiful she'd grown in the year since he'd last seen her. Sydney obviously agreed with her. He shouldn't have been so forward in his hello when he saw her at the morning tea, especially in front of her parents, but the way her cheeks had glowed when she'd spotted him, like the sky at dawn, made it hard to remain reserved. She was his oldest friend … only friend, really. That was all. He hated that she had to see him being treated like that at the Cecil, as if he was a dirty mongrel. Neither white nor black. Here nor there. And yet it irked him that Amelia had gone out of her way to point out that he was white. But he didn't want to dwell on it. There was enough to worry about with things heating up in the Pacific.

The pilots snickered, forcing Daniel back to the present.

"Mate, I'm signing up after work today," Kevin said. He was an average-sized bloke with dark hair that'd already started to recede. "The Rifles need all the help they can get." He was referring to the New Guinea Volunteer Rifles, a unit of the Militia formed in 1939 after the war had erupted in Europe.

Another pilot named James, a tall skinny guy with blonde hair, slapped Kevin on the back. "Mate, you've got two left feet. You think they want someone like you?"

Kevin punched James's shoulder. "The Army's taking anyone they can get. Johnno here signed up months ago." He flicked his head to the side towards the other pilot, a burly bloke whose hair had been shaved back to its stumps.

Daniel couldn't help but interrupt. "Anyone, you say?"

The three men turned to look at him, Daniel's face suddenly hot. James and Johnno looked away, but Kevin kept eye contact with Daniel. He cleared his throat and said, "Sorry, mate. It's supposed to be for Aussies and Europeans only."

"Yeah, you wouldn't want to put up with our lot," James added.

*I thought I* was *one of your lot?* Daniel looked to his feet, flicking his cigarette into the dirt, before stomping on it with his boot. "No worries."

"Is there a local division you could join?" Kevin offered.

Daniel sniggered. "Maybe." He walked away, kicking himself for thinking he could be considered one of them in the first place.

* * *

After easing his Junker into the hangars at Salamaua, Daniel walked towards

Logui Road. The towering palm trees that lined the main street of Salamaua swayed with the strong breeze that billowed across the bay. He kept his gaze towards the ground, not wanting to make eye contact with the whites who were strolling past. It was mostly pilots or New Guinea Gold executives, who were dressed in their usual all-white attire, on their way for a game of cricket or tennis. He smiled at a couple of houseboys who hurried past, then he turned off the path towards the small cottages Mr McKenzie provided to all his pilots.

Daniel's cottage sat on the edge of Salamaua Harbour, slightly away from the others but with a prime view. The water glistened in the late afternoon sun, speckled with canoes that bobbed idly, waiting for the fish to bite. He admired it for a moment, before turning up the steps, where he discovered Amelia.

"What are you doing here?" he asked, startled by her appearance. She was wearing an emerald-green gown that matched her eyes. The material swooshed as she stood. The puffy skirt accentuated her small waist, and the neckline sat low across her chest, accented by a large emerald jewel.

"I'm here to take you to the party," Amelia replied with a shy smile. She fidgeted with her dress, pulling it higher up her breasts.

Daniel couldn't help but stare, before eventually shifting his gaze and replying, "Party?"

"Yes. My parent's annual Christmas party? Surely you haven't forgotten?" Amelia bit her lip, face twisting in concern.

"Right. Of course." Daniel swallowed, wondering why his heart was beating so fast. It was only Meels he was talking to … his childhood friend who was in a beautiful dress that made it look as if she was a glowing green gem. "Uh, I haven't forgotten. I'm not going." He walked inside the cottage and tossed his pilot's cap on the single bed.

"Why not?" Amelia demanded to know, following Daniel inside.

He backed up against the teak dresser, heartbeat quickening as he looked to the door. "You know you shouldn't be in here. If anyone got word …"

Amelia pulled her shoulders back and tilted her chin up. "I don't care what anyone thinks," she said, but her voice didn't sound as confident as her body language suggested. Daniel opened his mouth and then closed it when she started again. “My parents won’t even notice if you’re at the party. All the other pilots are going … it’s only right that you come too.”

Daniel looked to the timber floor. “You know I’m not invited.”

“Rubbish!” she said. “You can be my date. It’ll be fun.”

He ran his hand through his moppy hair. “I don’t know, Meels.”

“Come on.” She stepped forward and grabbed his hand, and a shiver shot up his spine. “You’ve been every other year, so why should tonight be any different?”

He stiffened but couldn’t let go of her hand; her touch was inebriating. “Because your parents made it clear they don’t want me there. Their invitation even said, ‘Whites only’.” Daniel hadn’t known how to feel when he’d read that. Technically he was white – or half white, as Amelia had pointed out the other night – but he hardly felt it.

Amelia scoffed. “My parents are idiots. Or my mum is, at least. Dad definitely wants you there.”

But Daniel didn’t want to risk upsetting Mrs McKenzie on her favourite night of the year. Their annual Christmas party, held on the first Sunday of December, was the biggest event in the Mandated Territory, with Mr McKenzie flying in every European he knew from Wau, Bulolo, Rabaul and even Port Moresby.

“I … I can’t,” Daniel said, lowering Amelia’s hand, immediately wishing he hadn’t, the tips of his fingers now aching.

“Daniel? Don’t—”

“I said I can’t, Amelia.” His voice was firm this time.

Amelia’s mouth opened, before quickly snapping back shut. “Fine. I’ll go on my own then!” And she stormed out of his room, the swoosh of her emerald-green dress trailing after her.

* * *

Daniel slumped against a coconut tree and stared across the road at the Hotel Salamaua. The iron-roofed building was shaking as the band inside churned out "In the Mood". The dazzling white faces of New Guinea's finest spilled out onto the verandah. As expected, every person of European descent was there, strands of fat pearls dripping off the women, while the men braved dinner suits and quenched their abundant thirst with the champagne that was being carried around on trays by locals. Despite the war in Europe, Mrs McKenzie had spared no expense for this year's party, which would no doubt be more indulgent than the Carpenter's Christmas Eve Ball or the Burns Philps New Year's do.

Daniel lit a cigarette, kicking his boot into the sand as he replayed his conversation with Amelia. He hated disappointing her; that look of humiliation on her face was etched into his mind. But he knew it wasn't right for him to attend. It would only cause problems, particularly for him, as he depended on his job with Mr McKenzie – the man who'd promised to take him under his wing after Daniel's father had died of malaria a few years earlier. Daniel supposed Mr McKenzie *had* taken care of him, by offering him a job as a pilot – a privilege that no other Niuginian would ever be afforded. So Daniel needed to tread carefully, even if that meant jeopardising his relationship with Amelia.

Except she wasn't the same Amelia anymore. The way she had looked in that dress ... the way his body had responded when she touched his hand. Electrifying. He grimaced, wishing he'd told her how beautiful she looked. She deserved to hear that at least. He took another drag and closed his eyes as he leaned his head against the tree, the image of an emerald-green Amelia replaying in his head.

"What are you doing out here?" a voice said, interrupting his thoughts.

Daniel opened his eyes, jaw clenching when he realised who it was. Tom. "What does it look like I'm doing?" he replied as he held up his cigarette.

"You know there's no natives allowed at the party?" Tom said with a smug smile. Dressed in a full dinner suit, he was emitting an overpowering scent of musky aftershave that reminded Daniel of rotting fruit.

Daniel's jaw tightened again. "Good thing I'm not a native then."

Tom scratched his chin. "Huh. That's not the way it looks like to me ... and everyone else inside that party, to be frank."

Daniel pressed his fingers to his forehead. "What do you want, Tom? I was quietly enjoying myself until you came along."

"Thought I'd remind you of where you belong."

"Not to worry. You've done that every day since I was born."

Tom laughed, and the night echoed with his mirth. "Well, we can't have natives thinking it's normal to fraternise with whites. It would change the whole dynamic of the place."

Daniel pushed himself to standing, body tense as he tried to keep his temper under control. "It's our country—"

"You admit you're a native then!"

Daniel's muscles quivered, heat flushing through his veins. "Can you fuck off! Go enjoy yourself and leave me be."

"Don't worry, Danny *boi*. I intend to have a grand time tonight, getting rip-roaring drunk at the McKenzies' expense." He laughed again, more like a cackle this time, as he pulled at his shirt cuffs that were studded with their father's gold cufflinks. When he was done, he looked Daniel square in the eye and said, "I wanted to tell you to stay away from Amelia. Or I'll make your life very difficult."

"You already make my life difficult," Daniel spat back. His jaw muscles twitched. "You've taken everything away that Dad intended for me... cut me out of the business, out of the family, out of everything I've ever known—"

Tom snickered as he turned to walk away, before adding, "Don't kid yourself. You were never part of our family. How can you be when you don't look anything like us? You were a stupid mistake Dad once made and felt sorry for. Don't ever forget that."

# 3

# Amelia

Amelia lifted her dress, nearly tripping on the tulle as she walked up the narrow steps of Hotel Salamaua, stomach clenching as she felt everyone turn to look at her. She grabbed a coupe of champagne from a passing tray and gulped it down, the bubbles tickling her throat as she looked around the room for someone to talk to. What was she doing here? She hated these sorts of things and the society people her mother called friends. And without Daniel to help her weather the storm, she didn't think she could survive a night of their company. If only he had said yes; Amelia's body was still hot with shame at his rejection. She'd put on the stupid dress that her mother said would make her look beautiful, pinned her hair back so it didn't sit so awkwardly, even put on mascara so her eyes would pop, as her mother had claimed. She had done everything she was supposed to do to attract a man ... and yet here she was on her own. Was she foolish to think Daniel was attracted to her? That they had a connection beyond their childhood friendship? She thought she'd felt him shiver when she'd grabbed his hand, but it could've been her own body reacting to his touch. The night she'd envisioned would never happen now, and she wasn't about to endure it on her own. She gulped more champagne and turned to leave, bumping straight into an arriving guest.

"Apologies," she muttered, not bothering to look the man in the face as she pushed past, but he grabbed her arm, forcing her to look up. Her heart nearly stopped. "Daniel!"

The edge of his lips crept up, one of his dimples emerging as he stared at her intently. "I … I forgot to tell you something …" Amelia scrunched her brow. "… I forgot to tell you how beautiful you look tonight."

She felt her face flush. She wanted to look away, but the amber irises that were shining back had her transfixed.

"*I* should've changed, though," Daniel added as he straightened the collar on his shirt and looked around the room, his casual dress a stark contrast to the formal attire of her mother's guests.

Amelia shifted her gaze to follow his, sensing how out of place he felt, the throngs of people looking at them. "Maybe this was a bad idea …"

He took the champagne from her hand and downed the rest. "We're in it now."

She offered a reassuring smile as she assessed the room. Her eyes landed on her parents. They were saying hello to their guests, her father chortling as he shook hands with the men. Her mother stood poised, offering her friend Alice – or Mrs Middleton, as her mother would insist – a light peck on the cheek. She beamed in a crimson ball gown that was cinched at the waist and puffed out nearly a metre around her; her hair was twisted in an elegant chignon, and two large rubies dangled from each ear, matching a very large ruby that hugged her finger. Her chest sparkled with diamonds, which she touched ever so gently, her long fingers skimming the exquisite jewels. They were a vision … Amelia couldn't deny that. Mr and Mrs George McKenzie, in all their glory.

Her mother suddenly turned towards Amelia.

"Bugger," Amelia said. "She's seen us. We'd better say hello." But Daniel was already walking to the far end of the bar, gesturing to a local for a drink. "Thanks," Amelia mumbled as she grabbed another coupe and walked towards her parents. She waited as several other people in front of her said their hellos and her mother offered the same words of thanks over again, face beaming from all the praise. Amelia couldn't help but think how exhausted her mother must've felt — the constant upkeep, the ongoing performance, the suppression of feelings. Amelia was tired just from watching it. She looked back to see Daniel settled in at the bar, chatting to a group of pilots, looking relaxed with a drink in hand.

"Darling," her mother said when it was finally Amelia's turn. She tilted her cheek for Amelia to kiss. "Nice of you to join us."

"Wouldn't miss it for the world," Amelia replied as she kissed her mother, before turning to her father. "Hi, Dad."

"Meely …" he wrapped her in a bear hug, and she couldn't help but soften. "How's my wee lass this fine evening?"

"No doubt elated," her mother interjected. "I see you brought a guest." She nodded towards the bar and Amelia turned to see Daniel being encouraged to drink by the other pilots.

"I thought I told you he wasn't invited," her mother said through gritted teeth, turning Amelia's attention back to her. She was still smiling, but her eyes told a different story.

"Not now, Ruth," her father replied shortly.

Her mother's smile widened. "Have you seen your sister?"

"Which one?" Amelia replied and took another sip of champagne. The bubbles burst in her mouth, and for the first time that evening she relaxed, pleased she'd dodged the matter of Daniel for the time being.

"Sofia." Her mother nodded towards the other end of the bar. "She's in the corner with her usual entourage." Amelia turned to see her little sister sitting high on a bar stool, a group of young men around her. Her white tulle skirt puffed out, tiny diamantes stitched into the delicate fabric. "Would you be a dear and attend to her? You know how she gets with the boys," her mother said as she nudged Amelia in Sofia's direction.

Amelia frowned as she walked away. She had to give it to her. If her mother couldn't lecture her about Daniel, then she'd at least make sure Amelia was distracted for the night by her precocious little sister.

"Sofia," Amelia said as she approached, pushing between two men to get her attention.

"… and then I told her to stuff it!" Sofia was saying, paying no attention to Amelia. "I mean … you're my meri for goodness' sake, not my mother."

The men erupted in laughter as Sofia sucked on her cigarette. Her focus landed on Amelia, and she lowered her cigarette, her red lips turning into a sly smile. "Meels! To what do we owe the pleasure?"

"Mum asked me to check on you."

Sofia laughed. "See, gentlemen ... she's always watching!" The men laughed again, their adoration of her thunderous. Amelia could never understand why men worshipped the ground she walked on. Yes, she was pretty ... in an obvious sort of way, with her golden curls, rosy cheeks and full bustline. It didn't help that she flirted with anyone, lapping up every bit of attention men threw at her. She always had the perfect comebacks, her wit as sharp as her tongue, warding off their advances while still keeping them intrigued.

Sofia pointed her cigarette at Amelia. "Please tell Mum that I'm perfectly fine. I have these charming young men looking after me."

They all nodded with cheeky grins.

"Precisely why she sent me over here," Amelia replied.

"Oh Meels, lighten up. It's Christmas."

Amelia kept quiet this time, shifting her gaze towards Daniel. He was still at the bar, talking to a different group of men, laughing, shoulders relaxed and cheeks dimpled. He was so beautiful when he smiled. He gulped his drink and gestured for another. Amelia bit her lip, wondering if it was a good idea for him to be drinking so much. She decided it was; what better way for her parents to see that Daniel was like them?

"I see your boyfriend's here," Sofia said.

Amelia turned back to see her sister watching her with eyes narrowed like their mother's. "He's not my boyfriend," Amelia replied, holding her sister's gaze.

Sofia was the first to look away. She gestured for another cigarette and one of her admirers pulled out his silver case, a map of New Guinea engraved into it. He lit the cigarette as Sofia held it to her mouth; her chest expanded as she sucked in the smoke, before blowing it out the side of her mouth, straight into Amelia's face.

Sofia ran her tongue over her teeth. "Doesn't look that way."

"I could say the same," Amelia replied, looking at each of the men surrounding Sofia. For all their so-called charm, none of them had said a word since Amelia arrived.

"At least mine are the right colour."

Amelia tensed, a heat rushing through her body. She wanted to slap her. It took everything in her power to keep her hand around the stem of her glass. Her grip tightened as she sipped her champagne. Her head spun, but she managed to steady herself, taking a deep breath to calm her nerves. A clinking of silver against glass forced her to turn, the room quieting as the guests' attention turned towards her father.

"Thank you all for joining us this evening," he said, voice loud enough to carry across the Hotel Salamaua's open room. "With the war in Europe, I know it's a sombre occasion for many of you."

The women all nodded and looked to the floor; many of their sons had left in the past year and several of them had already been lost to Hitler's army.

"But thankfully, our lasses are safe here in New Guinea, and we can thank our lads for that."

"Not for long!" someone yelled. The room erupted into a hushed frenzy as they tried to find the culprit, but Amelia's father quickly settled them.

"Aye, well …" he went on. "It's unlikely the Germans will make it as far as New Guinea, so I think we're fine for the time being."

Amelia closed her eyes, her father's words comforting. He'd certainly changed his tune since that night at the Hotel Cecil. With the Japanese advancing on Asia, there'd been rumours New Guinea would be evacuated, and so she was relieved to hear her father say otherwise.

"But we're here tonight to celebrate our fortunes. This country has been kind to us … mostly." Her father laughed, and the bevy of guests followed suit, the men slapping each other on the back. "And despite its challenges, we've all reaped a reward. Business is booming, gold is rushing, and we're flying more planes than ever before." He raised his glass. "So, I'd like to propose a wee toast. As we soon farewell 1941 and welcome what's hopefully another fortunate year, let's give thanks to our formidable hosts." Her father looked towards a few of the locals in the corner, but their eyes were glued to the floor. "To New Guinea!"

The room roared in response, glasses clinking as the people chimed, "To New Guinea!"

"Now let's dance!" her father bellowed, and the band started up, a bugler belting out the intro to "Boogie Woogie Bugle Boy". People spilled to the side as a makeshift dance floor was formed, men twirling their wives in time to the beat. Tiger Lil took this opportunity to make her grand entrance. She was dressed in a strapless black velvet gown, with her full bosom, highlighted by a twinkling diamond necklace, spilling out above her tightly girded waist. Amelia's mother had been forced to invite her after Tiger Lil had unceremoniously asked about the party at the morning tea. She intruded on several of the couples dancing, grabbing the men and forcing them to spin her around as she tipped her blonde locks back, cackling with glee.

Amelia downed the rest of her champagne, hoping that someday she'd likewise have the confidence to do as she pleased. Now, with the threat of war at bay, she had time to pursue this thing with Daniel. Whatever it was that was brewing between them was hard to pick; Daniel's actions towards her these past few days were confusing to say the least. She didn't understand it, but wasn't willing to give up on it yet.

# 4

# Daniel

James tipped a glass of whisky into Daniel's mouth. Daniel's throat burned as the alcohol coursed through his body. He winced as he pressed the back of his hand to his lips, hoping he wouldn't gag. After the first drink, he'd told the boys *no more*, he'd had enough, but Johhno and James were persistent, like male dogs smelling a bitch in heat. It was too hard for Daniel to ignore their demands, especially in his position.

He knew he should've accompanied Amelia when she greeted her parents, but the thought of facing them directly when they'd explicitly said "whites only" was too terrifying. Plus, he was hoping they wouldn't even notice he was there, especially if he stayed out of the way – except the Aussie pilots weren't making that easy. He pretended to listen as they went on about the war, and the reasons why they hadn't gone to Europe yet. They were too scared of what could happen here, with the threat of the Japanese looming. Daniel begrudged them. He would've happily gone to Europe to fight Hitler – anything to be given a purpose. But since he wasn't Australian, and his father had never bothered to give him Scottish citizenship, he wasn't allowed.

He raised his eyebrows as he watched Amelia grab another glass of champagne, wondering how someone so little could stomach that much alcohol. She laughed as she drank, her body relaxing into the evening. This was her world – what she represented – and it seemed as if she fit into it so naturally, standing tall with her people. How could he ever stand next to her? Tom had made his position clear earlier; his words were still imprinted in Daniel's mind. Except Daniel was determined to prove him wrong.

He took another sip and offered a half smile as the boys talked about blowing the Nazis to bits. James was the one who'd yelled "Not for long" when Mr McKenzie had made his speech, though Daniel questioned what the bloke even knew about war. They were only young, twenty-something lads who'd been spoonfed their whole lives. What did any of them know about war? It was a foreign object, a vague idea. Something he prayed would never reach their shores. It'd been reassuring to hear Mr McKenzie declare they were safe for the time being ... the man had to have intel with the Aussie administration.

Daniel glanced at Amelia again, body tensing when he realised Tom was there. He was hovering over Sofia as if they were in on a secret, laughing like two brats who'd pushed a kid down on the playground. Daniel's nostrils flared, and before he knew it, he'd downed his drink and was walking over to them.

"Oh look ... here's that exceptionally tanned brother of mine," Tom said as Daniel approached. Everyone except Amelia roared with laughter, while Sofia didn't even acknowledge Daniel's presence. "Seeing as you don't respect the 'whites only' rule, I take it you don't have the necessary permit needed by mixed-race Kanakas to drink?"

While whites had an open-drink policy and blacks were banned from drinking completely, mixed-race people could apply for a permit that allowed them the privilege. Daniel had never bothered obtaining one, not usually caring for a drink the way white people did.

"Let's go," Amelia said and reached for Daniel's arm, but he pulled away. He swayed in his haste and stumbled into one of Sofia's admirers. The man jolted back.

"Woah ..." Tom said. "Easy there. Looks like you've had too much already."

"Have I?" Daniel replied, wondering if his voice was slurring.

Tom didn't say anything, turning towards Sofia instead. "The Kanakas are never any good at holding their drink." He eyed Daniel and added, "That's what my father always said."

Daniel felt his ears redden. "I'm not a fucking Kanaka!"

"Then what are you?" Tom asked coolly.

Daniel paused, inhaling slowly. He glanced at Amelia, whose face had blanched as if she were about to be sick. "I'm your brother," he replied, any hint of a slur gone. He stared at Tom, his face searching, pleading for recognition.

"Unfortunately," Tom said, and leaned in towards Sofia, blocking Daniel from the group. And then, possessed by rage, Daniel grabbed Tom by the collar. He pressed his fingers into his neck, squeezing so tightly it was as if their flesh was one. Sensing that the band had stopped playing, that he was being watched by the prying eyes who disapproved of his presence, he *wanted* to stop; he told himself to let go, but there was something inside that wouldn't allow it, a burning desire to put Tom in his place. All he could hear was the thrashing of his own heart against his chest.

The next thing he knew, Tiger Lil was between them, pushing Daniel away. "Easy there, fellas," she said as she lowered Daniel's hand, forcing him to release his grip. "Wouldn't want that brotherly love to get the better of you."

"Tell that to *him*!" Tom sputtered as he keeled over and gasped for air, a hacking cough escaping his lungs.

Daniel inhaled, trying to steady the rage that was shooting up his limbs. Blinking, he realised the music had stopped and everyone was looking at him. He turned towards Amelia, whose face was as white as a blanket of clouds.

"Daniel, love," Tiger Lil said. "Why don't you give me a spin around the dance floor? Show me those moves you Carmichaels are so famous for."

Daniel shuffled backwards, cheeks burning as he looked to the ground. "Uh … I'll have to decline, Mrs Millar. Think I've had a few too many."

"Probably best," she replied. "Go and sleep it off … God knows there'll be a few sore heads tomorrow—"

"Get the boy out of here," Mr McKenzie interrupted, his voice booming across the room. Two locals came out of nowhere and gripped Daniel's arms. He pulled away and walked himself to the door, head hung low. People whispered in a collective "tsk" as he went past.

"What are you all looking at?" Mr McKenzie added as Daniel was pushed out the door.

And with that, the band started up, Daniel already forgotten as people spilled back onto the floor. Then he remembered Amelia. He turned to look for her, but she was already gone, no doubt embarrassed by his little performance.

* * *

Sitting on the stairs of his verandah, Daniel stared at the waves that lapped at the ocean's edge, a light breeze rippling its surface. He sucked on a cigarette, imagining Amelia next to him, her head resting on his shoulder, the full moon creeping above the horizon, the soft yellow glow illuminating their desire, intoxicating… the end to what could've been a perfect night – if only Daniel hadn't stuffed it up.

He stubbed out his cigarette. He kept telling himself that it wasn't his fault, that Tom had gotten the better of him… again, his brother the king at stirring Daniel up. But he had to learn restraint, especially in front of *those* people, people who despised him simply because of the way he looked. Burying his face into his hands, he yelled, body shaking as his cries reverberated across the bay.

"Goodness," a voice said when he was finished. He looked up to see Amelia standing in front of him, hair sticking to her forehead and mascara smudged … and yet she still glowed beneath the moonlight. She sat on the step next to him. Daniel's pulse intensified as he was suddenly acutely aware of every nerve ending on his body.

"Meels, I'm sorry," he offered, knowing it didn't count for much. He'd embarrassed her in front of everyone and could never make up for it.

Amelia hiccupped. "Don't be. Tom was asking for it."

He ran a hand through his hair. "I never meant for that to happen. Whisky makes me wild."

"And champagne makes me floozy. I mean flouncy!" She giggled as she met his eye, the emerald irises shining back at him.

"That it does," he replied, holding her gaze. He licked his lips, but when she leaned forward, he couldn't help but stiffen. "You shouldn't be here," he added as he shot to standing.

"Then where should I be?" she asked in an icy tone without looking up. He stared at the back of her neck, the wisps of short hair that grew along the nape, above the line of freckles that tiptoed down her spine. His fingers reached forward, tingling, as his desire to trace the line surfaced, hovering closer, his desperation to know where they ended ... until .... Amelia pulled her shoulders back and Daniel pulled away.

He cleared his throat. "At home ... with your family, where you're safe."

She whipped her head around. Her smudged eyes were wet now, the image of her pain like a bush knife to his heart. "Do you honestly believe that? That I'm not safe with you?"

"You ... you should go," he said quietly as he walked inside his house.

"I'm not going anywhere," she replied, now standing at the door of his home.

His stomach tightened as he looked past her, praying no one was watching them. "Amelia, please ... if anyone catches you in here, I'll be done for."

She crossed her arms. "Not until you tell me what we're doing. I need to know how you feel about me."

"Meels, come on ..." he pleaded, but she wouldn't budge, forcing him to offer a response. He racked his brain for something suitable, something that would explain the way he felt about her. Except he didn't really know how he felt ... did he? She was his oldest friend, his only friend, really – that was it. Wasn't it? "I'm working for your father now, as an actual pilot. I can't risk that."

She stepped forward; the room was so small they were now only a metre apart. "Can't you?"

"Don't ask that of me. I'm not like you, I don't have the same opportunities."

"But I can help you, make my parents see—"

"It's not that easy."

"It's not supposed to be ..."

"They'd never accept us."

"They won't have a choice. We'll make them."

"And what about everyone else?"

"I don't care about everyone else ... all I care about is you."

"Meels ... please?" He glanced at the door, then back at her.

"Don't, Daniel ... don't tell me you haven't felt this, haven't known there's been something here for years." She drew in a breath, before taking the final step that closed the gap. They were inches from each other – he could feel the hairs on her arms standing on end. She lifted her chin to expose her long neck, the wisps of hair tickling his nose. She closed her eyes and parted her lips. He swallowed, moisture gathering as he stared at her mouth, breath quickening. Trying to steady himself, he inhaled, but his body was flooded with warmth as he smelt her perfume, lilies and vanilla, and before he knew it, his lips were pressed against hers. Their tongues met, slowly, searching for rhythm. She tipped her head back and he moved his lips along the side of her neck, her body shivering as she wrapped her arms around his back. He moved to extend the kisses along her collarbone.

The creaking of the door hinges startled him. He jumped back as Amelia turned towards the door, but there was nothing there, only the glow of the moon on the water's edge.

She laughed. "It's nothing," she said as she reached for him again, but he was frozen. "Nothing."

He blinked. "You need to go. You shouldn't be here."

She waved him away. "I told you, Daniel ... I'm not going anywhere. This is real, what's happening between us is real. I'm not going to run away from it anymore."

He pushed past her to the door and held it open. "Please, Amelia. Not like this ... there's too much at risk. You must go."

Her chin wobbled. "No."

"Fine!" he yelled, suddenly exasperated with her stubbornness. "Then I'll go." He rushed out the door and down the steps, running up the isthmus before Amelia could say anything else that'd force his heart to stay.

# 5

# Amelia

"Meels, get up."

Amelia tried to pry her eyes open, but sleep had crusted them shut. A dull ache thumped at her temples, the after-effects of too much champagne rearing its ugly head.

"Come on. Get up." It was Evelyn's voice.

Amelia peeled her eyes open. A flood of bright light hovered above her sister, who was still dressed in her nurse's uniform from last night's shift. "Go away," she replied and turned to the side, pulling the pillow over her face.

"I can't. Something's happened." Evelyn's voice was wobbly.

Amelia turned back. Evelyn was pale, her ashen skin even more ghostly than usual. "What is it? Are Mum and Dad okay? Sofia?"

"Come, will you?" she replied as she walked towards the door.

Amelia sat up, head still spinning as she took in the room that wasn't hers. The single bed, the teak dresser and front door that opened onto steps down to the ocean's edge. Daniel's room. Except he wasn't there. He had left.

Her body flooded with shame as she tried to piece together the events of last night. The party, that fight ... their kiss. And then Daniel's sudden departure, the look of fear that took hold when she refused to leave. She'd fallen asleep in his bed, hoping he'd come back, even though she knew he was right. If anyone had found her here, her reputation would be in ruins.

Her mother would be horrified, would put her on the next ship back to Australia, with no hope of ever returning. Luckily it was only Evelyn who'd found her. Though how had Evelyn known she was there? She followed her sister out the door, smoothing her hair back as they neared the main road, hoping she didn't run into anyone else she knew. But apart from the usual chatter of morning birdsong, Logui Road was eerily quiet and no one was in sight.

When she arrived home, she found half a dozen people gathered in their front lounge room; her father was huddled over a bunch of papers with three other men, while her mother sat with Sofia on the couch, worry sewn across their faces. The wireless hummed in the background as a man relayed a news report in a sombre voice.

Amelia looked down, remembering she was still in last night's attire. Her stomach clenched, and she stepped backwards, hoping to make a quick dash to her room before she was noticed.

"Meely, lass," her father said and hurried over to hug her. She wrapped her arms around her waist, hoping to hide her shame, when her mother turned her head.

"Dad?" she said, voice small under his warm embrace.

He squeezed her tighter and rested his chin on the top of her head. "There's been an attack," he said, his voice dimmed to barely a whisper. He looked her square in the face. "In Hawaii. The Japs have bombed Pearl Harbor." He rushed back to the table, where one of his associates was pointing to a map.

Amelia felt dizzy again. "An attack?"

"Yes," her mother replied as she walked over and hugged Amelia, the intake of her breath audible against Amelia's ear. Amelia stiffened when she realised she smelt of sweat and alcohol. "Over two thousand feared dead," her mother added as she retreated towards a chair and lit a cigarette with a shaky hand.

"America's declared war," Evelyn interjected.

Amelia's stomach hardened. "What ... what does this mean for us?"

"We'll have to leave, of course," Sofia replied. She was looking out the window towards the main road, dressed in a red polka-dotted, collared dress with buttons down the front, hair bouncing with fresh curls. Clearly the champagne hadn't had the same effect on her.

"We don't know that yet," Evelyn said.

Her mother took a long drag on her cigarette and asked Amelia, "Where've you been?"

Amelia felt her cheeks redden. She could only imagine what her face looked like right now. "Nowhere."

"Sofia's right," her father said, looking up from his papers. "We need to get you lasses back to Australia, where it's safe. Now that America's declared war, things are going to get hairy in the Pacific. New Guinea is what stands between the Japanese and Australia. It's only a matter of time before the Japs arrive, and if they make it to Port Moresby, then Australia won't stand a chance."

"What are you talking about?" Amelia was quick to reply. "You said last night we were safe here in New Guinea."

"That was before those dirty Nips launched war on us!" her father shouted. The room went silent; only the low hum of the radio could be heard. "We are now at war," kept repeating in the background. *War.* Bile burned at the back of Amelia's throat. "We're right in their firing line," George continued. "We have to get you out."

Her mother leaned back and rested her elbow on the armchair, smoke wafting in ringlets from the cigarette that was pinched between her fingertips. "He's right. It's not safe ..."

Amelia bit her lip. She opened her mouth to speak, but nothing came out.

"Why don't we wait for orders from the Australian Government?" Evelyn suggested. "In the meantime, we can make the necessary prep—"

"Good idea!" Amelia replied. "I'll start by letting the staff know." She hurried out of the room, not bothering to wait for her father's reply, knowing it wouldn't be what she wanted to hear. Plus, she had to find Daniel. She stopped on the front verandah and looked up. Flashes of white streaked the pale-blue sky, the clouds light and airy even on this, the heaviest of days. She let out a huge breath, willing her heart to stop racing. *It'll be okay,* she kept repeating to herself. It had to be.

"We're going." Her mother's voice came out of nowhere, forcing Amelia to turn and face her. As usual, her expression was unreadable.

"We ... we don't need to decide anything yet," Amelia replied, trying to keep her cool, though she could hear the wobble in her voice.

Her mother stepped forward. "It's decided."

Amelia held her gaze but didn't say anything. There was no point in arguing with Ruth McKenzie.

* * *

Having changed into a white linen shirt and khaki trousers, Amelia searched the hangars. The tin sheds were filled with her father's planes, but void of the only thing that mattered. Her stomach heaved as she ran through each one, uncertain if it was the remnants of last night or the heart-wrenching news they'd received that morning – her country was under threat of being invaded. She didn't know what that really entailed, but her parents' threats of leaving New Guinea kept running through her head, making the need to find Daniel even more desperate.

He was in the last hangar, crouched underneath his Junker, sleeves of his white-collared shirt rolled up to the elbow, like Amelia's.

"Daniel," Amelia said as she approached the aircraft, but he didn't stir. She brushed her fingers across the wing, the metal cold against her skin. Her nostrils flinched as the smell of diesel caused her stomach to churn even more. "Daniel," she said more forcefully.

He stepped out from under the plane and stared at her, a loose strand of hair covering his eye. She shifted on her feet, wondering how to act after last night, but he made the decision for her, dropping his wrench and rushing to wrap her in a tight embrace. She buried her face into his chest, body relaxing into his arms. He nuzzled her hair, and they stood holding each other as if it were the last time, no longer caring who was looking.

When they finally pulled apart, Amelia looked up and said, "I'm sorry—"

"Don't," he replied as he pressed a finger to her lips. She closed her eyes, savouring the touch of his calloused skin. He intertwined his greasy fingers with hers and pulled her towards the edge of the hangar. The rising peaks of the mountains that surrounded Salamaua were laid out before them, stretching as far back as they could see, until there was nothing but a faint trace of a line against the sky. In the foreground, tall kunai grass rustled in the breeze as little lime-green butterflies fluttered between each blade, while the banana trees danced in the wind, their splintered palms like fingers on a piano.

"What will you do?" Daniel eventually asked, breaking the silence. He continued to stare at the mountains, as if turning to face her, to hear the truth, would be too painful.

Amelia swallowed. "My father's talking about leaving ..."

He tightened his grip on her hand. "When?"

"I'm not going." Her voice was firm.

"Don't be silly, Meels. It's not safe here."

She tipped his chin in her direction, forcing him to look at her. His face was stubbled with a five o'clock shadow, while dark circles encompassed his eyes and a smudge of grease smeared across his cheek. She pressed her thumb against it. "I'm safe with you."

He shook his head and stepped back, their fingers breaking apart. "No, you're not."

She let out an exasperated sigh. "Daniel, please don't start that again. I'm happiest when I'm with you. That's all that matters."

"I meant it's not safe here—"

She crossed her arms and turned towards the mountains, knowing he was right. If the Japanese were to land in New Guinea, would the Administration be able to stop them? The NGVR had a few hundred soldiers, made up of men who'd hardly been trained to fight. If the Aussies didn't send more troops soon, they really would be in trouble, forced to fight the Imperial Army or escape through the treacherous mountains she was staring at. Her father used to tell her about the treks he'd made through those mountains when he first came to New Guinea in the twenties, before there were planes to take prospectors to the goldfields in Wau and Bulolo. It would take seven days, a trail of fifty local porters carrying the goods needed for the mines.

Hollywood actor Errol Flynn had even trekked it on his sojourn in New Guinea in the early thirties. Her father would scare Amelia with stories of cannibals like the Kukukuku who feasted off the blood of warring tribes. Could she really face such dangerous territory if the Japanese were to land? But could she allow herself to be evacuated with the other women, leaving Daniel to face it on his own?

She turned back towards him and said, "Come with us ... to Australia. We can finally go to flight school."

He offered a smile, but no dimples surfaced. "You know I can't do that. Australia has that whites-only policy."

"You're Scottish. They'll have to accept you."

Daniel winced, and Amelia wondered if she'd said something wrong, until he replied, "Yes, but I don't have any papers. As far as they can see, I'm from New Guinea."

She huffed. The world was at war, and because Daniel didn't have the right paperwork, he'd be left behind. "Surely my father would be able to pull some strings? Vouch for you?"

"Perhaps. But I'm not sure he'd want to."

Her shoulders slumped. She knew he was right – that her father could be unreasonable. It didn't matter that he was once best friends with Daniel's father; all that mattered was what people saw, and when her parents looked at Daniel, they saw colour.

"It's not an option, anyway," Daniel said. "Men are staying. It's only the women and children who will be evacuated."

Amelia suddenly felt lightheaded. Even if Daniel was allowed to enter Australia, he wouldn't be able to leave New Guinea. They were going to be separated. Before she could dwell on the feeling too long, Daniel pulled her towards him and said, "Let's get out of here ... while we still can."

# 6

# Daniel

Daniel grabbed Amelia's hand and raced towards the hangar that housed her Moth. It'd been years since the two had flown together, but they jumped into action, easily falling into a natural rhythm to prep the plane for flight. He pumped the propeller and moved the wedges from behind the wheels, before climbing onto the wing towards the rear pilot's seat.

"What do you think you're doing?" Amelia asked. She looked up at him, hand on hip.

"Uh ... flying," Daniel replied.

"So, you assume that because you're a man you get to take the lead?"

Daniel's lip inched upwards. "I'd never dare to assume anything with you, Meels." He reached down to pull her onto the wing, squeezing her hand as they paused to stare at each other, specks of brown colouring her emerald eyes.

He couldn't believe what a fool he'd been last night, letting her believe he didn't want this, didn't want her. Staying up all night to watch the moon make its way across the sky, setting behind the Hertzog Range until rays of sunlight peeked out from the other side, his mind churning the entire time, knowing he had to be firm with her – that he didn't have a choice. And yet that look of humiliation that had flooded her face wouldn't stop flashing in front of him. And he was the one who had caused it. He'd raced to find her as soon as he'd heard about Pearl Harbor, running into Evelyn along the way, who was also searching for her. She'd said Amelia wasn't in her bed that morning, and Daniel immediately knew she must've fallen asleep at his place, waiting for his return. As much as he wanted to go to her, to atone for his shame, he told Evelyn to fetch her. It was best she was with her family during this time. But as soon as he saw Amelia in the hangar, puffy cheeks and blotchy eyes, he knew what an idiot he'd been.

Now standing in front of her on the wing of a plane, her breath on his lips, he could feel every part of his body awakening. Their countries were at war, and he wouldn't waste one more minute pretending he didn't want this. She drew in a breath, and he could not help but kiss her. It started slow, both of them afraid of how the other would react, until they fell into a rhythm, like they had last night. When they were done, he rested his forehead against hers, his heart beating with hers.

She stepped into the rear cockpit and pulled a pair of goggles over her eyes while Daniel jumped back down to wind the prop. He gave it a couple of thrusts, heart racing from that kiss, before climbing into the front as the plane roared to life. Amelia eased it out of the hangar towards the top of the runway, vibrations rumbling beneath them.

"Ready?" she said into the Gosport tube that connected the two seats.

"Always!" Daniel replied, reaching his hand back.

Amelia's fingers immediately found his, squeezing tightly and only letting go as the plane took flight. Daniel looked below. Salamaua swept across a thin strip of land, the mouth of the Francisco River swelling into the ocean on one side, while the harbour glistened like a cold beer on a hot day on the other. Even though he did that take-off every day, it wasn't until that morning – his entire life now up in the air – that he truly appreciated how beautiful it was. He had to be willing to do anything to protect it.

"You sure you're ready?" Amelia said again.

"Ready for what—" But before he could finish, she was off, giving the Moth full throttle. They climbed vertically into the clouds until the plane sloped onto its back and looped into a full three-sixty circle. His stomach rolled with the exhilaration of weightlessness. She eased off the throttle and arced the plane down, coursing over the Huon Gulf, the Hertzog Range to their left, the treetops like broccoli, and the towering peaks of the Rawlinson to their right. She swooped into Lae, past Voco Point, Hotel Cecil and the terraced houses that hugged Mount Lunaman, its thick blanket of verdant foliage speckled with bursts of orange from the Flame of the Forest trees. She flew low over the aerodrome, past the Jacobsen Plantation, densely covered with thick raintrees, all the way out to the Edwards, Heath and Whittaker Plantations, taking care not to brush the towering palm trees that lined the dusty road, before pushing the throttle up again and looping the Moth back around.

"You're crazy, you know that?" Daniel said when she levelled the plane back over the ocean towards Salamaua.

Amelia laughed. "You could've taken over at any point."

"Wouldn't want to hold you back," he replied.

She landed the plane with an ease that came only to avid aviators, but when they climbed out of the cockpit, Daniel sensed how uneasy she was.

"What now?" she asked as she stepped onto the wing and looked out to the grey clouds that'd formed above the mountains. A low rumble of thunder echoed inland.

"I guess we wait," he replied, knowing that waiting was sometimes the hardest thing of all.

* * *

Daniel tapped his foot impatiently as he waited in line, the only person of colour in a sea of white. The other men looked at him curiously, as if he were a leper who'd escaped his colony. Daniel did his best to ignore them, a trick he'd learned from an early age. When he got to the front, he was met by the intense gaze of two middle-aged Australian men who were both dressed in khaki shirts with brass NGVR shoulder badges.

"I'd like to sign up for the Rifles," Daniel said, chin held high. The men looked at each other, as if waiting for the other to speak, which prompted Daniel to say, "I believe you need every man you can get?"

The man with a thin moustache replied, “Uh … we’re only accepting Australians or Europeans.”

“I’m European,” Daniel tried to say with conviction. “My father was Scottish. You may’ve known him? Harry Carmichael?” He hated using his father’s name, but he needed the clout it lent him.

“Afraid I don’t,” the moustachioed man replied and looked past Daniel, yelling, “Next!”

“Please, sir,” Daniel added, stepping forward so the man behind him couldn’t push past. “I’d really like to help. I’m young, fit and able. I can even fly a plane … I’m a pilot for George McKenzie, in fact.” Daniel pulled his shoulders back, hoping if he boasted with enough confidence he’d be able to convince them.

The other man raised his bushy eyebrows. “You’re one of McKenzie’s bois?” he said, enunciating “boys” in such a way that Daniel knew he was using the Pidgin word.

He gritted his teeth and replied, “No, sir. I’m a pilot for Mr McKenzie.”

“We don’t have any need for pilots,” thin moustache replied. “That’s what RAAF’s for.”

“But Kevin Parer told me he signed up. He’s a pilot.”

“Whose family has been here a long time,” bushy eyebrows said.

“So have I,” Daniel interrupted, trying to keep his voice levelled. “I was born here.”

“Clearly,” thin moustache said. “But still, the NGVR is for Europeans and Australians only.”

Daniel inhaled sharply. “As I said, I am European …”

Bushy eyebrows looked past him. “Not European enough. Next!”

Daniel slammed his hand on the table in front of them. “That’s ridiculous!”

“Look, *boi*, we don’t want your kind,” thin moustache said. “It’s hard enough getting natives to do their jobs properly, I sure as hell don’t want one of you watching my back when the Japs come. Now move aside so I can get through the other blokes.”

Daniel marched off, hands barrelled into fists, wishing he could punch something, but rational enough to know that he’d confirm their beliefs about him if he did. He kicked a coconut tree instead, again and again, channelling his rage into the land he loved so dearly. The land he wasn't even allowed to protect, all because of the colour of his skin. He was as able as they were, even more so being half their age and actually from New Guinea, with skills and knowledge they'd never possess – an ability to speak the language and appeal to its people. This wasn't even their country; they were merely custodians, wardens who were clearly in over their head. An entire region was protected by a few hundred blokes with a bunch of old rifles – against the might of the Imperial Army.

Who knew where the Japanese were, when they'd come and what they'd do? Daniel had heard enough reports to know they were fearless, well-trained soldiers ready to die for their empire. How would these blokes match up to that? They would've been lucky to have him, and yet he wasn't even given a chance because he didn't look like them, wasn't privileged enough to be born like them – even though, technically, he *was* like them. It was times like these he wished his father was still alive, the influence of men like Harry Carmichael and George McKenzie going far in the colony. He supposed he could always settle for the latter, even if he hated asking Mr McKenzie for help. But he couldn't let his pride get in the way. There was too much at stake.

* * *

"Mr McKenzie," Daniel said as he knocked on the door of his office, a windowless room in the back of the airline's hangar in Lae.

Mr McKenzie was bent over his desk, engrossed in a set of papers that reached to either side of the dark brown kwila wood. It took him a moment to glance up, glasses resting on the bridge of his nose. "Daniel, boy," he replied, and Daniel was unsure which version of *boy* he meant. "Aren't you on roster to fly today? The lads up in Bulolo really need those parts for the dredges."

Daniel stepped into the room but didn't dare take a seat. "I'm about to start but wanted to speak to you first—"

"What about?" Mr McKenzie cut him off, as if he was immediately suspicious.

"The NGVR, sir," Daniel replied, hoping his voice didn't convey his nervousness.

"Oh. Right." Mr McKenzie exhaled, looking to his papers again. "What about them?"

"I'd like to join, sir, but they're not allowing it." Daniel paused, waiting for Mr McKenzie to say something. Daniel rubbed the back of his neck as he glanced at the door, wondering if it was too late to abort. He'd been foolish to come here. Mr McKenzie would never help ... he had no reason to.

"Why?" Mr McKenzie finally said.

*Is he really going to make me spell it out?* "They say it's only for Aussies and Europeans—"

"No." Mr McKenzie leaned back into his chair, hands resting on his belly, the buttons of his collared shirt straining. "Why do you want to join?"

"Is that a trick question?"

"No, lad." His voice was firm, devoid of all emotion. "I ask all the lads the same question. Why do you feel the need to join the forces?"

Daniel shifted on his feet. What sort of answer did Mr McKenzie want? This honourable man, a man who had served in the Great War, who'd dedicated his life to providing for his wife and daughters. Surely, he'd understand Daniel's desire to fulfil his own duty, like any man should?

"Because this is *my* home," Daniel said instead. "And I sure as hell ain't going to let the Japanese stroll in here and take it."

Mr McKenzie narrowed his eyes again. And then a full body laugh escaped his lungs, echoing off the tin walls, allowing Daniel to relax a little. "Usually the lads give me a stock-standard reply about duty and what not, and while duty is important, it's not what's going to sustain you when you're arse-deep in mud and the bullets are raining down on you. Fighting for what you love is the only real thing that'll see you through. I'll talk to the recruiters at NGVR, see what I can do."

Daniel rocked back on his heels, a smile creeping up his lips. He wondered if his father's best friend was finally warming to him. He turned to leave, when Mr McKenzie added, "But there's something you need to do for me."

Daniel's stomach tightened, that feeling of accomplishment quickly diminishing. He swallowed and turned back to meet Mr McKenzie's gaze. "What's that, sir?"

Mr McKenzie waited a moment to reply, as if he was pondering his answer. "I need you to stay away from Amelia. I've gotten word evacuations will start in a few days. I can't have your relationship with my daughter complicating that. You know what she's like ... what she'll do to get her way."

Daniel opened his mouth, but nothing came out. He couldn't stay away from Amelia, even if he wanted to; it was as if there was an unexplainable power pulling them together. But he could always tell Mr McKenzie what he wanted to hear.

"Fine. I won't see her."

"It'll have to be more than that. You'll need to write a letter. Tell her you want to end things. That there's no future." He pushed a piece of paper and pen towards Daniel.

It was as if the lights had gone out. A sudden coldness hit his core. He couldn't do that to Amelia. It'd crush her. And it wasn't true, at least not in the long-run. There *was* a future, or at least there would be when the war was over. But she was leaving – she had to; the idea of her being here if the Japanese landed was even more bone-chilling than not seeing her again. Plus, he needed to do something to help protect his home, and the NGVR was the only option. If Mr McKenzie could get him in, then he wouldn't feel so useless, and maybe they'd be able to keep Salamaua in the hands of the Allies, and the unexplainable pull that Amelia and he had would see them together again in the place they both held so dearly.

He stepped forward, taking the pen and paper from Mr McKenzie, hoping to God this was the right choice.

# 7

# Amelia

"Z-day," Amelia's mother said to her daughters as she read from the notice that'd been issued to all households. They were sitting in the lounge room of their Lae house, Ruth in a wicker chair while the girls sat on the embroidered camelback sofa. A slight breeze blew through the shuttered windows of their plantation-style home. "That's what they're calling it."

Amelia grabbed the notice from her mother and read the words for herself.

*Lae and Salamaua have been fixed as embarkation points in the Morobe District and billeting arrangements will be made at those points. In order that arrangements may proceed with expedition it is requested that all concerned make the following preparations immediately:*

1. *Pack personal clothing, sufficient blankets, pillows and mosquito nets for use for themselves and children while awaiting embarkation at Salamaua or Lae. It is essential that you provide for all contingencies in regard to hygienic requirements.*
2. *Mothers should bring with them food requirements for babies.*

*At the moment it is not possible to inform you of the date you will be required to embark or to leave your home, but as soon as information has been received you will be advised either by the District Officer at Salamaua, the Assistant District*

*Officer at Wau, the Patrol Officer at Otibanda, the Patrol Officer at Finschhafen or the Assistant District Officer, Lae, as the case may be. Until further notice of movements has been communicated to you, it has been requested that you remain as near as possible to your homes.*

Amelia had read enough. She handed it back to her mother, who was immaculate in a cream-coloured afternoon dress with puffed sleeves and a belted waist. Amelia, on the other hand, was slightly dishevelled in her standard white-collared shirt that was tucked into high-waisted, wide-leg pants.

"It doesn't say when, though," Evelyn offered, placing a linen serviette on her simple button-down shirt dress. Evelyn never needed much in the way of fashion to look beautiful.

"Can't come soon enough," Sofia replied as she stifled a yawn with the back of her hand. She was also immaculately presented, wearing a long-sleeve pink floral dress with a contrasting white collar. Amelia didn't know how she stood it in this heat.

"I suggest you girls pack up your things today," her mother said, snapping her fingers at one of the houseboys to bring her a cup of tea. "Take only the necessities."

"Let's not be hasty," Amelia replied as she stood, pants swooshing as she started to pace the room. "It could be weeks before they get organised. You know how slow things move in New Guinea."

"Regardless, we should be prepared," her mother replied. She sat back in her chair, posture rigid as the bare-chested houseboy handed her a cup of tea with a shaky hand. Splashes of liquid pooled in the saucer. She pursed her lips and turned to him to say, "Polau, what is this?"

Polau, the Lae houseboy, looked to the floor and whispered, "Your tea, missus."

"I believe you're mistaken. Tea is to remain in a cup – while *this* is sitting in the saucer. Do you know how uncouth that is? To be served tea like this?"

Polau didn't reply, hands still shaking as he stared at the wooden floors. Clearly annoyed by his lack of response, Amelia's mother plucked the cup from its saucer and threw its contents of steamy liquid across Polau's chest.

He recoiled as the hot liquid scoured his skin.

"Mum!" Amelia shouted.

"Perhaps that will teach you for next time," her mother said, and she handed him the cup to take away.

Polau scurried out the room, a welt already forming where the tea had burned him. Amelia and Evelyn went after him, but he was quick to disappear outside, unwilling to accept their help.

"What were you thinking?" Amelia demanded, scowling at her mother as she re-entered the room. Evelyn sat back down, shaking her head silently.

Her mother looked at her fingernails. "As I was saying, we need to be prepared to leave at a moment's notice."

"How will I decide what to take?" Sofia replied, but no one paid her any attention.

Evelyn bit her lip and leaned forward. "What about me, Mum? Did you speak to Dad about what we discussed?"

Another houseboy returned with a perfectly poured cup of tea, which Amelia's mother happily accepted. She took a sip, the handle of the patterned cup pinched between her thumb and index finger. Amelia stared, mouth open, finding it hard to believe that her mum could have been so vicious.

"I did," her mother replied. "And we agreed you may stay. For now. The hospital needs you."

"Pardon me?" Amelia asked.

"The government has permitted nurses to stay," Evelyn said quietly, avoiding her sister's eye.

"Then women *can* stay?" Amelia replied, a jolt of excitement coursing through her body.

Her mother wiped the edges of her mouth with a napkin. "Nurses can stay, which Evelyn is—"

"*I'm* a nurse!" Amelia cut her off.

"No," her mother went on. "You would've been if you'd remained in Sydney and received your certification, instead of rushing back here ..."

Amelia placed a hand on her hip. "I know as much as Evelyn. Just because I don't have a piece of paper to show it doesn't mean I can't help."

Her mother stood, placing her napkin on the table before walking over to her daughter and resting a hand on her shoulder. "That's very admirable of you, dear, but I believe your intentions are elsewhere."

"They are not! I want to help!"

"Hmm ..."

"Why in God's name would you want to stay?" Sofia interjected, before turning to Evelyn and patting her knee. "No offence."

Ignoring Sofia, Evelyn turned towards Amelia. "Mother's right. It's too dangerous."

"Are you hearing yourself, Evelyn? How is it any different for me than you?"

Her mother squeezed Amelia's shoulder. "Evelyn's an experienced nurse, Amelia. They need her. You'll be much happier in Sydney, away from this mess."

Amelia flinched. "So, you're happy to leave *her* to tend to this mess, but not me?"

"I'm familiar with the hospital, Meels," Evelyn said. "I know the doctors and how to treat the various tropical diseases. That takes years of practice. It's too dangerous for someone who's not experienced."

Amelia threw her hands up in the air. "Everything's always too dangerous! Flying's too dangerous. New Guinea's too dangerous. Daniel's too dangerous—" Amelia's fingers flew to her lips, her boldness causing her stomach to lurch. She cleared her throat, raised her chin and, in a steady voice, said, "Isn't it about time you let me decide for myself?"

"Perhaps when you're mature enough—"

"I'm nearly twenty-one!"

"As I was saying, when you're mature enough, and when we're not at war, perhaps we'll start taking your wants into consideration. In the meantime, pack your bags. We're going."

* * *

It started the next day. Plane after plane flew into Lae, the constant whir of the propellers causing Amelia to jolt every time they whooshed past. Amelia hid near her Moth, watching as hordes of women and children – all friends of her mother, of their family – boarded with nothing but a suitcase in hand. They were allowed thirty pounds each, fifteen for children. An entire life condensed down to a mere valise. Amelia managed to dodge the first few planes, hiding out in the hangars and avoiding being where she was told to be while the planes were leaving. But she sensed her mother was becoming agitated by Amelia's sneakiness; Ruth's cigarette consumption had nearly doubled overnight.

As Amelia tinkered on her Moth, she wondered why she'd hadn't seen Daniel since they last flew. She figured he must've been busy with evacuation flights, but thought he would've sought her out by now, especially since Z-day had been announced. They needed to find a way for her to stay, or for him to come with her ... either way, they *had* to remain together. She polished the rudder as the Junker *Pat* came in for landing, creeping towards the terminal where more women and children were gathered.

"There you are," a voice said, causing Amelia to flinch. It was a voice she knew all too well. She turned to see her mother standing there, suitcase in one hand, a pair of gloves in the other. Sofia was standing behind her in a pair of white Harlequin sunglasses and matching wide-brimmed hat. "Time to go now."

Goosepimples crept up Amelia's skin. "I ... I'm not ready yet. I haven't packed."

Her mother offered one of her signature smiles. "Not to worry, I packed for you."

Amelia noticed that Sofia was holding two suitcases. "But—"

"No buts, Amelia," her mother replied. "We're going. Now."

"What about Evelyn? I'm not going without saying goodbye—"

"We said our goodbyes before she left for Salamaua. You were too busy avoiding us, so looks like you've missed out." Amelia's heart shrank. How could her mother be so cold, not even allowing her to say goodbye to her sister? It could be the last time she ever saw her ... saw him. "And before you say 'Daniel'," her mother pressed on, "your father received this letter from him." She handed Amelia a sealed envelope with her name on it. She stared at it briefly, wondering why Daniel would write a letter instead of seeking her out.

*Amelia,*

*Please don't put up a fight when the time comes to go. You must leave. There is no future for us. I'm sorry but it's better for us both if we end things here. Try to understand.*

*Daniel.*

She stared at it, unwilling to believe Daniel's words. How could he be so dismissive, when only days ago he'd declared his love? It couldn't be true.

"He ... he didn't write this," Amelia stuttered.

"Is it not his handwriting?" her mother replied.

It was. "Still, I don't believe it. Dad must've forced his hand—"

"Don't be so naïve, Amelia. Are you really willing to risk your safety, your reputation, for someone who clearly doesn't feel the same? Daniel doesn't love you ... not the way you love him." Amelia opened her mouth but didn't know what to say. Her mother's words held some truth. Didn't they? "Please ... get on that plane before it's too late."

"Okay," Amelia replied, not believing she was being so agreeable. "Let me finish up here—"

"Now, Amelia."

"Give me a minute, Mum!" Amelia shouted, matching her mother's tone. "It's not as easy for me to say goodbye."

"Make it quick." Amelia's mother turned towards the terminal where her husband was waiting for them.

Amelia rested her head against the aircraft. Could she really end things like that? Was that really the way Daniel felt? The words were as plain as day, but the sentiment felt wrong, unlike Daniel's character. He'd never be so cruel. She had to do something. She couldn't go without knowing how he really felt. Who knew what was going to happen? How long it could take for her to get back? She couldn't fly away without ever seeing him again, could she? Fly away? She bit her lip as she watched her father hug her mother goodbye, wondering how they made it looked so easy, her mother's face still unreadable.

It was because they didn't have a love like hers and Daniel's, a love born out of friendship. Their love had been forced; they'd met after the Great War, when couples were desperate to unite as a way to mask the pain. Amelia saw the way they interacted with each other, their lack of warmth for one another. Theirs was a necessary love; so many young men had been lost in that war that Ruth had been forced to accept George as her husband. And while Amelia admired her parent's tenacity – her mother had been one of the first white women to endure the harshness of this land – she wanted more than that, more than the stage production of her parents' lives. Looking at them now, she could see how cold they were to each other, bodies rigid and faces unmoving. Nothing compared to the couple next them, that pilot named Parer who was hugging his wife Nance and their three children goodbye. The family was cocooned within each other, emotions pouring out as they held on, the final goodbye breaking them. She couldn't go without having that with Daniel.

She glanced up at her Moth, wondering if what she was about to do was wise. It'd only make things worse, make her mother's dislike for Daniel stronger, but she no longer cared. She had to start living by her own rules.

* * *

Amelia jumped into the rear cockpit, flicked the ignition and pumped the thrust, before hopping back out to wind the prop. She pushed it down once, but the blades didn't go beyond a single rotation. She normally had a local to do this part for her, but gave a little thanks to her father for once showing her how to do it herself. She pushed the prop down again, adding a little more thrust this time, but it remained still. Scratching her head, she wondered if this was perhaps God's way of telling her not to go – to leave with her mother instead.

No. She wouldn't give up so easily. Not when it came to Daniel. She took a deep breath and tried one more time, arms pushing down with all their strength. The plane roared to life, and a shiver shot up her spine. She moved the wedges away from the wheels, hopped into the rear seat and steered the plane towards the top of the runway, passing her mother, who was staring back with her mouth wide open.

Amelia's heart raced – there was no going back now. Her mother waved her gloves, but Amelia thrust the plane forward, the tiny Moth picking up speed, faster and faster up the runway. The locals ran after her, yelling and waving, and she couldn't help but laugh, amused by the absurdity of the situation, again questioning if she should stop ... but when she looked ahead again and saw Salamaua in the distance, her beloved isthmus calling out to her, she knew there was no going back.

She shifted the throttle back, and the plane took flight, the boundless blue ocean at the end of the runway edging further away as the endless blue sky swallowed her up, while Lae trailed behind her, nothing but a tiny speck of sand.

# 8

# Daniel

Daniel heaved the spade into the ground. His blistered hands gripped tighter as he hurled another pile of mud over his aching shoulder. Streaks of sweat dripped from his face, the taste of salt and soil seeping into his mouth. He paused to wipe his brow, sniggering to himself as he looked around – the blokes were as black as the earth they were shovelling, matching the men they deemed beneath them. He guessed it didn't matter what colour you were when there were trenches to be dug.

*At least they're allowing me this.* Though it didn't count for much when every man on the isthmus had been asked to dig. In the last few days, he'd worked with Chinese and Australians, Salamauans and Europeans – all the men alike in their desire to protect their home. He was still waiting to hear from Mr McKenzie about the NGVR. Daniel was furious the Aussies were making it so difficult; he needed to be doing something. His hands were itching to work as he tried to mask the shame that leached from his skin. So long as he could help, he wouldn't feel so disgusted with himself for betraying Amelia, for writing that letter pretending he didn't care.

When he wasn't digging, he was flying evacuation flights to Moresby. Hundreds of women and children had already gone. He secretly hoped that Amelia would be on one of his flights, but suspected Mr McKenzie had rostered him so that would never eventuate. He took solace in their last encounter together, hoping it'd be enough to sustain him for whatever was to come, though it was getting harder as he witnessed the distress of the women leaving, sobbing as they clutched onto their husbands who stood strong. Daniel could see through the men's veneer – the way they held their wives and children, as if there was nothing more important than that final embrace. An embrace that Amelia deserved … that he could still give her.

*Mr McKenzie would never have to know.*

He chucked the spade into the trench and hurried to the hospital. Evelyn was hunched over a patient, diligently changing his bandage, the smell of rotting flesh causing Daniel's stomach to lurch. He held a hand to his mouth while Evelyn's face remained placid, her years of experience shining through. While a part of Daniel wished Amelia could stay like Evelyn, it was reassuring to know she'd be far away from here and whatever the Japanese would do.

"Evelyn," he muttered through his hand.

She looked up at the sound of his voice, surprise on her face. "Daniel? What are you doing here?"

"I need to find Amelia," he mumbled.

Evelyn glanced at the wound, then back up at him. "Wounds can turn quickly up here." He tried not to look at the pus oozing out of the patient's leg as Evelyn delicately picked debris from it. She squeezed the man's hand, her natural ability to comfort others a reassuring thought for Daniel. "I thought you'd spoken to her?"

"No."

"But that's what my father said. He told me you two said goodbye yesterday."

Daniel's stomach tightened, the smell of flesh no longer worrying him. "That's not true. He asked me not to see her. To end things."

Evelyn bit her lip, before looking back to the patient and applying iodine. The man winced as the liquid stained his flesh orange. She patted it with gauze and wrapped it with a fresh cloth.

"Where is she, Evelyn?"

Evelyn clutched the side of the patient's bed, unwilling to meet Daniel's eye. Daniel had always liked Evelyn, found her presence to be reassuring, especially when he felt anything but assured, though her behaviour in that moment was far from assuring.

Her eyes were wet when she finally said, "He promised me that he'd let you two say goodbye. That was our deal to get her on that plane. I even forwent my goodbye so there weren't any last-minute delays ..."

The back of Daniel's throat burned, acid rising up as he waited for Evelyn to say the unthinkable words.

"She's gone," Evelyn finally managed. "On the last flight out of Lae this morning ..." her voice trailed off, but Daniel couldn't bear the burden of Evelyn's sadness; the weight of his own despair was too heavy.

Amelia was gone, and he had no idea if he'd ever see her again.

* * *

Daniel resumed his duties in the trenches, mindlessly shovelling dirt to distract himself from the real pain he felt, his insides sunken like a hollowed-out punching bag. And it was all his own fault for bowing down to Mr McKenzie's demands when he should've fought harder for that goodbye, should've insisted to the Scotsman that it was the best thing for Amelia. Instead, he'd cowered, weakened by the white man who held all the power. Daniel had a mind to confront him, tell him of the pain he'd caused, but he still needed Mr McKenzie's help with the NGVR, and while he'd love to put the man in his place, there was too much at stake.

The trench Daniel was digging was parallel to the runway, and he glanced up to see a Junker landing. He wondered what it was doing here – until he saw Mr and Mrs McKenzie disembark, and a surge of hope rushed through him. But he stiffened as they approached.

Mrs McKenzie's lip curled in contempt. "Where is she?" she spat in an accusatory tone. "Where are you hiding her?"

Daniel wiped the sweat from his brow. "Where am I hiding who?"

Mrs McKenzie bent down and pointed a finger in Daniel's face. "Don't play dumb with me, boi. I know you two hatched a plan so she could stay. Don't you know it's illegal for a Kanaka to be with a white woman? I'll have you arrested!" She was breathing heavily, the normally composed woman apparently losing all control.

"I … I've been here, digging, for hours." Daniel shifted his gaze to Mr McKenzie, suddenly worried. In New Guinea, sexual intercourse between a white woman and a black man who were not married to each other was an offence for both. But if Mrs McKenzie was to have Daniel arrested, then she'd have to have Amelia arrested too. Surely she'd never do that. "I don't know what she's talking about, sir. I haven't spoken to Amelia, like we agreed." Daniel looked away, a flush of shame overcoming him again.

"Then it appears she's acted on her own accord, Ruth," Mr McKenzie said as he pressed his fingers to his brow. "Silly lass. Going to get herself killed by the Kukukuku before the Japs even get here."

"Kukukuku?" Daniel replied as he climbed out of the trench, realising he looked a mess compared with them, but he hardly cared. "Where did she go?"

"She took off in her Moth—"

"What about the letter? Didn't it work?"

"Evidently not."

Daniel exhaled, relieved Amelia couldn't be so easily fooled. And yet he'd still written the thing, his betrayal likely to break her heart.

Mr McKenzie looked around, then ran to the hangars, and Daniel followed, a tentative smile forming on his face. Amelia wasn't gone yet; he still had a chance. He could explain himself, how Mr McKenzie forced his hand …

"She isn't here," Daniel said.

"Isn't she?" Mr McKenzie replied as they turned the corner into the last hangar. Amelia's Moth rested inside. The smile grew on Daniel's face, but was quickly wiped away when Mr McKenzie glared at him.

"Tell me where she is," Mr McKenzie demanded.

"I … I don't know, sir," Daniel stammered, wishing he knew how to express himself better. "I briefly went to the hospital. She must've landed then."

Mr McKenzie steadied his breath. "Amelia needs to get to Moresby in order to meet the *Katoomba* before it sails tomorrow. Ruth, go ahead with Sofia. We'll look for Amelia and I'll fly her myself. She couldn't have gone far … the bloody isthmus is only so big." He turned to Daniel and with a contemptuous stare said, "Find her and you'll get your goodbye."

Daniel's breath was bottled in his chest, a floating sensation taking hold. He would get his goodbye, be able to make things right, and still fight to protect his home. He exhaled as he started to think of all the places she might be, his feet ready to run to the one place he knew to go.

"But Daniel," Mr McKenzie added before Daniel could leave. "If you don't bring her to me, then remember this." He paused, eyes full of disdain. "I won't do a thing to get you into the NGVR. And I'll make sure you never fly in New Guinea again."

# 9

# Amelia

Drawing in a breath, Amelia dove down deep, lips speckled with salt as she surveyed the colourful reefs that fringed the shores of Salamaua. The tepid ocean water was surprisingly refreshing against Amelia's flustered skin, and the beads of sweat that had pooled at the base of her spine quickly washed away. She kicked her legs to push herself further down, ears popping as she sank deeper.

It was disappointing that Daniel hadn't been at the aerodrome when she'd landed, but knowing word would soon spread – the locals' trusty wontok system no doubt helping with that – she knew exactly where to go so he could easily find her. It'd been their favourite spot since they were kids, the coral reef inside Salamaua Harbour a beacon of hope in troubled times. Amelia would come here whenever she was upset with her mother, Daniel escaping with her when life got difficult for him. They'd get lost amongst the kaleidoscope of colours, with the electric blue fish and dusty-pink fan corals dancing before them, lungs being pushed beyond their depth, ready to burst like balloons – until they couldn't go any further, and their bodies shot back up to inhale the sweet, sweet air, their worries left behind.

Her mind hummed in tune to the crackling corals as she considered the bold action she'd taken. Defying her parents like that would be met with grave consequences, but these were grave times that called for bold decisions. She didn't believe Daniel's letter ... there had to be more to it. She wasn't ready to give up; their love had barely been given room to fly. Didn't they at least deserve a chance?

Amelia glanced up to the sunlit surface; the lack of oxygen was causing her chest to tighten, but she wormed her way further down, determined to find the deepest part of the reef where she could let it all go. In her twenty years of life, she'd finally taken the first step towards finding the freedom she so desperately craved. She'd no longer be controlled by her parents – her destiny was her own to make, a destiny that had to include Daniel. She didn't know what was ahead or where either of them would end up after this war, but she vowed in this moment to always find her way back to him, no matter how difficult things got. Knowing their relationship would have its challenges – the world still working at learning acceptance – she was determined to forge her own path, a path that others could one day follow. She drew on the last bit of air she had tucked away, admiring the pristine marine life – its tenacity for life as it weathered the changing ocean patterns. The image of Daniel's smiling face came to her, before she flipped her body around to launch herself up.

As her head broke through the surface she gasped for air, a jolt of electricity surging through her veins. Tipping her head back to let the sun kiss her cheeks, body full of promise and hope, she sucked back the sweet air. When her breath had finally steadied, she looked towards the ocean's edge to be met with a beautiful sight ... her future standing before her. She swam to the shore to meet him.

* * *

"What have you done?" Daniel asked as he pulled her to his chest and buried his face into her dripping wet hair.

Amelia was suddenly conscious of how exposed she was and tried to shield her half-naked body from view. He'd seen her swimming before, but she'd always had her full costume on, never her bloomers and bra, and it'd never been when they had these feelings for each other. But when she felt his body relax against hers, the relief seemed to fill up the little space that was left between them, and she no longer cared. To be here, to see Daniel ... touch him ... hold him, meant more than anything ... and yet, there was still that letter. She wrapped her arms around his waist and listened to his beating heart, if only for a moment. They breathed in time with one another, matching the murmurs of a pair of Kokomos in the nearby trees.

"Your parents are livid," he said when he finally pulled away.

She steadied herself, not ready for the moment to end. But she knew, like all good things, it had to. "I don't care about my parents. Not the way you do."

He scratched at the stubble that shadowed his chin.

"They gave me your letter ..." She looked to the floor, feeling the hurt of his written words in the heat of her cheeks.

"I didn't mean it," Daniel was quick to say, tipping her chin up so she'd be forced to look at him.

"Then ... then why did you write it?"

"I ... I don't know. Your father convinced me it was for the best. That'd it be better this way." He looked away, face twisted as if he wanted to say something else.

"Is that what you believe?"

"No. Not exactly. But you have to go, Meels. Who knows what will happen to this place ..." He looked around the harbour, as if he was imprinting the view into his mind forever.

Amelia clenched her jaw. "Not you too. I've heard it enough from my mother."

"Well, she's right. Women and children have to go. It's not safe for you anymore."

She scoffed, the noise of the Kokomos suddenly bothering her. "What about Evelyn? Is it safe for her? Or the sisters at the missions who are choosing to stay? The Chinese women we're doing nothing to help? The thousands of local women we're leaving behind? Is it safe for them?"

"Evelyn is a trained nurse. I hope we never need her in that capacity—"

"I'm a nurse too, Daniel!" Amelia yelled. "Remember? My mother forced me to do it so she could keep me from flying, from doing what I love. I should put my training to use and help you lads."

"And what if the Japanese land?" Daniel replied, face reddening. "You think they'll spare a thought for a pretty Aussie girl like you? I hardly think so. You'll get eaten alive!"

"It won't come to that. The Aussie army won't allow it."

"Come on, Meels. You honestly think those blokes know what they're doing? Look around ..." He paused, waving his arm from one side of the harbour to the other. "The NGVR has a couple of hundred men here, men who've had no training, who are too ignorant to consider help from the local people. You think they'll be able to hold off the Imperial Army?"

Amelia crossed her arms. Daniel was right. The Aussies were hardly prepared, had left the entire territory to be protected by a few thousand men, most of whom were in Rabaul. If more troops didn't arrive soon, then Salamaua could be lost forever. She shuddered, the idea of losing her home, the only home she'd ever known, unimaginable.

"Fine," she said under her breath, refusing to meet Daniel's eye. "I'll go."

Daniel exhaled, his relief palpable.

"But not until tomorrow. I want one more night ... with you," she added quietly, looking up to meet his gaze. His lips were pressed tight, face distorted in a mix of fear and despair. His eyes ached with torment, as if he'd devour her right there on the beach, or just as quickly push her away, like a capricious sibling. She knew he was only trying to protect her, to keep her safe from whatever horrors would come their way, but she'd no longer be forced into anything. Her mother had done that her entire life – forced Amelia to speak and act and dress a certain way. No more. Amelia wouldn't take it anymore. "You owe me that after being so callous with my feelings."

He hesitated, running his hand through his hair. "Alright," he finally said, shifting on his feet, as if he was uncertain about his decision. "I know a place. But only for tonight. We must get you out tomorrow before it's too late."

* * *

They weaved up the hill, ducking under broken branches and climbing over fallen tree trunks, all the while trying not to trip on vines that snaked their way across the path. The jungle teemed with life. Daniel helped Amelia with her footing, the mud thick like molasses, sucking them back with each step. New Guinea could be a punishing place, testing one's will like a broken marriage, and yet at the same time, it was enthralling, filling the soul with its mesmerising beauty. It wasn't for everyone; it had spat many a settler out over the years, but her father was one of the more determined ones, and he had imparted a sense of adventure on Amelia that had given her nothing but appreciation for the place. To her, this was home.

She paused to catch her breath, watching as a birdwing butterfly fluttered past, its wings a phantasmagoria of greens and blues. When she looked up, she realised they were near the top; a panoramic view of Salamaua was laid out before them. The harbour glistened in the morning sun, beams of light shining onto the thick jungle that circled the town. The buildings that lined the isthmus rested quietly – too quietly, like a sleeping baby oblivious of its environment, while the aerodrome was still, a dozen or so planes resting easy. Goosepimples crept up Amelia's arm as she thought of how easy it would be for the Japanese to take Salamaua. Had she made a mistake by staying?

But when she looked up at Daniel – at the love that rested behind his eyes, the shy smile that lit up his face – she felt at ease. He clearly didn't mean what he'd said in that letter; he'd been convinced by her father, and yet it felt as if there was something more, something he wasn't saying. She chewed her lip as he pulled her further along, until they arrived at a small thatched hut that was tucked in behind the trees.

"It's the coast watcher's house," he said.

"Where is he?" Amelia replied. She bit on her fingernail and peered towards the entrance, hoping there was no one inside.

"They haven't actually assigned anyone to the post yet."

"Lucky for us, I suppose," Amelia said tentatively, remembering their earlier conversation about Australia's lack of preparedness. Daniel didn't reply, leading her into the hut instead, hands shaking. "I … I don't even have a blanket."

Amelia's heart quickened as she looked around the empty room that smelt of must and cockroaches. "It doesn't matter," she replied as she stepped forward to close the gap between them. This is what she wanted, and she couldn't back away now. She closed her eyes and tilted her head up, heart racing now.

Daniel's lips were against hers, hands still shaking as he slowly snaked them up her back. His stubble tickled her chin, her skin tingling as a surge of adrenaline coursed through her. She wrapped her arms around his neck and brushed her fingers through his thick hair, inhaling his sweaty scent, before tracing them along the crease of his back, across the firm shoulder blades and then the biceps that'd been carved out over the years, along his hard, muscled chest. Her fingertips prickled as they moved along his body. He shifted his mouth along the nape of her neck, planting slow kisses that awakened something deep inside her. He paused at her collarbone, and her hands shook as she loosened the buttons on her blouse and dropped it to the floor.

Daniel stepped back as Amelia unfastened her brassiere and slipped out of her trousers. He stared at her, eyes as wide as the ocean, and her cheeks burned as she stood before him in nothing but her bloomers. But the way he was looking at her, eyes full of wonder as he soaked in her near-naked body, pushed embarrassment aside. She quickly moved to remove his trousers, fumbling with the button, chest hiccupping into a laugh when she couldn't get it undone. He gently placed his hands on top of hers, quietly laughing as they tried to steady their breaths. She closed her eyes again and inhaled deeply, acutely aware of every smell – must and sweat and dirt; every sound – birds and insects and breathe; every feeling – nerves and shame and fire, and then she let it all go and her fingers took over to loosen his trousers.

She swallowed as her eyes took him in, and when he kneeled down before her, slipping off her bloomers she couldn't help by cry out in pleasure. He eventually pulled her down next to him, and she eased back against the hard wood, chest rising and falling like an ocean swell. He slowly moved on top of her, both dimples emerging as he looked down and smiled.

"I love you," he whispered and then lowered himself, raising his hips to shift inside. She winced as he slowly worked to penetrate her, his breath hot against her lips. She bit down on her tongue, wondering if sex always felt like this, until the static sensation of skin against skin shifted to a soft stream of fluidity as he eased himself deeper inside. He let out a deep, satisfied moan before pressing his hips harder against hers. She gasped, the sheer force of his craving nearly enough to make her scream. Their hips slowly moved together, tangled in a dance of desire, her breath quickening as they picked up the pace, whole body intoxicated by the feeling of every inch of his need as it moved harder and harder against her own until she was flooded with his warmth.

He fell into a heap on top of her, breathing heavily as he buried his face into her neck. His heart raced against her own, the two hearts beating as one. She stared at the ceiling, and the sights and sounds and smells of this place came back to her, and a tear fell onto her cheek as she thought of everything she was about to lose.

# 10

# Daniel

Daniel lay perfectly still, Amelia nestled in his arms, body warm against his. He pressed his nose into her hair and inhaled, savouring her unique smell and the fire that still flowed through his veins. It'd been better than he'd imagined, the mere sensation of entering her nearly enough to send him over the edge. She felt and tasted amazing, supple and ripe as if she'd been made for him. He wanted to do it again, and again and again, relishing in every inch of her body and the sensations she stirred inside him – but was conscious that this moment had to end, the reality of this new world still hard to comprehend. She was leaving, and there was nothing he could do it about it. He shouldn't have risked her staying the extra day, but the look she'd given him when she said she wanted to spend the night with him had been enough to send him mad. And that it did. Had it not been for the threat of the Japanese, and her father for that matter, he would've never left this hut; he'd have run away with her forever so they could do nothing but *that* for the rest of their lives.

He turned his head to look at her, wanting to soak up every speckle of green within her eyes, every freckle that dotted her nose, every wrinkle on her lips before it was too late – but when he did, he noticed her cheeks were wet.

"Are you okay?" he asked as he quickly sat up, but she refused to meet his eyes, chin trembling as she stared at the ceiling. His heart constricted.

"Amelia, please ... are you okay? I didn't hurt you, did I?"

She smirked and finally looked at him. "No, Daniel. That was the furthest thing from being hurt."

"Then what is it?"

She opened her mouth, as if she was about to speak, but quickly shut it, sitting up instead and planting a slow kiss on his lips. Daniel's insides stirred again, until she pulled away and said, "Nothing." She quickly dressed and walked outside, Daniel following her. She hovered at the edge of the tree line, looking out over the view, shoulders slumping as she took it in.

He knew she was lying, that there was more to that "nothing" than she was letting on. Had she been disappointed in the act; had his lovemaking not lived up to her expectations? She seemed to have enjoyed it at the time, that cry of pleasure when he kissed her down there enough to let him know it'd been satisfactory. Had she been ashamed of making love to someone who was not purely white? But the things she'd said to him in the past few days, the way she'd spoken about her love for him and the risk she'd taken by defying her parents suggested otherwise. He'd wanted to tell her about the deal with her father, but didn't think she'd understand that his need to protect his home had to come first. Lucky for him, she'd accepted his explanation. So, then, what was it? Perhaps, like him, she wasn't ready to say goodbye.

Daniel stepped forward, determined to get her to open up to him, to share her thoughts, her fears, and in return reassure her that he felt the same, but a loud chattering noise forced him to stop. He spun around, trying to figure out what the noise was and where it was coming from, his ears ringing, when his vision landed on the view of Salamaua ahead. In the sky was a swarm of planes. Daniel leaned in, a flutter forming in his belly. *The Aussies are here!*

But as quickly as that feeling of hope had arrived, it was sucked away. Large red emblems were on the belly of the planes – planes that were dive-bombing into the harbour, only yards from the water. It wasn't the Aussies ... it was the Japanese.

* * *

Pulse racing, Daniel grabbed Amelia's hand and sprinted towards the track, feet slipping as they manoeuvred down the mountain, gaze set on the coastline, watching as the Japanese swooped in. They opened fire, guns cracking, blazing away at the town, wave after wave of Zeros, a thousand feet high, diving down, thudding the isthmus with bullets. Amelia broke free from Daniel, eyes bulging as she watched the scene unfold from a clearing in the bush, her hands pressed to her ears, the raking of intense machine-gun fire like a file rubbing against an iron bar. Daniel flinched as the guns screeched, muscles tensing as his need to get down the mountain only intensified. He tried to pull Amelia again, but she was glued to her spot, body trembling, a gasp escaping her lungs when a wave of black bodies appeared, locals fleeing into the bush in every direction, while ringlets of smoke rose near the hospital at the far end of the isthmus.

The Zeros soared towards the aerodrome where Mr McKenzie's fleet was lined up alongside a RAAF Hudson and Kevin Parer's de Havilland Dragon, the planes like sitting ducks. Another Dragon was coming in for landing, its tail blazing red with fire. Daniel shook his head, not willing to believe what was happening, until the Zeros dove down, their machine guns ripping through each of the planes, splaying the metal with holes. Daniel's stomach plunged and a sour taste rose at the back of his throat as the Zeros shot back into the sky, looping around near the edge of the jungle, before dive-bombing the aerodrome again, this time aiming for the hangars. Again and again the Zeros dove down, shredding any semblance of life, before turning back for more and more and more, their thirst for death unrelenting.

Daniel blinked and clutched at Amelia's clammy skin. He yelled her name, but she didn't respond; she squeezed her eyes shut when a high-pitched whistling sound surfaced, and Daniel's own eyes widened as the Bettys swooped in. The ground shook as a loud whoosh took hold, bombs engulfing the runway. Amelia sank down and curled her face into her knees, body rocking. Daniel squatted next to her, his need to comfort her distorted by his need to get to the aerodrome to help. He took a breath – trying to sound out all the noise, the screeching, chattering, whistling, whooshing, the thrashing of his heart in his ears – and exhaled it all out.

"Meels," he whispered in her ear as he stroked her back. "Meels, it's okay. It's going to be okay." She was hyperventilating, back heaving against the palm of his hand. Another bomb rattled the earth. "Meels ... please ... look at me."

She drew in her own breath and peeked out from the safety of her cocoon, eyes wild.

"We need to get down there," Daniel pleaded.

"My ... my father," Amelia stammered.

"He'll be okay. That's what the trenches are for."

Amelia jolted as another bomb landed. Her voice hitched as she tried to speak. "What ... what about Evelyn? The hospital ... it, it looks like it's been hit."

He squeezed her face between his hands and, with certainty, said, "Evelyn will be okay. And so will you. But you need to get up. We need to get down there and help. The hospital will need you."

She absently nodded as Daniel pulled her up, his own legs weak but determined to carry her burdens, knowing there was no time to process their fear. The only thing that mattered was getting down that mountain and making sure everyone was still alive.

* * *

Forty minutes later they were at the aerodrome, the last Zero flying away in the direction they'd come from as Daniel and Amelia emerged from the bush. Daniel keeled over, panting heavily as he took in the devastation. Craters the size of Cadillacs were scattered across the runway, planes were blown to pieces, and the hangars had been replaced by raging balls of fire. His ears rang as he tried to steady his breath, the sound of the Japanese wreaking their havoc still reverberating in his eardrums. Now he was here, he wasn't sure what to do.

But Amelia forced him out of it as she staggered forward, stumbling along bits of debris while frantically yelling for her father. Daniel ran after her, the sharp smell of cordite causing him to cover his nose with his hand, eyes burning as they waded through the smoke. He tried to pull her away, terrified the Japanese would come back, or that more explosions would come as fire ripped across the aerodrome, but her will to find her father was too strong. She pushed him off and screamed for Mr McKenzie.

Daniel remembered the trenches, the ones he'd been digging just that morning, and where he hoped Mr McKenzie was hiding. If he could get Amelia inside them, they'd be okay, but as he turned to find a path to the perimeter of the aerodrome, out of the corner of his eye he caught something moving. A person, being helped out of the cockpit by someone. Two souls still alive. But it wasn't just any person; it was Kevin Parer. He was being pulled out of his burning Dragon by another pilot, Clarke. Daniel ran to help, but as Clarke was heaving Parer out of the plane, another Zero swooped in out of nowhere.

Daniel dove under the cover of Parer's plane, which was in flames, but still the safest place as the Zero flew only fifty feet above them. Daniel's skin singed as the flames moved closer, and he knew it was only a matter of time before the fire hit the fuel tank and sent them all up in smoke – but that time was stolen from him as a burst of machine-gun fire ripped along the plane, the sound of bullets against metal like balloons bursting. He pressed his hands to his ears as Clarke collapsed, clutching at his legs, which were weeping with blood. Daniel moved to help him, when he saw Amelia still sitting on the runway, a stupefied look on her face as she watched the Zero soar back into the sky. She hadn't sought cover like he thought. Daniel ran to her and this time forced her to listen.

"We have to get out of here!" he yelled. "It's not safe."

"I have to find him," she replied, trying to pull away, but Daniel gripped her tighter. He glanced over his shoulder through the smoke-filled haze and saw three men running out of the trenches to help Clarke and Parer to safety.

"He'll be in the trenches," Daniel yelled. "We have to get to the trenches!"

Amelia nodded, allowing Daniel to lead her carefully through the debris until they reached the trenches. The eight-foot hole was full of men.

"Dad!" Amelia yelled as she ran along its edge.

The men stared up at her, their eyes lighting up to see another uninjured, living soul. But none stepped forward; her father was not amongst them. She fell to her knees, tears pouring down her cheeks.

Daniel crouched beside her, desperate to make her pain go away. Even though Amelia could get frustrated by her parents, he knew she still loved them, her father especially, and losing them would be hard to swallow. The shock of all of this was bound to haunt her for years to come.

"Amelia," Daniel whispered in her ear, still trying to comfort her but not having much luck. She was unresponsive, grief overcoming her. "Meels," he tried again, but he was overshadowed by a booming voice.

"Meely, lass? Is that you?" Mr McKenzie said as he stumbled back from Parer's plane with the group that'd helped to pull the men to safety. His shirt was torn and his beard caked in mud, and there was a large gash across his cheek.

Amelia's head spun in his direction, body sagging in relief as she laid eyes on her father. He pulled her from Daniel and wrapped her in a bear-like hug. Daniel's chest deflated as he watched Mr McKenzie effortlessly comfort his daughter, stroking her hair while shushing into her ear. She relaxed, chest slowing to a steady rise and fall as if the last hour of terror had never happened.

Mr McKenzie eventually pulled away and with a warm smile said, "You're alive. I was so worried—"

She laughed. "You were worried? I was terrified they got you."

"I'm not that easy to get rid of." Mr McKenzie eyed Daniel when he said this, causing a shiver to run down his spine. "But you, lass, this is why you should've gone with your mother and sister. You're lucky you weren't killed!"

She looked to the ground. "I know. I'm sorry. But I'm ready to go now. You can take me. I'll be on the next plane—"

"Look around you," Mr McKenzie replied, shifting his gaze to the aerodrome, or what was left of it. "It's all gone. The bastards got every last plane."

Daniel's chest tightened as Mr McKenzie's words sank in, a burning sensation forming in the back of his throat. All of Mr McKenzie's planes: the fleet of Junkers and de Havillands he'd acquired over the years, even Amelia's old Gipsy Moth ... his whole life's work, everything he'd built – destroyed in an instant. Which meant there was no longer a way for Amelia to safely leave Salamaua.

Daniel could no longer contain the bile that'd been rising ever since that first Zero swooped in. He bent over to let it all out, chest heaving as the terror of the last hour expelled itself from his body. When he was finally done, he glanced up to see Amelia looking at him with a strange expression, as if she didn't know whether she should go to him or not.

"We can't worry about that right now," Mr McKenzie said, bringing Amelia's attention back to him. "They're going to need you at the hospital."

"Evelyn!" Amelia cried.

Mr McKenzie squeezed her shoulders. "She's okay. She radioed to say they hadn't been hit and that we can bring the injured and dead."

Amelia exhaled but then said, "Dead?"

"Yes, lass," Mr McKenzie replied. With a heavy intake of breath, he removed his glasses, face pained. A fresh surge of nausea was surfacing in Daniel's throat as he prayed that whoever was dead wasn't someone he knew, that Amelia knew – the shock of losing someone close to them would be too much to bear – when Mr McKenzie said, "It was that lad, that pilot ... Kevin Parer."

# 11

# Amelia

Amelia's hands shook as she blotted her father's cheek with alcohol, the man barely flinching against her shaky touch. He was resting on a hospital bed with his eyes closed, bushy brows furrowed as if he was deep in thought. Amelia didn't know how he could sleep; the hospital was a whirlwind of chaos as Evelyn and Amelia tended to the throngs of men who'd been hurt during the raid – mostly cuts and grazes, except for the pilot Clarke who'd been shot twice above the knee. Evelyn was tending to him while Amelia worked on the minor cases, her nerves still too shaky to take on anything else.

The relief of finding her father alive had passed as the reality of their situation sank in. All she could say was she hoped she never had to experience that sort of panic again; the fear of not knowing if someone you loved was alive was worse than watching the Japanese attack. She couldn't even look at the body of Kevin Parer, who'd lain limp as a group of local men carried him up the isthmus to the hospital. They were saying that he'd landed when the Japanese swarmed in, and had tried to take off again but was hit by a cannon shell; he'd died immediately, though Clarke couldn't have known that when he was trying to pull him to safety.

Amelia shuddered when she thought of Kevin's wife, their last embrace at the aerodrome singed into her mind. She couldn't imagine the utter devastation that was about to fall upon poor Nance Parer, and pushed the thought aside as she returned her attention to her father. She blinked back tears as she secured a bandage to his face, thinking how she could easily have been Nance dealing with the death of a loved one. But her father wasn't dead, and neither was Evelyn or Daniel or anyone close to her. She'd been lucky this time, but who knew how long that luck would last?

How foolish she was for not leaving on the plane with her mother and Sofia. It was hard to believe that was only yesterday. Amelia's whole life had changed; a collection of life-altering moments had been jammed into a single day. She could no longer convince herself that defying her parents had been a wise decision. Even though she'd been able to share that wonderful experience with Daniel, the repercussions of that choice were earth-shattering and yet to fully unveil themselves. Especially now that the Japanese were on their doorstep and there was no longer a safe way out.

Her father stirred and opened his eyes. "Meely, lass. You shouldn't be bothering with me. I'm sure there are plenty of lads who need tending to."

Amelia managed a half smile. "I don't think my nerves can handle it. The men have been bandaged up anyhow." She fiddled with the items on the trolley to ensure the gauze and tape were in perfect order.

"They're lucky to have such competent nurses," her father said. "Clarke especially. And Daniel … the boy's lucky he wasn't burned alive. This whole thing is his fault. I told him to find you and bring you back, but instead he took you away. If only he'd stuck to our agreement, then you wouldn't be here right now."

Amelia frowned. "What agreement?"

"How do you think I got him to write that letter?" A painful tightness was forming in Amelia's throat as she stared at her father blankly. "He agreed to end things in return for me getting him into the NGVR."

"But he didn't mention that—"

"Why would he? Doesn't make him look very good, betraying you like that. I thought it was a fair trade, if only the boy stuck to his side of the bargain."

Amelia stumbled backwards, reaching for the trolley to steady herself. Daniel had gone behind her back to conspire with her father. She told herself she could understand his need to help, especially now, after seeing the devastation caused by war. Did she need to look past her own needs and try to see the good in this, in Daniel?

"Perhaps he was trying to do his part? He doesn't have the same options as everyone else."

Her father waited a moment to reply. "I thought that myself, until I saw how eager he was. Even suggested writing the letter himself. And then when I saw him at the aerodrome yesterday, he agreed to bring you back when I promised to keep him flying. Clearly the boy only thinks of himself."

Amelia felt dizzy, spots flashing in her vision. She'd risked everything ... and for what? For someone who was willing to betray her when he was presented with something better. She inhaled deeply, trying to breathe oxygen back into her trembling limbs. The realisation that she couldn't trust Daniel anymore felt like having her head held under water, like she'd never breathe again. But she had to find a way out of it, her gut telling her there was more to the story than her father was letting on.

"Regardless of what Daniel promised you, I believe his intentions were honourable. I love him, Dad. Doesn't that count for something?"

Her father looked as if he'd been punched in the gut, his face twisting like a contortionist's. He cleared his throat. "No. Love will only get you so far, Amelia. A life with Daniel would be far too complicated. You must see that?"

Amelia bit her lip. Her father had a point, but still, she couldn't deny her heart. "He loves me too," she said, though it didn't sound so convincing.

Her father narrowed his eyes. "No. I don't think he does. How could he possibly love you when he hardly loves himself? You would spend your days second-guessing his feelings for you, twisted about whether he loves you or loves the idea of you. A white girl who could bring endless opportunities to his life? Aye? You know this is true? If it wasn't, then he wouldn't have betrayed you so easily. Would've fought harder. Don't make another foolish mistake, lass. You've put your mother and me through enough."

Now it was Amelia who felt as if she'd been punched in the gut, her father's words triggering a doubt she'd been suppressing. Daniel's feelings for her had been so wishy-washy these past few weeks, his willingness to solidify his love only surfacing when they shared that moment of intimacy. Had he used her for sex? To feel what it was like before war was truly upon them? It was clear now. Daniel didn't care for her the way she cared for him. Her father was right. He had used her. And to top it all off, now she was stuck on an isthmus with the threat of the Japanese invading. What a fool she'd been.

* * *

A curl of smoke rose from the cigarette that was pinched between Amelia's fingers, a centimetre of ash threatening to fall upon the sandy path outside the hospital. At the time she'd asked for it, she'd hoped it would steady her nerves, but it'd failed miserably, along with everything else since that morning's attack.

Daniel took the cigarette from her hand and tapped the ash to the ground before sucking back on what was left of it, his chest expanding in a slow inhale. "Talk to me, Meels," he said after exhaling the smoke. "How are you feeling?"

Amelia wasn't sure how to answer that question, a mixture of feelings swirling inside. Terrified. Relieved. Devastated. The thought of Daniel conspiring with her father disgusted her. The image of their shattered town crushed her.

She shrugged instead.

Daniel stubbed the cigarette into the sand. "I should've listened to your father when he told me to bring you back. I'm such an idiot."

Amelia cringed. So willing to listen to her father, all for his own benefit. But she had to remember it was she who had forced him to let her stay. "It's not your fault."

"Still. I should've known better." He kicked a nearby palm tree. Amelia stared at him blankly, unable to muster the energy to comfort him, and luckily didn't have to as Evelyn walked outside.

"How are you holding up?" Evelyn asked. She looked weary, dark circles encompassing her eyes and hair frizzled by the heat. Amelia jumped up and wrapped her arms around her sister, taking comfort from the person who knew how to give it best. It'd been so hectic after the raid she hadn't had the chance to express her relief that her sister was still alive. Evelyn exhaled against her, the two women holding on to each other as if it were the last time – until, out of nowhere, Amelia was overcome with laughter. She pulled away and bent over, trying to contain the odd feeling of amusement that was escaping from her chest. "I can't believe we're here. That we're the last Australian women in Salamaua!" Amelia's chest hiccupped at the hilarity of the idea while Evelyn looked at her as if she'd gone mad.

"It's certainly something you'd only read about in war novels," Evelyn replied quietly.

"That's why it's so hilarious!" Amelia tipped her head back, no longer knowing if she was laughing or crying.

Her father's voice interrupted her outburst, forcing Amelia to compose herself. "What's gotten into you two?"

"Nothing," Evelyn replied, always quick to come to Amelia's rescue. She turned towards their father and looked at the bandage on his cheek. "Looks like Amelia patched you up nicely."

"Hmm. That she did."

Amelia looked away, not used to the praise about her nursing skills. It'd never been her strong suit; even while she was studying, she was always at the bottom of the class, so it was nice to hear that she had some ability, especially in their current predicament. Her gaze landed on Daniel, who was still standing by the tree, watching closely but not saying anything, like he always did. She wanted to go to him, to ease his burdens, but was still enraged by his betrayal. She turned towards her father instead. "Did you manage to get any rest?"

"No," he replied. "I was speaking with the Administration staff. Looks like we're going to evacuate. Inland to Butu in case the Japs try to land. From there we'll have to figure a way out. We've gotten word that Rabaul may've been taken … they've been off the wireless since the raid. It's only a matter of time before they get to Salamaua, to Lae. We're not prepared for that, and the few NGVR lads the Administration has assembled won't cut it when the Nips do come."

Amelia stiffened. It was disconcerting to hear her father confirm Daniel's earlier beliefs, that the Australian Administration really had abandoned them. She glanced at Daniel again, who was looking as if he was deep in thought.

A thought suddenly came to her. "All of us are going, then?" she asked.

"Aye. All the remaining men. Silas too. Most of the natives scurried into the bush but whoever's left can carry our goods."

She nodded. They were leaving Salamaua, but this time she didn't know if she was happy that Daniel was coming with her or not.

# 12

# Daniel

Mud sucked at their feet, making the trek in the pitch-black night all the harder. The track was a quagmire from the pouring rain that'd refused to cease since the first droplets had fallen earlier that evening while they were burying Kevin. Daniel had shivered as they lowered his body into the wet ground, even though the air was sticky with heat. He was pleased the lad would at least have a spectacular view of the Huon Gulf as his final resting place, though doubted that would mean much to his wife and children.

At least they'd given Kevin a proper send-off. Would anyone think to do that for *him*? Amelia would, but without being his wife, what right would she have to lay claim to his final resting place, especially if she was in Australia and he was here? He shook his head and told himself to stop thinking such morbid thoughts – he was alive and so was she … that's all that mattered. And she was getting out, no thanks to him, but at least there was a plan. He hoped the Japanese didn't land before they were able to see it through. A report had come through that Kieta had been taken too. Without a coast guard stationed at Salamaua, who knew if the Japanese were within range of the isthmus? And with all the aircraft destroyed, walking really was the only way out, even if the conditions were near impossible.

He squinted through the blinding rain, trying to determine whether Amelia was struggling as she walked ahead of him. She'd never admit it outright, her pride sometimes getting the better of her. It'd hurt that she couldn't even convey her feelings to him after the raid, and that she'd been so easily comforted by her father when Daniel's words had seemed to fall short. He needed to get through to her, to find that connection again, like they had in the hut, before everything had turned to shit. Who knew how much time they had left?

"Meels," he said as he grabbed her hand and pulled her off the track. A branch scratched at his leg as a line of men marched past, their bodies outlined in the blackened night. He was glad it was near impossible to see, not wanting any prying eyes on them. "You need to talk to me."

"I don't need to do anything, Daniel," she replied, voice hard to hear as the rain fell against the leaves. "My father will have a fit if he discovers I'm no longer behind him."

Daniel clenched his jaw. She was worse than before; there was a clear shift in her mood that he couldn't put a finger on. He wiped the rain from his face and said, "Fine. But when we stop, we need to talk."

"Stop telling me what to do, too," she said, before falling back in line with the men.

Daniel let out a heavy sigh. What had changed so dramatically between them? Obviously, the attack had rattled her in a way she was finding hard to shake, but shouldn't grief and fear bring two people together, rather than pull them apart? And if she wouldn't turn to him, then who was Daniel supposed to turn to? He had no one without Amelia.

* * *

They arrived at Butu in the early morning, the local villagers welcoming them with curious looks as they set up camp, no doubt wondering why more than a hundred men and two women were suddenly thrust upon their village. The white man, or "waitman", was only seen a few times a year by visiting Administration men called Kiaps, who were assigned to administer the law Niuginians were to abide by as part of the Mandated Territory. So to be suddenly bombarded by more than a hundred of them must've been baffling, especially after the attacks. *They* were supposed to be the ones in charge – and here they were, fleeing.

Daniel tried to reassure the villagers by offering a warm smile, but he still felt the intense scrutiny in their eyes, as if he was the strangest component of it all, his non-conforming skin colour rearing its ugly head again. But with the Japanese on their heels, all that mattered now was getting Amelia to safety. He took a moment to wipe the mud from his face and body, thankful the rain had cleared, even if the humidity had risen in its wake, and went off in search of Amelia. He found her instantly; spotting a woman amidst a hundred men was like finding gold in Edie Creek. But when he realised who she was speaking to, he couldn't help but stiffen.

"Look what the cat dragged in," Tom said as Daniel approached. Tom was wearing a clean white shirt and khaki shorts, with white knee socks that didn't have a speck of mud on them.

"Tom. Where did you come from?" Daniel replied, trying to hide the shock in his voice. He hadn't once thought of his brother after the attack, which he couldn't help but feel ashamed about. Even if he hated the bloke, he was the only family Daniel had.

Tom refused to look at Daniel, saying to Amelia instead, "I was with the last group who arrived from Lae. We left Salamaua not long after you. The *bois* helped me find the way." He turned his head to a group of locals who were resting nearby, mud slicked across their bodies.

Daniel scratched his chin, wondering if the "boys" had carried Tom, which would account for his immaculate appearance. He glanced at Amelia, who looked as if she was thinking the same thing, brows furrowed in suspicion.

"What's the word in Lae?" Amelia asked. "Was it as badly hit as Salamaua?"

Tom spat in the mud. "They came in pretty hard, the dirty bastards, thrashing away at the town as if it were theirs to take. The aerodrome was hit badly, the Guinea Airways dispensary and powerhouse were flattened, their aircraft and hangars too. Everyone bar the NGVR evacuated up Markham road. I wanted to check what happened at Salamaua but when I got there the remaining NGVR told me you'd left. I would've gone back to Lae, but the Administration decided to destroy it."

Amelia gasped. "What do you mean, *destroy*?"

"Scorched-earth policy," Tom said casually. Daniel carved his hands through his hair, knowing what that meant, but Tom provided an explanation anyway. "The Administration said to burn it all, to leave nothing for the Japs in case they land. It's gone … all of it."

Amelia pressed her hand to her mouth, while Daniel shook his head, the thought of Lae being burned to the ground hard to fathom. At least there were parts of Salamaua still intact: the hospital and hotel, and several of the houses and trade stores, which meant there was still a chance of reclaiming it if the Aussies could get enough soldiers back in time. But if the Administration thought it best to burn Lae, then there really mustn't be any hope for an eventual return.

"Was that McNicoll's idea?" Daniel asked.

Tom continued to look at Amelia, whose face had blanched. "McNicoll's gone. Evacuated out of Lae yesterday due to ill health. He left his deputy, Melrose, in charge."

Daniel released the grip on his hair, not willing to believe it. They really had been abandoned by the Aussies, left to navigate themselves through a dangerous land with the threat of the enemy beating down their necks. Who would help them now?

Mr McKenzie approached, Evelyn in step behind him.

"Right," Mr McKenzie said, instantly commanding the group's attention. Tom and Amelia turned towards him. "I've spoken to Melrose, and the plan is for the young and fit to head up the range to Wau with Penglase, while the elderly and sick will be led by Melrose down the coast to Buna, then inland to Kokoda airfield for evacuation."

Daniel exhaled. While he was angry with Mr McKenzie for forcing his hand, at least the man knew how to take charge and get things done, which was exactly what they needed.

"So, then we'll head up to Wau with you?" Amelia asked.

"Afraid not," Evelyn replied in lieu of her father. She was dishevelled from the trek, loose strands of hair sticking out of her bun and streaks of mud slicked across her arms. Stepping forward so she was in line with Mr

McKenzie, she added, "The sick men will need us on the journey to Kokoda."

Mr McKenzie squeezed Amelia's shoulder and added, "Aye, lass. The trek up the Black Cat is much too difficult for those who aren't young and healthy, which is why we need you and Evelyn to accompany them down the coast. It'll be much more comfortable for you all."

Amelia glanced at Daniel. He held her gaze but was unsure of what his eyes would convey. Mr McKenzie's plan was logical. A clear division of the group would be easier to manage and prevent them from being detected by the Japanese, and yet he knew what that division would mean for the two of them. He was young and fit, and she was needed to care for the sick.

Yet Amelia wouldn't concede so easily. She looked back to her father and asked, "Why don't we all go to Kokoda together, then?"

"I need to find out what state Wau is in," Mr McKenzie replied. "I lost my entire fleet at Salamaua. Who knows what's happened up in the Highlands. We can't get much off the wireless, except reports of the occasional Jap sighting. Bulolo was attacked in the raids, but we should be able to fly out of Wau."

"I don't want to leave you, Dad," Amelia said, voice cracking. Daniel's heart twisted, wishing she'd said his name instead of her father's.

"Aye, lass," Mr McKenzie replied as he pulled Amelia to his chest. "But the trek is much too difficult for the lads who are sick. They need you and your sister, and I don't need you fighting me on this one."

Amelia nodded and left it at that, which surprised Daniel a little, but he didn't have time to dwell on her behaviour.

He pulled his shoulders back and stepped forward to say, "Sir, what do you need me to do?"

Mr McKenzie met his eye. "Help Silas and the boys divide the materials. Both parties will need adequate supplies to make the journey. The injured will leave for Laukanu this afternoon."

Daniel's heart sank. He now knew how long he had with Amelia. A matter of hours. He swallowed and offered a curt nod in return.

"So ... so soon?" Amelia replied, voice wobbling.

Mr McKenzie scratched his beard, puffing out his cheeks as he expelled the air from his chest. "I know, lass, but it's no longer safe here – for any of us, men included. We need to get you and your sister out before it's too late. But not to fret, Tom will be with you."

Daniel jerked his head back. "Tom?" He fixed his gaze on his brother, who was standing there with a smug look on his face.

"I ... I was injured in the raid," Tom said, still unwilling to meet Daniel's eye. "That's why the natives had to carry me here. George agrees I should be evacuated with the other injured men."

"You don't look injured to me," Daniel said with a snarl.

Tom scowled, finally meeting Daniel's eye. "What would you know, Danny *boi?*"

"More than you."

"It's fine, Daniel," Amelia interjected, grabbing his forearm and squeezing, but Daniel snatched it away. He stepped towards Tom, who cut him off.

"You think you're so clever," Tom said, head tilting to the side. "A Kanaka who thinks he's white. Well, think again, *boi,* because you're not."

"That's enough, lads," Mr McKenzie interrupted, voice firm. "Your father would be ashamed of your behaviour, especially in a time like this. I've agreed Tom can go with the injured men, while Daniel will come with me to Wau. If there are any planes left up there, I'll need a good pilot to fly them out."

Daniel glared at Tom for another moment before turning on his heel and storming off, not even bothering to relish the compliment Mr McKenzie had paid him.

* * *

"There you are," Amelia said as she walked up behind Daniel. He was at the edge of the village, fiddling with the packs of stores that would see Amelia and the injured men through the next several weeks as they made their way up the Morobean coast to Buna. It was harsh territory: croc- and mosquito-infested swamplands with long stretches of exposed beach. The group would have to be mindful of not only the elements, but also the threat of Japanese planes flying overhead, especially when they didn't have the jungle for protection. He wanted to make sure she had everything she needed to make the trip as comfortable as possible, though didn't know why he was even bothering, since she had Tom to look after her.

Looking over his shoulder, he offered a half smile. "Here I am," he said as he shoved a raincoat into the pack.

She hovered next to him, biting her fingernails. Daniel opened his mouth, but wasn't entirely sure what to say. Amelia shifted on her feet, glancing over her shoulder, before finally taking a seat on a patch of grass opposite him. She pulled her knees to her chest and rested her chin on them, biting on her lip as she spun a blade of grass between her fingers. A symphony of insects hummed, the only noise between the two of them. She cleared her throat, as if she was going to speak, but no words came.

"I guess we better say goodbye," Daniel finally offered, trying to break the pulsating tension.

"I'm surprised you want to," Amelia muttered, gaze still set on the grass.

Daniel tensed. "Why would you say that? Look at the lengths I went to before the raid."

Amelia looked up. "The lengths you went to? I ran away from my parents so I could see you. Look how much good that's done me now."

"You couldn't have known what was going to happen."

"No. But I still risked it. You can hardly say the same."

Daniel flinched, skin tightening. *Does she know?*

"Why didn't you tell me my father offered you a place in the NGVR in return for ending things with me?"

*She does.* Daniel looked away. "I'm sorry, Meels. I shouldn't have done that."

"No, you shouldn't have."

The silence between them stretched on again, the lack of words screeching in Daniel's ear, like fingernails scraping a chalkboard. He wanted to offer an explanation, to help her understand why he'd betrayed her, but everything he could think of fell short.

"Right, then. I guess I'd better go," Amelia said as she stood.

Daniel swallowed, throat choking as he tried to think of suitable words. Were they really going to leave it like this? Amelia stared at him, eyes pleading, desperate for recognition of her pain, but he didn't know how to express himself; his thoughts were muddled. She offered a slow nod – as if she understood that nothing was coming from Daniel's pathetic mouth – and turned to leave.

"You know ..." she said, stopping short. "I don't regret what happened before the raid. Everything we shared leading up to it, and what ... what we did in the hut." She paused, as if she was remembering that moment, before saying, "But something changed in me when those Zeros swooped in. A realisation of how selfish I'd been. My parents don't deserve that. No matter how awful my mother can be, she deserves for her daughter to respect her enough to leave when she's asked. And my father definitely didn't deserve to worry about whether I'd been killed or not, and certainly doesn't deserve the stress I've now added to the situation. I ... I'm lucky he's even alive." Her voice choked on the last word.

Daniel rose, ready to comfort her, but she stopped him by adding, "I love you, Daniel. I always have. I was ready to do anything to preserve that love, to fight until the end to give it a chance. But I'm not so sure anymore. There's too much uncertainty, not only with the war, but with how you feel about me."

He didn't know what to say. He didn't want to leave things this way, but he couldn't find the words to change it. She was right. He'd betrayed her when it mattered most. There was so much uncertainty – not just because of the war, but with Daniel himself. How could he be there for her when he didn't even know how to be there for himself? "Amelia—"

She put her hand up. "Don't. It's easier this way."

And with that she walked off, turning her back on Daniel, just like everyone else in his life had done.

# 13

## Amelia

Amelia swallowed back the tears, determined not to let Daniel see her cry. *It's easier this way.* She had to keep telling herself that. *It's easier.* Daniel betrayed her. She'd sacrificed it all for him, for a chance at a life together, a chance of a future – and he'd thrown it all back in her face. He'd been so willing to fight for his country, and yet he couldn't even muster a few words to fight for her. She could no longer trust him. Her father was right. A life together would be challenging. War was here. The Japanese were coming. Her life was in danger.

And still ... it felt as if she'd made the biggest mistake of her life. But she had to hold firm, so she kept her goodbye with her father brief, inhaling the familiar scent of her childhood as she imprinted every line of his face into her memory, telling herself over and over again this wouldn't be the last time. She did the same with Silas, fully embracing the little man, no longer caring who was watching, before gathering her pack and falling in step with the group as they marched out of Butu. Evelyn was by her side, the only saving grace in this entire mess.

They trekked up an old goat trail, and the rain fired up again with a vengeance, the downpour a mirror to Amelia's mood. Her boots were sucked off her feet several times, but she hardly cared, her heart the only thing she could feel. She stumbled, thankful for the group of locals from Butu who'd volunteered to help, carrying the stores and the sick men on old pinnaces while helping Amelia and the others with their footing in the mud. Tom was being carried in a pinnace, one arm resting behind his head and his Akubra hat tipped forward over his eyes, while his thin lips were turned slightly upwards. She shook her head. Did Tom really have the audacity to make these men carry him the entire way? But with no energy left to fight, she let it go. The events of the past twenty-four hours had changed everything. All she could do now was look forward and continue to put one muddy boot in front of the other as she walked further away from everything she'd ever known, praying she'd be lucky enough to get out of this alive.

* * *

Amelia dumped her pack on the ground and slumped down next to a tree. Her mud-slicked limbs ached along with her broken heart. They'd been walking for several hours, trudging through mud as thick as cassava. She was thankful when Melrose made the call to rest at Laukanu – a village five miles east of Salamaua – before they were to journey around the point on canoes. From there they'd hike again until nightfall. Amelia closed her eyes, focusing on the cacophony of jungle sounds echoing off the trees – anything to distract her from the look on Daniel's face when she'd refused to say goodbye – until the citrusy smell of Earl Grey brewing pulled her back to the present. She opened her eyes to see Evelyn standing above her with a cup of tea.

"Drink this," Evelyn said as she wiped the sweat from her forehead. "A cup of tea makes everything better."

Amelia accepted, her body relaxing as the tea coursed down her throat.

"We need to rebandage the men before we carry on," Evelyn said. "It's important we to keep their wounds clean, or they'll risk infection."

Amelia exhaled and savoured the final sip before standing up. "Righto. Where would you like me first?"

"Start with the men with the ulcers."

Amelia fished her medical kit out of her pack. She worked through a dozen or so men, dousing their wounds with iodine and wrapping them in fresh bandages. They were in fine spirits, thankful for Amelia's care, which helped to brighten her mood. There was comfort in providing comfort. She was finishing up on the last of the men when Tom came out of nowhere.

"Aren't you going to tend to me?" he said. That ridiculous smile of his was plastered across his face, and not a smudge of mud across his all-white attire.

Amelia swatted a fly away. "You look alright to me—"

"My ankle is killing me."

Amelia glanced at his foot. Tom suddenly winced as if he was in pain. She bit her tongue while pulling out a roll of bandage, then squatted to inspect his foot. She gently removed his boot and sock and checked for swelling, digging her fingers into his flesh to see if he'd react, but all he could do was smile down at her.

She stood up and said, "I'd better check in with Evelyn before we leave."

She glanced over his shoulder towards the village that was nestled in between the palm trees lining the black-sand beaches. Several locals were helping to pack the canoes, loading the pinnaces up with the supplies they'd carried from Salamaua and the men who were too sick to sit. Children splashed in the waves, completely unaware of the world around them, their bouts of laughter comforting. There would always be innocence.

Amelia offered Tom a half smile as she stepped past him, her mother's standards so ingrained in her she couldn't help it, but a loud whooshing stopped her cold. She looked up, searching for the plane that had made the noise, hopeful it was the Aussies out on reconnaissance. Her stomach seized. It was a large gunmetal-grey plane with red emblems emblazoned on the belly. The Japanese, back for more. Amelia stumbled backwards, tripping over Tom into the mud, where she cowered like a turtle in its shell. She pressed her hands to her ears, heartbeat thrashing, the plane no longer audible, only the distant sound of her name being called. A name she no longer wanted, a person she no longer cared to be. It wasn't until several minutes later – or hours; she wasn't sure – that the thrashing stopped. She peeked out of her shell to discover she was in Tom's arms.

"It's alright, Meels. They're gone," he said as he stroked her back.

She was suddenly aware of his skin against hers, the heat of his breath.

She stiffened. "What was it?"

"Just the Japs surveying the area. They kept going up the coast."

"Are you sure?" She looked around as if she was expecting the Japanese to jump out of the bushes. But all she could see was the injured men she'd tended to earlier being loaded onto the canoes.

"Of course I am," Tom replied matter-of-factly and pulled her closer to his chest. He pressed his nose into her hair and inhaled, causing Amelia to flinch.

She pulled away. "We'd better get to it then, if we want to get past the point before nightfall. We're lucky we weren't out there when they flew past." She walked towards the pinnaces, not daring to give Tom a second look, to give him any ideas; her willingness to take comfort in the arms of the first man she fell in was a worry.

* * *

Sweat seeped from every crevice as the sun singed Amelia's skin. The canoe spliced through the water that glimmered like an aquamarine. What she would give to jump into the ocean, to wash the sticky, pungent aroma from her body. They were moving at a snail's pace, the local who was paddling taking his time to guide Amelia and Evelyn around the point safely. No one was ever in a rush in New Guinea … even with the threat of the Japanese flying overhead at any minute, the locals would always take their time. Amelia's stomach roiled, the meagre lunch they'd had before they left threatening to expel itself. She turned her head to watch the trail of canoes and pinnaces behind them, like a mother duck leading her ducklings along – ducklings that were more like sitting ducks out here.

Amelia glanced back at Evelyn, whose face was tipped towards the sun.

"Do you think we're foolish for not going with Dad?" Amelia asked.

Evelyn opened her eyes, a soft shade of hazel staring back at Amelia. She found it incredible that the three sisters all had such different features.

"We didn't have a choice," Evelyn replied with a smile. "These men need us." Evelyn's smile wasn't as reassuring as usual. It wavered, like Daniel's love.

"But what if the Japanese catch us?"

"We can't think like that."

"Still ... aren't you scared?"

Evelyn took a moment to answer. "I've learned that nurses don't have that luxury. We must remain calm. The injured already have so much to contend with. As hard as it can be, we must be strong for them."

Amelia nodded, wondering how she could ever muster that sort of strength. She was not the reassuring type and found it very difficult to control her emotions; she was always the first to fire up, her father's Scottish blood flowing freely through her veins. She only had to look at how easy it was to get angry with Daniel to know she could be quick to react. Now that they were miles apart, separated by mountains, jungle and seas, she wondered if perhaps she had overreacted.

"Ev," she said quietly, wondering how to phrase the thoughts that'd been whirling in her head ever since she walked away from him.

"I know you're hurting, Meels, but I think you made the right decision," Evelyn replied, instantly knowing her sister's thoughts.

"You do?"

"Yes."

Amelia bit her lip, still not reassured, prompting Evelyn to continue.

"War changes things. Everything, in fact. You cannot make the same decisions without factoring that in. War will change you. It will change Daniel and it will change this place. The hard truth is that New Guinea is no longer our home."

"How can you say that? Lae ... Salamaua, they'll always be our home."

"Think about it, Meels. What do you think will be left when the Australians and Japanese are through? Look at what the Aussies did to Lae, what the Japanese did in one air raid."

Amelia looked past Evelyn at the receding coastline, the staggering green peaks that enveloped the valley that Lae sat in. Heavy clouds hovered above the town, the town that was now engulfed in smoke, swallowed up by its own forced destruction. Amelia shivered when she thought of what else was to come, what Daniel would be left to face. And yet, what choice did she have? War was here. Change was coming. Daniel wouldn't be the same person when this was over, and neither would she. The events of the past two days had already cemented that. Who would she be in a year, or five years from now? This war could drag on for years. Everything would be different when it was over. She had to trust her decision, that what she was doing was right, even if it was breaking her heart.

# 14

# Daniel

Daniel fell to the back of the line, boots dragging through the mud as they ascended the range. He kept glancing over his shoulder, hoping she'd appear, desperate to have him back, forgiving him for his transgressions. But all that was behind him was jungle as dense as his steely heart. A bevy of birds bellowed high above, their song piercing his ears like a screeching baby. Normally Daniel would take pleasure in the sounds of nature, the elements around him and the indistinct beauty of the bush, but every agonising step only deepened his distance from Amelia.

He could've slapped himself for not speaking up when she came to say goodbye, for not fighting harder for their love and its place in this world. But she did have a point – he'd betrayed her, to her father, no less, put his needs before her own. And there was so much uncertainty, so much unknown before them ... yet the one thing he was certain about was his love for her. So then why couldn't he say that? He swatted at a vine that hung across the path, wishing he was better at expressing himself. He always held his emotions close, whereas Amelia wore hers like a shield. She'd been ready to fully commit herself, but he'd wavered, torn between his two desires.

She said it was easier this way, but none of this felt easy. The only thing that'd been easy was the way he felt when he held her in that hut, the delicate lines of her body pressed against his. He closed his eyes and inhaled, still smelling her perfume, praying it never faded. But it'd be impossible to hold on to, with what was ahead. How could they find a place together in a society that would never accept them? He was too busy fighting for a place for himself, let alone the two of them together. She must've seen that, which was why she was able to walk away so easily. She was right. It was easier this way. He'd have to soldier on without her, even though his shattered heart was screaming not to.

* * *

For every white man on the track, there were two to three black ones carrying his goods, blindly trudging up this mountain on the faith of their master's word. He had to give it to the locals who'd stayed. Most of them had fled into the bush after the Japanese swooped into Salamaua. He supposed for some, like Silas, working for the waitman was the only life they knew. They were far more loyal and brave than they were given credit for. Silas was directly in front of him, dressed in a lap-lap that hung above the knee. His torso was seared with scars, the history of his life written on his body, a preview into the daily hardships that Niuginians faced. He was carrying a spear carved out of bamboo that was tucked into a sheath made of kunai grass. His head slowly shifted from one side of the jungle to the other, like a meerkat watching for predators.

Mr McKenzie was in front of Silas, trudging along purposefully, even though the trek would've been taxing on a man his size. Daniel still hadn't spoken to him since the attack, worried he might have blamed Daniel for Amelia missing the evacuation flight. Daniel was angry with him for allowing Tom to go with the injured men. The lying weasel clearly wasn't hurt, and yet Mr McKenzie had let him get away with it. And Daniel was still angry with Mr McKenzie for convincing him to betray Amelia. He was angry about it all. But there was no point in arguing about it now.

The line came to a stop as the men ducked under a fallen tree that was blocking the path. When it came to Mr McKenzie's turn, he stepped aside to let Silas go ahead of him. Then as Mr McKenzie bent down under the mossy log, his trousers got caught on a branch that ripped straight through the khaki material.

"Christ!" he cried as he clutched at his thigh and blood poured out. Daniel ripped one of the sleeves from his shirt and crouched under the log to tie it around the wound.

"Thanks," Mr McKenzie mumbled. Daniel didn't reply, but stepped back to the other side of the tree. He shifted his pack, the weight of his cargo digging into his shoulders.

"You coming, lad?" Mr McKenzie asked, eyes concealed by the fog that shielded his glasses. Even at altitude, the jungle was still steamy with heat. "Wouldn't want you to be left behind."

*You sure about that?* Daniel carefully ducked under the tree, mindful of the branch that got Mr McKenzie, but was so weighed down by his pack that he fell arse over in the mud.

Mr McKenzie chuckled and reached out a hand. "You should really let one of the bois carry that for you." Daniel was the only one who'd felt the need to carry his own pack.

"I'm capable of doing it myself," he replied as he took Mr McKenzie's hand and pulled himself up.

Mr McKenzie patted him on the back. "Course you are, lad. But it's still nice to have the help."

Daniel didn't say anything, waiting for Mr McKenzie to start back up the track. But the man hovered, as if he wanted to say something but didn't know how. Daniel looked around, watching as a palai slinked up the branch, listening as a gecko clicked, suddenly very aware of the intricacies of the jungle.

Mr McKenzie coughed before saying, "You know why I wanted you to come with me to Wau, don't you?"

"You needed a pilot," Daniel replied.

"Aye. That's true. I sure as hell wouldn't trust Tom in one of my planes. He can't fly to save his life." Daniel couldn't help but smile at that. It was nice to hear his brother being criticised for once. "But that's not the only reason ..." Mr McKenzie continued, lowering his glasses, his impenetrable stare forcing Daniel to meet his eye. "You remind me a lot of your father. That's why it's hard for me to say this, but it has to be said. This thing between you and my daughter must come to an end."

Daniel held Mr McKenzie's gaze, searching for the man his father had been so fond of, but the old man's eyes revealed nothing, forcing Daniel to look away. "I already know your sentiments on that, sir. So, if you don't mind, can we keep moving? I don't want to be left behind." He stepped ahead of Mr McKenzie, but the man grabbed him by the arm and said, "I don't care what you think you know, I need you to confirm that it's over between the two of you."

Daniel snatched his arm back. He was sick of being pushed around by this man, desperate to put an end to the inexplicable power he held over him. Daniel lifted his chin and looked him square in the eye. "And what if it isn't? What are you going to do about it? You can't threaten me anymore. I've lost everything that's ever meant anything to me. My father's dead, my home's destroyed, Amelia's ..."—he swallowed—"gone."

"I told you I'd make sure you'd never fly again—"

"Who gives a damn! There aren't any planes left to fly, and if there *are* any left they'll likely be seized by the Air Force. Even if I wanted to, they'd never let me join anyway. I'm too black! So enough with your threats. I'm done." Daniel spat the words out. He wanted to press on with the trek, but something was keeping him in place, an itch to know how Mr McKenzie would respond to such a bold outburst.

Mr McKenzie scratched at his beard as he took in Daniel's words. He ran his tongue along the inside of his mouth, before turning to spit into the bush. "You *are* too black," he said, meeting Daniel's eye again. "At least you are to the Aussies. But that's not the reason why I don't want you to be with Amelia ... well, not entirely."

Daniel had heard enough, and yet still he couldn't move, beholden to this man's opinion.

"It's because Amelia has enough to deal with. Leaving here will hit her hard, harder than it will be for her sisters and mother. Like me, she's drawn to New Guinea in a way that can't be explained. To be separated from it, with the potential of never returning, will be difficult for her. She doesn't need anything else to exacerbate the situation. Pining over you for the next several years won't help."

"Don't you think that's up to her to decide?"

"No. As her father, I know best. And I know that leaving you behind once and for all is what's best … what's easiest."

*It's easier this way.* He gasped. "It was you … you're the one who convinced her to finish it."

"I had to. There was no other choice."

"What did you say to her?"

"I convinced her to think rationally for once. After what she put me and her mother through, she owes us that at least."

"Why? Why are you so convinced this will be easier?"

"Because …" Mr McKenzie said slowly. "This war will kill you, and I don't want my daughter's heart to be broken all over again when it does."

# 15

# Amelia

Amelia tossed in her hammock, the incessant noise of cicadas chirring making it hard to sleep. Or was it her own troubled mind? Either way, she knew in situations like this it was easier to get up and get on with the day. The injured men would need tending to before another day beneath the blazing sun, and she wanted to do it on her own this time, allowing Evelyn some extra rest.

She walked to the hut that housed the sick. The air was cool ... pleasant, the only time of day when the temperature was tolerable. Several of the men were sleeping soundly, like Tom. She rolled her eyes and started on the men who were actually sick, the ones who were shivering with fever. Their moans were like the cries of feral cats. She mixed a tincture of salts, hands shaking as she carefully tipped it inside the first patient's mouth. She sponged the next one, the tepid water doing little to alleviate the heat from his sweating body. Most of them were suffering from typical diseases seen in the tropics – malaria, yaws and dysentery; these were able-bodied men knocked down faster than if they'd been punched by Joe Louis. There were a few who'd been hit by shrapnel in the attack, their wounds already festering with infection. But the worst was the pilot Clarke, the man who'd pulled Parer out of his plane. He stared at the thatched ceiling, his blue eyes clouded with tears he was clearly trying to hold back. His leg was wrapped tightly, but pus had already oozed through the bandage, crusting the cloth.

Amelia tried to steady her hands as she peeled it back to expose the weeping wound. She held her breath to mask the smell of rotten flesh.

"How's it looking, miss?" Clarke asked in a strained voice. His teeth were chattering.

Amelia swallowed. "Not great."

"At least you're honest. Do you have anything for the pain?"

She nodded and hurried to administer a dose of laudanum, before redressing the wound so it was fresh for the journey ahead. She didn't know how these men could stand to be in the hot sun, and made a note to think of them whenever she thought to complain. When she was done, Clarke closed his eyes, the painkillers already taking affect. While his infection wasn't the worst she'd seen, Amelia could tell he was masking a deeper pain. Attempting to pull Parer from that plane had clearly shaken his psyche, and there wasn't much Amelia could do to ease those troubles. She didn't know how Evelyn did it every day.

Desperate to escape the smell that swallowed the sick, she stepped outside and drew in a deep breath. The air was warming as the sun peeked over the horizon, and miles of coastline stretched out before them. It would be another long day. One of many as they slowly made their way to safety.

* * *

Evelyn heaved over the side of the canoe, her morning's breakfast expelling itself. Fish nibbled at the bits of vegemite-stained rice that floated on the ocean's gleaming surface. It was the second time she'd been sick that morning, the seas not as accommodating as they'd been in the previous few days.

"Get me out of here," Evelyn moaned.

Amelia handed her the canteen of water. "You need to keep your fluids up. You'll get dehydrated if you don't."

Evelyn snatched it out of her hands. "Don't you think I know that?"

Amelia didn't reply, knowing Evelyn wasn't herself. The canoe bobbed along, swaying with the ocean's current, water slapping the hull like a seal fanning its flipper.

"Sorry," Evelyn eventually said. "I never expected for this to happen. I really need to stay well for the men."

Amelia rubbed her sister's back. "Of course. We'll get you a kulau when we get to shore … it'll be sure to replenish you."

Evelyn offered a half smile and closed her eyes. They spent the next several hours rocking along, Evelyn vomiting another two times, staining the turquoise waters around the Fly Islands yellow with her bile. Amelia relished the kaleidoscope of blues that danced before them – assorted aquas and azures, contrasted by deeper shades of cobalt further out. A pod of at least fifty dolphins cruised past, leaping from the ocean in such a playful way Amelia couldn't help but laugh, the first time in days.

Evelyn groaned.

"Sorry," Amelia said. She was still stroking her sister's back when she was startled by a noise – one she knew all too well. Her gaze shot to the sky; she was no longer entranced by the water but desperate to know if the Japanese were back for more. She frantically searched the patches of cloud, pulse picking up pace as she waited for a plane to emerge, praying it wasn't them. And then … when it did, her breath escaped in a loud exhale.

It was a Hudson, flying north towards Salamaua. She wondered if the pilot had seen them, if he'd send help, find them an easier way to get out. Though she'd flown enough to know their canoes would look like nothing more than a tiny blip across the ocean's vast surface. There wasn't any help to send anyway. The Administration had failed them. They were all alone out here. Nothing more than a few sick men, the fate of their future left in the hands of two flailing sisters.

* * *

"Look, Ev," Amelia said a few hours later even though Evelyn couldn't lift her head. "We're coming in to shore."

They were approaching the mouth of the Eia River, the water shallowing out as beds of sand emerged out of nowhere. Amelia was thankful they were being guided by a local from the area, each day's journey being led by the villagers they'd camped with the night before. The swell was up, making the navigation into shore even trickier as large waves propelled the canoe forward. Amelia gripped her seat, praying they wouldn't capsize, unsure that she'd be able to get Evelyn safely to shore in her current state. Another wave took hold, and they surged forward, the wave crashing as they landed safely ashore. Amelia exhaled as she released her grip. She helped Evelyn hobble to a nearby coconut tree, then yelled to their steadfast captain, who was dragging the canoe up the beach so it could be hidden amongst the trees.

"Wantok. Yu kisim sampela kulau?" She pointed to the coconut tree above.

Within seconds he was shimmying up it, his limbs like a catapult thrusting him towards heaven. He reached the top and pulled two coconuts off, before sliding down like a fireman. With his bush knife, he peeled the husks and pierced the eyes, before handing the coconuts to Amelia.

"Yu laikim sampela moa, missus?" he asked, a wide smile crinkling his eyes. His teeth were as red as a beetroot, lips and tongue stained with betelnut.

"No. Tenkyu, tru."

Amelia tipped the coconut water into Evelyn's mouth. "Thanks, Meels," Evelyn mumbled. Her face was blanched, cheeks hollowed and eyes watery. A sour smell lingered. Amelia made a note to give Evelyn a sponge bath as soon as they'd set up camp.

She took a sip of the sweet drink, watching as the local man helped the other canoes to shore. She grimaced when he spat a large glob of buai into the sand, staining it red. Nearly all of the canoes had made it safely to shore when Amelia realised the two pinnaces – one with the very sick men and the other that held their food supply – were still further out, stuck on a sand bar.

Amelia ran to the water's edge to join the legions of men who were disembarking their canoes. They were helping the locals to get the canoes up the beach, even though they couldn't do much in their wearied states. Tom jumped out of his, the waves soaking his white socks through. Amelia smirked as he sulked over to her, leaving the local who had navigated him in to drag the canoe on his own.

"Bloody hell," he said, his shirt soaked to his skin.

Amelia was watching the pinnaces again to see if they had moved. "Bloody hell is right," she said. "The pinnaces are stuck on the sand."

"So?" Tom replied.

"So, if we don't get them off, we could lose them!"

"What do you want me to do about it?"

Amelia scoffed. "Nothing, Tom. Absolutely nothing." She ran into the sea, the saltwater stinging her sunburnt skin. Another set of waves was coming through, the crash of them landing like thunder pounding the heavens. She watched them carefully, and then dove under. A whitewash of water engulfed her, pushing her forward, backward, upwards and down, and her body searched for the surface, the breath of air she would soon need. When she pushed through the top, she gasped, relieved to be beyond the break. Her arms cut through the water as she broke into a freestyle, pushing through the current that was determined to send her back. When the water was shallow enough to touch sand again, she waded through a new set of smaller waves, waves that were crashing against the hull of the pinnace, tipping it back and forth. The Aussie bloke who'd been captaining it was standing in the water, desperately trying to push it off the sandbar without much luck, the veins on his face bulging against his red, blistered skin.

Amelia keeled over to catch her breath, noticing the bags of stores piled high inside the pinnace. She exhaled, relieved it wasn't the pinnace with the sick men. Still, they needed those stores to see them through the next few weeks. Watching the Aussie bloke, she jammed her shoulder into the side of the boat, but even with her added weight, it wouldn't budge. She shifted her stance so she was towards the starboard side of the stern. She caught the Aussie's eye, and they gave it one more push together. The boat moved, but instead of going forward, the hull tipped towards the port side, flipping itself and all its contents into the ocean.

Amelia gasped.

"Crikey!" the Aussie yelled. He waded further into the water to try and salvage the bags of rice that were starting to sink. Amelia gaped, unable to move, until her body caught up with her mind and she ran in after him. Except she forgot to time her entrance, and the first wave pummelled her down. Her throat choked and her lungs heaved, a hacking cough escaping in between her gasps for air. She kicked, struggling to keep her head afloat, considering whether to stop, let go, concede defeat and finally be free of it all. It'd be easier. But then she thought of Evelyn and her father, of Daniel, and of what her death would mean to them. She thought of Kevin Parer's wife – the emptiness that grief brings – and knew she could never voluntarily do that to those she loved. She had to keep fighting. If not for herself, then for others. She kicked her legs until she touched sand, then crawled up it, heaving in every last breath of sweet air.

That's when she noticed something sailing in the distance, out towards the setting sun. It was the other pinnace. The one with the sick men. It should've made it to shore by now, escaping the fate of its friend here. But it was nowhere near land. It appeared to be moving further out to sea, being pushed away by the strong current of the river, soon to be swallowed by the horizon. Her mind raced. What should she do? Attempt to push through the waves again and find a way to save them? As a nurse, she had a duty of care. What would Evelyn do? The thought of her sister made up her mind and before she could change it, she dove back into the foamy waves, hoping she was a strong enough swimmer to save them.

# 16

# Daniel

Silas dug foot holes into the steep hill, helping Daniel and Mr McKenzie with each step. They were slowly finding their way up the near-vertical incline, Daniel gripping onto the wall of dirt, fingernails encrusted with earth, the ceaseless rain making the track boggy. If he slipped, he'd be sure to die. Just as Mr McKenzie had predicted. Except Daniel wasn't willing to allow him the satisfaction. The old man was heaving with every step, an endless stream of sweat slipping from his skin. The trek was taking its toll on all twenty-eight of the men – men who were supposed to be fit enough to survive this. Today's efforts were creeping into their eleventh hour, the never-ending hills getting steeper and steeper. The men were taking it in their stride, but Mr McKenzie seemed more put out than the others. A surprise, since he had climbed it so many times before.

Daniel focused on each step, losing himself in the jungle – every branch, every root, every vine imprinted into his mind. If he ever had to come back, he wanted to be prepared. Who knew in what capacity he would help once they got to Port Moresby? If the Aussies didn't want him, he'd be sure to find another other way to serve. He'd gather the Papuans and form his own army if he had to. Or go out on his own, a lone ranger. Niuginians were the greatest of warriors, Scotsmen too ... it was in his blood to fight, even if it killed him.

Mr McKenzie stopped halfway up the hill, chest heaving as he sucked in air. They were on an incline with nowhere to sit, and breaks had to be kept to a minimum until they arrived at the next village. Silas was above him, hand extended while he waited to help Mr McKenzie with his next step. Mr McKenzie's face was pale, and his shirt soaked through. It was hot, but not that hot, the air cooling considerably as the altitude increased. Mr McKenzie winced as he tried to lift his leg, and that's when Daniel noticed the problem. The man's shorts had risen up his thigh to expose his bandage, which was stained with blood and pus. The skin around it was raging red, the cut he'd suffered from the broken branch clearly infected. Daniel remembered what Evelyn had said about wounds that day at the hospital, how quickly they can turn up here. They still had another two days until they were due to arrive in Wau, and had to stay on course for fear of being left behind.

"Sir, are you alright?" Daniel asked, taking the few steps up so he was at the same height as Mr McKenzie. "Your leg doesn't look too good."

"Och," Mr McKenzie replied. "It's fine. Nothing I haven't encountered on this hellish trek before. Why do you think I started the airlines? So I'd never have to climb these mountains again!"

Daniel knew Mr McKenzie's moods well enough not to reply. A mosquito swarmed in his ear and he swatted it away, not wanting to succumb a fate every bit as dire as Mr McKenzie's, a bout of malaria being the last thing he needed. He rubbed at the stubbly beard that'd grown over the past week, wondering how they were going to get the man off the side of this mountain. They weren't far from the top; the trees were clearing only a few hundred feet above them. They'd made it this far, and Daniel sure as hell wasn't going to go back now.

"If you give me a push, I should be right with Silas pulling me from above," Mr McKenzie said. "Silas! Pull me up while Daniel pushes."

Silas nodded, but Daniel saw him look to the ground, not out of shame but as if he was assessing the situation. "I don't know, boss," he said. "You could slip."

"I won't slip if you do your job!" Mr McKenzie yelled. "Now hurry up! I'm desperate for a cup of tea." Silas shook his head but did as he was told, bending down to grab Mr McKenzie's hand. "Right, lad," Mr McKenzie said to Daniel. "You ready?"

Daniel looked down. The wall of dirt extended several hundred feet below until it opened into a deep ravine that was covered in a web of vines and trees. Silas was right. One of them could easily slip and fall to their death before they'd even have time to comprehend what was happening. Daniel refused to let Mr McKenzie's prediction come true, and yet couldn't help but think that it'd be an easy way to rid himself of the burden of him once and for all. Daniel bit the inside of his cheek and said, "If you say so."

Mr McKenzie shifted his rifle across his back and extended his good leg into one of the foot holes while Silas grabbed his hand. Daniel pushed up against Mr McKenzie's buttocks, muscles straining against the weight of a man, who easily weighed over fifteen stone. He gritted his teeth and held on tightly, even though his feet were slipping, the ground like banana peels beneath him. He *could* let go and watch as Mr McKenzie plummeted to his death, except his arms wouldn't allow it, wouldn't take a life so easily. Not yet, at least. He shoved his shoulder into Mr McKenzie's arse instead, throwing all his weight into it, just as a loud whooshing sounded from above. A plane was flying overhead. Turning his head to search through the canopy of trees, heart accelerating at the thought of the Japanese finding them, he lost his grip, his feet slipped from beneath him and his body hurled down the mountain, with no end in sight.

* * *

Daniel opened his eyes, a vision of Amelia dancing before him, glimmers of emerald green fading away as the canopy of rainforest came back into focus. The rain had eased into a light pitter-patter, everything else quiet except the usual sounds of the jungle. No plane. No voices. No one but him. He sat up – every muscle aching as he moved – and looked around. The jungle was as quiet as Daniel had feared. A snake slithered past, its cold skin brushing his arm. He flinched, and the creature slunk away, as if it hadn't even noticed Daniel was there. It was a death adder, with a flattened, triangular head and a thick body with bands of red, brown and black. Daniel shot to standing and scurried away. Taking a minute to calm his racing heart, he looked around to discover he was at the bottom of the ravine, the one he'd been sure would kill him. He'd fallen, terrified by the sound of the Japanese plane overhead.

He pieced together the last moments before it happened – how, ironically, he had ended up taking the fall for Mr McKenzie. Was that his plan all along? And now that Daniel had fallen, would he at least send the locals to help, or would he leave Daniel here to rot, finally getting his wish? Would anyone else come? Silas would, but would be forced to do as his "masta" said. Would the others even notice he was missing? Probably not – to them he was just another black man.

*I'm more than that. Aren't I?*

He spat out the mud that'd gathered in his mouth, eyeing the wall of dirt in front of him, the mountain he'd already climbed once that day. He squeezed his fists, ready to prove Mr McKenzie wrong. His body took control, stepping forward to start again. Mr McKenzie wouldn't be getting his wish – at least, not today.

* * *

Daniel hobbled into Skindiwai village, the roar of the men's laughter and smell of bully beef leading the way. He was desperate for a good feed and smoke after conquering that mountain again, and couldn't wait to see the look on Mr McKenzie's face when he strode into camp in one piece. But his reaction fell short. Mr McKenzie barely batted an eyelid.

"About time," Mr McKenzie said, extending a cup of tea out to Daniel.

"No thanks to you," he replied, taking the cup and throwing its contents into the fire. A few of the other men eyed him curiously, but said nothing.

Mr McKenzie sipped at his own cup. His thigh was propped up on a log, freshly bandaged though still the colour of cooked lobsters. A sheen of sweat glistened from his forehead. "Aye, well ... you couldn't have predicted the Japs flying overhead at that exact moment, but should expect that sort of thing when you're at war. Those bastards will come out of nowhere, so you'd better get a thicker skin about you, lad, or you won't even make it to Wau."

"That's what you'd prefer, isn't it? That I die out here? Then you'll be rid of me for good! That's why you didn't send anyone to help!"

Mr McKenzie shifted his leg slightly and winced. "I didn't send anyone to help because I knew you'd be alright on your own."

"How could you have known that?"

"Because your father survived the same fall when we were lads. Nearly same circumstances, in fact. Trying to help my fat arse up the range. These mountains are in your blood."

Daniel's mouth fell open. "You did this climb with my father?"

"Of course. You know that. Harry had been up and down the Black Cat at least a hundred times until we built the aerodrome in Wau. He was searching for gold, after all."

Daniel huffed, taking a seat next to Mr McKenzie as he warmed his hands above the fire. The talk of his father had settled his anger; Mr McKenzie always knew how to defuse a situation. Maybe the old man didn't want him to die after all. He eyed the men around him, who were sitting in nothing but their underdaks; their clothes were strewn over a rail that'd been erected near the blaze, washed of all mud and nearly ready to be worn again. A light mist lingered, the rain gone for now. Daniel noticed how the men were sitting in pairs, huddled close as they talked, the occasional laugh surfacing, while empty plates that'd been licked clean lay by their sides. There was a satisfied and sleepy look across each of their faces.

Daniel's stomach grumbled. "Is there any more food?"

Mr McKenzie hissed, and a local Daniel didn't recognise came scurrying up. "Givim dispela boi sompela kaikai," Mr McKenzie said, nodding towards Daniel. The local quickly returned with a plate of what looked like roast pig, but it had the rankest of smells. As hungry as he was, Daniel knew he'd be sick if he ate it.

Mr McKenzie grumbled. "Yu no ken ting?" he said to the local. "Givim sampela pawpaw, sampela suga cane." He shook his head and tsked, before saying to Daniel, "We're out of rations. Cooked up the last of the bully beef before you arrived. That cup of tea you threw into the fire was it until we get to Wau. The natives from this village went out and killed a boar for us, but as you can see the beast is as rank as my arse."

Daniel's shoulders slumped at the thought of nothing but fruit to satisfy his aching hunger, but was too tired to ask for anything else. He tucked into the plate of pawpaw the local man brought back for him, slurping up the slippery flesh that sailed down his throat until he couldn't eat anymore. All he needed now was a smoke, and he felt around in his pockets until he remembered he was all out. He looked around at the other men, but Mr McKenzie said, "We're all out of tobacco too."

Daniel's heart sank until Mr McKenzie added, "But I traded with the Kanakas in the village for some brus. Not as good, but it'll do the job." He handed Daniel a cigarette rolled out of banana leaves and lit it for him.

Daniel toyed with the taste of the first inhalation; it was incredibly strong compared to tobacco. *It's something at least.* He leaned back against a tree and closed his eyes, knowing this would be the first of many changes he'd have to endure.

* * *

Daniel shivered; the early morning air was bitterly cold. Mr McKenzie was lying next to him, face glistening with sweat as his body convulsed in chills. There was no doubt that he was suffering from infection, but there wasn't much they could do until they made it to Wau. He sat up briefly to stoke the fire, hoping the flames would help to warm them both, when he noticed that the other men were huddled close together, sucking the warmth from one another. Daniel inched closer to Mr McKenzie so his stomach was pressed against the old man's back.

"You trying to coorie me, boy?" Mr McKenzie asked, the tremors of his body vibrating through Daniel's.

Daniel stiffened but didn't move. "I'm trying to keep you warm."

Mr McKenzie grunted but allowed himself to be held. "Hope you're not thinking of my daughter."

Daniel scoffed. "Trust me. That's the last thing I'm thinking about." He relaxed and closed his eyes, though it was hard not to think of Amelia now, not to wonder whether she was travelling alright. New Guinea was a harsh place, a dangerous land. Her journey would be different to what Daniel was experiencing, but that didn't make it any less difficult. And with all those sick men to care for, Amelia had an extra challenge. At least she had Evelyn by her side, the company of a loved sibling. And Tom too, of course, but he pushed that thought aside, thinking instead of his friendship with her over the years, the close bond they shared and the ease that came with falling in love with your best friend. She was likely too consumed to think of anything except what was in front of her, but Daniel hoped that in those quiet moments before the day dawned and unveiled its gruesome self, in those occasional breaths of respite where she was able to sit, to think, to reflect, that she thought of him too.

# 17

# Amelia

The only thing Amelia could think about right now was getting Clarke and the other sick men safely to shore. Managing to reach their pinnace at the same time as two of the canoes, she climbed on board to discover the wounded were none the wiser about their situation. Clarke was gazing up at the sky – now fading into the blue hour – with a vacant stare. The Aussie man who was captaining this boat was trying to keep his cool, giving Amelia a stern look to warn her to keep quiet. She helped him tie the pinnace to the back of the canoes, then tended to Clarke as they were pulled towards shore.

She helped Clarke onto land, then lay him under a coconut tree before going to assess the damage to the pinnace. Evelyn was up on her feet, a touch of colour returned to her cheeks, and she helped to unload what they could salvage of the stores. All of the sugar, tea, biscuits and most of their rice was gone, sodden with sea water. Amelia sank to her knees.

"We might be able to dry it out," Evelyn said in that encouraging way she was known for.

"What will we do?" Amelia asked, a desperate tinge to her voice.

Evelyn sighed and sat next to her. "What we always do. Get on it with it."

Amelia nodded, but didn't know how much more they could get on with without the appropriate supplies. The sick men needed nourishment, the able-bodied ones hope. The kind of hope that comes at the bottom of a cup of tea. They still had weeks left of their journey, being only halfway to Buna, from where they'd trek inland until they reached Kokoda. From there, they'd hopefully be evacuated by air – but weren't certain Kokoda's airfield was even operable. She loved Evelyn, but her sister's overly positive nature was hard to stomach when they were faced with truly difficult circumstances. Sometimes she wanted to wallow in their misery. The rest of the trek would be near impossible without their stores; their reliance on the locals and their generosity would increase tenfold. And even though Amelia knew it was selfish, the idea of facing long days at sea and even longer nights without a cup of tea to look forward to was heartbreaking. She swallowed, throat burning as she held back the tears that threatened to spill out, the little hope she had left for the remainder of their journey sitting soaked on a beach in the middle of nowhere.

* * *

The huts that housed the sick were stifling, the smell of decaying flesh mixing with the pungent aroma of ammonia and sweat. Amelia held her breath as long as she could, but soon got used to the misery that swallowed these men, the hope for their survival diminishing each day. Their moans rattled in her ears. She and Evelyn had barely stopped since they'd arrived that afternoon, for the men who looked as if they had fared okay on the pinnace had taken a turn for the worse. Thankfully, Evelyn was well enough to help, having fully recovered from her bout of seasickness. But two nurses could do little to alleviate the trouble these men were in. Whenever she had finished tending to one man, she was summoned by the agonising groans of the next. The rain had started again too, a thunderous storm rolling in from the mountains, with bolts of lightning illuminating the hut and the worrying state they were in.

Clarke was by far the worst, with his wound slowly eating away at his flesh. He thrashed in his cot as he dozed in and out of delirium. Evelyn had changed his bandages and administered the only painkillers they had. Amelia remained by Clarke's side for the rest of the night, feeding him sips of water whenever she was able to get him to hold still for long enough. He knocked the spoon out of her hand on several occasions and spat the liquid in her face whenever she did manage to get a small amount inside. He lunged at her twice, but she was able to thwart his swoops, his body too weakened to put up much of a fight. She patted his forehead with a wet cloth; the air was so sticky with heat she knew it wouldn't do anything to cool his temperature, but she refused to give up.

When he finally settled, she stepped outside to catch her breath. She sat on the steps and listened as the rain splattered against the thatched roof. She pressed her face into her hands and cried, the release of emotion finally coming in her solitude. The salty tears stung her blistered cheeks, a reminder that she was, in fact, still alive. She thought of everything they'd been through this past week and what was still to come. There was no guarantee she'd make it out alive; the wilds of New Guinea unleashed themselves at every bend, this country she loved so dearly finally showing its true self. She could see now what a sheltered life she'd lived, gallivanting between Lae and Salamaua in her father's planes, her biggest worry being whether her mother would reprimand her for wearing pants or not. She'd never had to experience the true hardships of life up here, not the way Niuginians had, and certainly not the way Daniel did.

Her chest hiccupped. The realisation of what her life had been up until that point made her laugh. And laugh she did, until all the feelings had released themselves from her body, and Amelia was finally ready to get on with it.

# 18

# Daniel

"Sir, we'd better get going," Daniel said as he shook Mr McKenzie's shoulder to wake him. "We'll fall behind if we don't."

Mr McKenzie opened one eye; the whites were clouded over in a yellowy sickness. "Och. We'll be right. I know these mountains better than any of those men. I'll get us to Wau when I'm ready."

Daniel sat back and watched as the rest of the men marched out of camp, jealous that they were on their way. In normal circumstances, Daniel would've been pleased to remain in the village for the day, getting to know this particular tribe and the customs that shaped their lives, but with the threat of the Japanese beating down their backs, Daniel wanted to put as much distance between the coast and himself as possible. Having heard several planes over the past few days, he was worried the enemy was back for more. While the rainforest offered a canopy of protection, Daniel couldn't help but pray those planes were the Aussies finally coming to help. Wau was the last airfield between here and Port Moresby, so getting there was more imperative than ever.

Daniel rubbed his feet. The sores were bubbling and oozing pus like little volcanos erupting. Even though he wanted to get to Wau, the thought of putting his boots back on was nearly enough to make him thankful of Mr McKenzie's condition. This was the longest time he'd spent with the man since he was a kid, since his father had brought him to Salamaua. Born in

Rabaul to his Tolai mother who'd died in childbirth, he'd spent his early years in the village with her family until his father came for him when he was nine. As a pioneering gold miner, Harry Carmichael had lived all over New Guinea, first in Rabaul in the early twenties, where he'd enjoyed the spoils of his labour and gallivanted with local women while his family remained in Australia. When he heard of the Royal brothers striking it big in Edie Creek, he headed to the Highlands to make his mark, and had only taken claim of Daniel when he was wealthy enough to get away with his previous indiscretions.

They lived with the McKenzies for the first year at Salamaua. And the friendship between Daniel and Amelia – two kids who felt out of place in their worlds – was forged. Mr McKenzie treated him as his own back then, no doubt forced to out of respect for his best friend. And then when Daniel's father died, Mr McKenzie took him under his wing again by teaching him to fly and giving him a job. Tom had denied him any claim to his father's fortune, so if it wasn't for Mr McKenzie, he'd be back living in the village. He sometimes wondered if life would be easier that way.

He knew he owed Mr McKenzie a lot – the Scotsman didn't have to help him – but surely the score was even now. Daniel had fought his feelings for Amelia, denied his heart and betrayed her, all so he could remain in good stead with him. But Daniel had done enough to prove his worth. It was time he went his own way, forged a path that'd see him live his own life, on his own terms in a place he knew better than anyone. Mr McKenzie may've pioneered these lands over a decade ago, but New Guinea was in Daniel's blood ... his heart ... his soul. As soon as they got to Wau he'd be rid of the ties that'd bonded him to a world where he hardly knew his place. For the first time in twenty years, Daniel's life would be his own.

* * *

When he'd rested enough to walk again, Mr McKenzie had them leave Skindewai early the next morning, a day behind the rest of the group. They went along the mild Buisaval Track, Mr McKenzie explaining it'd been cut in the twenties to enable ponies to carry cargo to the goldfields. But it'd long since grown over, the route abandoned now that aeroplanes ruled the land. Daniel longed for the sight of Wau's aerodrome, a notoriously hard place to fly into, the heavy cloud and rolling hills that surrounded it making it nearly impossible to land on. It was Mr McKenzie himself who had accompanied Daniel on his first-ever solo flight into Wau.

"If you're going to learn to fly, lad, then there's no better place to start than Wau. It will teach you all you need to know about landing," Mr McKenzie had said from the co-pilot seat of one of his Junkers.

Daniel had taken care to dodge any peaks that were covered by cloud, his stomach rolling as they approached the runaway – a narrow strip of kunai grass that sloped upwards. Hopefully the three thousand feet ahead of him would be enough to allow him to stop, or else they'd become permanent additions to Mt Kaindi, the mountain that sat at the end of the runway. Daniel eased the plane down, forcing his eyes open as he pulled on the brake, knuckles white as they crept closer to the looming range.

"Well done, lad," Mr McKenzie said, slapping Daniel on the shoulder when they stopped. Daniel's hands shook as he pried them off the steering wheel. "Now let's get this fellow unloaded, and then you can have real fun taking off."

Daniel's stomach plunged again at the thought of rolling the plane down the runway into the adjoining mountains. But if he was going to be a pilot, he'd have to be brave, and from that day forward, he came to work with the courage and discipline needed to fly. It had served him a perfect flight record, right up until Salamaua was attacked and his life changed forever.

Now, Daniel didn't care who flew him out of Wau, as long as they could get the hell out of there. He was done with these mountains. They paused to catch their breath in the last few miles before they were due to reach Wau. Rising fields of kunai were spread out before them, the blades of grass as sharp as razor blades, while Crystal Creek was on the horizon, connecting to the Bulolo River: a wide torrent of water studded with mossy rocks and surrounded by forest, thick brush and rolling hills so verdant it was like staring into Amelia's eyes. It was the last river they'd have to cross before reaching Wau, and thankfully the water was only at hip level today. They'd crossed several other rivers over the past few days, some as high as their chests, with raging currents as strong as a charging bull. They would use a rope to help them cross, Silas leading the way.

Daniel removed his boots and slung the tied laces around his neck as his bare feet pressed into the stony creek bed. The water was icy, and a trail of goosepimples snaked up his arms. What was left of his khaki trousers was rolled up to the knee. His shirt had been abandoned in Skindewai, thc piece of white cotton in tatters from the thorny track. With Silas now halfway across the river, it was Daniel's turn to enter. The rocks were slippery; Daniel was thankful for the rope. His pulse accelerated, the risk of being swept away or taken by a croc suddenly crossing his mind. Why was it his mind always turned to the worst when he was in difficult situations?

Mr McKenzie paused in the middle of the river, struggling to move his solid frame through the rampant torrent. The water was rising quickly, well above their waists now, the sound of it roaring in his ears. Silas had made it to the other side, and Mr McKenzie should've nearly been there, but it was as if he was stuck. Daniel pushed his way through the current and stopped behind Mr McKenzie to shout, "Everything alright, sir?"

"My foot is stuck," the old man yelled. He was trying to yank it free, body swaying against the whooshing water. Even a man as big as Mr McKenzie was no match for a raging river.

Daniel crept so he was facing Mr McKenzie, ensuring he always had one hand on the rope. "Take my hand and I'll pull you out!"

Mr McKenzie nodded and reached for Daniel with his free hand. Daniel gripped onto his wrist and tried to yank him forward, but the old man wouldn't budge. They tried two more times with no luck, until Mr McKenzie finally became so exasperated that he let go of the rope to try to pull his foot free.

It was like watching it in slow motion, the way he slipped backwards as his foot finally freed, the water scooping him up, body sprawled, arms flayed, the current pushing him down like a log. All Daniel could do was stare, limbs frozen, hand gripping tightly to the rope. The river rushed for miles, all the way to Bulolo Valley. The old man was sure to drown.

That's when Daniel saw a bank of sand half a mile up. His body responded before his head. He pulled himself safely to the other side and ran up the riverbank. Silas followed until they were level to the sandbank. Daniel dove in again, pushing through the torrent until he was in shallow enough water to crawl onto the bank. He took a moment to catch his breath, but there was no time to dwell on his discomfort, as Mr McKenzie's body was hurtling towards him. Daniel reached out, grabbed the old man's arm and pulled him to safety.

Mr McKenzie hacked up a lung, nearly half of the Bulolo River gushing out. When he was done, he rolled onto his back, chest heaving as he stared at the sky. Silas was shouting at them from the riverbank, but Daniel needed a moment to process the relief that sailed through his veins. He lay next Mr McKenzie and pressed his hand to his own heart, waiting as the beats of his chest steadied, the egg-blue sky and its perfect flying conditions helping to ease his worry. He turned his head to Mr McKenzie, whose eyes were clouded with tears.

"You saved me."

Daniel nodded, and the world went silent around him. The last week had been a whirlwind, a convolution of emotions as they were thrown into the chaos of war and the life-altering decisions that came with it. While he'd come to resent Mr McKenzie for that decision, for a lifetime of feeling like he didn't belong, it was reassuring to know that when it came down to it, Daniel still knew how to do the right thing. He could still save a man's life even if he hated him.

Turning back to look at the picture-perfect sky, the place he always found solace, he was met with an alarming sight. A charge of planes shooting across, bright red emblems blazing under the metal wings. Daniel bolted upright, mesmerised, as they coursed towards Wau in perfect formation. He stared as pebbles started falling from their bellies, turning the land below them into giant clouds of smoke. The sound of the earth rattling finally awakened him to his reality. The Japanese were back for more.

# 19

# Amelia

They arrived at Mambare the next day, an Anglican Mission with an attractive Elizabethan-looking house sitting in an alcove not far from the beach. It was home to Father Gill, a Sussex man, who welcomed their group. They were to remain for the night. They finally learned news of the war after having been off the wireless for a week. Rabaul had been captured by the Japanese, who now had twenty-three of their ships in its harbour. The AIF were resisting in the hills outside the town, and although the RAAF had bombed four of the ships, the Japanese were now in control. Amelia was devastated by the news; the entire group was as the reality of war set in. Just like that, their home had been taken.

It'd also been announced that the evacuation of all civilians from Papua had been ordered and flights to Australia had commenced from Port Moresby that week. That was reassuring, as Amelia realised her father would be forced to leave with her and Evelyn, provided they all made it to Port Moresby.

"Any news of Wau?" Amelia asked Father Gill as they sat in his main living room, a light breeze blowing in from the bay. She glanced at Evelyn, who was absently peering out the window, the outline of her chest bones peeking through the opening of her blouse. She'd already lost a considerable amount of weight – another worry for Amelia. Tom was sitting across from her, acting as some sort of liaison for the Administration. Having conducted the inquiries into the war, it appeared as if Tom was now contemplating their next step, and his face was stitched up in concentration.

"Wau?" Father Gill replied, his blue eyes full of warmth and kindness. "Well, it was bombed. The other day, in fact."

Amelia's stomach hardened, the buzz of a mosquito in her ear suddenly very audible. "Bombed? Are you certain?"

"It came through on the wireless last night. There was one death and one person injured."

Amelia looked again at Evelyn, whose attention was now on Father Gill. Her face had drained of all colour as she asked, "Did they say who?"

"Afraid not," Father Gill replied. "They never do, but rest assured, they'll be working hard to evacuate the remaining civilians."

"Which is why we must press on tomorrow," Tom interrupted. He stood and eyed Amelia and Evelyn, as if it was time to let Father Gill have his peace. "We must get to Kokoda as soon as possible. Thank you, Father, for your generosity."

Father Gill smiled. "But of course. I thought you'd also be interested in the stores that were left behind by a group of miners. After hearing of everything you lost on the sandbanks, I'm sure you'll need the supplies more than we do here."

Tom ushered the women out of the house, annoying Amelia by assuming he was in charge. He took off in the direction of the Administration men, while Evelyn started to walk towards where the sick were resting, but Amelia pulled her back.

"Do you think it was Dad who was killed?" Amelia asked.

Evelyn's thick eyebrows drew together. "I don't know, Meels. It could be anyone. There were more than twenty-five men in their group, plus all those Wau civilians who were yet to be evacuated. We must not fret about Father. He knows what he's doing."

Amelia's lip began to wobble; Evelyn's words were doing little to stem her worries. She opened her mouth, but her own words were trapped by the fear that'd seized control.

"It's okay, Meels," Evelyn said as she pulled her into a hug. Amelia rested her chin on her sister's shoulder as she stared at the calm ocean, the alcove that shielded them failing to calm her nerves. "*He'll* be okay too," Evelyn whispered in her ear.

Amelia knew exactly who she meant, though this time it was difficult to share her sister's blind faith. Wau had been bombed, and Daniel could be dead.

* * *

Their canoes navigated their way into shore after another day of rough seas. The sight of the next mission was heavenly. Evelyn had been sick again and took to her hammock as soon as they arrived, while Amelia got acquainted with the two Australian women who helped with the mission – Miss Mavis Parkinson, a teacher from Ipswich, and Sister May Hayman, a nurse from Adelaide. They were most welcoming, Sister Hayman tending to the sick men while Miss Parkinson made Amelia feel at home, feeding her cups of tea and biscuits and doing her washing.

"I can't thank you enough," Amelia said as she rested on a mat on the floor of Miss Parkinson's small mission school. It was made out of reedy walls of sago stalk and had a lingering musty scent. She was immediately taken back to her night with Daniel, but pushed the thought aside, happy to have the company of Miss Parkinson to distract her. "It's been an ordeal these past couple of weeks."

"I can only imagine," Miss Parkinson said. She was wearing a simple button-down collared dress, her dark curly hair sitting above her ears. She looked to be around Amelia's age, this young woman who'd dedicated her life to teaching the local Gona people. She handed Amelia a tub of cream and said, "This will help with your sunburn. Sister Hayman makes it from pawpaws."

Amelia pressed her fingers to her cheeks, feeling the flakes of skin that hung loosely from the raw flesh. "You're too kind. I'm sure I'm a real sight at the moment."

Miss Parkinson waved her away. "You look far better than the blokes you're travelling with. You're welcome to stay with us as long as you need."

"Thank you, Miss Parkinson—"

"Please, call me Mavis."

"Thank you, Mavis. As lovely as that sounds, I'm sure the gents will want to press on in the morning. Now we're nearly at Buna, we'll have to make arrangements to get these men inland to Kokoda."

Mavis nodded as she hung Amelia's brassiere and bloomers out to dry. The school was built around a pretty path bordered by hibiscus and crotons, with a number of tall trees and palms scattered about. It was as picturesque as Salamaua, and yet was enveloped in eeriness, as if it too was waiting for the Japanese to attack. "That's quite the journey, especially when they're so sick," Mavis said, peering into the adjoining room, where Sister Hayman was busy administering medicine to the men.

"It's been trying, to say the least."

Miss Parkinson smiled, her thin lips exposing a set of straight teeth. "You're a good Christian woman. God will remember this."

Amelia bit her lip, offering her own sort of smile. She'd never been overly religious, often skipping church on a Sunday to spend the day flying. Her father was a Catholic, her mother an Anglican, and the two had found their way together in a world that didn't approve of interfaith marriages. Religion had ended up taking a backseat in their family, her parents never bothering to reprimand her when she'd skipped church. Was that why the move to New Guinea had been so seamless for them ... was it a place for them to escape the norms of society? Even if her mother was obsessed with following conventions, New Guinea was a place where different rules applied. Perhaps putting religion to the side had allowed them to find their own way forward.

As if Mavis had sensed her unease, she broke the silence by asking, "Do you think the men could do with staying on a few days?"

"I'm sure they could, but with the Japanese now in control of Rabaul, it's not safe." Amelia looked out to the bay and shuddered. "Will you and Sister Hayman be evacuating soon? Surely you don't want to be here if the Japanese land."

"We're not considered civilians," Mavis replied. "The decision is made by the Bishop of New Guinea, Reverend Philip Strong. He's decided we should stay."

"Has he? That's awfully short-sighted."

Mavis shifted on her feet. "Not entirely ... women missionaries have been given the option to leave, but Sister Hayman and I have decided to stay."

"May I ask why?"

"It's what's expected. Who will teach my students if I go?"

"Who will teach your students if you're killed by the Japanese?"

Mavis shrugged, but Amelia noticed a flicker in her eye. Fear. The one emotion that's hard to mask.

"As the Bishop said in his speech over the wireless to us," Mavis continued, standing a little taller as she repeated the words, "'God expects this of us. The church at home will surely expect it of us. The universal church expects it. The tradition and history of missions requires it of us. Missionaries who have been faithful to the uttermost and are now at rest are surely expecting it of us. The people whom we serve expect it of us.'"

Amelia shook her head. Expectation. She knew something about that. Her whole life Amelia had been expected to act a certain way, to live up to a certain standard of behaviour as a daughter and a woman – a white woman, to be specific. And then ... when she had finally gained the courage to do things her way, it came back to bite her on the arse.

Mavis handed Amelia her laundered clothes, looking down at her with warmth and love. "Have faith, dear, for God will protect us."

* * *

Amelia considered Mavis's words, the blind faith she harboured. How could it be so easy to trust in something you couldn't see, to believe that everything would be okay because you simply wanted it to be? Was it really that simple? Amelia tried to have faith when it came to the safety of those she loved – she had to, when it came to Daniel and her father, even though it was hard not to panic at the thought of them being killed in Wau. But to believe that faith would keep you alive when the enemy knew no bounds was hard to fathom. Though Amelia supposed that was the definition of religion – a blind faith.

So, was it religion that kept Evelyn so positive? Amelia had never thought of her sister to be the religious type, though it was starting to make sense. Her willingness to stay when all other women were being evacuated. Her dedication to the sick as she tirelessly saw them through this journey. Her belief in Amelia's ability to do the right thing. Could Amelia do the same? Have faith and pray that all would be okay? No. Because no matter how much faith Mavis had, the reality of their situation was clear. Amelia had seen it herself. The Japanese were here, and they didn't care what you believed.

A trickle of fear ran up her spine at the thought of Mavis and Sister Hayman being captured. It was foolish for them to stay, but then Amelia knew she had no right to judge. She had acted the same way by choosing not to get on that plane with her mother. For believing that her love for Daniel would protect her. For not seeing how dangerous their situation was. *Is that what love does: lead you to believe in something greater than yourself?* Lead you to have faith in the impossible? Mavis's love for God was clear, and would see her through whatever was to come, even death. What did Amelia love more than life itself?

Daniel, of course. Except that love was over now. Her love for him hadn't been enough. She'd turned her back on him when things had gotten tough, had lost all faith in their ability to be together. Even if they both survived this war, their love wouldn't be able to withhold the challenges they would face as an interracial couple. Her father had made that clear.

Or would it? Maybe all she needed was to have a little faith.

# 20

# Daniel

The smoke from the bombs was blinding, a cloud of ash as thick as cement. Daniel shielded his face as he ran through it, desperate to get to the other end of the runway, to prove that what he'd seen wasn't an illusion. They'd run all the way from the river, the Zeros leading the way, but it was too late by the time they got there; the aerodrome was engulfed in smoke so ferocious that to see it was like looking at death. Mr McKenzie and Silas had come to a stop at the edge of the fire, but Daniel kept going, adrenaline surging, in a plea to find his last way out. He'd seen it, from back at the river. Or at least he was convinced he had. A plane. An Aussie one.

A loud whoosh erupted, followed by a high-pitched ring that drowned everything else out, and the blinding smoke started to eat away at his eyeballs, like acid burning through flesh. But he kept on running; until his own failing body gave in, consumed by a wheezing cough that choked his airways, forcing him to his knees. The kunai grass runway was scorched to ash. This was it. The reckoning that Mr McKenzie had predicted. Daniel still wasn't ready, but his body was giving in, bending to the will of warfare. He tipped his head back and forced his eyes open, searching for that perfect patch of blue, a last look at the heavens above, but all he could see was blackness. He began to relax as his lungs gave into the asphyxiation, a sense of calm clouding his mind, Amelia dancing before him ... until ... hands were gripping onto his arms, dragging him away from the hell he'd succumbed to, the hell that would make all the heartache go away.

He came to sometime later in a sort of ditch, his lungs attempting to resuscitate themselves by sucking in the clean air.

"Are you mad?" It was the indistinct sound of Mr McKenzie's Scottish accent. But it was faint, somewhere in the distance, trying to compete with the shrill ring that had highjacked his earlobes. "Running into that hellfire! You're lucky you weren't killed! Or was that what you were trying to do?"

Daniel curled into a foetal position, chest still panting for air. He rubbed his eyes open to find a wall of dirt before him. They were in the trenches, Mr McKenzie lying next to him, while Silas was peering out over the side.

Silas tsked and shook his head. "Yu no ken ting." He was gripping his spear, the veins on his hands bulging against his calloused skin.

Daniel ignored him, trying to find the words to explain himself. "Did you see what was ahead of all that smoke?" The two men didn't reply, allowing Daniel to continue. "It was a Lockheed. One of the Carpenter ones."

"And you thought you'd board it as it was being rained on by bombs?" Mr McKenzie asked. His voice was clearer now, the ringing subsiding.

"It took off before they started bombing. Didn't you see the Japanese chase after it? Lucky Lockheeds are fast. It got away without any damage."

"Then why'd you go after it, if you knew it had already taken off?"

"I was hoping to find another plane. But there weren't any. Not a single one."

"That's a good thing, lad. Or else they would've been bombed like my lot was back in Salamaua." Mr McKenzie rose from the dirt and stood next to Silas to peer out over the edge of the trench, rifle raised. His glasses were smudged with mud – his whole body, in fact – and the bandage on his leg was coming loose, revealing what was still a red, raw wound. Daniel didn't know how he'd managed to run to the aerodrome all the way from the river, but then remembered what adrenaline could do.

"Looks like they've gone, but let's give it a few minutes to be sure," Mr McKenzie said.

"But if there aren't any planes here, how will we get out?" Daniel asked.

Mr McKenzie removed his glasses and wiped them on a bit of shirt that had yet to be stained. "We don't know that there aren't any planes."

Daniel sat up, another cough forcing itself out like a seal's bark. When he was done, he wiped his mouth and said, "I'm telling you, there weren't any planes. The Lockheed was the last one."

"Och. I don't believe it. The Administration wouldn't leave us here," Mr McKenzie said, but his voice wavered on the last word.

"Wouldn't they?" Daniel replied, that sinking feeling he'd felt when they left Salamaua settling in his gut once again.

* * *

"The bloody bastards have left us here!" Mr McKenzie roared. They were in town, or what was left of it, in a makeshift shack tucked behind the trees, which was being used as NGVR headquarters. He was talking to the NGVR Commanding Officer, Bill Edwards, an Aussie bloke who looked to be similar to Mr McKenzie's age. The two men were on either side of Bill's desk, while Daniel and Silas hovered near the door outside, the waitmen's conversation easily heard through the flimsy walls.

"Calm down, George," Bill replied. "It's not that cut and dry."

Mr McKenzie baulked. "Isn't it? You did it to us in Salamaua. And now they've gone and done it again!"

"We tried to get the men out, but the bloody Nips came in too quickly."

"It's been a week since they hit Salamaua and Bulolo. Surely you knew they'd be back for more?"

"What do you want me to say, George? We've been working round the clock to get the fellas out. Had two planes flying in and out all week. We got most of the men out but you lot arrived too late."

"That's it? Two planes. What about the Junkers and Fords that normally operate up here? Where are they?"

"Their bloody pilots took them back to Australia! Against the RAAF's orders!"

Mr McKenzie went silent, and Daniel sensed his anger rising. Bill tried to fill the silence by adding, "Did you see they nearly got Clive Burnard as he took off in his Lockheed? The bloke's lucky he got out."

"At least he got out! What about Bulolo? What's left of it after the raid?"

"Gone. The new Kanga Force major ordered it. Said to scorch it all. Reckons the Japs will be dumping airborne troops in the Highlands as soon as the cloud lifts."

"What does an Aussie major know about this place? I bet he's never even stepped foot in the Highlands before."

Bill chuckled. "The bloke's only twenty-five and is now in charge of all the operations up here."

*Twenty-five!* Daniel's mouth fell open. He peeked into the room, to see Mr McKenzie shaking his head. At least he and the old man agreed about something. Navigating the perils of New Guinea was no place for a waitman fresh off the boat. But he supposed that would be inevitable now that war was here.

"And Wau?" Mr McKenzie asked.

Bill didn't reply, the silence between the men enough to answer the question. Wau would be scorched too. Daniel shuddered at the thought of another town being so callously destroyed. What would be left of the place when the war was over?

"Where does that leave the men that are left?" Mr McKenzie asked.

"Most have enlisted with the Rifles. The ones who are injured or too old will make their way to Moresby by foot."

"Foot?" Daniel could hear the disbelief in Mr McKenzie's voice.

"There's a track up the Kaindi Range, past Edie Creek through the old Bulldog mine. It connects to the Lakekamu River."

"I'm familiar with the Bulldog Track, Bill, but I didn't expect the Administration to ask a bunch of injured old lads to walk across it. That's no man's land. Kukukuku territory!"

"There's no other option, George."

"You Aussies have made a real mess of things. If I had half a mind, I'd make my way down to Canberra so Curtin can hear what an idiot he is. But I'll stay here with the rest of you lads and fight. So go on ... add me to your ranks. Would've done it months ago but have been waiting to see what happened first."

Bill waited to reply, the hesitation in his response reverberating through the bamboo walls, until he eventually said, "That's very honourable of you, George, but you know it's not possible. You're too old."

"I'm only a few years older than you, Bill!"

"Even so, the Administration only wants blokes under fifty."

Mr McKenzie scoffed. "How old are you? Clearly the rules can be broken."

"Even so, you're not fit to fight. Look at that leg. I can nearly see the bone!"

"My leg is fine," Mr McKenzie grumbled. "Having walked up the Black Cat, I think I can manage."

"We can't risk putting injured men on the front."

"But you can put a bunch of young lads who know nothing about New Guinea out there? They'll be lucky to last five minutes."

"I'm sorry, mate. It's Kanga Force orders. Go home to your wife and kids. You'll be happy you did."

Mr McKenzie didn't reply, which surprised Daniel. The silence between the men lingered again, the usual sounds of the surrounding jungle filling the gap, while a light mist hovered over the tree line. Daniel glanced at Silas, whose eyebrows were squished together as if he was thinking hard. He'd been shaking his head and tsking throughout the conversation, his disdain for Bill's directives clear. Daniel didn't agree with him either ... the Aussies should be taking whoever they could get. Which led Daniel back to his original idea about joining the NGVR. Would they take him now that the threat was real?

As if Mr McKenzie could sense Daniel's thoughts, he asked, "What about the Kanakas? Will you be using them, now we know what we're up against?

"You know the answer to that question, George. Do I really need to spell it out?"

"Hell's bells. Bunch of fools you are. You're wasting a capable bunch. The Japs are here and the Aussies are in over their heads. Rabaul's gone. Salamaua and Lae will be next if they haven't already been taken. Those dirty Nips could be lurking outside right now, and you won't use the next best thing you've got?"

Daniel couldn't help but stiffen at that comment, eyes scanning his surrounds for any sign of the enemy.

But all was still until Bill spoke again. "It's policy. Tell your boi he can join up in Moresby. There's a native group called the PIB over there. No doubt you'll want him to accompany you over the Bulldog anyway. It sure as hell won't be an easy climb."

* * *

While Mr McKenzie tended to the rest of his business, visiting what was left of the general store with Silas to collect what supplies they'd need for the trek, Daniel thought of the conversation he'd overheard.

Mr McKenzie was right. The Aussies had made a mess of things, practically leaving New Guinea for the taking. The Administration had had years to prepare for this, yet here they were, asleep at the helm, left to burn down their towns while a makeshift militia made up of a bunch of untrained misfits manned what was left of the fort. It was beyond belief. No wonder Daniel ran into the bombed aerodrome, desperate for a way to get out, though he was starting to suspect the real reason he did it.

And still, they wouldn't accept anyone they deemed to be unfit for duty. Not only the injured like Mr McKenzie, but young capable men like Daniel, who were desperate to fight. There would've been a thousand more Daniels out there if the NGVR were willing to look beyond their own stubborn ways. Young Niuginian men who were willing to do anything to protect their home. And yet they were expected to sit back and let the invasion happen. To hide out in their village and be good bois. Sure, they'd still be used in other ways to help the waitman, like guiding the men through the rough terrain as Silas had, all the while being expected to carry their goods and cook their food, but they'd never be allowed to fight the way any man should be allowed to fight – to fight for what was rightfully theirs. It was foolish of the Aussies, to say the least.

This talk of the PIB sounded like the way to go. Clearly the Administration in Papua had more foresight than the blokes in the Mandated Territory. Even if it meant having to trek over another range of mountains, a range that was considered far worse than any other in Papua or New Guinea. The Bulldog was thought to be wetter, colder, steeper and higher than Kokoda and the Black Cat. And with the Kukukuku lurking around every valley – an isolated mix of tribes that were known to be the last cannibals, fearless men who didn't abide by any waitman's law – Daniel couldn't help but wonder if they stood a better chance staying here with the Japanese. Even Silas was terrified of the Kukukuku, and he was from this region.

Daniel knew he couldn't stay. There was no longer a place for him here, that'd been made clear. So he'd take his chance on the Bulldog, even if it meant slogging it out with Mr McKenzie a little longer. At least the Scotsman was being forced back to Australia. Amelia would be pleased about that. He wondered if she'd made it to Moresby yet. Unlikely, since her journey was expected to take the best part of a month. Hopefully he'd get there in the next few weeks, depending on what sort of trouble they got in over the Bulldog. That's when a little flicker of hope lit up his insides – his longing to see Amelia one more time, to rectify their last goodbye and do it right burning bright. That was the reason he'd been so desperate to find a plane out. He'd made the wrong choice with Amelia, he could see that now. But if he was lucky, they'd both make it to Moresby at the same time, and he'd be reunited with her once more.

# 21

# Amelia

"Sir Murray radioed to say Moresby's been raided," Tom said. "Luckily, the damage was minimal and the aerodrome's still intact. They'll be able to send a Ford when we get to Kokoda."

They were standing on the beaches of Buna. The black sand was swarming with sandflies, and red welts were quickly surfacing on Tom's thighs above his socks. Since a simple bug bite could turn into a deadly infection up here, Amelia was grateful her long sleeves had withstood the elements over the last couple of weeks. Evelyn hadn't fared as well; her blouse was ripped at the cuff, exposing her arms, which had already suffered badly from sunburn.

Evelyn scratched a bite on her arm as she squinted at a grove of coconut palms that extended at least a hundred yards inland. "How long do you think it will take us to get there?"

"Depends on the state of these blokes," Tom replied, flicking his head at the sick and injured men who were lying on mats under the palms. Half of them had succumbed to dysentery and were covered in their own stinking filth, which the locals were helping to clean up. The other half were suffering from infection or malaria, in and out of states of delirium as they grappled with high fevers, seizures and body aches.

"They can't walk," Evelyn replied in a firm tone, her stoicism stitched across her face even though Amelia could see how frail she was after days heaving up her own guts. Her cheeks were sunken and eyes sockets hollowed.

"But *you* certainly can," Amelia interjected, eyeing Tom's supposedly injured leg.

Tom ignored her. "What about Clarke? How's he going?"

"He'll need to be carried," Evelyn replied. "His wounds are badly infected."

"I can walk," Clarke called out from under the tree. He was gripping his leg that was wound tightly with gauze, eyes wide and alert as if he was waiting for the enemy to appear. "Don't waste a carrier on me."

Amelia bit her fingernail, wondering how they'd manage to trek eighty miles with these men. "We should've stayed at Gona longer," Amelia replied, voice full of longing, still missing the short time they'd had with the missionary women.

"You know that wasn't an option," Tom replied, swatting at the sandflies on his legs. "The Japs have Rabaul. It could be a matter of days before they land on the northern coasts. We must head inland and get to Kokoda."

"Are you sure we can even get out from there?" Amelia asked. "What if they don't send a plane?"

"Sir Murray said he would," Tom replied. "I believe in the ability of the Papuan Administrator to keep his word."

"As much as you believed in the ability of the Niuginian one?"

"You have too many opinions, Meels. You should learn to hold your tongue."

Amelia stepped forward, raising her hand in readiness to slap Tom, but Evelyn stepped between them. "Enough! Arguing about the unknown won't help. If Sir Murray says to go to Kokoda, then we'll go."

Tom glowered at Amelia before turning on his heel. He swatted away at sandflies while shouting over his shoulder, "I'll round up some bois from Buna. Four for every man, myself included!"

Amelia glared at Tom, lips pursed as she thought of all the things she wanted to say to him.

"What's gotten into you?" Evelyn asked, pressing her fingers into Amelia's arm.

Amelia snatched her arm away. She didn't feel like being scolded by Evelyn right now. "I'm tired of listening to these people who think they know what they're doing."

"Amelia, don't be so arrogant, or else you're just like them."

"I'm tired of trusting in a government that has no idea what it's doing. Look at Mavis and Sister Hayman. They're staying when everyone else is going. Maybe we should too?"

Evelyn let out a bark of laughter. "Please tell me you don't believe that? Salamaua was only two weeks ago. Surely you remember what the Japanese are capable of?"

Amelia huffed. "Of course I do. It's why I'm here … fleeing up the coast with a bunch of injured blokes. I'm terrified of the Japanese, but I wonder if there's something more we should be doing. Look at Sister Hayman and Miss Parkinson. *They're* staying …"

"It's different for them."

"Is it? They're women with a sense of duty, just like us."

"The church requires it of them."

"Maybe that's what we need too?" She couldn't stop thinking about her conversation with Mavis about the expectations put on her by her religion and fuelled by her faith. If Amelia could find faith too, then maybe everything would be okay. "Would you consider yourself religious?"

Evelyn furrowed her brow. "Why would you ask such a thing? I had the same upbringing as you, the same parents who didn't instil much of any religion into us."

"Then how do you do it?"

"Do what?"

"Believe in what these people are telling us? Believe that everything will be okay, that Dad, that"—her voice hitched—"that Daniel is okay."

Evelyn sighed, shoulders slumping as she stared out across the sea. Gentle waves lapped at the shore as a pair of pigeons flew overhead. "I don't know, Meels. I just do. Doesn't mean it's easy, though. Like I told you when we left Salamaua, we have to get on with it and hope tomorrow will be a better day."

Amelia leaned her shoulder into Evelyn's. "I know that, Ev. The last few weeks have clearly shown me that. All the whingeing in the world won't change a thing, but still, I can't shake this sense of dread that's taken over."

"I know."

Amelia swallowed. "What if I never see this place again? Never stare out at that ocean, never smell a frangipani or eat a Rabaul mango again?"

"They have oceans and mangos and frangipanis in Australia too."

Amelia shot her a look. "You know what I mean. What ... what if I never see Daniel again?"

Evelyn squeezed her sister's hand. "You will. Wars don't last forever."

"But they can last for years. I can't imagine being away that long. This is my home."

"Then come back."

"How?"

"Enlist. They're going to need nurses when things do kick off up here. I plan on signing up as soon as we get to Sydney."

Amelia's mouth slackened. She didn't know why she'd never thought to enlist, but it sounded like an intriguing idea, a way for her to come back safely. "But I didn't finish my exams. They won't take me."

Evelyn pulled her sister in tighter. "Since when have you let anything stop you doing what you want?"

* * *

Trudging through the swamps further inland from Buna was like walking through wet cement, the mire of mud as thick as the sago that lined its perimeter. Amelia held her breath; the fetid smell from the ponds of water, mixed with the overhanging mangroves, gave the place a dank and eerie feel. At least they were protected from the Japanese flying overhead. Amelia finally breathed a sigh of relief as they headed away from the exposed coastland. She knew her objection to Tom's plan made no sense; while she'd miss the sight of the glistening beachheads that extended down from the Huon Gulf, she knew they needed to put as much distance between them and the Japanese as they could – and as quickly as possible.

Evelyn was in front of her, and a web of Orokaiva men with tapa cloths around their waists trailed behind her, carrying the hammocks that held the sick men. Several of them were curled in the foetal position as the dysentery hammered their insides, while others moaned in agony, their infections getting worse. If they were lucky, they'd arrive at Kokoda in a few days and be on their way to Port Moresby shortly after that, though Amelia was terrified the sick men would run out of time.

She chewed on her lip, contemplating what else she could do to help them. She'd have to become more diligent with her care, forsaking sleep so she could remain by their sides each night. Except she'd already been doing that. She could up the ante by reading and singing to them, and could be more patient when they resisted her treatments, more understanding of their pain and their struggle – but she'd been doing all of those things too, which made her think that she wasn't such a terrible nurse after all.

Perhaps Evelyn was right. Enlisting could be a way to serve a purpose during the war while also bringing her home, even if it was a long shot to hope she'd be posted back here. She'd likely be sent to the Middle East, where she last heard Australian nurses were serving, though she wondered if they'd be brought back to Australia now that things were heating up in the Pacific. It was hard to predict anything when there was so much unknown, but the idea of coming back thrilled her. She laughed out loud at the irony of it all. Here she was trying to escape the place while at the same time mapping out a way she could safely come back. While she'd wanted to get to safety, the idea of walking away from her home – of doing nothing to try and protect it – was like walking away from Daniel all over again.

What was it that bonded her to this place? What was it, beyond its beauty and intrigue, and the life and memories she'd built for herself? And why couldn't she be more like her mother or Sofia, willing to leave without even batting an eyelid? A smile crept up her lips when the image finally came to mind – a dimple-cheeked man with big brown eyes. Eyes full of hope. Hope for a better life. It was hard not to think of Daniel when she thought of New Guinea, the promise of seeing him again causing her stomach to curl. Her anger with him had subsided, and yet she still didn't know how they'd find their way in this world. If he was even alive ... that thought was surfacing again. She pushed it aside and focused on her steps, on what she would need to do to get these men through the next few days. Though it was nice to have something to look forward to, a sliver of hope in these uncertain times.

# 22

# Daniel

They'd joined a group of miners from Bulolo who'd also been left behind, a burly bunch of blokes who'd been deemed unfit for service. There were over two hundred of them, the men split into groups of twenty to make them less conspicuous. Most of the lads from their original party had stayed on with the NGVR, while a few of the others had been evacuated by plane. Arriving that extra day early, before the Japanese attacked, had made all the difference for those men; if Mr McKenzie's injury hadn't forced him and Daniel to stay behind, *they* might have been evacuated too. A group of locals from the Watut area had joined their party, adhering to a strict rule of the Territory that forbade locals from different clans from working together, for fear of sparking the centuries-old warfare between the sub-clans in the region. Luckily, Silas was from Watut, though Daniel figured it didn't have so much to with luck as Mr McKenzie getting his way.

The trek from Wau to Edie Creek had started well, Silas and the other Watut men leading the way in the familiar territory. It was a trail that'd been commonly used by Europeans and locals since the goldrush days in the twenties. Mr McKenzie knew the track as well as Silas, the two men sympatico with their navigation. They crossed through the gorges skirting the villages of Kwembu and Winima, the surrounding mountains so dense the area was like a hidden valley. Silas described it as an old trade route –

a way the people of the coast, islands, floodplains and the highlands could come together. For Daniel and the others, it was the only way out.

Up and down they went for days, slipping and sliding along the muddy track, the temperatures freezing as they crossed limestone peaks of over ten thousand feet high. It was the coldest Daniel had ever been, and he was clothed in long sleeves and a blanket for warmth, unlike the local carriers, who had nothing but their lap-laps on. Daniel watched as Mr McKenzie and the other waitmen slapped the carriers on their bare backs, their handprints visible on their skin like brands on cattle. He asked the old man what he was doing, what right he had to hit the locals when they were doing nothing more than carrying goods.

"Why we're bashing the coons? To keep them warm," Mr McKenzie replied and proceeded to do it again. The local he was striking recoiled at the old man's touch.

Daniel scoffed. "You don't have to hit them! Why don't you give them clothes? Blankets. Like us."

Mr McKenzie chuckled. "Don't worry, lad. They like it. It's part of their warrior nature. They respect us more for it."

Daniel bit the inside of his cheek. He couldn't imagine the men liked being hit. But then he wasn't a pure Niuginian and couldn't comment on how they felt. It wouldn't make a difference anyway. Mr McKenzie would continue to behave in the way he was accustomed to.

They set up camp in a dank, wet forest that night, a heavy rain making it hard to sleep amongst the freezing temperatures that wouldn't allow for a fire. The waitmen "cooried" together, as Mr McKenzie would say, clinging on to one another as if their life depended on it, the little warmth their bodies exuded seeing them through the long night.

They departed at four the next morning, after successfully trading with the local villagers and stocking up on supplies of sugar cane and pawpaw in exchange for items such as salt and tobacco. Silas warned that by the time the sun rose, they would officially be out of Watut area and into the land of the Kukukuku.

Daniel didn't think they had much to worry about with the Kukukuku, and was more concerned with crossing paths with the Japanese. As Mr McKenzie had said to Bill Edwards back in Wau, for all they knew the Japanese could've already made it to Lae, or even Port Moresby. Or they could be making their way there through the mountains, lurking in the trees, ready to run a bayonet through them. Mr McKenzie was relying on Silas and the other locals to choose the best route, having admitted he was out of his depth as soon as they left Edie Creek, though he couldn't help but chime in to insist they kept near densely covered forest in case a Japanese plane flew above.

Daniel diligently followed suit, trusting that these men knew more about these lands than he ever could. Apart from keeping his eyes and ears peeled for any sign of the enemy, all Daniel could do was focus on his steps, desperate not to fall down a ravine again. The ranges were relentless, the narrow tracks as steep as the ones they'd seen on the Black Cat, overgrown with vines and trees that were nearly impossible to manoeuvre through. He was surprised Mr McKenzie was handling it so well, though suspected Silas had whipped up some concoction for him to drink. He was considered a bit of witchdoctor in the village, something most of these men were in need of, with their worrying hacking coughs and wheezes. For that reason, conversation was kept to a minimum. Daniel couldn't imagine trying to speak when it was hard enough just to breathe with each ascending step. He kept a moderate pace nonetheless, determined to get over the Bulldog as quick as possible.

The rain continued to beat down, making the track as slippery as an oil spill. He didn't know how the local men managed the sleet-like conditions in bare feet while carrying upwards of fifty pounds each, even more if they were carrying one of the men who was too sick to walk.

*These men are the real heroes.*

Daniel hoped there would be a place for them in this local army Mr McKenzie and Bill had been talking about. He hoped there'd be a place for him; for a mixed-race Niuginian, fighting in Papuan Territory posed a whole new set of issues.

He paused to wipe the rain from his face, gazing up to see the afternoon sun peeking out from a clearing in the tree line. They were nearly to the top of the range after twelve hours of continuous climbing, and a sudden lightness took over Daniel's aching limbs. He took the final few steps, closing the gap on the ascent, gaze landing on a magnificent view of sprawling jade mountain tops dusted with cloud, range after range extending as far as the eye could see, the sun hovering above the highest peak. Beams of light radiated through the cloud, as if God was shining on the land, while a light mist hovered in the valley below. Daniel inhaled the thin mountain air, his breath steady again. A slow smile crept up his face as he took a moment to enjoy the sight before him. For all the horrors the past few weeks had brought, he couldn't deny the beauty that ran deep within these lands … even if they were dangerous, by God he was ready to do anything to protect them.

* * *

"We'd better get to it," Daniel said to Silas. The two men were sitting at the top of the range after a quick rest. Mr McKenzie had already gone ahead with several of the other men and locals, navigating their way down the mountain while it was still light.

Daniel turned a corner to begin his descent – and let out a cry that echoed across the valley below.

"What is it?" Silas asked, running up next to him with his spear raised.

But Daniel couldn't respond; his jaw clenched as he took in the sight before him.

Silas laughed and lowered his spear. "Ahh. You see? We are in Kukukuku territory. It's their smoked bodies."

A chill shot up Daniel's spine. He blinked, twice, assessing the sight of three mummified bodies that'd been decayed to the bone, their eye sockets hollowed and skeletons slicked with ochre. They were crouched on the cliff ledge, overlooking the valley below. One was still clutching a spear, small and weathered, as if he'd been sitting there for at least fifty years. The other looked to be a woman, the subtle rise of her chest giving way to the small child she held to her bosom.

Silas slapped Daniel on the back, causing him to jump. "It's okay, Daniel. There's no need to be scared. The Kukukuku believe the bodies keep away evil spirits. We are safe."

But he didn't believe it, wanting to put as much distance between him and the bodies as possible. He reached for his knife and proceeded down, not daring to look back, the haunting image of the fallen warriors imprinted in his mind.

Silas followed after him, laughing to himself as they went. "How will you fight the Jap man when you're scared of a smoked body? These are merely traditions, a sign of respect for their elders."

Daniel shifted his backpack. "I'm not scared. I'm ready to fight the Japanese now."

"You think you're ready, but this wokabout will do you good. Teach you how to be a man."

"All this walk will do is kill me."

"We have a saying in my village ..." Silas's voice lingered behind Daniel. "Mipela bai kirapim bilong mipela hat wokabout."

*We will start our hardest journey now.*

Daniel didn't doubt that this was the hardest thing he'd ever done – physically, at least. He'd lived a cosy life compared to the locals, never having had to journey through the bush or trek for hours to visit his gardens, hunting and foraging along the way. He hadn't seen much of New Guinea at all, apart from the view of the jungle from his Junker.

"And what do you think it will be like when we start fighting?" Daniel asked over his shoulder as the cry of a Raggiana echoed from high above the dewy treetops.

"Not good," Silas replied, voice solemn. "Many will die."

"Do you think we'll stand a chance against them? And by 'we', I mean the Papuan and Niuginian people."

"This is not our fight."

"What do you mean?"

"This is the waitman's fight. The Jap man's fight. Leave us out. It is not our war."

"It's on your land! Surely that's enough reason to fight."

Silas tsked, his disapproval resonating. "Of course we will help, like we always do, but I hope the waitman will remember the sacrifices we will make for them. But it will be difficult for our people without the right leader. Papuans … Niuginians, we are warriors. For thousands of years, we have fought each other. It is in our blood. But without someone to lead us in our cause, I fear we will spend too much of our energy fighting each other, rather than fighting your enemy."

Daniel rubbed his beard as he navigated a tricky bit of the path, contemplating Silas's words. He had a point: the Papuan and Niuginian people were notorious for their intertribal warfare. At least that was one problem the Australians didn't have to deal with amongst themselves – their commitment to mateship one of the things that would see them through this war. There were over eight hundred cultures and languages throughout the two territories, and even getting two groups to agree when they couldn't even converse with one other made the idea of a local army seem impossible. But, as Silas said, with the right leader to bring them together, perhaps they stood a chance.

"Will you sign up?" Daniel asked, wondering if someone like Silas was the person to harmoniously join the tribes. He would've only been around forty – the right age to lead.

"I will do as my masta says," Silas replied.

Daniel clenched his jaw, frustrated that Silas could still be so subservient to Mr McKenzie. They were at war and needed every able-bodied man they could get. Out the window with these colonial rules … it was time to fight!

* * *

Daniel hadn't realised how much they would need to rest. At least a day was spent at each village in between trekking days. The men were too sick not to, and even the healthy ones needed time to soothe their aching muscles and blistered feet. The villages they stopped at were friendly enough, the chiefs, or luluais offering bits of meat from a pig, wallaby or tree kangaroo they'd killed, and a dry place under their huts to sleep. The luluai told them of the pisin seen flying in the direction the men were headed – planes with red spots on their bellies. The news put Daniel further on edge. Had the Japanese made it to Moresby? While he could've stayed in the cocoon of the village for days on end, relishing in the safety of the remote location, he knew they had to get over these mountains as soon as physically possible. Mr McKenzie's health was deteriorating again, Silas's medicine only doing so much to counter the effects of tropical disease. He needed to see a doctor, and quick fast, or he risked losing his leg.

"Och! Don't worry about me, lad," Mr McKenzie said as they sat by the fire. "I'll be right. We'll be to the river soon and then it'll be all downstream from there."

A throb of drums echoed from the village as the locals wailed into the night. It was a Haus Krai for a little boy who'd suddenly died. Life in New Guinea was much more dangerous for its own people, children especially. Daniel shuddered and turned his attention back towards Mr McKenzie, who was having his wound tended to by Silas. He peeled back the pus-crusted bandage, the stink of putrefaction quickly overtaking the smell of smoke from the fire. Daniel dry-retched and looked away, wondering if he'd ever be able to stomach the sick. He lit a cigarette, his thoughts drifting again, this time to Amelia. She'd be facing all sorts of ailments on her journey with the sick, and he wondered how she'd be fairing. She'd no doubt get on with it, like they all had to – the realities of war forcing them all to adapt beyond their wildest imaginations.

"How do you think the girls are getting on?" Daniel couldn't help but ask, meeting Mr McKenzie's hazel eyes to avoid looking at the wound.

A sudden shadow crossed Mr McKenzie's face. "I suspect they're alright. My lasses are tough. They won't let New Guinea get in their way."

"What about the Japanese? Aren't you worried they'll get caught?"

"Of course I'm worried! I'm worried enough that the bastards are already up here. God knows they've reached Salamaua by now. Can only hope they haven't landed anywhere else up the coast. Once the lasses get to Kokoda they can get the next plane out."

"When do you think that will be?"

Mr McKenzie eyed him curiously over the rim of his glasses. "Hard to say. You know how unpredictable flying is in this country, and that's if they have a plane. Look what happened to us."

Daniel didn't reply, fear seizing his guts as he thought of Amelia stranded in Kokoda. He'd been so focused on getting over the Black Cat, trying to get out of Wau and now through the Bulldog, he hadn't considered that things might not be going so smoothly for her.

"Why do you care?" Mr McKenzie asked. "I thought you said things were finished between you two." Daniel looked away, preferring to focus on the rotting flesh than have to face Mr McKenzie's scrutiny again. The old man tsked at the lack of response. "Thank heavens the Japs are here and I've got a reason to get her out."

Daniel scoffed, taking the bait. He took a drag on his cigarette before stubbing it into the grass. "You'd rather see your home destroyed than have me be with your daughter?"

Mr McKenzie scowled back, swatting Silas away. "I'd prefer you two finally see sense. There's no future for Amelia if she's with you. She'll spend her best years waiting to find out if you survive this war, when you'll likely be dead in the jungle."

"Why are you so certain I'll die? I have as much chance as any of those Aussie blokes do. More, seeing as I actually know the land."

"You might. But if you do, even if we can come back after all this is over, then what? There's no easy future for you two. You'll be outcasts! Pariahs in the worst sense. Surely you see that? Why would I want to subject my daughter to that?"

"Because I love her more than anyone else ever will. Doesn't that count for something?"

Mr McKenzie waited to reply, running his tongue along his teeth. Daniel wondered if he'd finally said something that'd gotten through to the old man, made him see how much he would do for his daughter. Mr McKenzie lay down, rolled onto his side and said, "I'm afraid not, Daniel. Love will only get you so far in a world like ours."

He closed his eyes and went to sleep.

Daniel glared at him across the fire, finally realising that no matter what he said or did, he'd never be able to prove his worth. Daniel would never be good enough for Amelia's family. Even if his education and employment were as good as any other European man, his skin was still too brown for their taste. It'd always be a battle with them, no matter what he did. He lowered himself to the ground and curled into the foetal position, the beating of the drums soothing his rage, a final thought coursing through his head as he drifted off to sleep: *You're wrong. Love is the only thing we have left in this world – and I'll damn well be sure to fight for it.*

# 23

# Amelia

"I don't think he'll make it through the night," Evelyn said as they stood over Clarke's limp body. He was lying on a mat on the floor, another makeshift haus sik – hospital – they'd set up in a hut at the village of Illimo where they'd arrived late that afternoon. They weren't far from Kokoda; another day's walk through the gold-rich Yodda Valley and they'd finally be at the government station that housed the last safe aerodrome outside of Port Moresby. But Clarke had taken a turn, developing a septic throat, his infection slowly spreading through his wretched body.

Amelia tipped a spoonful of laudanum into his mouth. Evelyn checked his pulse and made a few notes in her diary.

"Don't worry about me," Clarke croaked. He was dripping with sweat, his skin as hot as burning coals, while his body shivered. Next thing they knew, he was seizing, violent tremors coursing through his limbs as if he was being electrocuted.

Amelia looked at Evelyn, eyes widening. "What do we do?"

"We ... we need to cool him," she replied frantically, trying to tip Clarke's head to the side as a frothy white foam leaked from his mouth. "But without any ice, I'm afraid we can't."

Amelia's mouth went dry. "What else? Can't we give him something?"

Evelyn looked around the dimly lit hut. "I don't have anything else. We're out of penicillin. We've used the salts ... the sulphur. Besides, they haven't worked to stop the infection. In New Guinea, the sick must learn to live with fever."

Amelia stepped backwards, staring at Clarke's shaking body, lost as to what to do.

"Meels, I have to check on the other men."

Amelia swallowed. "Can I stay with him? He shouldn't be alone."

"Of course." Evelyn retreated to the other end of the hut, where she crouched into the corner and quietly wept.

Amelia sighed, wanting to go to her, but knew moments like this were best spent alone. She bent down next to Clarke instead, reaching for his hand as she started to sing "Somewhere Over the Rainbow", knowing her voice was nothing like Judy Garland's but hoping the words would be soothing enough.

* * *

Amelia raced through the Yodda Valley at a feverish pace, glancing over her shoulder every few minutes to make sure the carriers were keeping up. Clarke had made it through the night, but was in and out of consciousness, his breath becoming shallower and shallower. She was determined to get him to Kokoda and on the next plane out, hoping they could finally put this hellish journey behind them.

One of the locals who'd been travelling with them since Buna offered to carry her pack, which Amelia couldn't refuse after another long night. He led the way through the rich valley, where ridges of mountains had been cut out on either side, the rifts that ran down each range like the lines that stretched down the palm of Amelia's hand.

"Wanem nem bilong yu?" Amelia asked the man's name in Pidgin, trying to make conversation to help pass the time. She turned her head to look at him, noticing his features for the first time – a thick beard that covered his face and dark brown eyes. A thin piece of tapa cloth was wrapped around his hips, detailed in an intricate light-brown pattern, while necklaces of shells hung loosely across his chest.

"Ambogi," he said, keeping his gaze on the path in front of them.

"Nice to meet you," she replied. "Are you from Northern Province?"

"Yes, missus."

A bird whistled from above, and a symphony of calls sounded through the valley. A cassowary hovered near the tree line where the mountains began, and a wild boar rustled in the bush. They really were in the wild out here. Amelia stiffened, wondering if the Japanese could also be skulking in the jungle. Turning her head to Ambogi again, she said, "You must think we're all mad. A bunch of white men running away from the Japanese when we're supposed to be the ones in charge."

"Waitmen are weak. Us Orokaiva people would stay and fight."

Amelia eyed him sideways, shocked by his boldness. Papuans and Niuginians never spoke their minds – not to white people, anyway. But he wasn't wrong. "I wish we could stay, but I'm afraid we're out numbered. Hopefully the Australians will be back soon with reinforcements." Ambogi didn't say anything, forcing Amelia to fill the silence. "Thank you for helping with carrying our sick men. We wouldn't have been able to do it without you."

"It's time for your people to leave."

"Pardon me?" Her voice rose in pitch.

"Time for you to leave New Guinea," he went on. "Nothing good has come to our people since the waitman came."

"I'm sorry you feel that way."

"You murder, you rape, you steal. We tried you out and you have been harsh on us. Maybe it's time we try the Jap man out. He might be better."

Amelia tensed, suddenly aware of how vulnerable she was. A white woman being led by a group of Orokaiva men who clearly harboured hostilities. She didn't know the specific history of Ambogi's people, also known as the Binandere, but knew that there had been much killing on both sides when white men first arrived in this area in the late 1800s. The miners had journeyed as far north as the Mambare River, into the deep valleys of Yodda, Gira and Waria, exploring for gold, meeting fearless tribesmen along every bend and dip. They eventually found common ground and the tribespeople had come to live with the white folk as every other tribe had done in Papua and New Guinea ever since it was first colonised, but Amelia imagined there were deep-seated resentments still lingering in some of the locals.

She left the conversation at that, not wanting to push Ambogi any further. She picked up the pace instead, the need to get to Kokoda mounting, her legs moving as quickly as the swift-flowing waters of the Ambosi River.

* * *

They arrived later that afternoon; the sight of an old government station had never looked so pleasing. Kokoda sat atop a perch, overlooking the deep valleys that were sombre with scrub, vast jungles climbing high into the Owen Stanley Ranges. Amelia let out a cry of relief as they approached, and immediately searched for Tom so they could make a plan. He was at the back of the line with Evelyn, instructing the locals to set up camp. The rest of the group were still a day or two behind, their need for rest along the way having slowed them down.

"Bloody hell," Tom said as he slumped onto the ground. "I'm buggered." He had been forced to walk the last leg of the journey after several of the locals had deserted them as they moved further inland. His legs were covered in grazes, his socks torn and sodden, while his white-collared shirt was speckled with mud – a stark contrast to how he'd looked when they first embarked on this journey.

Amelia chuckled to herself before saying, "What's the plan?"

"I'll speak to the gents, but we'll need to radio the Administrator in Moresby," he replied.

"We don't have a lot of time," she said. "Clarke urgently needs to see a doctor."

"I'm well aware of that, Meels."

"How long do you think it'll take for them to respond?"

"Meels, why don't you leave it for now?" Evelyn interjected in a hushed tone. "There's nothing we can do now. It's nearly nightfall."

"But if Tom sends the message now, the plane can come first thing tomorrow," Amelia replied, shooting her sister a look.

Evelyn glanced at the sky, and Amelia's gaze followed. Dark clouds were rolling in from the mountains, a rumble of thunder sounding in the distance. "Look at the weather. You know they'll have to wait until it clears."

Amelia stomped her foot. "I'm sure they'll manage. It's only cloud, for heaven's sake." But she knew cloud could lead to death up here.

"Don't worry, Meels," Tom mumbled. "We're all desperate to get out of here. The Administration will send a plane as soon as they can."

* * *

But they didn't. Day after day they waited, and still no plane came. Tom and the Administration blokes blamed it on the weather, for the thunderous clouds had turned into a violent storm that lashed the area for several nights. Amelia knew it was more than that. Be it due to the lack of planes or care from the Administration, she soon came to believe they'd be stranded here indefinitely. A formation of four Hudsons flew overhead on the third day, and a tickle of excitement coursed through Amelia's veins as she waited for them to land, but when they kept on over the mountains, she was left gawking at the white smoke trail remaining in their wake.

By some miracle, Clarke was still alive, barely, fighting through the fever as Evelyn had predicted. Amelia continued to sing and read to him through the night while Evelyn tended to the other men. Ambogi returned to Buna with the other carriers, Amelia relieved he was no longer in their midst. His words had unsettled her; the idea that the locals mightn't remain loyal to the Aussies made what lay ahead even more terrifying. She'd be getting out – eventually – and while she'd do everything she could to come back safely as a nurse, she couldn't help but feel a deep sense of dread whenever she thought of Daniel. She hated the way she'd left things, especially now there was time and distance between them. While it had been wrong of him to conspire with her father, he'd only done it out of desperation, the need to protect his home. Her father wielded so much power, especially when it came to Daniel ... no wonder Daniel had folded to his demands. And while her father may've had a point about life being easier without him, she no longer cared about taking the easier path; the last few weeks had shown her how strong she could be. Life wasn't meant to be easy; it would be boring if it was. Life was meant to be lived. She knew that now, had known it ever since she first climbed into a Moth and took to the skies.

Waiting idly at Kokoda as the sick men wasted away, dependent on a government who cared little about their survival, constantly looking over her shoulder in case the Japanese came calling, she knew, more than ever, what she wanted. She knew now not to betray her heart for what was easier.

And when that familiar sound of an engine came whizzing in over the mountains, and a "big fella binntang", as the locals would say, came zooming down the aerodrome, relief spread through her bones, and she realised she was now willing to do whatever it took to fight for what she loved most.

# 24

# Daniel

Daniel squealed as he dipped his toes into the water's edge. They'd made it to Lakekamu River; the treacherous mountains were now behind them and there was nothing but easy sailing ahead. Hopefully. It'd still be days until they reached the Papuan coast, but at least they'd be days cruising instead of trudging through muddy slopes. He splashed the cool water on his face, rinsing away that morning's mud. He stripped down to nothing but his underdaks, and the sand was coarse against his skin as he scrubbed at his legs, his feet, his body, ridding himself of the layers of dirt.

The other men were doing the same, black and white alike, even Mr McKenzie, who was using the water to clean his festering wound and the sweat that was dripping from his skin. The infection was back, and Mr McKenzie could no longer hide it. Daniel thought to offer him help, but knew the old man wouldn't take it, not that there was much Daniel could do anyway. He wasn't a doctor, wasn't anything apart from a man wanting to protect his home.

He focused on the squeals of delight that echoed through the jungle instead, the men like birds of paradise calling to one other. Even though they still had to figure out how they'd make it up the river, shaping rafts out of their limited supplies, there was an air of excitement amongst the men, the worst of their journey behind them. Daniel couldn't help but relish the moment;

this was one of the few times he'd felt joyous in the past few weeks. He sat in the shallows and tipped his head back as he dug his hands deeper into the sand, the weight of the river pressing against his fingers comforting in a way. The middle finger of his left hand brushed against something hard. He pinched it with his thumb and forefinger and pulled it from the sand. A glimmery nugget of gold shone back at him. His mouth dropped open, a jolt of excitement crawling up his skin.

He couldn't believe it. Casually happening upon something so rare! Though it *was* the legendary Lakekamu River that had been home to flocks of miners in the early 1900s. That was why the track was called the Bulldog, after all, named after the vessel that used to take the diggers up and down the river in their hunt for gold. The expedition had dried up by the end of WWI, though there was no reason why gold couldn't still be found in the area. Daniel squealed, imagining what he could do with the money if he sold it. Perhaps he could buy a plane, start his own company, find his way out of Mr McKenzie's hold. The opportunities seemed endless when you had something to start with. But all that would have to wait ... there was a war to be fought and a river to navigate first.

He stood and pulled on his trousers, slipping the nugget into the deepest fold of his pocket. Skimming his surrounds, he took in what they'd be able to harvest to make into a raft, the sorts of trees that would work best to support their weight. Reaching for his knife that sat in the backside of his trousers, he noticed something moving further up the riverbank and wondered if one of the men had wandered off. He squinted to get a better look at the figure, when he realised it was a black man standing on the edge of the water, his hair tied at the top of his head. In his hand was a club, and across his body was a cape made out of bark, different to the lap-laps the carriers normally wore. Daniel's eyes flicked beyond the man into the thick jungle that lined the river's edge, falling upon more black bodies ... at least a dozen of them, each with a weapon in hand, some with bows and arrows but a few with star-shaped clubs. His heart hammered as he turned to look at his own group of men; they came to a standstill, realisation dawning, their focus set on the foreign men. The air of excitement was immediately zapped away, replaced by a surge of fear. The Kukukuku had found them.

* * *

"What do we do?" Daniel whispered to Mr McKenzie as the Scotsman and Silas sidled up to him. Mr McKenzie already had his rifle in position, gaze set on the Kukukuku.

"We fight," he replied through gritted teeth.

"But they haven't attacked," Daniel said.

"Doesn't matter. They're savages. Uncontainable. The worst of their kind. If we don't get them now, they'll come back for us later. Raid our camps, killing us when we least expect it. It's what the Kukus are known for."

"But they don't look like they're after a fight." Daniel's eyes flicked to the line of men, their weapons at their side as they whispered to one another.

"Och. They are. The more remote and unknown the natives are, the further from civilisation, the blacker, shorter, uglier and more violent they become."

Daniel twitched. As nervous as he was amongst these men, who were known to be bloodthirsty and vicious, he couldn't help but want to give them the benefit of the doubt.

"Why don't you let Silas speak to them?" Daniel suggested. "He'll be able to avoid a fight."

Mr McKenzie hesitated, and Daniel used the opportunity to push Silas forward. "Silas, can you reason with them? See what they want."

Silas nodded and yelled at them in Pidgin.

The Kukukuku man Daniel had first seen tilted his head to the side, as if he didn't understand Silas.

"I don't think they understand Pidgin," Daniel said.

Mr McKenzie stepped forward with his rifle.

"Aiyo," Silas replied and reached for something in his pocket, prompting the group of Kukukuku to raise their weapons. Silas raised a knife and axe into the air and asked if they wanted to trade. "Tret? Yu kisim sampela naip, tamiok?"

The Kukukuku looked at each other, and then at the items Silas held, but didn't lower their weapons.

"Christ. Let's shoot the bloody savages," Mr McKenzie said.

Daniel shot him a look. "They don't want a fight. It's only because you're holding a gun that they have their weapons raised."

Mr McKenzie spat into the water. "What do you know about it, boy? I've seen this lot before. They're evil. They don't want to trade, to learn from us. We've tried to teach them and we've failed. No European can ever hope to rescue these natives from their own savagery. We must kill them all."

Heat flushed through Daniel's body. He wasn't about to risk getting killed by the Kukukuku because Mr McKenzie wasn't willing to reason. "Don't mistake them for the Japanese. There's a better way to go about this."

"A fatal mistake is made by those who place any reliance on the apparent friendliness of the native races."

And that was when another group emerged out of the tree line, their numbers now well over thirty. But it wasn't men who appeared this time, but women, one holding a baby and the others with small children by their side.

"See," Daniel added. "They're with their families. They won't risk the women and children."

"He's right," Silas added. "Kukus won't fight in the presence of meris and pikininis. Their hunting parties where they kill and cannibalise are men's work only. I believe we are safe."

Mr McKenzie grumbled and lowered his rifle. "Fine. But if they come back later, I'll have your head. That's if they don't eat it first." He laughed to himself.

Daniel rolled his eyes and crept up the riverbank, Mr McKenzie and Silas following. The Kukukukus were no more than five feet tall, with a strip of grass arranged around their groins held in place with a thin plaited vine, like a sporran. Their hair was cut short except for a tuft on top. From one earlobe of each man hung a tassel of fur, and pierced through the nasal septum was what looked like a shard of bone. Necklaces of teeth lay across their chests, like trophies marking their conquests. Goosepimples crawled up Daniel's skin, and he shifted his gaze to the women, who were bare chested, wearing nothing but grass skirts that were full in the front and back but bare at the flanks. Around their necks were necklaces made from cowrie shells, woven tightly on thin fibrous ropes. Daniel's eyes widened when he realised that the woman was holding a baby, but a small piglet, who was happily sucking at her teat. He averted his gaze and reached in his pack for his own selection of trade goods, presenting the men with salt, tobacco and shells.

The chief Kuku shook his head at Daniel but nodded at Silas instead. In his own dialect, he mumbled a few words and reached for the knives and axes Silas still held.

"Kukus only like to trade weapons," Silas said, eyes remaining on the men. One of them walked up to Mr McKenzie and reached out to touch him, prompting the old man to lift his rifle again, but the Kukukuku merely stroked his skin, as if he was fascinated by its colour.

Mr McKenzie pulled away and said, "Bloody natives. You'd think I was the King of England or something."

The woman with the piglet stepped towards Daniel and looked at him strangely, curiosity mixed with confusion crossing her face. Her chin was stubbled with wisps of black hair, her eyes dark like coal. She glanced at Mr McKenzie, then back at Daniel, comprehension suddenly dawning on her. She shook her head, reaching for the shells before walking away.

Daniel's neck stiffened. He'd never belong.

The chief Kuku handed Silas a bilum of sweet potato and instructed his group to leave, watching the group of white men as they went.

Daniel exhaled loudly, relieved that was over. Walking back to their belongings, he said to Mr McKenzie smugly, "See … that wasn't so hard. Look what you can do when you're willing to reason."

"Och, lad. You've got so much to learn."

* * *

Working tirelessly together, the men had managed to build a raft out of the pine and pandanus trees that ran wild in the mountainous region. By the end of day two, they were left with four sturdy rafts, three larger ones that could hold six men, and a smaller one that would hold the remaining two, plus their supplies.

"That's not enough," Daniel said, realising the rafts would only fit twenty people.

"It's enough for us," Mr McKenzie replied, glancing at the group of miners who were getting ready to embark.

"What about the carriers? You're going to leave them behind?"

"No, lad. The bois will make their way by foot."

"That's outrageous! Surely we can build them rafts too?"

Mr McKenzie winced as he limped to the raft, and Daniel realised how much weight he had lost, his thick calves that had once resembled tree trunks reduced to scraggly twigs. He hoped he was well enough to make it up the river.

"Don't get your nose out of joint," Mr McKenzie said. "It was Silas's idea. He thinks it's best for them to journey ahead to tell the neighbouring villages that we're coming. We don't want another run-in with the Kukukuku."

"We can handle the Kukukuku. It's the Japanese we need to be worried about."

Mr McKenzie snickered. "I'm also in no position to keep walking, and neither are the other lads. So are you coming? Or would you like to stay here and coorie up with the Kukukuku?"

Daniel looked around, realising the other men had left, leaving him and Mr McKenzie with the small raft. He groaned, annoyed to be left with the old man on his own. But, knowing he didn't have any choice, he grabbed the pole he'd fashioned out of bamboo and stepped onto the wooden logs, balancing his weight as the raft wobbled from side to side.

"Help me up, will you?" Mr McKenzie said, reaching towards Daniel, who lifted him on board, the two men on either side of the raft to balance the weight. Mr McKenzie sat, elevating his leg on a bag of rice, the skin around his wound blazing red. "Thank Christ we're done with walking. Think my leg would've fallen off if I had to climb one more mountain."

Daniel didn't reply. He used the pole to push them out of the shallows, the current of the river helping the raft to gain a slow but steady speed. Mr McKenzie leaned back against a chest to rest. The river was eerily quiet as they made their way up its twists and bends, the other rafts too far ahead to be seen. Stooping branches hung overhead, twisted with vines that drooped down like that Kukukuku woman's breasts. A low grunting noise echoed across the river – the sound of the cassowary foraging for food – and the water wrinkled in various spots from the insects that rested beneath. Daniel bent down to trail his hand in the water, cool to touch.

"I wouldn't do that if I was you," Mr McKenzie piped in. "You'll get it bitten off by a croc."

Daniel snatched his hand away. "I know that."

They stayed silent for the rest of the day, Daniel enjoying the peace for once, glad to get a break from Mr McKenzie's condescending tone. He was tired of being told he had so much to learn, even though he could admit he knew little about village life and the true hardships that Papuans and Niuginians faced. What he did know, now more than ever, was what he wanted when this was all over, and with every dip and bend of the river, each stroke of his paddle, he put himself one step closer to getting it back.

# 25

# Amelia

"What do you mean, you don't have a record of them?" Amelia asked the government official in Port Moresby. They were sitting in a makeshift barracks at Seven Mile, a bunker of offices that'd been erected to support the Australian Army. "They were expected to arrive from Wau a few weeks ago."

"I'm sorry, Miss, but we don't have anyone by the name of McKenzie or Carmichael arriving from Wau. Are you sure they were evacuated?" the government official replied.

"No, I'm not sure! I haven't seen them since we left Salamaua."

The official looked to his desk of papers and shrugged. "There's nothing more I can do for you for the time being. Why don't you wait with the others outside while we make the necessary arrangements for your evacuation? It's incredible you're all still alive after everything you've been through."

Amelia glared at the short, balding man whose thin moustache stood out against his round, blotchy face.

"Useless Administration," she mumbled as she took a seat next to Evelyn.

"No luck, I take it?" Evelyn asked in a small voice. She was rubbing her hands down the front of her trousers, thigh jittering up and down.

"No wonder the Japanese have waltzed in. The Aussies are bloody hopeless! That insipid little man can't give me any indication of where Dad and Daniel are ... if the men were evacuated from Wau at all."

"I'm sure they're perfectly fine, Meels," Tom replied from the bench opposite. "Your father knows those mountains better than anyone else, and as long as Danny boy doesn't cause any trouble, then I imagine they'll be arriving in Port Moresby any day now."

Amelia fixed a cold stare on Tom. "Why do you always assume it's Daniel causing trouble?"

Tom met her gaze with his piercing blue eyes. "Why do you think?"

Amelia threw her hands up and huffed. "You're unbelievable!"

"Simply speaking the truth."

"How do you think we managed to survive the past three weeks? *You,* especially – carried half the way!"

He leaned back against the bench, resting his arms over the back in a casual way. "I have to admit they can be handy sometimes, especially when it comes to washing and cooking, carrying goods and other hard labour. But it doesn't extend beyond that."

"Perhaps if you opened your eyes and gave them a chance?"

"Please, Amelia. You've seen what they're like … they'll never change. No amount of giving up dancing and other foolishness, no amount of embracing Christianity, no amount of going to work or learning English could make a native an equal."

"That's enough, Tom," Evelyn interjected in a firm voice. "It doesn't do us any good to listen to your nonsense."

Tom looked at his fingernails instead. "I do hope they have a plane for us to travel on today. I'm desperate to get out of these clothes and into something clean."

Amelia opened her mouth to reply, but Evelyn beat her to it. "Won't you be staying?"

"What do you mean?" Tom replied. "You heard Sir Murray … he's ordered all men to be evacuated as well."

"All men over fifty. You're fit, you're young … surely you'll enlist to fight?" Evelyn said, the shock clear in her voice.

"Don't be foolish, Evelyn. You've seen what a mess they've made of this. I'm not going to stick around and get myself killed while they figure it out."

Amelia scoffed. "Your arrogance knows no bounds, does it?"

Tom shrugged again, but with a cheeky smile plastered across his face this time. "My arrogance is what makes me a man."

* * *

Amelia paced the halls of the barracks in the same clothes she'd worn on the trek, trousers torn and slicked with mud. There were no women left in Moresby to lend her any clothes, not that the government officials even noticed, the bureaucrats being too busy planning the ways in which they could stuff up this war. They were waiting for the Hudson that would evacuate them to Townsville, where they were due to be met by the Red Cross before boarding a train for Sydney.

It was all rather hasty; the lot of them were being rushed out as soon as the Administration could organise it, which Amelia found ironic, seeing as they weren't in any rush to get them out of Kokoda. At least Clarke and the other men were stable, in the hands of the doctors that still remained in Port Moresby, due to be evacuated with them.

She couldn't believe Tom ... the guy had some nerve, ripping into Daniel about his perceived inabilities, when Tom wouldn't even consider staying to help. He was a coward ... weak and despicable, the furthest thing from a man. Daniel would've volunteered in an instant. That must've been why he wasn't in Port Moresby: his nobility was forcing him to stay in Wau to fight. But that still didn't explain why her father hadn't arrived. As a man over the age of fifty, he should've been evacuated. Unless of course they'd both been killed in that last raid on Wau. No. She couldn't keep thinking like that, had to remain positive, to believe that her father ... that Daniel was still alive.

She glanced at Evelyn, who was lying on the bench asleep, her face the colour of off meat. She'd lost at least two stone, her cheeks so hollow it looked as if her eyes were bulging from their sockets, while her lips were dry and cracked, like the scorched drought lands out west. The last few weeks had taken a toll on her, more than she was letting on. Her sister's stoicism was heroic, in a way. She'd been terribly jittery all day, as if she was frantic to leave, when she was usually the calm one. Amelia supposed it was the cumulation of events – finally reaching safety making Evelyn fall to pieces, no longer able to carry everyone's burdens. She tucked a loose piece of hair behind Evelyn's ear, pleased her sister was finally sleeping.

A door creaked opened, and the government official Amelia had spoken to earlier emerged from his office.

"The Hudson should be here soon to take you," he said as he walked past. "You should gather your things and wait on the aerodrome for its arrival."

Amelia snickered. *What things?*

"Please, sir. You must have more information about my father." She grabbed his pudgy hand and forced him to look at her. "He said he'd be evacuated from Wau, which should've been several weeks ago."

The man looked to the door, then glanced at his watch. "I'm sorry, miss, but I'm not at the liberty to divulge government information."

"What does that mean? Government information? Do you know something you're not telling me?"

The man pulled his hand away, pausing for a breath before exhaling loudly, his fat cheeks squishing his eyes further into their sockets. "As I said, your plane is due to arrive soon. Best you make your way to the 'drome so you don't miss it."

Amelia's eyes welled up, the struggle to fight her tears proving impossible as she pleaded with him. "You must tell me something. You"—her voice cracked—"you can't expect me to leave without knowing what happened to my father."

*To Daniel.*

The tears fell down her cheeks at the thought of him.

"I'm sorry," he said and walked away.

Amelia leaned against the wall, slowly sliding down to the floor as the tears poured out. It was a relief that after everything they'd been through these last few weeks, they were finally getting to safety. But having to say goodbye to the place she loved, without ever knowing if the person she loved most was still alive – and if he too still loved her – made her think it might be worth staying.

# 26

# Daniel

Two days after setting off down the river, they washed up on a large sandbank. The raft flipped up, stern over, and the limited supplies they had left were flung into the air, while Daniel and Mr McKenzie were thrown into the murky water. Daniel dragged the old man up onto the sand – his body was hot to touch – before running back to the water to salvage their goods.

"Don't even think about it, lad," Mr McKenzie managed to say between coughs.

Daniel halted, knowing he was right, that it wasn't safe to enter the river; crocs were abundant in these parts. He slumped onto the sand as the last of the kerosene tins of rice were pushed downriver by the current. If they couldn't enter the river, and their raft was now in pieces on the sandbank, then what else could they do? They were stuck here, completely out of ideas. Staring at the canopy of rainforest – at the birds that flocked from one tree to another, their cries echoing across the wide expanse of river – he felt as if he was finally ready to give up. He'd been holding on to slivers of hope these past few weeks – of getting on a plane out of Wau, of getting over the Bulldog, of getting to Moresby – so he could have a chance of seeing Amelia and make things right. Every single one had been shot to shit. What was the point in hoping anymore? It was futile.

Mr McKenzie started up with his coughing again, this time a raspy wheezing sound escaping his lungs. The old man was not faring well, and this time there really wasn't anything Daniel could do. He crawled over to where Mr McKenzie lay in the sand and patted his back. Mr McKenzie eventually passed out from exhaustion. Daniel closed his eyes, and the next thing he knew, he was woken in the dead of the night by terrible moaning. Mr McKenzie was lashing in his sleep, his head whipping back and forth as his body shook uncontrollably.

"Get down! Get down! The Japs!" Mr McKenzie yelled, but when Daniel looked around, all he could see was trees billowing in the pitch-black night. "Where is she? They're coming. Shoot them before it's too late!"

Daniel shook Mr McKenzie, but it did nothing to shake him out of his delusions. The fever had seized his mind, and without Silas and his witchdoctoring to help, Daniel wasn't sure he'd make it through the night. He stared at the old man for a minute longer, thinking of his father and the similar way he went, dying of malaria's unremitting fever.

Daniel had stayed by his father's side for days, holding his hand as the doctors tried to bring him back to the land of the living, while his father's blue eyes stared blankly into the distance, devoid of all feeling. Daniel wiped the sweat from his auburn brow with a cold cloth, running it down the length of his cheek as he looked at this man who'd given him everything, this man who was his only connection to the world he so desperately longed for. His chin trembled as he thought of his life without him, wondering how he would manage with no one to love him. His father blinked, a small smile forming as his gaze came into focus, and two dimples pressed into his cheeks.

"Daniel, son," he said, voice raspy as he forced the words out. "You'll be okay. George will look after you. I know it."

Daniel swallowed. "But he's not you, Dad."

"No. But he'll ensure you have a place in this world." His father closed his eyes for the last time, and Daniel's heart shattered.

Now, watching Mr McKenzie fade away in much the same way, he felt little emotion for the man who'd found him a place that was much different to what his father would've imagined. Daniel turned to his other side and forced himself back to sleep, wondering how long it would take before *he* would go too. Without food and water, was he destined to die out here? And would Amelia ever know how much he truly loved her?

* * *

Daniel woke to soft whimpering, the sound akin to the morning birdsong that reverberated through the trees. Rubbing his eyes, he sat up and glanced at Mr McKenzie. He was still alive.

Daniel snickered. *Of course the bull won't go so easily.*

Mouth sticky, he crawled to the water's edge, trying to ignore the pains in his stomach, the ache in his limbs and head, and slurped the brackish water. He knew he was bound to end up with dysentery for it but didn't care. When he'd had enough, he pulled a leaf from a fallen branch and scooped water into it, which he poured into Mr McKenzie's mouth. He groaned in acceptance. Sweat trickled down his brow, and a greyish tinge stained his cheeks. He opened his eyes, the whites tinged red as he stared blankly at Daniel.

"Can't believe you're going to be the last thing I see," he managed to say with a chuckle. "At least it's not that halfwit Silas, though I could really do with one of his potions right now."

Daniel swallowed, unsure why he was feeling this way, when only last night he'd felt indifferent towards Mr McKenzie. This was what he wanted, wasn't it? For Amelia's father to be out of the picture so he had a chance at being with her. But each time it was close to happening, something inside of Daniel stirred. Whether he liked it or not, he was attached to Mr McKenzie. Daniel couldn't put his finger on it, but the feelings were there nonetheless. And yet again, he didn't know how to communicate them. He opened his mouth, but the words were trapped, twenty years of emotions refusing to surface.

Mr McKenzie saved him the trouble. He mumbled, "Promise me you'll look after her," before closing his eyes again, chest easing into a slow rise and fall.

Daniel tilted his head to the side. *Did he really say that?* A last wish by a dying father? A blessing?

Whatever it was, Daniel didn't have time to dwell on it, for a loud rumbling noise, like a plane, sounded overhead. Looking to the sky, he searched through the treetops for the Zeros and Bettys that had already wreaked so much havoc on their lives, but came up with nothing. The sound was too low to be a plane, too constant, more of a dull put-put-put like a boat would make.

*A boat?*

Daniel stood and looked down the river, that sliver of hope surfacing again. He tried to push it away, to force himself to accept the reality of their situation, that they were stranded on a sandbank in the middle of nowhere – but that was the thing with hope … it was always there, worming its way into his heart.

And then, there it was: a boat, cruising around the riverbend, a waitman at its helm. Daniel let out a laugh. The absurdity of it all. Being saved by the white man in the end. He was wearing a long black robe and tight white collar – a priest, accompanied by a group of locals, one of whom was Silas.

"Hallo!" Silas yelled as he waved from the bow.

Daniel smiled and waved back, knowing who the true saviour was.

* * *

"He hasn't woken in three days," Daniel said to Silas as they stood over Mr McKenzie's lifeless body. His breath was shallow and rasping as it slowly escaped his lungs.

They were in the haus sik on Yule Island, a Catholic mission fifty miles from Port Moresby. The priest Silas had found was from Terapo Mission at the mouth of the Lakekamu. Silas had convinced him to send a boat in search of Daniel and Mr McKenzie. The priest and Silas had taken them down the river, where they were met by the miners, and then Silas and the boys had carried Mr McKenzie another forty miles up the beach to Yule Island. It was a haven for the group of battered men who were in desperate need of care. First founded by French missionaries of the Sacred Heart in 1885, it had been a stopping point for nuns and priests on their way out to Australia from the Notre Dame. The fact that it was still open even though war had been declared was something of a miracle, a true Godsend for Mr McKenzie and the other men.

But Mr McKenzie wasn't getting any better.

"He needs to rest," Silas kept saying. "You all do."

"We don't have time to rest," Daniel replied impatiently. "I need to get to Port Moresby before it's too late."

Silas narrowed his eyes. "Ah … yes. This Papuan group you're so desperate to join. And what will you do if they don't take you? You are from New Guinea after all."

"I'll figure something out." Daniel bit his lower lip, looking around at the beds of sick men, the other miners who'd made their way across the Bulldog. Apart from sore and blistered feet, he was thankfully feeling okay, ready to press on. The fact he'd been given another chance at life cemented his need to let Amelia know how much he loved her.

"There's no reason why you have to stay," Silas said as he pressed a cold sponge to Mr McKenzie's forehead. He met Daniel's eye and added, "Go. You've done all you can for him. He is thankful, even if he can't say it."

"What if he doesn't make it? How can I ever look Amelia in the face again knowing I walked away when her father was dying?"

"Amelia knows the good that flows through your heart. That's why she loves you. She will not blame you for her father's death."

Daniel nodded, fighting back the burning sensation that was creeping up his throat. "And you? Will I see you again?"

Silas smiled. "If my masta has his way, I'm sure you will."

Daniel scratched his chin, but left it at that. He squeezed Silas's shoulder while whispering, "Tenkyu tru."

Silas offered a curt nod and refixed his attention on Mr McKenzie. Daniel whispered his own words of goodbye to the man, not daring to say anything out loud for fear of tears escaping. He turned on his heel, walked out the hospital doors and was met by bright blue skies that were the same shade as the adjoining ocean. He shielded his eyes from the harsh sun, wondering what now. How the hell was he going to get to Port Moresby and find Amelia all on his own?

# 27

# Amelia

The sisters hobbled across the runway; the ground was dusty and the air sweltering, and the chafing between Amelia's thighs stung with each step. Ahead of them, the sick men were being loaded onto the plane, Tom practically skipping towards the Hudson that was gearing up for take-off. How he'd managed to get out of duty in his perfectly fit state was beyond Amelia's comprehension, but she imagined it had something to do with his privilege. She stuck her tongue out at him, wishing her eyes would burn a hole in the back of his neck.

"You're something," Evelyn said with a little laugh. The energy it took her to say that made her convulse into a coughing fit. Amelia stroked her back and waited while Evelyn caught her breath. When she had settled, Evelyn added, "But Tom's a right jerk. He deserves every ill wish against him."

"I'm glad we can agree on that … I wish we weren't leaving without knowledge of Dad and Daniel."

"Me too. I'm sick with worry about it. They really should've been here by now. Should we stay a few more days? See if they arrive?"

A flicker of excitement surged up Amelia's spine at the thought, but was quickly diminished by the sight of the pallor of Evelyn's face. They couldn't stay any longer. "You know we can't do that, Ev. You need to see a doctor, and God knows we're both in desperate need of a change of clothes," she added, trying to make light of the situation.

The Hudson roared to life, deafening Amelia's muddled mind. She thought she'd have been more excited to be near an aeroplane again, but a sense of dread had seized her stomach. Even though she could barely hear her own thoughts, she swore she could hear her name being called and turned to look back at the hangars. She squinted into the bright sun, but could only see the verdant hills that rolled on for miles. There was a group of locals gathered on the other side of the fence that lined the aerodrome, at least twenty of them with their faces pressed to the metal. One of them waved as if he knew her. She raised her hand above her eyes to get a better look through the blinding sun, but it was too hard to see. Then, out of nowhere, came a loud buzzing noise, like a swarm of bees. She looked to the sky and stiffened. What looked like tiny birds were moving into a V formation, but birds wouldn't make such a penetrating sound … only planes. Enemy planes. The Japanese had made their way to Port Moresby.

Amelia turned to Evelyn, who looked cadaverous with fear. And then a piercing scream – the "red alert" – sounded, and the drome ascended into overdrive. But there were no Allied planes to counter the attack. Only the lone Hudson they were trying to escape on. A crack of bullets came thudding down, a tune of noises that were loud enough to leave anyone rooted to the spot. Amelia ducked to the ground, pulling Evelyn down with her. She threw her arms over them as their bodies shook in tempo to the downpour of bullets falling around them. Her heart had taken off like a prize filly, but she could barely move. Through it all, she could still hear Evelyn whimpering, her once resilient sister reduced to a cowering lamb. In that moment, she knew it would be up to her to get them out.

"Come on!" she screamed through all the noise, pulling Evelyn towards the Hudson. A loud whoosh exploded near the building they'd been waiting in earlier that day. She pushed Evelyn inside the plane, jumped in after her, and secured the door as the wheels gained speed. Evelyn cowered in the corner, knees to her chest as she rocked back and forth. Tom was also inside, eyes alight. Amelia lunged towards the window to peer outside as they whooshed up the runway.

A high-pitched whistling sound was followed by the whomp! whomp!

of exploding bombs. Pillows of smoke shot into the sky. The locals who'd been waiting at the fence had all fled into the bush, except for one, who was jumping and running as the plane went past. Amelia gaped, wondering who'd be crazy enough to stand around while bombs came pouring down, when another one exploded behind the man, and he was engulfed in a cloud of smoke.

Amelia looked away as that familiar feeling of her stomach dropping took hold, the nose of the plane lunging upwards as she silently said her final goodbyes to her beloved home.

# 28

# Daniel

Determination proved to be as futile as hope. Journeying up the remaining Papuan coast and into Port Moresby wasn't as simple as Daniel had hoped. Food wasn't the main problem – he'd been able to fish along the way – but the locals were wary and reluctant to help. The villagers he came across were clearly unsure of what this light-skinned black man wanted from them. Daniel supposed they'd been accustomed to visits by the waitman and his entourage of locals through the patrols that'd taken place since Papua was first made a protectorate of Britain in 1885. But to have a lone man whose skin was the same shade of brown as theirs but who clearly wasn't one of them made them suspicious.

When he finally got to Port Moresby three days after leaving Mr McKenzie, he was convinced his search for Amelia would turn up empty. It'd been nearly a month since he last saw her. That look of devastation was still seared into his brain. She had to have left for Australia by now; Daniel estimated a journey up the New Guinea coast would have taken no more than two weeks. But perhaps, like him, she'd been delayed along the way. At the very least, he could find out what'd happened to the group of injured men who were to be evacuated from Kokoda, and gain peace in knowing if she'd safely made it to Australia.

After searching out the appropriate office amongst the buildings scattered throughout Port Moresby, Daniel was told to head to the aerodrome at

Seven Mile, where the RAAF were headquartered. No one would give him much more information than that, the whites being as unwilling to help a dark-skinned white man as much as the blacks had been.

"What is it you're after?" a pudgy man at headquarters asked him. They'd refused to let Daniel inside the building, so the man had grudgingly met him at the front entrance.

"I'd like news of the party that escaped Salamaua," Daniel replied.

The man sneered. "What's it to you?"

"There's family of mine in the group."

"We haven't any news of the men who escaped over the Black Cat. They were supposed to arrive in Moresby by now. In fact, I had someone else enquiring about them this morning."

"I'm not referring to the party of men who made it to Wau. Though surely you should know of their whereabouts? You were the ones who refused to send a plane."

The man looked at his watch, before glancing back at Daniel. "Was there anything else? You've taken up enough of my time already."

Daniel swatted a mosquito away. "I want to know what happened to the group of sick men who were evacuated from Kokoda. They journeyed down the coast with two women … two nurses?"

"Oh … that lot. Yeah, we managed to get them out – the men and the nurses."

Daniel's shoulders relaxed, his body suddenly light.

*Amelia's okay.*

"Only yesterday, in fact. They got delayed due to bad weather over Kokoda. Due to be evacuated to Australia today. In fact, their Hudson should be leaving any minute now, which is a relief, as one of the women in the group was in bad shape." He nodded at the aerodrome, but Daniel was already on his way, feet moving faster than the fat man's lips.

His legs pushed him over the rolling hills that lined the runway, cutting through the wafts of kunai that scratched at his calves. Over the rise, he saw a plane with the distinct angular tail of a Hudson Lockheed. He paused at the top of the hill, watching as men on stretchers were loaded onto the plane.

One of them looked like Tom. And behind them, two women, hobbling across the tarmac, their looks so similar it was hard to tell who was who.

He yelled her name. It would have been hard to hear over the roar of the Hudson's engine, so he ran down the hill to get closer and was shocked when he came to bottom to find a barbed-wired fence blocking his way. A group of locals were hovering at the fence, watching in awe at the "big fella binatangs" who were about to take off. Daniel screamed Amelia's name again through the fence, but she kept walking. He cupped his hands to his mouth and tried again. This time she stopped and turned to look in his direction. Waving his arms frantically, he prayed she could see him through the blinding mid-morning sun that was pointing in her direction. He kept screaming her name, mustering every last bit of sound he could expel from his lungs, but it didn't seem to cut through the noise of the engine.

And then came another sound, one he'd become all too familiar with over the past few weeks. He looked to the sky and spotted them immediately: the Japanese Zeros and Bettys with their distinct chattering noise and red emblems. The chatter was soon drowned out by the wail of sirens and the whoosh of bombs meeting earth. Daniel looked back at Amelia, who seemed frozen in place, staring at the sky as if she could change the course of the war, until out of nowhere she started moving, pushing Evelyn into the plane that was gearing for take-off.

He screamed her name one more time, gripping the fence, throat burning as tears poured down his cheeks, his desperation for her to know how much he loved her finally materialising into actions. And then the plane gained speed, coursing up the runway. Daniel ran along the length of the fence after it, another loud whooshing sound the last thing he heard before everything went black.

# II

# Part Two

*May 1942*

# 29

# Amelia

The train rattled north, the carriage shaking around each bend. Amelia sat in a window seat, her posture stiff and ankles crossed behind her. She watched as Sydney sank further and further away, the whistling of the train's engines steaming ahead. It was hard to believe she'd been back in Australia for two months now. There'd been no word from Daniel or her father.

When Amelia arrived back in Sydney, her mother had met her with little emotion. She gave Amelia her usual look of disdain, while fussing over Evelyn and ushering her off for immediate medical attention. Amelia suspected her mother's anger was more at being defied than at Amelia's staying behind, and the tension between them was so palpable it was like a bulging vein. She couldn't understand why her mother wasn't overcome with relief that *both* her daughters had been evacuated safely, no matter the circumstances. Her apologies seemed to make no difference. Ruth hardly cared, or wouldn't show it if she did.

When Amelia got off the train twenty minutes later at Lindfield station, the sight overwhelmed her. Masses of people, men and women, all dressed in the RAAF and WAAAF uniform, the women in pale-blue shirts with navy blazers, skirts, ties and berets. She shuffled out of the station with them to the adjacent bus terminal, and they piled into overcrowded, stinking, hot buses that wheezed along to Bradfield Park, where she and hundreds of other recruits reported for their first day of training.

It'd seemed in the days following the Darwin bombings that all Australians had the same idea. Everyone felt compelled to do something. Amelia had secured her nursing certification and immediately enlisted, and she'd received orders to report to training the following week. At least she'd be close to the aeroplanes, even if she couldn't fly them. Evelyn had also enlisted, but was told to return home to rest, as she was still emaciated from their journey. Even Sofia stepped up to the plate, forgoing her plans to be a debutante and joining the Red Cross instead. With still no news from their father – or from Daniel – the women were more determined than ever to do their part.

After Amelia received her service and hut numbers, she reported to her drill instructor, a tall, lanky fellow with red hair and freckly skin. Amelia stepped forward to introduce herself, extending her hand, but was immediately told to step in line.

"Ladies," the drill instructor said. "I'm Section Officer Mitchell, your commanding officer for the next four weeks. We'll begin with the basic march sequence, which I'm sure you're all clever enough to manage."

Amelia took her place towards the front, figuring she had to get herself noticed if she was ever to get sent back to New Guinea. She stiffened her posture, arms firm by her side, and looked at the back of the girl's head in front of her.

A group of RAAF blokes were watching and heckling them. "Looks like we've been issued women instead of blankets!" one of the men yelled out. The others erupted into laughter as the women held their stance.

Officer Mitchell did nothing to stop them, yelling instead, "Now lift your feet, you lot of crabs, and if you swing your arms, I'll cut them off! Left. Left. Left, right, left. Left. Left. Left, right, left."

The words echoed in Amelia's ear. She took a step with the left foot, but her stride was too long and she stumbled.

"Sister McKenzie!" Officer Mitchell roared. "Are you with us or are you off with the fairies?"

The RAAF blokes chuckled. "Think the bird is off with the bloody fairies."

Officer Mitchell paid the men no attention, but said to Amelia instead, "Let me know if you have two right legs and I'll make a fortune."

Amelia bit her tongue, focusing on the pain of her teeth pressing into her flesh rather than the constant berating. She wanted to yell at them: at Officer Mitchell, for singling her out, and at the men for being lazy sods. What did they know about flying? What the difference was between a Dash and Junker? Nothing, probably. But she couldn't say anything, no longer being allowed an opinion. She shot the men a look and nearly fell into the girl in front of her again.

Then she realised who was laughing at her. *Tom?*

His lips curled into one of his ridiculous smiles – he'd known it was her the entire time. She turned her attention back to her steps, determined to get this right if it killed her.

"You've got four weeks until your passing-out parade, where you'll be given your station locations," Officer Mitchell said when the marching was complete. "You'll likely remain in New South Wales or be sent to Queensland."

"What about overseas?" Amelia asked.

"Fat chance of that happening," Officer Mitchell replied.

"But surely they're in need of our assistance in Port Moresby?"

"Absolutely not. Minister Drakeford has made it clear all Air Force women will remain strictly on Australian shores. Now …"

But Amelia was no longer listening; a recurring thought was running through her head. She'd never make it back. She wanted to do whatever she could to help, but couldn't it be somewhere where they needed her? Her knowledge of New Guinea, her time spent there, her understanding of the language and the culture had to stand for something? Maybe Tom would know. He was leaning back on his heels, hands in his pockets, waiting for Amelia to approach him.

"Sister McKenzie," he said with a salute as Amelia walked up to him.

Amelia saluted in return. "Tom. What in God's name are you doing here?"

He looked at his feet. "Seems as if conscription is still a thing."

Amelia smirked, pleased he couldn't get out of this one. "Do you know where you'll be posted?"

"Not yet. Though I suspect it'll be New Guinea. They're sending all available troops up there."

"Not women," Amelia mumbled.

"Nor should they. Look how much trouble we went to, to get you birds out. We sure as hell don't want to send you back to that mess so quickly."

"You realise Daniel and my father are stuck in that mess?" She was still hopeful they were alive.

He pressed a hand to Amelia's shoulder and offered a conciliatory smile. "That sort of thing suits Danny boi. They'll put him to good use, I'm sure."

"Have you heard anything … from Daniel?"

"I'm the last person the government should be contacting about Daniel."

"You're his brother—"

"Only by accident," he nearly spat back. "Do you know how offensive it would be if the government sent a letter to my mother's home regarding the half-caste her husband fathered?"

Amelia crossed her arms. Perhaps she needed to give Tom a break. Whilst it wasn't Daniel's fault what his father did to Tom's mother, it would've been heartbreaking for her and Tom. "I didn't think about it like that."

Tom's face reddened. "That's the problem, Amelia. You don't think. You live in a fairyland where we all get along. No thought for past actions or their repercussions, no thought for standards or decorum, no thought for anyone other than yourself and your utopian views."

Except, as always, Tom couldn't help being an arrogant prick. Amelia pointed a finger in his face and said, "Well, you, Thomas Carmichael, are still living in the last century, where women are expected to obey their husbands, where men are more concerned about the size of their manhood than doing the right thing, and where you're so blinded by prejudices that you can't see something good right in front of you."

He tipped his head back in laughter. "That's true. The size of my manhood is very serious business, so thank you for acknowledging that. As for Daniel … he's where he belongs."

* * *

"How's training going?" Ruth asked. Her attitude towards Amelia had shifted slightly in the weeks since Amelia had enlisted, as if she was finally satisfied with her daughter's choices. They were sitting at the dining room table of their Mosman home, her mother at the head, with Evelyn and Sofia on either side and Amelia in the chair across – her father's chair. The table was loaded with the pastries and preserves Amelia had purchased from the bakery on her way home from training that morning. Between living on rations whilst evacuating and the ghastly food at training, Amelia had learned to appreciate a good meal. But since her mother had yet to readjust to life without house boys – content with a cup of tea and piece of toast most mornings – Amelia had used the last of her rations to splurge.

"Fine," Amelia replied, as she lathered a scone with butter and jam. She reached for the silver coffee pot and inhaled the aroma as she poured the steaming dark liquid into her mother's gold-trimmed bone china cup.

Her mother looked up from her newspaper, eyes crinkling around the edges, freshly formed wrinkles having surfaced in the months since she left New Guinea. She was wearing one of her frocks from Lae – the brown swing dress with embroidered burnt-orange flowers – which was most unusual, seeing as she normally preferred to wear a new dress. Amelia supposed the rations were catching up with her too.

"Surely the Air Force is better than 'fine'?" her mother asked.

"It'd be better if they put me in a bloody cockpit," Amelia replied, shoving the scone into her mouth and savouring the sticky taste of raspberry.

"Language, Amelia! Not to mention manners."

Amelia licked the jam from her fingers. "Sorry. But it's true. Our home has been taken, practically handed to the Japanese on a silver platter. Haven't you read the papers? They sailed into Lae and Salamaua without any opposition, any care from the Australian Government."

"I'm well aware of what's happening up there. I spent weeks waiting for news of you and Evelyn after that foolish decision you made." Her mother fixed her with such a penetrating stare that she couldn't help but look away.

"The government is doing the best they can," Sofia added in a small voice.

Amelia scoffed. "Best they can? You really believe that?"

Sofia looked at her nails. "You know what it's like up there. The people—"

"Mum's right, Meels," Evelyn interjected. "Most of our boys are still fighting in Europe. Australia's doing what they can under the circumstances."

Amelia wanted to scoff at Evelyn too, to tell her she was wrong – but when she looked at her older sister, who, despite the weeks of rest at home, looked weak and frail, Amelia didn't have the heart to yell at her. Instead, she focused her frustrations back on Sofia and her mother.

"The people, when dealt with correctly, are New Guinea's greatest strength. Exploit and abuse them, then they'll abuse you back. But respect them, and they'll return it to you tenfold."

"Of course," Evelyn said, reaching her hand across the table and placing it on Amelia's. "The locals have done so much for us. We wouldn't be here without them—"

"And yet we're supposed to sit back and watch as they get blown to bits?"

"No," her mother replied. "We're supposed to do what you're doing, what your sisters are doing, by helping out where we can—"

"The Red Cross is doing tremendous things," Sofia interrupted, a similar smile to their mother's sewn across her face. "Last week we raised fifty quid from our cake and quilt sales."

"Whoop-de-do!" Amelia replied, her sister's charm doing nothing for her. "It's going to take a lot more than fifty quid to save New Guinea."

Sofia huffed and crossed her arms.

"Amelia," her mother said in a stern voice. "Don't mock your sister. Every bit helps."

"Oh please, Mum!" Amelia shot to standing and glared down at her family. "We all know that the only thing that helps – that *really* helps – is the men who are over there putting their lives on the line. Not a stupid fete or parade! If this government had any sense, they'd let us women help where it matters."

Her mother pressed her fingers to her temple.

"And what about Daniel?" Amelia continued. "Dad? The government doesn't give a toss about them! For all we know they're lying dead somewhere in the bush, eaten alive by the Kukukuku."

Sofia gasped. "Do you really think … Daddy's been … ea-eat-en?"

"Of course not," her mother replied as she squeezed Sofia's hand. "Amelia, will you please calm yourself? Your little outburst isn't helping anyone."

"The time's over for being calm. If we don't—"

"For Christ's sake, Amelia!" her mother yelled, slamming her cup on the table, spilling tea all over the saucer and linen. "Enough with these tantrums of yours. It doesn't do any of us any good!"

Amelia opened her mouth and then closed it again. She hated being reprimanded like a naughty schoolgirl. Didn't anyone care what was happening in New Guinea? They'd heard nothing of Daniel and her father for months now, nothing of the state of the country or what they were doing to hold back the Japanese. Australians had been called up to do their part, and yet they continued to be kept in the dark like children. She was going to take her seat again when the doorbell rang.

"Who'd be calling so early?" Evelyn said as she looked to the door.

Amelia peeked outside the window. "It's a man … in a suit." She looked back at her mother, whose face blanched.

"Only one?" her mother asked, voice small.

Amelia nodded.

Her mother pulled her shoulders back. "Let him in then."

Amelia toddled to the entryway and rested her hand on the door, heart racing. *It's a man in a suit, nothing more.*

* * *

"Mrs McKenzie?" the man said with a stony face when Amelia opened the door.

"That's my mother," Amelia replied, chin held high – until she glanced at the letter in his hands, which caused it to tremble.

"Is she home?" he asked.

She stepped to the side. He walked inside and paused at the entryway to the dining room. Amelia had wanted to follow him, but she couldn't move.

Her legs had seized, heavy like wood. She watched the man's back, the way he stood rigid and tall.

He cleared his throat, removed his hat and said again, "Mrs McKenzie?"

"Yes?" her mother's voice echoed up the hall.

"Mrs McKenzie, I am with the government and have news of your husband."

The man paused, waiting for a reply, but nothing came. Amelia imagined what her mother's face looked like at that moment – jaw set and lips pressed tight, eyes cold and unwavering. Was it surprising that even a moment like this couldn't draw Ruth McKenzie out of her shell? Amelia followed the man up the hall and got to the dining room just in time to see him handing her mother a letter. Amelia sprang into action. She wouldn't let her mother have it. She rushed forward, nearly knocking the man over as she snatched the letter from his hands.

"Amelia!" her mother said curtly, but Amelia didn't care, knowing her mother wouldn't lower herself to snatching it back from her. She took a few steps backwards and stared at it. Her father's fate rested in the small envelope.

"Well, go on then," her mother said.

They were all watching her. Sofia's lips trembled, while Evelyn wore a small smile, a look of hope. The eternal optimist. Her mother's arms were crossed, her lips pursed. She raised her eyebrows in impatience, but resting behind her eyes was something else. Fear. The same fear that had encased her eyes in dark circles and wrinkles, like crevices allowing a glimpse of her soul.

Hands shaking, Amelia opened the letter. She skimmed over the official details at the top, desperate for the guts – the all-capital letters in blue typewriter ink.

IT DESIRES ME TO TELL YOU STOP CIVILIAN OF LAE/SALAMAUA GEORGE MCKENZIE + OTHERS EXPECTED TO BE EVACUATED BY AIR VIA WAU FAILED ARRIVE DESIGNATED TIME STOP DEEMED MISSING STOP ALL PLANES DESTROYED STOP WHEREABOUTS UNKNOWN STOP SECURITY CANNOT DIVULGE PLACES & TIMES

STOP FURTHER INFORMATION FORTHCOMING STOP GOVT REP. WILL FOLLOW WITH RESIDENT CALL STOP SINCERE SYMPATHY MINISTER FOR THE ARMY.

Amelia's hands went limp. She watched in slow motion as the letter fell to the floor. The three of them stared at her, waiting for her to say something, but she couldn't repeat the words she'd read. She'd known it for weeks: that her father and Daniel were missing. Lost in the jungle, the wilds of New Guinea their only hope.

Her mother scooped up the letter. "Missing," she eventually said, barely above a whisper.

Sofia wailed and Evelyn stifled a sob.

The government man cleared his throat again. "Not just missing, ma'am." He paused, making sure to look everyone in the eye. "He's presumed dead."

Dead. Their worst fears had come true. Amelia's chest ached. Her throat burned. The room was spinning, and yet she was perfectly still, trying to absorb the word that'd changed everything. Dead. Her eyes welled with tears, but she blinked them back. She knew that once she opened the floodgates, there'd be no stopping them.

Evelyn was crying, quiet tears rolling down her face. She was solemn, and yet reserved – like their mother. Across from her, Sofia's eyes were puffy and red, streaks of mascara cascading down her cheeks. Sofia had never had a problem showing her emotions, like their father.

"Then it's not certain?" her mother asked. "That he's dead. It's only presumed?"

"Yes, ma'am. But—"

Her mother held her hand up. "That'll be all."

"But don't you want details on what happened?" the man asked.

She looked to the letter and then up again. "It says he failed to make his evacuation flight."

The man stiffened. "Correct. There was an attack … on Wau. Planes, houses and even a few people were taken out—"

"But not George?"

"No. Mr McKenzie took off with a group of miners that were still in the area at the urging of our local force. An Allied force."

"The Volunteer Rifles?" Amelia asked eagerly, wondering if Daniel had finally been able to join.

The man looked at Amelia. "I can't divulge that information. All we know is the group is missing. We've had no word. The government wanted you to know that it is a grave situation and to prepare yourselves for the worst."

"The worst," her mother said in a sarcastic tone. "Always the worst."

The man scratched his cheek. "Well, yes, it is New Guinea after all."

Her mother offered a half smile. "Was that everything?"

"Uh. I suppose."

"Good. Amelia, please see him out."

"But … Mum?"

"Now."

Amelia ushered the man to the door, desperate to get back to her mother and have it out. How could she be so callous? To show indifference when told her husband was dead? What sort of person does that? She didn't know, but she wasn't going to put up with it anymore. She stormed back into the dining room, to find her mother upright at the table, reading the paper, teacup resting between her index and thumb, pinky flicked outwards.

"Honestly?" Amelia said, with a hand on her hip.

Her mother glanced up. "Pardon?"

"That man …" Amelia paused, trying to steady her voice, "told us Dad is dead – and you're reading the paper?"

Her mother placed her cup down. "No. He said your father is *missing* and *presumed* dead."

The heat was rising in Amelia's body. "So, because he said 'presumed' you won't take it seriously?"

Her mother exhaled. "If I had a shilling for every time someone told me your father was missing over the years, I'd be a very rich woman."

Amelia shook her head. "This isn't 'someone', Mum. This is the Australian Government telling you Dad is dead!"

"Presumed."

"Honestly!"

"She's right, Mum," Evelyn added. "We should take him seriously."

Her mother glared at Evelyn. "Why?"

"Because he's from the government," Evelyn said slowly.

Her mother scoffed. "Amelia said it herself. The government doesn't know what they're doing up there, so why in God's name should I believe them?"

"I'm sure they wouldn't make such a grave claim if they weren't certain," Sofia said, her face red and blotchy.

Her mother threw her napkin on the table. "The government doesn't know a thing! Believe what you want, but until they turn up on my doorstep with a body, I will continue to believe that my husband is alive. No one knows New Guinea better than he does. No one! And God knows George McKenzie won't bow down to the Japs. He'd rather be skinned alive and eaten by natives than surrender to those mongrels."

Her mother scowled before gracefully departing the room as if she had somewhere better to be.

"Well, good then!" Amelia threw her arms up in the air. "We'll continue to carry on with our perfect lives, like we did back home, like Mum's always taught us! No worries if Dad is missing, dead somewhere in the jungle ... as long as we look the part, then all is well."

She glared at her sisters, heart pounding, but they didn't say anything. "Unbelievable!" she yelled as she stormed out of the room.

* * *

Amelia stared at the cloudless sky, mesmerised by the pale-blue expanse. Instead of lying in her mother's garden, she wished she could be up there, soaring through its never-ending reach, looping and gliding in her Moth. She took a drag of the cigarette that was burning idly between her fingers, and was horrified when her lungs exploded into a raging cough. She rolled onto her side, convinced her chest was going to burst; her body was heaving with such force she was sure she'd never breathe again. When she finally caught her breath, she stubbed the cigarette into the grass and vowed to never touch another.

"You should be happy smoking doesn't agree with you," her mother said. Amelia looked up to find her standing behind her. "Filthy habit."

Amelia stomped to the wrought-iron table on the patio, picked up the cigarette case she'd stolen from Sofia earlier and pulled out another.

Her mother plucked the cigarette out of Amelia's mouth. "You always were my wilful one." Amelia curled her lip and reached for another, but she snatched the case away. "Don't test me, dear. Not today." She lit the cigarette for herself and sat on one of the wrought-iron chairs. "Sit."

Amelia huffed as her mother sucked on the cigarette, chest expanding easily. She blew the smoke out the side of her mouth. "Why do you insist on challenging me?"

Amelia crossed her arms.

Her mother shook her head and laughed. "Oh, Amelia. Just because I don't wear my heart on my sleeve, doesn't mean I don't care. You've a lot to learn about life."

"I know more than you think."

"Perhaps you do. This war will certainly teach you things ... force you to discover a side of yourself you never knew existed."

"It already has. I learned a few things trekking up the coast."

Her mother took another drag and narrowed her eyes. "Perhaps you did. It certainly isn't an easy place to survive. But if anyone can do it, it's George McKenzie. Be it the Japs, or the Kukukuku or any of the other savage cannibals that lurk in those jungles, your father can handle it ... *has* handled it. He pioneered those lands, along with Harry, all those years ago."

"And what about Daniel? Do you think he's alive?" Amelia's skin tingled as she waited for her mother to reply – for her confirmation, her belief that Daniel was okay.

"Harry taught Daniel everything he knows." She shook her head and laughed. "He was a funny old bloke, that Harry. Didn't care about race or colour ... thought we were all one being. He brought out the best in everyone, your father especially. I'd never seen two Scotsmen so different, and yet still the best of mates. Your father hasn't been the same since his death. I guess that's why he's taken to Daniel so much. Wants to make sure that boy has a place, even with all his shortcomings." Amelia bit her tongue as her mother stubbed out her cigarette. "Do I think Daniel is alive? Yes. That boy is as determined as you, even more because he's black."

"Half," Amelia said.

"Same difference."

"Is that why you hate him?"

"I don't hate him. I just don't want him anywhere near my daughter."

"Because he's black?"

"Yes, Amelia. Because he's black! It's hard enough as it is being a woman. And if you really do plan on becoming a pilot after the war, you'll face even greater difficulties. Do you think I want you to be held back by him as well?"

"But don't you see, Mum? Daniel's never held me back; he only wants me to shine."

"Being with Daniel will pose huge challenges—"

"But what if I'm okay with that?"

Her mother shook her head. "You think that now, but life would be very difficult. Cut your losses and be rid of him once and for all. This is where you belong."

# 30

# Amelia

Amelia scratched at the studs that pressed into her neck; the collar of her uniform was suffocating. She longed to rip the whole thing off, especially the skirt, which was too tight to march in and not the least bit practical. Instead, she stiffened her stance and waited in line as the day's proceedings got underway. There was a slight chill to the air as the late May sun beamed down on the group of women, the smell of freshly cut grass lingering. Rows of chairs were assembled, and several hundred people had gathered on the RAAF's open lawn, while a succession of drums beat in time with Amelia's own pounding heart. She'd made it to her passing-out parade and should've been beaming with pride, yet she couldn't get her conversations with Tom and her mother out of her head.

Were they right? Was Daniel where he belonged? Was this where *she* belonged? A cog, lost in the works of army bureaucracy, marching, obeying, following without any opinions or say? Her sisters, her mother and the hundreds of women surrounding her were happy to do it without any hesitation. Why couldn't she be like them? Why couldn't she choose the conventional, ordinary life that was laid out before her? Because she'd never be that sort of girl. She'd never settle for ordinary. Life in New Guinea had shown her there was another way. Deeply rooted to this extraordinary place, like the hundred-year-old raintrees that sheltered Lae, she couldn't imagine settling for anything less. Only those with a true connection knew how New Guinea lives inside you, deep within your bones, resting within your heart, like a child in the womb. It was where she belonged. She'd made a vow to find her way back and couldn't let others get in her way.

The line started to move as the women took the field. Amelia repeated the order of steps in her head for the millionth time as she stood tall, posture stiff and gaze set forward.

"Recruits!" Officer Mitchell yelled. "You have trained hard over the past month and have diligently learned what is required as a nurse of the Royal Australian Air Force. It's been my pleasure to lead you, and even a greater pleasure to witness your induction today. Go forward with pride as you serve your nation."

Officer Mitchell saluted the women, and they returned the gesture without flaw. Amelia's heart swelled as she held her fingers to her forehead, her lips turning upwards in the smallest of smiles. She *was* proud of herself.

* * *

When the ceremony was over, the women waited as they were given their postings. Amelia bit her bottom lip as she moved through the line, nearly tripping on her feet. She'd managed to march perfectly but was still so clumsy when it came to life. The audience had dispersed and were waiting on the sidelines as each new recruit received her envelope. Amelia watched the outward displays of affection – young women hugging their loving fathers, women crying tears of joy. Now that all the pomp and ceremony was over, they were really letting themselves go.

Amelia took a step forward as she looked through the displays of love to find her family. But there was no one there.

"Good work, Miss McKenzie," Officer Mitchell said as he handed her an envelope. "I'm sure you'll be pleased with your posting."

Amelia blinked and looked back at him. But before she could muster a reply, she turned her head towards the crowd. She thought she'd seen something – something she'd never imagined seeing on a day like this. A ghost. The ghost of her father. Or was it?

"Dad?" she whispered, not even realising the words had left her lips.

"Pardon?" Officer Mitchell replied, but Amelia was already gone, legs taking flight as they ran across the lawn and the ghostly figure took shape – a haggard shape, half the size he once was. Her father limped towards her, his once-broad frame now skeletal. He was cleanshaven, his skin ashen, cheeks and eyes sunken. Wrapped around him were her mother and sisters, the three women taking care as they helped him walk. Amelia stopped, eyes wide as she drank in the sight before her. Her father, her family – together again.

"Hello, lass," her father said, chin trembling and eyes watering. "That was a fine job you did up there."

Her legs felt weak; her knees buckled. He wrapped his scant arms around her, and before she knew it, she was a blubbering mess, face hot with tears.

"Shh ... shhh," he whispered in her ear as she collapsed against his body. The other three women joined in and held what was left of her father.

When they finally pulled away from each other, Amelia looked up and smiled. "How?"

He let out a jolly laugh. "Not too sure about that myself. I was convinced that place was finally going to get the better of me."

Amelia shot her mother and sisters a look. "But why didn't you tell me?"

"We only got word last night," her mother replied. "We didn't want you to miss your parade, and figured this would be a nice way to celebrate."

Amelia wiped her eyes. "It's more than nice ... it's ... it's unbelievable. But I don't understand! They said you were missing, presumed dead?"

"They had to, for security reasons. They censored the information so we could get out. Over the Bulldog Track, to Yule Island on the south coast. The kept us there for several weeks to recuperate." He paused to shake his head. "I tell you, I thought I was done for. Even after all my years exploring the Highlands, this was something else."

"No wonder you look so terrible," Amelia said.

"Thanks, lass." He ruffled her hair and wrapped his arms around the women again. "And you, Meels, gone off and joined the Air Force. What a thing!"

Amelia looked at her feet. "It's only as a nurse. I won't get to fly."

"I couldn't be prouder. What you're doing … what you're all doing"—he looked at Ruth, Evelyn and Sofia—"is remarkable."

There were tears in her father's eyes again. She wanted to savour this moment, to wrap herself up in his love, but she remembered why they were all here in the first place. War. The war in which Daniel was still fighting.

Her stomach twisted. "What about Daniel? Where is he?"

Her father ran his hand over his face. "That boy is as stubborn as you. But he saved me in the end. Got me to Yule, though I haven't seen him since."

Amelia's stomach plunged. Daniel was still missing.

Her father placed a hand on her shoulder as if he sensed her uneasiness. "Not to worry. I sent Silas to find him. If he made it to Moresby, I suspect he's joined the Papuan Infantry Battalion."

"What about you, Meels?" Evelyn's voice chimed in. "Did you receive your posting?"

Amelia blinked. She looked at her hand and realised she was still holding the envelope Officer Mitchell had given her. "Well … what are you waiting for? Open it."

Amelia skimmed over the typed writing, the words of gratitude for her service flying over her head, and her mouth fell open as she read the two words she'd never expected to see.

"Well?" Evelyn asked.

Amelia looked up. Four eager faces were smiling back at her. "Port Moresby," she whispered. "They're sending me back."

III

# Part Three

*January 1943*

# 31

# Daniel

Daniel crawled forward, body caked with mud. Sweat dripped from his forehead; the early morning air was sticky with heat. A mosquito buzzed in his ear – their relentless pestering was insufferable – and smoke from the village campfires choked his nostrils. He inched towards the clearing that opened onto the village, near the mouth of Kumusi River, north of Buna. They were on the hunt for the last of the Japanese, who were hiding after the Battle of the Beachheads. This morning's mission was to determine how many were left.

It was something Daniel had become all too familiar with since joining the Papuan Infantry Battalion last May. He'd finally found an outfit that would take him, and after a couple months of training at the barracks in Moresby, the men had trekked over the Owen Stanley Ranges to patrol the northern beaches. The PIB's baptism of fire on July 23 was seared in Daniel's memory, that first kill hard to shake. The feeling of pulling the trigger – the rifle shuddering as the bullet charged out and struck its target with exact precision – was exhilarating. His heart had pumped as adrenaline surged through his body, something he'd never felt before, not even in those brief moments of passion with Amelia. But when he'd watched his targets fall, the lives of young Japanese soldiers taken in an instant, he couldn't help but think of Amelia, and how she'd feel if he was killed. It was this feeling that stayed with him more than the exhilaration of firing a gun. The images of the men falling and the thoughts of their heartbroken loved ones coursed through his head day after day.

He tried to banish the thought, telling himself it was not like he had a mother or father to mourn him; it was only Amelia who'd suffer, and she'd eventually move on, if she hadn't already. After the raid in Port Moresby, he decided he couldn't hold onto anymore slivers of hope. Not when he had a war to focus on. Mr McKenzie was right: it wasn't fair to make her wait for him. Not when he was likely to die up here. It was easier to continue on this path, to let their love go. She was better off without him. But the thought of her mourning was enough to keep Daniel soldiering on, even after the blast at the 'drome that had knocked him unconscious for a month, even through multiple bouts of malaria, tropical ulcers and the threat of the Japanese lurking in every tree. He'd managed to stay alive this long and wasn't about to let today's mission change that.

A twig snapped, forcing Daniel to freeze. He glanced over his shoulder. An American from the 41st Division and an Aussie private from another company was lurking behind him. He'd been used to patrolling with the Papuan men who made up his unit and wasn't sure what to make of these newbies. Their movements were abrupt, the men not used to the guerrilla tactics used in the jungle. A chill shot up Daniel's spine each time they banged a bush or knocked their rifle against a tree. He raised a finger to his lips.

The Yank named Pocock was the first to snicker. "Yes, sir," Pocock said mockingly, not bothering to whisper. He was an average-height seppo in his twenties whose hairline was already receding.

The sweating, pasty-faced Aussie private named Morris eyed Pocock sideways, but didn't say anything.

Daniel gritted his teeth. If it wasn't their clumsy movements, it was reckless behaviour like this that was going to get them killed. And Daniel hadn't come this far to die on a routine raid because some seppo was too arrogant to listen to someone he deemed beneath him. Daniel had found this was the attitude of several of the American soldiers, but it was nothing he wasn't used to. At least the Aussies' attitudes towards the locals had improved, most of the men amongst his ranks treating them respectfully.

He peered through the thick foliage that blocked their view, watching as the village came to life under the early morning light. The villagers went about their business, the women tending to the hard labour while the men smoked brus and talked around the fire. Daniel bit the inside of his cheek, wondering if he should approach his countrymen like he'd done many times before, appeal to their likeness. But he knew he couldn't trust them, even if he was more of a local than the whites; he was Niuginian and they were Papuan, practically worlds apart. Plus, the Japanese had already taken them under their control, like many villagers in this area, forcing them into submission through beatings and killings. Daniel didn't blame them – they had to do what they could to survive – but he didn't want to battle Papuans if he didn't have to.

Daniel waited, counting his breaths, constantly wondering if they'd be his last. The Japanese would show themselves eventually; they always did – no one could escape the watchful eyes of the "green shadows". And then, more than a dozen of them emerged, returning from the river, bare chested, wearing only trousers. They yelled something at the men around the fire, who quickly got up and scurried off towards their huts, while the Japanese sat and lit their cigarettes. As billows of smoke curled into the air, Daniel considered whether it was a good time to go forward with the ambush and catch the Japanese off-guard. But he knew better, knew to stick to his orders.

Pocock stifled a sneeze, and one of the Japanese looked up. Daniel tensed as the man's eyes penetrated the tree line. Daniel signalled for Morris and Pocock to retreat; they'd gathered enough intel for now. But Pocock didn't listen. He crept forward so he was now in line with Daniel at the edge of foliage that surrounded the village.

Daniel grabbed Pocock's arm and forcefully whispered, "What are you doing? We've got to get back."

Pocock pulled away. "Bullshit. We're in a good position for an attack."

"We don't have orders for an attack," Daniel said through gritted teeth.

"Don't mean we shouldn't jump at the chance," Pocock replied. "I wanna kill a Jap, put a bullet in the head of those yellow-skinned mongrels."

"There's three of us and twelve of them." Daniel eyed Morris, hoping the Aussie would back him up, but Morris appeared to be torn; his face twisted as he looked from Daniel to Pocock and back, as if he was wondering whose side to take.

Daniel exhaled. "Hooper wants us back."

"I don't answer to Hooper," Pocock said in a condescending tone. "So why don't you go back, and me and Morris here will try to win this war."

Daniel shook his head. Typical. A few months into the job and he thinks he can single-handedly win the war. "Look, mate, I've been tasked with keeping you alive and I intend to do that. So why don't you do what you're told and head back with me now."

"I ain't your mate," Pocock said, his southern drawl ringing in Daniel's ears. He gestured for Morris to follow him, and the two men inched forward, the bush rustling against their movement.

Daniel's heart picked up pace. He had to act now or risk giving their position away. He grabbed Pocock by the ankle and pulled him back.

"What the—" Pocock said, but Daniel was already on top of him, one hand over Pocock's mouth, the other raised to his lips, gesturing for silence. Pocock squirmed against Daniel, but Daniel only pressed down harder, putting all of his frustrations into his hand. All he needed was to make one strong statement and exert enough power to force Pocock to listen.

Morris turned around and with wide eyes said, "He can't breathe."

Daniel watched as Pocock turned from white to the lightest shade of blue. How much further could he go? What was one more life? He'd already taken so many. Staring into his pale-blue eyes – eyes of a colour that Daniel would never have – he watched as they clouded over, his life slowly slipping away.

Daniel released his hand; it wasn't worth it. It never was.

Pocock gasped for air as Daniel forced his attention back to the tree line, trying to steady his racing heart. "Right. You lads ready to listen?"

"You nearly killed me," Pocock said between breaths.

"Yeah, well, take it up with your captain. Now, let's move. For all we know the Japanese are already onto us, and I want to put as much distance between us and them as possible."

Pocock looked to Morris, as if daring him, but Morris inched towards Daniel. "Come on, mate. Like he said, take it up with the captain when we get back."

Pocock pushed himself up so he was eye to eye with Daniel. "Look, nigger. I ain't gotta listen to a thing you say. You're nothing but a coon."

Daniel ran his tongue along the inside of his mouth. "I may be a coon, but I've been here far longer than you. So you best do what you're told before you get us all killed."

Pocock tilted his head to the side as he balled his hand into a fist. Daniel stiffened, ready to counteract the blow, but Pocock didn't have a chance to land it. A noise from the bushes startled them. They slowly turned towards the faint whimpering sound. The men glanced at each other and propped their guns under their arms. Daniel listened for the noise again, for the click of a rifle loading, but all he could hear was his heart thrashing in his ear. Pocock stepped forward, his boot crunching on a twig. Daniel winced, certain they were going to be shot at any second now. He pressed his finger against the trigger and waited. Each second passed like an eternity. Pocock was right in front of the bush now, Daniel behind him and Morris at the back. Daniel watched as Pocock pushed the tip of his rifle against a branch to clear the way, a prime target for whoever was hiding behind it. In normal circumstances, Daniel would've shaken his head, told him what an idiot he was for walking straight into a trap, but there wasn't any time for that, because before they knew it, out it jumped.

A dog. A scraggy-looking village dog.

Pocock and Morris lowered their rifles and laughed, patting the dog that was now panting with joy. Daniel watched them from the corner of his eye but kept his attention on the bush. It lay completely still, but he wasn't convinced. The Japanese were clever, fearless warriors who didn't care about dying. He narrowed his eyes, waiting for it to move again, for the click of the rifle and blast of the bullet, but nothing came.

"Oh, give it a break," Pocock said, pushing Daniel's rifle down. "Was only a dog."

Daniel looked at the panting dog waiting for a pat. Exactly. A dog, which could bark any second, giving their position away to the Japanese who were lurking beyond the trees. "Let's go."

Pocock and Morris followed, finally submitting to Daniel's commands. They crept back in the direction they'd come from, Daniel's heart racing the entire time.

* * *

Camp was buzzing when they got back. The men were divided into their usual groups: Papuans huddled around a fire towards the back, while the Aussies and Americans assembled around their own fire. Daniel glanced at the Papuans – a mix of Kerema and Central men who'd been part of the PIB since before Pearl Harbor. They were all muscle, their exposed chests hardened by years of hard labour, and their lean legs were covered in lap-laps that were tied with a belt that housed their rifles. Daniel didn't approve of their uniform, a skirt not being the easiest item of clothing to trek or fight in. He was fortunate his CO had allowed him to wear the Aussie dress of khaki shorts and shirt. He'd had to dye it green for camouflage, and the ink ran whenever there was heavy rain.

Sitting with the Papuans was Silas, the only other Niuginian besides Daniel. He wasn't sure how Mr McKenzie's right-hand man had found him after they'd parted at Yule Island, but suspected the wantok system had something to do with it. Nothing went unnoticed amongst the locals, and word would've spread between villages that a Niuginian had joined the PIB. It'd been nice to have Silas by his side the past nine months; he was a link to Daniel's past that he wasn't willing to shed, especially as he figured out his place in this new world. He was desperate to join the Papuans by the fire for a hot cuppa but, knowing he had to take care of business first, he turned towards Lieutenant Hooper's tent.

Lieutenant Hooper was huddled over a map, and he glanced up as Daniel paused to salute him. Hooper looked down and tapped repeatedly at the map as he mumbled something about forced leave. He liked Hooper – a no-nonsense Aussie bloke who took the time to get to know the men in his unit, even learning Police Motu, the lingua franca the Papuans spoke when dealing with the waitman. He was young, maybe a few years older than Daniel, with brown hair and barely a whisker on his face. His teeth were gapped and his smile warm, and he was fair and reasonable in his commands and respected by the unit of Papuans he led.

"Don't bother," Hooper eventually said. "Salutes are a sign of respect, something you clearly have little of."

Daniel lowered his arm and scratched at his beard. It was overgrown and due for a shave. "I have the utmost respect for you, sir—"

"If you had respect for me, Sergeant, you wouldn't have pulled that shit out there! Do you know how much trouble this is going to cause me with the Yanks?"

"I'm sorry, sir. That's why I'm here … to apologise."

"I don't want your apologies. You should've known better."

"He provoked me—"

"And? You think it's okay to nearly choke someone every time you're provoked? After months of training, discipline, drills … has the Army taught you nothing?"

Daniel looked down.

"Look at me when I'm talking to you, Sergeant," Hooper said in a firm yet amiable voice. Daniel pulled his shoulders back and lifted his chin, meeting Hooper's sharp eyes. "You're a smart bloke, Carmichael, much smarter than some of these chaps. You should've known better. Even if they provoked you, even if they're a bunch of arseholes, you have to do better."

"Why?"

Hooper jerked his head back. "Pardon me?"

Daniel exhaled. "Why does it always have to be me? Why not Pocock, or any of the other white men who treat us like shit?"

Hooper exhaled. "Because, Sergeant … the world is unfair. Haven't you learned that by now?"

"What if I want to change it? The world?"

"Look how much good that's done the Japs."

"That's not what I mean—"

"I know what you mean." Hooper leaned back in his chair and ran his hand over his chin, watching Daniel carefully as he considered his words. "It's not every day you get the entire world coming together to fight the injustices of few. The world is changing, hopefully for the better. But it won't happen overnight, and it won't happen by you fighting with blokes like Pocock. It will happen if you take the time to listen, to learn. It's bloody bullshit what you lot have to put up with, but for right now, it's how things work. Hopefully, over time, by following the right processes, we'll be able to make improvements, but you've got to work with me."

Daniel pressed his lips together. He was tired of being told to accept the norm, to wait for change. But what could he do? He was subject to the will of the Allies' command, a mere soldier amongst many.

"Anyway," Hooper pressed on, "you can take it up with your new CO. I'm taking leave, effective immediately."

"New CO?"

"I'll introduce you. It'd be good for him to get to know you. It takes a bit to get the Papuans to take to us, and I'm sure the new CO could use all the advice he can get from you, seeing as you're both."

"I'm Niuginian, actually ..." but Hooper wasn't listening; he was already calling for the new CO to come in.

"I just realised he has the same name as you."

Daniel tensed as soon as Hooper shouted the new CO's name.

"Sergeant Carmichael," Hooper said. "Meet Lieutenant Carmichael."

"Danny *boi* ..."

Daniel's stomach hardened as *tha*t smile stared back at him.

"Long time, no see," Tom added. "I'm honoured to be leading you boys on the next part of this journey."

# 32

# Daniel

Daniel took a long drag, thankful they'd been able to get decent rations again after the Allies took back Kokoda and its airfield last November. The Japanese had made it as far as Ioribiwa, only twenty miles from Port Moresby, before being forced to retreat. Their soldiers had been exhausted by the difficult terrain and were nearly starved to death without sufficient rations. The Aussie men who'd had to slog up and down that track, outnumbered five to one by the Japanese, so sick with dysentery they had to cut holes out of their trousers so the shit could run down their legs – they were the real heroes. Not the pricks like Tom who waltzed in thinking they knew everything. It was hard to comprehend he was here in the Northern Province, serving as Daniel's new CO.

As if his brother could sense his unease, Tom came waltzing up to the fire with that obnoxious grin. "Bois, that's enough tok tok. Time to get to work. We're moving out after the raid tonight."

Daniel smashed his cigarette into the ground with his boot. "Alright. We'll get the carriers to pack up camp."

"No need," Tom replied. "I've dismissed them."

"Who'll carry our goods? You know we need at least two carriers for every soldier."

"Not anymore. I don't trust these Northern Province natives. Too many reports of defecting villages. We'll carry our own goods."

"That's at least fifty pounds each! How can we be expected to carry that and still be on the hunt for the Japanese?"

"*We*"— Tom pointed to himself, Pocock and Morris, who were hovering nearby—"won't be carrying anything. You natives will carry our stores to Buna. Pocock and Morris will come with me on the raid."

Daniel's eye twitched. "But it's our bloody unit! We're the ones experienced at taking out the enemy."

That slow smile crept up Tom's face, like the Cheshire Cat's. "Not anymore. It's my unit now, and what I say goes."

Daniel stepped forward, the two brothers eye to eye. Daniel's nostrils flared as he took in the stench of arrogance and the twinkling blue eyes that screamed privilege. Hooper was wrong. Nothing had changed. It never would. But what could he do?

"Do you have a problem with that, *boi*?" Tom added.

Daniel gritted his teeth and forced himself to say, "No, sir." He picked up Tom's pack and signalled to Silas and the Papuans to follow suit.

Tom snickered as they marched past. "Here comes the boong train."

Daniel paused, which caused Silas and the men to stumble into him.

"Aiyo!" Silas said, shaking his head. "Hurry up before masta gets cross."

"He's not your master," Daniel replied through gritted teeth. "And I don't care if he gets cross ... he should be hauling his own gear."

Silas tsked. "Yu bikhead."

"How am *I* the big head?"

Silas didn't reply, but nudged Daniel forward instead. Daniel huffed, hating being spoken to like a naughty schoolboy. Why did Silas always have to be so self-righteous? Wasn't there ever a time he felt like giving up? Daniel had done everything right, had supported the Allies, led his men and respected the Aussies enough that they made him sergeant. And all for what? To be placed back at the bottom, given the lowliest job? This was a part of the war he'd been lucky enough to avoid so far. For the most part, the men in the PIB had been treated like their Aussie counterparts; they'd been allowed to use locals from various villages to carry their bedding, clothing, mess tins, ammunition and mortars. The carriers sometimes worked up to twenty hours a day for days on end, their bare feet like leather against the slippery slopes of the Owen Stanley Range. Though they were underfed with measly rations, they carried the white soldiers who'd been struck down by the horrors of jungle warfare and were paid with a stick of Emu Twist tobacco and a sheet of newspaper for each day's work. Many had deserted, running back to the protection of their villages, but many others took it in their stride, rarely complaining. No wonder they were called fuzzy wuzzy angels. He hated that the Papuans had to be used this way, exploited as indentured labourers, the old ways of the Aussie Administration still intact. Come to think of it, the Papuans were the real heroes.

* * *

Tom, Pocock and Morris strutted into their next camp like cockerels gearing up for a fight, slapping each other on the back in congratulations. They dumped their guns and ammo and grabbed a plate of tucker from Silas, digging into bully beef and damper by the fire, shovelling food into their mouths like starving orphans, lips smacking and crumbs falling in pieces around them. Pocock hissed at one of the locals to bring them tea. They slurped it back like camels at a watering hole and tossed their plates onto the ground. Pocock and Morris retreated to nearby coconut trees for a kip. Tom was following, picking the food out of his teeth with his fingernail, when he spotted Daniel sitting at the edge of camp. He turned in his direction instead, and Daniel focused his attention on his gun.

"We got them," Tom said as he approached, chest puffed out like a goura pigeon. "The dirty lot of them. Took the defectors out too. Serves those Kanakas right for betraying us."

Daniel shuddered. The callous destruction of life – of Papuan lives, no less – was hard to digest.

Tom smiled. "How was your trek?"

"Fine. These men aren't afraid of hard work." Daniel immediately wished he hadn't said that, not knowing what else Tom would do to abuse his power.

"Good. Because we have a lot of ground to cover. Moresby wants me to take you lot to Morobe while the Allies finish up here. Can't believe I'm back in this hellhole when we went to so much trouble to get out of here."

Daniel pushed a brush into the chamber of his Owen gun. He forced it in and out with jagged movements, and bits of mud and residue came out. "I forgot you were here last year," Daniel said. "Though I imagine it would've been a pretty easy trek for someone fit and healthy like you?"

"It was a bloody nightmare. Long days under the hot sun with little food. Thank God for Evelyn and Amelia, tending to the sick men."

"Sounds like them. You lads were lucky they were there."

Tom shrugged. "Hopefully the RAAF sorts out Meels."

"The RAAF?"

"Yeah, she enlisted after we got back to Australia. We both did," he added, jutting his chest out. "We were in training together in Sydney before we went on to Brisbane. They wouldn't let her in a cockpit – rightly so – but she's being put to good use as a nurse. Have to say, she's still feisty as ever … that's why it's been hard for her to find a fella. Oh, wait, that's right … you two are together. Or *were* together? It certainly didn't look that way when I saw her out dancing with all those American coons. She really has something for black fellas, doesn't she? Such a shame."

Daniel stood and balled his hand into a fist, adrenaline surging up his arm. He glared at his brother, at that stupid smile and look of indifference. How easy it would be to punch him. To smack that smile off his face. But then, as Hooper said, what good what it do? Tom would always be Tom, would always win. Daniel had to learn to rise above, to walk away. He turned on his heel and walked towards the beach. It wasn't worth it.

* * *

The warm water lapped at Daniel's feet as the sun rose over the horizon, beams of light creeping higher, the blue hour blazing into a fiery palette of reds. Wading further out, he closed his eyes, the swell of nature luring him into its fold – salt brushing his lips, waves crashing in his ears, the smell of sea tickling his nostrils. Inhaling, he dove down, the warm water cleansing, the pressure of his lungs building, the sensation of his life slipping, his muddled mind releasing, until he could take it no more and kicked his way back to the surface, lungs gasping for air. When he could breathe easily again, he leaned back and floated, letting the roll of the waves bounce him up and down.

It'd been so long since he'd seen someone he knew, someone from his past, he hadn't realised how much it meant to him to see a familiar face, even it if was Tom's. It'd been easier to close off his feelings this past year, keeping everyone at bay, than to risk letting someone in. Focusing on the war – on keeping his unit of men alive – had allowed him to push Amelia aside. But seeing Tom had made it all come back to light. He realised what he'd been searching for: familiarity, the sense of ease that comes with being around someone who'd known you your entire life. He craved the comfort of companionship. Longing for Amelia was like his longing to belong. Hearing she was getting on with her life in Brisbane had been hard to stomach – not because he didn't want the best for her, but because it meant she was distancing herself from New Guinea and the life he pictured with her. He knew Tom was only trying to get a rise out of him, but still … what if Amelia didn't want him anymore? She was his only real family, the only person besides his father he'd ever loved. He couldn't bear to think that was gone. What was he fighting for, if it wasn't for her? For them? For a new world where it was finally okay to be together? What was it all for, without Amelia?

# 33

## Daniel

"Change of plans," Tom said after ordering the locals to pack up camp again. "Headquarters has radioed with reports of a few Japs still lurking."

"You said you got the lot of them in the raid?" Daniel replied.

"Apparently not," Tom mumbled. "We're to head back towards Popondetta and finish them off. You bois will carry the goods until we get closer, and then I'll need you on the ground."

"Where are Pocock and Morris?"

"They've been sent on leave," Tom grumbled as he swatted away a mosquito that was lingering on his thigh, a red welt already surfacing. He pulled up his socks, readjusted his slouch hat and marched out of camp with only his gun across his back, the rest of his pack left for someone else to carry.

Daniel shook his head. Every other Aussie soldier he'd met had carried his own pack. Tom's arrogance knew no bounds. But knowing he needed to lead, to show the men in the unit that not all was lost, he picked up Tom's pack and trudged after his clueless brother.

When they got to the next village at the end of the day, the locals eyed them carefully, like eagles hunting for prey. The men were clutching their spears, shell necklaces hanging from their bare chests and a thin strip of tapa cloth covering their genitals. Whispering in their Binandere language, the women – whose faces were tattooed with patterns that matched the print on their tapa cloth – hurried inside their huts, the musty smell of the dried leaves that were wrapped around their biceps lingering. Daniel noticed an older woman who'd remained outside. Her face tattoo had faded into her skin and been replaced with wrinkles that extended down to her sagging breasts. Tufts of black whiskers lined her chin. She stared at him, eyes penetrating like the sun on your skin, forcing him to look away.

"We'll rest here," Tom said, gesturing for Daniel to give him his pack.

Daniel bit his lip. "Are you sure? This bunch doesn't look very friendly."

"I thought you said we could trust the natives?"

"Of course we can," Daniel mumbled, not wanting to admit that they still needed to be on guard. While this village had pledged their allegiance to the Allies, several of the villages in the area had defected to the Japanese over the past year. It wasn't far from here that a local had betrayed a group of Australian missionaries, including two women and a six-year-old mixed-race boy, handing them over to the Japanese, who'd beheaded them all. While he didn't think that would happen now the Allies had taken control of the Northern Province, he'd make sure each of them took a turn as guard just in case. He left Tom to join Silas and the Papuans around the fire, greeting the village chief as he went. He was a youngish man with a colourful feathered headdress that dripped with tiny shells, flowers, and pig tusks that looped into his nose. Daniel shook his hand and asked if he knew anything about lingering Japanese, but the chief shook his head and looked away.

When Daniel joined the men, Silas handed him a plate of sago, a favourite of the locals, since it grew in abundance in the swamps around the river. Daniel tucked into it, and the starchy substance stuck to the roof of his mouth. When tea was finished, the men took to bed, curling up into balls by the fire. Daniel was on first watch, gun resting by his side as he scanned the village. It was quiet, apart from the usual jungle noises; the mating calls of a million male cicadas were like a crescendo of pheromones that rose then faded away into an eerie silence. He reached for the cigarette behind his ear and leaned forward to light it on the fire. He drew back on the cigarette, savouring the sweet sensation of his lungs filling.

"Can I bum a smoke?" Tom asked as he took a seat, stretching his legs out in front of him.

Daniel tensed, not in the mood for Tom's company. But since there was something he was itching to ask, he offered him one. Tom lit it and the flames cast him in a shadowy light.

"If you were in RAAF training with Amelia, how is it that you're here?" Daniel asked.

"What do you mean?" Tom was quick to reply.

"This is an infantry battalion, a land-based unit."

"I ... I decided to transfer."

But Daniel didn't have a chance to reply; his ears pricked up as a twig snapped. He reached for his gun and shot to standing, the barrel pointing into the blackened jungle. Tom stumbled upright, lifting his own gun, while Daniel listened carefully. But the crackling of the fire, mixed with the mating cicadas, was all he could hear. He slowly lowered his gun and turned to Tom, who was still waving his gun about in jerky movements.

"Will you put that thing down?" Daniel said. "You're going to get someone killed."

"Yeah ... a Jap, I hope!"

"You know most of the men fighting out here haven't even seen a Japanese? They could be twenty feet away and you wouldn't even know they were there."

Tom lowered his gun. "How have you managed to stay alive so long then?"

Daniel shrugged. "Luck, I guess."

"A man needs more than luck to survive."

"I disagree. Luck always comes into play. It's what made you white and me black."

"No ... luck had nothing to do with you being black. That was our father's mistake."

Daniel's chest constricted. He felt as if razorblades were scratching at his throat, but before he could reply, a loud bang sounded off. Tom clutched his leg and keeled over.

* * *

Daniel dropped to the ground, gun raised as he commando crawled towards Tom. His thigh was pouring with blood, his screams of agony ringing through the night. The other men had woken and formed a line around him. One of them grabbed onto Tom's uniform and dragged him to the trees for cover. Daniel skimmed the area, trying to determine where the shot had come from, the thud thud thud of his heart hammering in his ear. His gun moved from hut to hut, the fire offering a faint light over the thatched houses that otherwise would've been swallowed in darkness.

Then the ground next to him shot up, tiny pebbles spraying his face as the taste of dirt seeped into his mouth. He rolled away as another bullet crashed down, and another, and his eyes watered as clouds of dust engulfed him. Pop pop pop, a shrill scream, voices yelling, a baby wailing – noises ringing through the air. He didn't know what to do, where to go – he wished he could curl up and let fate take its course, but his body wouldn't let him, adrenaline surging through his veins. Before he knew it, he was up, running towards the huts, index finger pressing down, melting into the trigger, a thousand jolts of electricity shooting up his spine, matching the force of each bullet. The dirt around him shot up, his feet dancing like an Irishman's as he navigated the bullets coming at him. He sensed someone next to him, their presence moving him forward along the same deadly path. He dove under one of the huts for cover, his companion doing the same. The blasting bullets came to a halt. His heartbeat slowed, slightly, the thuds retracting, replaced by a dah-dump, dah-dump as he gulped in the air that would fuel his next move. He looked over to see Silas with his face covered in dirt and blood, eyes as wide as the moon.

"luluai's haus," Silas whispered through jagged breaths.

The shots came from the chief's hut. Daniel had been right not to trust him.

"Are you sure?"

Silas nodded. That was enough to know what Daniel needed to do next. He blinked, fingers slippery with sweat as he fumbled with reloading his ammunition. They tingled as he pushed the prop into its holster, the seconds slowing until he was off again, back on his feet and surging towards the chief's hut with Silas by his side. Time sped forward, a flurry of activity, and yet he felt every movement – finger tapping against the trigger, shrapnel scrapping his shins, beads of sweat running down his spine. But as quickly as the shots had come, they stopped again. Silence.

He climbed the steps into the chief's hut and burst into the house to find the young man standing tall as a Japanese soldier sat at the window reloading his gun. Daniel closed the space between them, the soldier's eyes full of fear as Daniel shot the soldier point blank. He collapsed backwards. Daniel exhaled as a pool of blood seeped into the floorboards. Then he turned towards the chief and, without hesitation, shot him too. The young man's life was gone before it even began.

Daniel kicked the man, devastated it'd come to this – that another local man had fallen because of someone else's war. Just like Silas had said. He turned to look for Silas, for the words of comfort he knew he'd need, but the room was empty. Silas was no longer by his side.

* * *

Daniel spun around, searching for the faithful companion who'd been with him all these months. Had he tripped, fallen, stumbled in the commotion? Daniel retraced his steps, backing out of the hut, with his gun raised in case the enemy was about. But the air was still, eerily so, the smell of death and grief surfacing. Daniel crept backwards, watching as the villagers slowly emerged from their huts. It wouldn't be long before they realised their chief was gone, and Daniel didn't want to risk the repercussions of their backlash without appropriate backup. He and Silas had to get back to the men and get the hell out of here. But where was Silas?

Daniel stumbled, tripping on a large lump that wasn't there before. His mouth went dry as he realised what – *who* – it was. Silas. Lying face down in the dirt. Daniel rolled him over and felt his hands covered in a warm stickiness.

"Silas," Daniel said as he tried to shake him awake, but the man didn't move. "Silas!" Daniel said more forcefully this time, watching as the villagers made their way to the chief's hut. "We've got to go!" Daniel looked down, squinting to see what was wrong with him. He ran his hands across his face, his neck, his shoulders, feeling along his arms, his chest, finally settling on his stomach. It was wet. "Silas!"

Silas stirred. Daniel leaned over his face as he slowly opened his eyes. "Daniel," he whispered.

"Silas," Daniel cried out in laughter, cheeks wet with tears he didn't know had fallen. "You've got to get up."

Silas smiled and reached his hand up to cup Daniel's cheek. "Look after yourself. Look after her. Without each other, you will be lost."

"I need to look after *you*," Daniel pleaded. "Please ... get up."

"Yu gutpela waitman ..." Silas's smile faded, eyes closing as he exhaled. Daniel shook him again, but he didn't move. His chest was perfectly still. Daniel's chin trembled as shouting ascended from the chief's hut. He grabbed Silas's hand and tried to drag him away, but the dead weight of his body was too heavy. His muscles seized, frozen against the weight of his grief.

"Lau!"

The old woman from earlier was standing above him.

"Lau!" she yelled again in Motu.

Daniel stared at her blankly.

She pushed his side. "Go!"

Daniel blinked; the villagers were rounding in on him. And then he was running, back the way he came, praying he had what was needed to make it out alive.

# 34

# Daniel

Daniel waded through waist-high swamps, mangroves as thick as oak casting a blanket of protection, while the roots snaked through the brackish water. A flood of mosquitos preyed on every inch of exposed skin, their incessant buzzing ringing in Daniel's ears. Four of the Papuan soldiers carried Tom above their heads, their arms bulging and torsos tight, while Daniel plodded behind, gun raised, heart surging, eyes peeled, watching… waiting… wondering when the villagers would come.

They'd run steadily for the first couple of hours through dense jungle, navigating the pitch-black terrain with torches, adrenaline pushing them forward, but had been forced to stop when the land turned into a quagmire, their boots sinking into mud like quicksand. Daniel wanted to press on, not willing to take on the villagers without backup. But Tom's injury made it difficult. A bullet lodged in his thigh caused an endless stream of screams. Daniel had knocked him out with a heavy dose of painkillers, which gave them a few hours of reprieve, but once the sun had risen, they trudged onwards, through the swampy backcountry that led to Popondetta.

Daniel shivered, even though the water was at least eighty-five degrees. Silas was gone. His chest constricted each time the realisation hit him, a wave of grief so powerful he didn't know how he was even standing. Adrenaline, he guessed, the need to escape the angry villagers, to get to somewhere safe, away from this bastard of a place.

He couldn't understand how the chief could have betrayed them like that. Turned on his fellow people and shot up members of the PIB, men who'd been put there to protect them. He'd obviously had a bad encounter with the Allies. The Orokaiva people could be vengeful, harbouring resentments that dated back to the 1800s when the waitman first set foot on their land. That's what enraged Daniel about this place: the ruthless retribution that ran deep in its people, hatred that had been passed down through generations, acted on by chiefs who were trying to make their mark. That chief had made *his*; he'd be forever remembered for killing Daniel's closest ally.

He'd have to radio headquarters when they got to Popondetta. Someone needed to collect Silas's body, to clean up their mess. The villagers would have to be held accountable for their actions, punished for their betrayal. There had to be consequences for traitors. Even if the locals were in a difficult position, stuck between two countries that didn't belong here, they had to remain loyal, would pay if they didn't. Daniel would make sure of it. He'd pay as well. While it was Tom's fault for putting them in that position in the first place, Daniel should've known better, should've tried harder to make sure their unit was safe. How would he survive the rest of the war without Silas? How would he live in this new world without the man who'd helped him find his footing? Perhaps living without Silas would be payment enough.

* * *

Daniel squinted; a discombobulated object was floating ahead. He was starting to fatigue, a wave of dizziness washing over him, the last few days a blur. The lack of sleep was taking effect, and his body was blistering with a sudden onset of fever. Daniel pressed his finger to the trigger, but realised the floating object was already dead. A Japanese man, mouth infested with maggots, body ragged and devoid of life.

It wasn't uncommon to see their bodies scattered about the region; thousands of them had been killed in the past several months. He stared at it as it moved along, wondering if the body would suddenly spring up and put him out of his misery. It'd be easier if it did. Mr McKenzie's prediction would finally come true. He could die a hero, like Silas, forever remembered for his bravery and sacrifice. They'd sing songs about him, erect statues – the brown-skinned boy who gave everything, paying the ultimate price. He'd be glorified, loved by all, no longer having to contend with his place in the world. A lazy sort of smile crossed his lips as he watched the body float away, a sense of euphoria taking hold.

He stumbled up the shoreline sometime later, the sludgy slop sucking at his boots. Sweat seeped from his skin, his body convulsing in shivers as he collapsed into the mud. They had to be close; days of trekking had to mean they were nearly at Popondetta. But he didn't think he could go on. The ground was spinning, his body overcome with sickness. Malaria or some other tropical ailment was wreaking havoc. They'd lost so many men to it the last few months. Maybe that would be the thing that finally took him.

Daniel peeled his eyes opened and through a hazy gaze watched as his fellow soldiers re-dressed Tom's leg. Tom was lucky to have them. It was these men who deserved to be celebrated, deserved to get out of here. Boy, did he want out of here, this land he no longer recognised. He wanted to be back in the arms of the one he loved, the only place he felt safe. He had to remember Amelia once loved him – maybe still did – and that his life was worth fighting for because of her. All of this was for her. He had to go on … for her.

* * *

Daniel stirred, the light pitter-patter of rain bringing him back to consciousness. His head was pounding, clouded in a sickly haze that caused everything to ache. But he could hear a plane overhead, the whoosh of the propellers. His heart picked up a beat. He pried his eyes open, adjusting to the light that only made the pain worse, and commando crawled to where Tom had been sleeping. Rain trickled down his cheeks, past his chin, onto his arms that were crusted with mud and blood. It took every measure of strength to move forward, but they had to get to that plane. They had to get out of here.

Except Tom wasn't there; his stretcher was lying empty. Daniel pushed himself up, exhaling as he looked around, the muddy swamps merging into thick jungle. He tried to stand but stumbled back in a wave of dizziness. And then he heard voices yelling, feet running, and through the trees appeared the men from his unit, Tom limping behind them. The Papuan soldiers scooped up Daniel by his underarms and dragged him into the jungle. He tried to keep up with their pace but kept stumbling.

"Where are we going?" he mumbled.

Tom, hobbling next to him, said, "The Japanese are hiding out in an old government station. We need to get out of here before they find us."

Fear shot up Daniel's spine. "Where's my gun?"

"You're holding it," Tom replied.

Daniel felt his Owen pressing against his back, breathing a sigh of relief. "We can't go," he said, forcing the men to stop. "We have to kill them first."

Tom paused, keeling over to clutch his thigh. Beads of sweat dripped from his forehead into the puddles of mud beneath them. "Don't be ridiculous. You're in no state to fight."

Tom was right. Daniel could barely hold *himself* up, let alone his rifle. And while Tom was well enough to move again, he didn't know how to take on the Japanese in a close-range situation. But they couldn't leave them to kill someone else, not after what they did to Silas. They had to be taken out.

Daniel inhaled, the steamy air coursing through his veins. "I'll be right. We can't leave them for someone else. We have to go back and ambush the fuckers one last time before we get the hell out of this shithole."

The Papuans looked at him and nodded, while Tom chewed his lip. "Fine. But it's on you if anyone else dies."

* * *

They prowled through the jungle, branches thick with leaves and vines that clouded them in green shadows. The leaves rustled in the wind, the breath of air cooling Daniel's hot skin. Up ahead, the sun shone through the tree line, and the government station where the men had spotted the enemy peeked through. Daniel focused on his breath, ignoring his splitting headache, the heaviness in his joints. He had to get through this, to avenge Silas's death, to finish what his brother had started.

He emerged from the trees, the Papuan men in a staggered formation behind him. Tom had stayed behind, much to Daniel's relief. He didn't need him stuffing this up. A small hut surrounded by a pile of waist-high dirt lay before them. They crept past it, four of the men veering off to either side to scan the perimeter. Daniel climbed the stairs, the last two of his men by his side. Pausing to steady his racing heart, he pushed the tip of his rifle against the door. A loud creaking noise made him stiffen. He stepped inside and was overcome by a festering smell of rotting flesh. His stomach lurched.

Daniel held his breath as his eyes readjusted to the dark, the room slowly coming to life. He scanned the inside, instincts forcing his gun towards the right-hand corner. There was a dead Japanese man, maggots crawling out of his eyes and mouth. The acrid taste of bile burned Daniel's throat. He let out his breath and took another, the smell so bad that what was left in his stomach came hurling out. Daniel panted as the Papuan men inspected the dead body for booby traps. Forcing himself to stand straight, he skimmed the rest of the room; the line of danger had not yet been fully averted. His eyes landed on the other corner, where another Japanese was curled up on his side, eyes shut and body still. Daniel crept towards him, heart racing as the floorboard creaked with every step.

He hovered over him, gun pointed at his chest as he took in this gaunt shell of a man – starved to death, skin grey, rib bones protruding. This man, like many others, who'd come to his land and tried to claim it as his own. This man, who'd taken everything he ever loved away from him. This man, who'd changed everything. And yet he couldn't help but feel a pang of sorrow for him, for his family, *his* Amelia.

Daniel kicked him in the stomach, and the man rolled over onto his back. His eyes flew open. Daniel froze, whole body paralysed with fear for a split second. Then his finger was on the trigger and a bullet was piercing the enemy's heart. Blood poured from his chest, matching the rush of blood that soared through Daniel's veins. His heart hammered so loudly in his ears, a deafening thumping of fear, like kundu drums in a sing-sing, that he barely noticed the faint hissing coming from the man. His eyes scoured the room and landed on the pineapple-shaped explosive that had fallen from the dead man's hand. Daniel's heart stopped; time expanded into an infinite passage. He couldn't believe he'd made it this far, only to be fooled into death.

His voice surged from his lungs, the word *grenade* bursting from his mouth as he ran towards the door and leapt over the pile of dirt that lined the hut. A loud whoosh engulfed his ears, the pop pop of gunshots barely audible over the shrill ring that echoed. He collapsed onto the ground, dirt flooding every crevice – eyes, mouth, nose, and ears seething with earth as he lay there, unmoving, body finally melting into the arms of death.

# IV

# Part Four

*February 1943*

# 35

## Amelia

Amelia wiped the sweat from her brow. The canvas tent was like a sauna. The wet season's morning deluge of rain had ceased, and the surrounding foothills around the 2/9th Australian General Hospital were steaming up. The two-thousand-bed hospital had been set up outside of Port Moresby the previous October, spread over a mile of long narrow terrain near Rouna Falls, the Owen Stanley Ranges hovering behind. Steep hills were intersected by eroded gullies, where, after heavy rains, torrents of water flowed through, turning the site into a quagmire.

It was six months before Amelia actually arrived in Port Moresby; nurses had only been allowed back when the hospital opened. She spent the time training in Brisbane, advancing her skill set and learning more about the tropical ailments she'd be treating. Evelyn had joined her after completing her passing-out parade with the Army. Amelia was thankful to have her sister by her side. Desperate to discover where Daniel was, she sent letters to the Papuan Infantry Battalion and enquired of any returned soldier she met whether they had come across a mixed-race soldier. But a year later she still hadn't heard anything. Every time she treated a new patient, a little pang of hope pulsated inside.

Nearing the end of her shift, she stifled a yawn as she skimmed through the chart of a newly admitted patient, another one who'd been evacuated from Popondetta with malaria. Malaria was by far the biggest threat the

Allies had to worry about, thousands of men having succumbed to the illness over the past few months. She slowly approached his bed, heart picking up pace … until he turned over, revealing his pasty white skin. She exhaled; her pulsating heart diminished.

Beads of perspiration dripped down the man's face, and his body convulsed with chills. She sponged him with cool water and, with the help of an orderly, changed his sweat-soaked sheets, before administering a dose of quinine. But it did little to relieve his suffering. Desperate to help him, she remained by his bedside for the next several hours, dismissing the nurse who came to relieve her and ignoring the pangs of hunger that gnawed at her stomach. The man was in and out of consciousness, his cries clawing at Amelia's insides like a feral cat.

She imagined Daniel out there, alone, never knowing how much he was loved. It was his face that got her through the mounds of suffering that surrounded her. The hospital couldn't keep up with the influx of soldiers coming back from Kokoda, thousands of blokes battered by the deadly track. It was the Battle of the Beachheads – the Allies advancing on Buna, Gona and Sanananda – that'd been the deadliest. Over two thousand mangled bodies had returned from the very place Amelia was last year. And that was just the Aussies. It didn't account for the thousands of Americans, the thousands of Papuans who'd also been killed or injured.

She'd heard the PIB were assigned to patrol the beachheads. Any one of those fallen soldiers could've been Daniel, and she would never know. For all she knew, he was dead. The hope she was holding on to was fading, like the last light before the blue hour took hold. But she had to hold on, had to keep believing he was out there. Alive and looking for a way back to her.

* * *

Amelia lugged an oxygen cylinder up the ward, boots sinking into the boggy mud. The rain pelted down on the canvas roof like a freight train hurling forwards, making it hard to hear anything other than her own spiralling thoughts. She paused to catch her breath and looked up to see that one of the patients had gotten out of bed. He was commando crawling in the mud as if he was back on the battlefields of Kokoda. He paused and screamed for everyone to take cover as he shielded his head with his arms. Amelia ran to his side and gently pressed her hand on his shoulder, worried his delirium would cause him to lash out. But he cowered in the mud instead, whimpering like a small child who'd lost his mother. She softly stroked his back as she swallowed back a sob of her own, thinking of everything he'd been through. When his body finally relaxed, she helped him sit up – and reeled back in shock.

"Tom!"

A woozy sort of grin inched up his face. "Meels."

"What in heavens are you doing here?"

"I was shot ... outside of Buna."

She looked him up and down, eyes landing on his leg that was bandaged above the thigh. "Are you alright?"

His eyes glassed over, as if he was masking something, and she couldn't help but feel sorry for him. He'd been through the worst, and thankfully made it out the other side.

Amelia pulled Tom to his feet. She let him lean his weight on her as she helped him back to bed. "I haven't seen you since Brisbane," she said once he was tucked in under the covers. I didn't realise you'd been sent to the front. What division are you with now that the RAAF—"

"They stuck me with the Papuans out in Buna," he replied quickly. "Thought I might know a thing or two about managing the locals."

A surge of hope shot up Amelia's spine. "Did you see Daniel? Was he there? You know he's supposed to have joined the Infantry Battalion ..."

Tom scowled. "I wish you'd stop asking me about him."

"I ... I just thought—"

"That's the problem. You don't think."

He turned away, and Amelia's surge of hope shifted back to the heaviness she'd been carrying the past year. It was foolish to think Tom might know where Daniel was. There were tens of thousands of Allied soldiers spread across the Northern Province, the area as big Wales. She wondered how

Buna, Gona and the other areas had changed in the year since she was last there, thinking of Mavis Parkinson and Sister Hayman … their tragic deaths. She'd read in the papers they had been "annihilated" by the Japanese, whatever that was supposed to mean. Having heard stories of what the enemy was capable of, she figured it wasn't pretty. During battles, they would push the locals they had recruited to the front, so the Allies were forced to shoot them first. The Japanese beheaded many of the locals for being traitors, all the while raping and killing women and children. But the Allies weren't innocent either. Her heart ached for Mavis's and Sister Hayman's families, what this loss of life would've meant to them. In spite of everything, the two women had never given up hope, always stuck to their faith. Could Amelia do the same with Daniel?

She turned to continue her rounds when she saw Evelyn running up the ward. The sisters rarely found time for each other with the demands of their shifts – Evelyn in particular, as she worked on the ward where the very sick men went – so it was a pleasant surprise to see her face.

"Ev, what are you doing here?" Amelia asked, stepping forward to give her a kiss on the cheek.

Evelyn was panting, chest still weak after last year's ordeal. "Meels," she said between breaths. "You have to come …"

"Come where? I'm in the middle of my shift—"

"Yeah … she's looking after me," Tom chimed in.

Evelyn ignored Tom and stepped closer; her hazel eyes speckled with flickers of hope. "Meels, it's Daniel. He's here."

# 36

# Amelia

Amelia ran, heart racing as she followed Evelyn to her ward. Rain poured down her face, her boiler suit sticking to her skin as her feet slipped with every step. But she wouldn't slow down, wouldn't stop until she got to him. Her muscles were tight, stomach hard, adrenaline coursing through her veins. Daniel was here. Daniel was alive.

Evelyn led her through a long row of injured soldiers, men crying out like babies. Her stomach lurched at the sight of their broken bodies, their mangled minds. But she couldn't focus on them. When she arrived at Daniel's bed, her heart nearly stopped, breath so tightly wound in her chest she had to force herself to inhale. She peered through the mosquito net covering, eyes welling as she took in what was left of him.

Half his head was wrapped in bandage, which wound above his left eye and over his ear, a patch of dried blood seeping through. His face was barely recognisable; a thick woolly beard covered his gaunt cheeks, while his eyes were sunken like craters and his body like a malnourished child's. He was shivering – a blanket pulled up to his neck seemed to offer little warmth – and while he appeared to be asleep, the low whimpering cries that escaped his lungs suggested his slumber wasn't a very restful one.

"He has scrub typhus resulting in high fever, and a lateral head wound caused by a grenade," Evelyn said. Amelia looked up to see her sister on the other side of Daniel's bed. She was pressing a washer to Daniel's forehead, which caused him to flinch. Amelia wanted to reach out, tell her to stop, not to hurt him, but she remained rooted to the spot, unable to move. "His unit was attacked outside of Popondetta. They lost several men, but Daniel somehow survived. It's likely he'd been fighting the typhus before he was hit."

Amelia stared at him, unable to speak.

"He's in bad shape, Meels ... we can't get his fever down."

She reached out to touch his face, but when he cried out even louder, she snatched her hand away.

"We've been at it for hours ... our best nurses ... but nothing's working."

Amelia blinked, wondering how they'd all got to this point. How one day they were carelessly living their lives in Lae, and the next they were ripped apart by war. How her life had been turned upside down, and now Daniel's life nearly taken. And then something in her snapped, the blood rushing back to her limbs as she realised what could happen if she didn't act. She grabbed the washer from Evelyn's hand.

"Meels ..."

Amelia met her with a deathly stare. "He needs me."

Evelyn nodded and retreated as Amelia looked towards Daniel. She swallowed as she watched him wither in agony, questioning whether she could manage this, whether she had the ability to bring him back to the living. She gently pressed the washer to his forehead and cupped his cheek with her other hand. Daniel flinched again.

"I'm here," she whispered into his ear, a tear caressing her cheek. She rested her hand on his chest, feeling the rise and fall, the tempo of his beating heart. "You're home now."

* * *

The next few days were exhausting, a never-ending cycle of constant care. Daniel's temperature continued to rise – to 103° by the second day. Very little could be done to lower it. Without any special treatment available, Amelia had to rely on fluids, a dose of salts, cold sponge baths and considerable patience.

"He's not getting better," Evelyn said as she helped Amelia to feed him. She stood next to his bedside, holding his arms down as Amelia spooned warm broth into his mouth.

Amelia twitched. "What do you mean? He's far better than he was two days ago."

"Meels, he doesn't even recognise you ..."

"He does too," she said, but noticed the wobble in her voice. She turned back to Daniel, whose eyes were closed, head drooping to the side. She wedged the spoon into his mouth and gently tipped the broth in, but was met with a forceful response. His eyes flashed open, wild and full of rage. He lashed out, freeing his arms from Evelyn's grip and backhanding the spoon out of Amelia's hand. She jumped back and gasped as Evelyn lunged for Daniel's arms and held him down while he violently tried to shake free.

"Get up ... get up!" he screamed, head thrashing from side to side. Amelia threw herself on top of him, using her body as a shield against his pain, but he only got angrier, using a resurgence of strength to try to push the women off.

Amelia pressed her hands to his hot cheeks, trying to hold his face in place to calm him. "Daniel, it's me," she said enthusiastically, but he stared at her with vacant eyes. Her heart shrank. "It's me," she whispered this time, throat so choked she was surprised she could even get the words out, but he continued to look at her from a faraway place.

And then he whipped his arms free again, pushing Amelia away as he screamed. "Get up!"

Amelia staggered off him, suddenly dizzy. She could hear Evelyn yelling at her to help, but she couldn't move. And then an orderly was there, pushing Amelia to the side as he helped Evelyn hold Daniel, all the while whispering "mate" incessantly in his ear. Daniel relaxed, arms falling to his side as he rested his head against the pillow.

Amelia's knees shook as she watched this man, this stranger, soothe Daniel into submission. Daniel's eyes rolled back as he drifted off to sleep. The orderly left, and Evelyn immediately came to Amelia's side.

"You know it's nothing to do with you, right? It's the delirium," she said with a forced smile.

Amelia stared at her, unable to speak. She flicked her eyes to Daniel, who was resting peacefully now, chest slowly rising and falling. She pressed her lips tight and looked away.

"Meels ..." Evelyn said, forcing Amelia to meet her gaze. "Have you thought about next steps?"

"What do you mean?"

Evelyn shifted on her feet. "Evacuation ... to Australia."

Amelia laughed for the first time in days. "You aren't serious, are you?"

"I am. He needs better care."

"Who could give him better care than me?"

"You know what I mean. He needs to be in an Australian standard hospital."

"Australia doesn't give a toss about him!" she yelled, noticing several of the other nurses were now looking their way.

"That's not true," Evelyn said calmly.

"Even so ... he's fine here. I've got it under control."

"Meels ... you're exhausted. Look at you – you've barely slept in days, and I don't even want to know when you last showered. Your hair is in tatters and the circles under your eyes are as dark as the mud on your feet. Imagine what Mum would say!" Evelyn's lips curled into a smile, which Amelia was tempted to match, but she didn't want to give her sister the satisfaction. "At least take the night off ... you need to rest or you'll get sick too."

"I'm fine."

"Meels, I'm speaking to you as your sister and not a nurse. Trust me when I say you need a break. What you have done for him so far has been incredible ... honestly, I've never seen such attentive nursing. But this job is demanding, taxing in other ways than physically. It's emotionally exhausting to care for someone all day."

Amelia crossed her arms in front of her chest. She was tired of fighting ... so bloody tired. "Fine. But only if *you* look after him."

"Of course."

"You have to give him fluids every ten minutes and sponge baths every thirty."

Evelyn squeezed Amelia's shoulder. "I know."

"I'll be back first thing in the morning. If anything happens ... you come and get me, okay?"

* * *

Amelia fell into a fitful sleep, stretcher squeaking with every turn. The air in the six-sleeper marquee was still, the mosquito netting that engulfed her bed suffocating. The sound of rats scuttling in the roof above, mixed with the clicking of geckos, ebbed in and out of her restless consciousness. She couldn't stop thinking about the turn of events, how she'd ended up here, in this place she no longer recognised. She knew it'd been her choice, her need to get back to Daniel having prevailed over logic, but she couldn't stop wondering if she should've stayed in Australia, worked her way up to officer rank and found a way to fly again. She'd heard reports of a small group of women in England who'd done that, who'd been chosen by the RAF to move planes around the country. That could've been her, doing something she loved, instead of being here, nursing a man who didn't even know who she was.

It had been naïve of her to think everything would fall back into place. She and Daniel hadn't spoken in a year; they were two completely different people from what they'd been that last night at Salamaua. Daniel had been through hell and barely made it out, while Amelia was learning what life as a woman was really like. Daniel would never be the person she once knew. Would she be willing to accept who he'd become? She loved him, but once again questioned if love would be enough. If he even still loved her. He'd been alive this whole time and hadn't written a word to her. Couldn't even let her know he was alive. How could their love withstand the bruises that were unwilling to fade?

* * *

Amelia drifted between sleep and consciousness, the vibration of her shoulder being shaken no match for the exhaustion that'd finally overcome her. She could hear someone's voice, but didn't know if it was real or only in her dreams, taunting her with the promise of something else. But then the vibrations grew stronger, and the voice louder, and she couldn't help but peel her eyes open to see Evelyn standing above her, that same worried look etched across her face.

Amelia shot up. "What is it? What happened?"

"His temperature is out of control, up to 106," Evelyn said, her normally steady voice wobbling.

Amelia was out of bed in an instant, throwing her dirty boiler suit and gumboots on, not bothering with her hair, before racing back towards Daniel's ward. Nurses and orderlies surrounded his bedside, wielding every technique they could think of to help him. Daniel was convulsing, lying flat on the bed in a fit that shook his body so violently it was as if he was possessed. They held him down as one of the orderlies ripped off Daniel's shirt, his once-broad chest now bony and thin. One of the nurses pulled a towel out of a bath-sized bucket that sat next to Daniel's bed and wrung it out, before wrapping it around his torso. She did it again and again, covering his body from his neck to his feet with wet towels. The convulsions slowed but did not stop. Amelia peered into the bucket and saw a mixture of ice and water.

She stepped forward as she began to unbutton her boiler suit. "Get him up," she said to the orderlies on the other side of the bed.

"We shouldn't move him while he's seizing," the nurse who'd been sponging him said.

"We need to cool him." She reached under Daniel's shoulder as she stared at the two orderlies with such force that they couldn't help but mirror her actions. The three of them carefully lifted him into a seated position, his body still shaking as the men held him up. Amelia stepped back and wiggled her way out of her clothes, letting them fall to the ground as she stood in nothing but her Department of Defence–issued brown Milanese bloomers and bra.

The nurse gasped. "What are you doing?"

"Going in with him," Amelia casually replied as if she'd done this a million times before, even though her heart was racing. She glanced behind the nurse to Evelyn, who was standing at the end of Daniel's bed. Evelyn gave her a curt nod, and then moved to help the orderlies lift Daniel. Amelia stepped into the bath, the water piercing her skin like a million bee stings. She grabbed onto Daniel's waist as Evelyn and the orderlies lifted him in, his cries ringing in her ears as they plunged him into the water. She swallowed her own cries as she lowered herself, and kneeled in front of him while they rested his head on a rubber pad against the edge of the bath. They seized his arms as Evelyn tipped a cup of water over his head. His face twisted and he let out fitful screams that lashed at Amelia's heart. She winced but wouldn't let go. He tried to swing his arms out of Amelia's hold, but she tightened her grip. Evelyn tipped the water over him again and again. Daniel's screams increased in pitch but Amelia only held on tighter.

When the submersions no longer made him lash out, Amelia began to briskly rub his body with her hands, moving from his shoulders and arms to his legs and feet, making sure to stay away from his abdomen like she'd learned in training, ensuring circulation was moving through each extremity as his body slowly started to relax and the convulsions came to a stop. She ignored her own shivering pangs of cold, the tingling sensation of her toes and fingers numbing, as she rubbed faster and faster.

"Amelia, I think that's enough," Evelyn eventually said. "He's stopped seizing." But Amelia shook her head and kept rubbing, moving her hands up and down his body until Evelyn's grip on her wrist forced her to stop. Amelia's hand went limp as Evelyn lifted her out and wrapped her up, while the orderlies did the same for Daniel, resting him back on his bed in a womb of blankets. His body was still, his breath slow but steady. The nurses and orderlies moved to clean up the mess, giving Amelia curious looks as she sat shivering at the end of Daniel's bed.

Evelyn placed a hand on her shoulder. "It was the right call."

Amelia glared at Evelyn, a flash of anger suddenly seizing her. This never would've happened if Amelia had been there. But her teeth were chattering too much to reply.

"We'll take his temp in half an hour, see what effect the bath had. In the meantime, why don't you change into something decent?"

Amelia eyed her dirty boiler suit on the ground, and would've laughed at the fact that she was sitting at the edge of Daniel's bed in her underwear, freezing, if it wasn't for the shivers that'd seized control. "Can't. Leave. Him. Again," she managed to say.

"Meels, he's stable. Go sort yourself out while you can." Amelia opened her mouth, but Evelyn raised her hand to stop her. "Don't try to argue with me about this. You did the right thing, but getting half-naked with a soldier is going to have major repercussions around the hospital. Get dressed and make yourself presentable while I deal with this mess."

# 37

# Amelia

Amelia looked into the small mirror that sat above the portable washbasin, noticing the effect war had taken on her. Her eyes were bloodshot, the dark circles that encased them puffy and swollen; her skin was blotchy, in desperate need of soap and creams to bring it back to life, while her lips were dry and blistering with cracked skin. She looked far from presentable, at least by her mother's standards – something she normally wouldn't care about if it weren't for the fact that she needed to keep this job, needed to remain by Daniel's side.

She smoothed out her hair and pinched her cheeks, pressing her thumbnail into her skin, barely noticing the pain. As she walked back to the ward, she watched the sun peek out over Hobrum Bluff, another beautiful dawn rising out of the misery of war.

When she got inside, she pressed the back of her hand to Daniel's forehead. "How is he?"

"102," Evelyn replied with an encouraging smile. "But if it goes over again, we'll need to do another ice bath."

Amelia nodded. Her initial anger with Evelyn had subsided, but something was still festering inside that she couldn't shift. She didn't have the energy for it, though, and ran her fingers down the side of Daniel's face instead. She stroked his cheek and arm, then found his upturned palm and squeezed his hand. She stiffened when she thought she felt the faintest hint of a squeeze back and glanced at his hand, then his face. Both were perfectly still.

"Matron Nelson wants to see you," Evelyn said, forcing Amelia to look up.

"Why?"

Evelyn raised her eyebrows.

Amelia snickered. "Honestly. I was doing my job."

Evelyn didn't reply, busying herself with feeding Daniel fluids instead. The ward had come to life, several men sitting up looking surprisingly better than they had the day before. A pang of hope fluttered in her belly until she saw Matron Nelson approaching.

Amelia let go of Daniel's hand. "Matron Nelson."

"I understand there was an incident this morning?" Matron Nelson said without any introductions.

Amelia fiddled with Daniel's sheets, unable to meet her eye. "I'd hardly call it an incident. A patient was in a state of hyperpyrexia ... I merely administered an ice bath to cool him."

"In your knickers?"

"I thought it'd be easier without my uniform weighing me down."

"Look at me when I speak to you, Sister McKenzie." Her voice was stern. Amelia lifted her head and met Matron Nelson's deathly stare, the intensity of her dark brown eyes burning into her. "You understand there are protocols we must adhere to as nurses? One being not to get undressed in front of the patients, especially native ones."

Amelia shifted on her feet. Her instinct was, as usual, to point to Daniel's European heritage, but something made her hesitate. Apart from his father, Daniel hardly had a connection to Scotland. He *was* Niuginian. But that wouldn't be enough for Matron Nelson. "He's Scottish ..." Amelia enunciated her words carefully.

"Doesn't look it to me. Either way, we're here to work and uphold the standards of the Australian Army Nursing Service."

"With all due respect, ma'am, I'm part of the Royal Australian Air Force Nursing Service—"

Matron Nelson scowled, the vein on her neck pulsating. "And I'm still in charge, regardless of which service you're in!" She stepped towards

Amelia and pointed a finger in her face. "If I get wind of you tarting around with the natives again, you'll be on the first plane back to Australia, do you understand?"

Amelia flinched as Evelyn dropped her spoon and turned towards Matron Nelson. "If you want someone to blame, then blame me, as I was the senior sister on duty. Amelia was merely doing what she was told."

Matron Nelson whipped her head towards Evelyn and spat out, "I don't care. She should know better! We have a standard to uphold, and I won't have her sullying it with the likes of him!" She pointed at Daniel, who was lying peacefully in bed.

Evelyn's cheeks reddened. "It's not in your jurisdiction to comment on who Amelia spends her time with." Matron Nelson's mouth dropped open, ready to retort, but Evelyn pressed on. "Lieutenant Carmichael is a respected member of the Papuan Infantry Battalion who has served our country faithfully this past year. He's also an old friend of our family, someone our father, George McKenzie, the person who pioneered these lands, has come to hold with great admiration." She smiled at Daniel, her warmth easing Amelia's heart.

"Like hell it isn't!" Matron Nelson roared. "This is my hospital, my girls, my rules. You best remember that, Sister McKenzie, or you'll end up in the same boat as Amelia."

Evelyn straightened her collar. "I wouldn't be so nonchalant about the importance of your nursing staff. We're at war and you need every single one of us if you want any hope of getting these boys out alive."

Matron Nelson curled her lip. "I suggest you both get back to work."

A heat flushed through Amelia's body, but she smiled coolly and said, "Love to."

"On *your* ward," Matron Nelson added.

Amelia paused, muscles quivering, ready to explode. But she took a deep breath instead and stepped forward, carrying on in the usual way, like her mother had taught her.

* * *

"How is he?" Amelia asked as soon as Evelyn walked into the mess. It'd been two days since Amelia had been banished back to her ward, two long days filled with caring for patients who weren't Daniel.

"The same," Evelyn replied dejectedly, before grabbing a tray and entering the line for tea. The mess was busy as usual, the change of shift bringing in tired and overworked nurses by the dozens, all of them eager to see what rations would be dished out. Amelia loaded her tray with food – a banana, a scone lavished with jam and cream, orange juice, jelly and tea – anything to settle her stomach. Evelyn placed a cup of tea and toast with a side of marmalade on hers.

"It should be me in there," Amelia said. They sat at an empty table, Amelia not touching her food. "He needs me."

"What he needs is time," Evelyn replied as she scraped her toast with butter. "Scrub typhus patients can have swinging temperatures for weeks, and combined with a head injury, it could be much longer."

Amelia reached across the table and squeezed Evelyn's wrist. "I'm glad he's got you. And thank you for standing up to Matron Nelson for me."

Evelyn waved her away. "No big deal. The old bat needed to be put in her place."

Amelia offered a small smile, wishing it were as easy as that. "Anyway, it's probably best I keep my distance. You were right … he doesn't even recognise me. I was foolish to think things would be the same."

"You shouldn't give up on Daniel so easily."

Amelia was quick to reply. "Who says I'm giving up? I'm accepting the reality of our situation."

"And what reality is that?"

"Things are different. Too much time has passed. We're different people now. You said it when we were leaving Salamaua. War changes everything."

"You may be different, but your heart is still the same."

"He doesn't know who I am anymore"—she pointed to her chest—"Heck, I don't know who I am anymore. I had all these dreams, these grand plans for my life … flight school, a career as an aviatrix, flying around the world like Earhart. Now none of that will happen."

"This war won't go on forever. Our dreams are merely on hold."

"And what if I'm tired of waiting?"

"We're all tired, Amelia. War is a tiresome business."

Amelia nodded, knowing her quibbles were nothing compared to the true atrocities that so many had faced. They were in fact just that: quibbles. But still, it felt nice to get it off her chest.

"You know, it might help if you told Daniel how you feel."

* * *

Amelia sat at Daniel's bedside and rested her hand in the palm of his. She watched the steady rise and fall of his chest, the soft puff of breath escaping his lips. His face was shaven, the scruffy beard he'd had when he arrived erased, exposing his gaunt cheeks and layers of skin peeled back from too much sun. His body was warm to touch, and yet his hand felt cold against Amelia's. She traced her thumb along his, fingers tingling.

"So ..." she said as she looked at their hands together, their palms the same colour. She glanced behind her, wondering if anyone was watching, but could only see the usual hustle of the ward as nurses and orderlies attended to patients. "It's hard to concentrate with all that noise," she went on as she watched a nurse pin down a man who'd lost both his legs, before turning back to Daniel. "That's one of the things I dislike ... the noise. The constant screaming and moaning, the beeping and buzzing of the machines, and the air raids ... the bombers during a full moon, when they woosh overhead, I swear I'm going to wet myself looking at them." Her chest hitched in a small laugh. "Can you believe it? Me, afraid of an aeroplane?"

She looked at Daniel with a smile, but his face was perfectly still. Shaking her head, she looked towards his hand. "How ridiculous am I? Thinking you'll reply. This whole thing is ridiculous, if you ask me. Me, trying to be a nurse? You know how much I hate blood, how little patience I have, how frustrated I get if something doesn't immediately work. Nursing is the last thing I should be doing. But what choice did I have? It was either this or sit around in Australia and wait ... and I'll tell you, the waiting has been unbearable. Not knowing where you were ... if you were alive."

She swallowed back the burn that threatened to spill out. "And now you're here, alive, and all I feel is disappointed. Disappointed we didn't get the reunion I'd dreamt of ... disappointed you don't know who I am ... disappointed that I have the audacity to feel disappointed when you're the one lying here, barely alive! Silly me, thinking it was going to be like one of those war stories – you a handsome pilot, me a dedicated nurse, coming together to save our home. How foolish I was ..." she pressed her fingers to her temple and closed her eyes, a fresh wave of exhaustion sweeping through her body. "But what can I do? I made this decision and now I have to live with the consequences. I chose not to get on that plane out of Lae and had to witness my home getting destroyed. I chose to walk away from you, to turn my back. I chose to be a nurse and now I must live up to my choices. That's life, isn't it? Enduring the consequences of the decisions we make, with the hope we'll eventually make the right one? I really thought this was the right one, was ready to do whatever it took for us to be together. I don't know why I'm complaining. It's not like there's an alternative. I'll never be able to do the things I want. It's simply not on the cards for us women."

She stroked the inside of Daniel's palm, tracing the lines that were etched into his calloused skin, the creases along the joints of his fingers, the dry skin that clung to the edges of his fingernails. She could no longer hear the screaming that haunted her dreams; the men's cries for help had faded. Her chest felt lighter, her limbs no longer weighed down by her burdens. Evelyn was right – talking was good.

She knew what she had to do. She'd made this choice and she'd have to live with it. No matter the outcome, she'd hold her head high and get on with it. Because that's what women did. She inhaled, breathing in the warm tropical air, a faint scent of frangipani lingering. This was still home. Or a version of it. She'd make the most of being back in the land she loved so dearly, even without Daniel by her side. Life must go on.

Pulling her shoulders back, she let go of his hand – but the pulse of his fingers stopped her. She stiffened, the tempo of her heart increasing as she shifted her eyes from his hand, up his arm, to his shoulder, his neck, his chin, and finally his face … and the gleam of his brown eyes shining back at her.

A slow smile brightened his face, a flicker of a dimple emerging. He drew in a breath and said, "Aren't I glad to see you."

# 38

## Daniel

Daniel stared at the fine curves of Amelia's lips, the little wrinkles around her eyes, the freckles that dotted her cheeks, the line across her forehead ... the small things he loved about her. She was staring back at him in disbelief, her mouth gaping open, while the emerald jewels he'd longed for were wide with wonder.

"Are you okay?" he asked, trying to push himself up, but his body was too weak to sit upright. Amelia rushed to grab his arm, and his hand gripped onto her elbow as she steadied him back down. He paused, heaving in air, before looking back up at her. "You look very pale."

Amelia laughed. "*I* look pale? You should look in the mirror."

He smiled again. "That's okay, I'm enjoying my view."

Amelia shifted on her feet, moving to smooth her hair back. "Yes ... well, not exactly the same as when you last saw it."

"It's even better."

Amelia looked away. Daniel wondered if he'd overstepped the mark. It'd been so long; so much had changed. He coughed and asked instead, "Could I get some water?"

"Of course." She poured him a cup and lifted his head as she slowly tipped it into his mouth. Most of it dribbled down his chin.

He sneered. "I'm an invalid."

"Don't be silly. You're sick – incredibly weak and malnourished. You're lucky to be alive."

He stared at the ceiling. "I don't even remember what happened."

"They evacuated you out of Popondetta. You have a severe case of scrub typhus and a head injury … which they said was from a grenade."

Daniel swallowed, the memories coming back to him. "Something like that. Where's Tom?"

"Tom?"

"Yeah, he was my CO the last few days. Got shot … along with—" Daniel couldn't finish, the pain still too raw to say his name.

"That lying bastard. He told me he hadn't seen you."

Daniel shrugged. He didn't want to talk about Tom, didn't want to think about those last few days with him.

"I can't believe you're here. You"—Amelia's chest hitched—"you were so sick."

He reached for her hand. "I'm okay now … I think. My head is killing me, and everything hurts—"

"We'll get you something for that," Amelia interrupted as she moved away to look for medicine, but Daniel gripped onto her hand.

"Later. I want to look at you for now."

Amelia smiled, cheeks blushing. Daniel's eyes welled up, the sight of her causing his heart to suddenly feel whole again. It'd been so long since he'd looked at anything this beautiful. He couldn't believe he'd pushed his feelings aside this past year. He knew he'd done it so he could get through each day, not knowing if he'd make it out alive, and not wanting to give her false hope. But now she was in front of him, he realised what a fool he'd been. He finally saw that it was his love for her that had gotten him through it all.

* * *

"I don't understand, though," Daniel said later that day as Amelia helped to feed him. "How are you here? In Moresby?"

Amelia was positioning several pillows behind Daniel's neck, propping him up into a slightly elevated position. "I was sent up last October. I wrote to tell you. I've been writing you every week, in fact."

Daniel looked away, the heat of shame creeping up his neck.

"It's okay," Amelia replied quietly, but pulled her hand away.

"No, it's not, Meels. I should've done more to fight for you. Should never have let you walk away like that after Salamaua. I've been kicking myself every day since, every day we slogged over those mountains, every day while fighting. I'm an idiot. Need to do better at sharing my feelings with you.

"I'm sorry. I'm so sorry for what I put you through. For betraying you to your father, for letting you walk away, for not getting over the Bulldog fast enough to get to Moresby in time to say all this before you left on that plane that day."

Amelia scrunched her brow. "Moresby?"

"That day you flew out. I was at the aerodrome, on the other side of the fence. I swear you saw me."

Amelia gasped. "I did. Or I thought I did, but then the bombs came and we had to get out of there. You were jumping up and down like a madman."

Daniel laughed. "I was. Nearly got me killed."

Her shoulders slumped. "Oh, Daniel. What a mess we've made of this."

"Not anymore. I promise not to let anything else get in the way." He reached for her hand and stared into her eyes, heat radiating through his body. She leaned forward, her breath hot on his lips, and closed her eyes. Heart racing, he closed the gap between them and gently pressed his lips to hers, savouring the soft touch of her mouth. The one thing that made everything better.

# 39

# Amelia

Daniel was up and about two weeks later. The relief of seeing him get better, of slowly returning to his former self, was palpable, like the first breath of air after a deep-sea dive. Colour had returned to his cheeks, the blotchy patches of skin around his nose had healed and the dark circles under his eyes had lightened. The bandage around his head had been removed, revealing a light pink scar that had formed across the side of his shaved head to the tip of his left brow. While his frame was still weak, rib and chest bones exuding from their cavities like a prisoner of war's, he'd regained his appetite and was slowly putting on weight again. Amelia was beginning to think she could relax, that they were over the worst of it.

She entered his ward with a slight spring to her step, on her first day off in a month. She was hoping they could spend the day outside under a raintree, away from the prying eyes of others.

Daniel ran to the entrance to meet her. "I've got news!" he shouted, pulling her into his arms. Her body softened under his slight frame, but the moment was quickly snatched away when she noticed Daniel had stiffened. She followed his gaze, realising the other patients and nurses were watching them. He let go and walked towards the entrance. She could feel the eyes of the patients burning into the back of her head as she followed him.

"What's this big news you want to tell me?" Amelia asked.

Daniel glanced at the patients before looking back at Amelia. "They're letting me out. For the night. The doctor thinks some R & R will do me good."

Amelia bit her lip. "Are you sure? You're finally getting better, starting to look human again. Are you sure you have the energy for a night out?"

"You bet I do!"

"What if we just found a quiet spot outside—"

"I need this, Meels … need to get away from all of this." He gestured to the nurses and soldiers, and Amelia looked over her shoulder to see several people watching. She met the eyes of the patient next to them – an older bloke who had lost his leg – but he quickly looked away.

"What did you have in mind?" Amelia asked tentatively.

"I'm not sure. Where do *you* normally go?"

"Sometimes there's a film in the mess—"

"Didn't you hear me? I need to get away from here."

"There's the Officers' Club, near town?"

"Yes! Perfect. Let's go there. Is there dancing?"

"I believe so …"

He leaned back on his heels, with a jubilant smile, said, "Excellent. I heard you enjoyed dancing in Brisbane?"

"Who said that?"

"Tom. When we were in Buna."

Amelia rolled her eyes. "Of course he did. Tom didn't like that I would dance with anyone but him."

Daniel's dimples surfaced in a warm smile that melted Amelia's insides. "Well, get ready, Sister McKenzie, you're finally going to dance with that someone special."

Later that day, as they walked to the jeep Amelia had borrowed, she toyed with the thought that what they were doing wasn't smart. Daniel was still weak. Even if he was allowed out for the evening, she hardly believed the doctors were okay with him going out dancing. Plus Amelia had rules to follow, Matron Nelson's warning being cemented in her mind. But it'd been so long since she'd had fun, so long since Daniel had had a break, that she didn't want to be the one to spoil it. A night out wouldn't kill them, but they'd have to be careful. Except they were already facing their first roadblock: Tom, leaning against the door of the jeep with a cigarette pinched between his thumb and forefinger.

"Well, look at that," Tom said, the scorn in his voice as hot as the afternoon sun.

Amelia glanced at Daniel, who was a few steps behind – the distance he always kept when he walked with her – before turning back to Tom to say, "Tom. How are you? How's the leg?"

Tom ignored her. "Danny *boi* … all better, I see?"

Daniel stepped forward so he was in line with Amelia. "Your leg's alright then?"

Tom flicked his cigarette to the ground. "Just fine. And you? Alright after you got all those Kanakas killed?"

Amelia spun towards Daniel, feeling his body tense as he looked to the ground. She opened her mouth, ready to come to his defence, but Tom pressed on. "Shame Silas was one of them … I was starting to grow fond of him."

Amelia gasped. "Silas is dead?"

"Sure is," Tom replied, his casualness causing Amelia's skin to crawl. "Danny *boi* here got him shot when he tried to take down the Jap that attacked me."

Amelia's chest constricted; the hot afternoon air was hard to swallow. A sudden heaviness seized her limbs, the finality of Silas's death so sudden … so absolute. She'd held on to the thought that when this was over, when they were finally able to go home, things would go back to the way they were. But now that would never be possible. She would never see Silas again. Things would never be like they were.

Daniel's hand was shaking next to hers, and she imagined what it must feel like for him. What it was like to lose the person who'd been by his side this past year. Her grief was nothing compared to what he must be feeling.

"Thank you, Tom, for that callous delivery, but we were about to leave." She moved to push past him, but he grabbed her arm.

"So that's it?" he replied, digging his fingers into her flesh. "After everything we've been through?"

Amelia snatched her arm away. "What are you talking about?"

"Our time last year evacuating up the coast. Training together in Sydney. In Brisbane?"

"Tom, I saw you on a handful of occasions until you were kicked out of the RAAF for reckless behaviour. Why the Army would take you beats me, but I suppose they're after any man they can get."

He pleaded, ignoring her jab. "Jesus, Meels, can't you see? There's no future with him, not a real one. He can't offer you what I can."

Amelia's lips parted, the realisation dawning on her. Tom loved her. It all made sense now. His arrogance. His disdain for Daniel. It was all a front for the pain he felt inside. It can't have been easy for him to watch Daniel get everything that he had longed for. And it wasn't the first time it had happened. Harry had walked away from Tom and his mother, had chosen Daniel over him. Tom had been the one standing in Daniel's shadow all along.

She opened her mouth, ready to let him down easy, but Daniel cut her off.

"Let's go, Meels," he said, stepping towards the jeep. "He's not worth it."

Tom scoffed. "And you are? You're nothing but a Kanaka, and always will be, no matter how much you try to disguise it. Dad never loved you – he only took you in because he wanted to be the saviour, wanted to feel like he was needed. She's the same ..." Tom flicked his head towards Amelia, though his eyes never wavered from Daniel.

She stepped between them, fire radiating through her body now.

"How dare you," she spat. "Just because your father left you and your mother, doesn't mean he felt the same about Daniel. Harry loved him! As do I ..." Her eyes moved to Daniel, whose eyes were clouded in sadness. She held his gaze and said, "I love him more than you will ever have the benefit of knowing, because no one will ever love you like that. I'd rather any future with him than what I'd have to suffer with you!"

* * *

Daniel pressed on the accelerator, speeding through the hills that wrapped Moresby in a rolling encampment of dirt and dust. Amelia gripped onto her seat, the deep ravine that hung off the side of the road causing her stomach to plunge. But he was driving in the wrong direction, and so she asked, "I thought we were going to the club?"

He forcefully shifted gears as they turned around a bend, and they drove in silence but for the roar of Rouna River alongside them. Eventually Daniel turned towards the entrance of a camp. He slipped through the gates after speaking to the guard in Motu, and parked the jeep at the back.

"Where are we?" Amelia asked as she stepped out and took in their surrounds. Like the hospital, the camp was encased in lush rainforest and boggy hills. Rows of tents were scattered about. But Daniel didn't reply; he marched towards a hill, giving her no choice but to follow. He led her through a dark forest of mossy trees with roots so deep they were woven into the ground like a web, until he finally stopped on a small circular enclosure of grass that overlooked the camp.

She lifted her hand to her forehead and squinted through the glaring sun that was dipping down towards the harbour. "Is this the PIB camp?" she asked. But he didn't reply, and when she looked in his direction, she realised he was crying.

Her arms were around him immediately, his cheeks wet against her chest. There had been so much he'd been holding in. Silas's death. The role Daniel had played in it. She was surprised he'd lasted this long without saying anything. Then again, Daniel had never been good with words. But she suspected there was more to it, that Tom may have hit a nerve. Even though it seemed that Daniel's father had loved him, Amelia wondered if it'd been an enduring love, or something manifested from Harry's sense of duty, his need to be seen to do the right thing. Had Daniel felt this all along? Was that why he was so unsure of his place in the world? He'd had his father's love, but was it the right kind of love, a love that would give him legs to stand on? While Amelia struggled with always being controlled by her parents, she knew their behaviour came from the right place. It was her father's love that allowed Amelia to be so forthright with her own convictions. Without it, she never would've become so sure of what she wanted. But now she could see that maybe it wasn't the same for Daniel.

She held him tighter, hoping he knew that Tom had been wrong about one thing. Her love for Daniel was absolute.

When enough time had passed, the sun descending a little further in the sky, Daniel pulled away and wiped his cheeks. "Sorry," he said, not meeting her eye.

Amelia reached for his hand. "Please … don't ever feel you have to say that, not after what you've been through."

He looked at their hands and nodded. "Do you want to know? What I've been through?" he asked, voice barely above a whisper.

She squeezed his hand, giving him the courage to go on. He told her everything – the words spilling out so fast she could see the tension releasing, like a bird taking flight. He talked about how he'd risen through the ranks, working to unite the men until he was promoted to sergeant. He spoke of how rewarding those months were, how he'd finally had a sense of purpose, a place. He'd been united with the Aussies under a joint cause and, for the first time in his life, felt as if the colour of his skin didn't matter. Until it did. Until he had an altercation with an American who pushed him too far, forcing him back down, his sense of purpose lost. And then the reappearance of Tom, and a surge of hope that things would be different, and the sad realisation that they weren't, that they'd never be. And how it all came crashing down – the encounter with the Japanese in the village, the betrayal by the Papuan chief and the doubt about whether he made the right choice in killing him in return, the loss of Silas, his reckless behaviour that had cost the lives of the men in his unit, his sickness that had spiralled into a manifestation of his own sadness. And now he was here, trying to crawl his way out of it, of that anger that still churned inside.

Amelia felt her own unexpected release of tension as she finally learned what he'd been through. She'd never understand the toll it'd taken, but at least she could help him weather some of his burdens, be the ground he needed, the stability that would enable him to move forward. She stroked his cheek, wiping away a tear as she soaked in the fine lines that etched his eyes, the lines she'd been so eager to see this past year. He swallowed as he finally met her gaze with a desperate look.

Before she could think, her lips were on his, quenching her thirst with the taste she'd been aching for. He responded with the same intensity, his hands cupping her cheeks, as he pressed his tongue inside. His face scratched her chin, and the sensation filled her with a sense of nostalgia of their first kiss, so long ago. She longed for everything that could've been – everything the war had stolen. They sank down and wrapped their legs around each other as he ran his fingers along her neck, tracing a line down the centre of her spine. She shivered and coursed her fingers through his hair, the soft strands cut short to military length, another reminder of everything lost. She grabbed his hand and pushed it inside her blouse, arching her back as he squeezed her breast. He brushed her nipple, flicking it with his finger as if he'd done it thousand times before. She kissed him harder, biting down on his lip. She'd waited so long for this, never imagining it would truly happen again. She needed him, like she needed air. All of him, right then and there. And she knew he felt the same, his groin hard against her thigh.

Sometime later, when they were all out of breath, the desperation released from their bodies, she rolled onto the grass and stared up at the cloudy sky. He pressed the back of her hand to his lips and held it there. It'd been worth the wait, and would always be worth it, as long as they remained willing.

* * *

Amelia emerged from the forest, body light, filled with warmth and love. She and Daniel would be okay. She knew it now, had to hold on to this feeling, remember it whenever things got tough. They walked hand in hand through the quiet camp, no words spoken as they savoured the simplicity of being able to touch each other without the prying eyes of others. As they approached the mess, Daniel tried to let go, but she held on tighter, not letting anyone take this away.

The mess was teeming with shirtless Papuan men, chests glistening with sweat, faces expressionless, hard like their bodies. They were gathered around a large fire and stood as Daniel approached, their faces softening as soon as they saw him. He dropped Amelia's hand as the men swooped him up in bear hugs, surrounding him with warmth and love. They enquired in Motu about his whereabouts, the tok tok they'd heard about his time in the jungle. These were the men Daniel had served with, the ones who loved him. When all the welcomes were done, Daniel looked to Amelia, who held his gaze with teary eyes.

"This is Amelia," Daniel said, with his shoulders pulled back. Their faces flickered with recognition before they looked down and nodded at her – the usual greeting a Papuan or Niuginian man would offer to a white woman.

"I'll have none of that," Amelia chimed in, making sure she met each of the men's eyes as she pulled them into a hug. They all stiffened under her embrace, but her smile never wavered, though tears rolled down her cheeks. When Amelia was done, they looked to each other, slightly alarmed, but Amelia wiped her cheeks and laughed.

"Mi lukim yu wantaim wantok … wantaim brata. You are my friends, my brothers," she repeated in English, unsure if they'd understand Pidgin.

Daniel wrapped his arm around her as they sat by the fire. He kissed her cheek and she rested her head on his shoulder. She inhaled, the smell of smoke and cloves lingering, while beyond the fire a group of dancers had emerged, signalling the start of the sing-sings. The kundu drum began to beat – a low drubbing sound mixed with the high-pitched chants of the dancers. Bodies of oiled men bounced around, their hips gyrating as their feet stomped in time to the measured beat. On top of their heads sat feathered headdresses, and their faces were painted with colour that was rubbed deep into their beards. Their eyes were lit up like the rising moon, the expression of their dance a glimpse into their warrior past. Amelia watched the mesmerising act, the rich history and culture that was laid out before her, the reflection of their souls enchanting hers.

# 40

# Daniel

Daniel loosened his tie as they walked up the dusty path towards the Allied Officers' Club, a sense of dread gnawing at his gut.

"Are you sure you want to do this?" Amelia asked, brushing his fingertips with hers.

He cleared his throat. "Of course." But he wasn't so sure. They'd enjoyed a wonderful afternoon, finally finding each other again, and he didn't want to ruin that. But this was their reality, their world, and he had to find a place within it. He glanced at a family of Papuans resting under a tree – a man dressed in a lap-lap, a naked small child at his side. Standing behind them was the mother, bare-breasted with a grass skirt around her waist. Across her forehead, cutting through the fuzzy curls of her black hair, was a bilum – a bag woven out of string – that was holding a sleeping baby. His insides warmed at the thought of one day having a baby with Amelia, until he was met by a long frowning stare of incomprehension from the mother.

He averted his gaze and picked up the pace until they approached the club – a large hut built on stilts that sat over the pale-blue waters of Ela Beach. Potted plants lined the front windows that opened to a large verandah. Loud jazz music and the smell of sweat floated outside to mingle with the scent of the sea. Through the windows Daniel saw Papuans dressed in coloured lap-laps, with red hibiscus in their hair, waiting on the tables of loud American men. There was a line-up to get in, hordes of uniformed men swarming the entrance. Several of them stared at Daniel and Amelia.

"Do you think they'll ever accept us?" Daniel asked, as they hovered at the back of the line.

"Who do you mean by 'they'?" Amelia replied slowly.

"Papuans. Niuginians. Australians … everyone, really. Do you think we'll ever be okay in their eyes?"

Amelia turned to look at him. "Does it matter?"

"Yes … no. I don't know. It'd certainly make things easier."

The doorman stopped them when they got to the entrance.

"No natives," he said in a whiny American accent. He looked behind them and gestured for the next pair of men to go in. They immediately pushed past, shoving into Daniel's shoulder and causing him to lose his balance. Amelia reached out to steady him, but he shrugged her off.

Amelia shifted on her feet, looking between Daniel and the doorman. She cleared her throat and said, "He's Scottish and a loyal member of our Allied army, as am I. We have every right to be here."

Daniel stiffened next to Amelia as the doorman repeated, "No. Natives."

"He's not—"

"Meels, leave it," Daniel interrupted and pulled her away.

"But it's not right," Amelia replied and scowled at the doorman.

Daniel came to a stop some distance away from the club and dropped her hand. "Not like we can change it."

"We can try …"

He shook his head and buried his face into his hands, before letting out a loud groan, looking up at her again. "Can we? Really? Can we actually do anything that's going to make a goddamn difference!"

She flinched. "Sure, we can. We can fight back, make them see that they're wrong."

"And what is it that they're wrong about?"

"Well for one … that you're not a native."

"But I am."

"Yes … but you're also Scottish."

He threw his hands up in the air. "You love to point out the fact that I'm

Scottish."

Amelia crossed her arms. "Well, you are—"

"I've never even been to Scotland! I know nothing about the place. This"—he stamped his foot and pointed to the ground—"is my home. I'm Niuginian ... I'm a native!"

"Sure ... but you're more than that, and people should know it."

"Do I need to be? If I wasn't half white, would you still love me?"

"Of ... of course I would." Her voice was shaky. "I'll always love you, regardless of where you're from. Haven't I proved that?" She grabbed his hand, but he pulled away.

He paced up and down the path. "And yet you continue to let the colour of my skin define us. That's what it's always about with you. Colour! You go out of your way to make sure people know it's okay to be with me. You constantly challenge their beliefs, point out their prejudices—"

"So what? I'm standing up for you ... for what I believe in!"

"While knocking me over in your wake? You think I want to always be reminded that I'm different, that us being together is something to be baulked at? I live with it every day, am reminded of it all the time. I don't need it from you too."

Her mouth fell open, but nothing came out. She kicked the dirt, shoulders slumping as she refused to meet Daniel's eye. "Look ... I get it—"

"You don't get shit!" he roared. "You have no idea what it's like; you're not one of us!"

"Don't you dare!" She stepped forward and pointed a finger in his face. "I know exactly what it's like to be treated as inferior, to have to play second fiddle, to watch as men be given precedence, all because I'm a woman and deemed unfit! So, don't give me that, because I deal it with every day!"

# 41

# Amelia

Amelia stormed inside the club, heart pounding. She brushed past the men with a confidence she didn't normally possess and tried to order a gin and tonic from the Papuan behind the bar. She huffed when he told her they didn't serve alcohol. She turned towards the open verandah and saw Evelyn sitting in the corner by herself, foot tapping to the beat of the music.

"What are you doing here?" she asked, after she'd marched through the throngs of men who'd tried to pull her onto the dance floor.

Evelyn glanced up, then turned her attention back to the band. "Listening to music, of course."

Amelia sat in the chair next to her. "But you never go out. You don't even go to the mess, apart from mealtimes …"

Evelyn didn't reply, taking a sip of her drink instead, the condensation from her glass leaving a ring of water on the white tablecloth.

"Evelyn?"

She placed her glass on the table and turned towards Amelia. "Fine. I came to chaperone you and Daniel. The other nurses heard you talking—"

"Of course they did," Amelia muttered.

Evelyn looked around her. "Where *is* Daniel?"

Amelia stared out to the bay, watching as the full glow of the yellow moon rose from the horizon. "We got into a fight."

"About what?"

Amelia held her gaze on the rising moon, its incandescence, before shifting her eyes to meet Evelyn's. "What else?"

"Surely you two have moved past that by now?"

"We had. Or at least I thought we had. We were at the PIB barracks before, where I met all the soldiers he served with. We watched these sing-sings, and for a moment I thought everything would be okay, that we'd be able to make it work. But as soon as we got back here, it all came to surface again."

"Then why come back?"

"What choice do I have?"

"I mean when this is all over ..." Evelyn looked around the room, forcing Amelia to follow her gaze. An air of superiority clung to the men – the relaxed, jovial nature of the officers, the way they barely acknowledged the Papuans who served them, laughing and dancing as if there wasn't a war happening right outside. "Why stay in this world?"

Amelia chewed her lip. "It's all I know?"

"You said it yourself ... what an incredible time you had when you were at the PIB barracks? So then, why not, when this is all over, think about living here, with Daniel, on his terms?"

"How? Who would even give him a job? If it wasn't for Dad—"

"Listen to yourself, Amelia," Evelyn interrupted, voice harsh. "Daniel is smart. He doesn't need our parents' charity to see him through life."

Amelia pulled at her collar, suddenly hot even though a breeze blew through the windows. For so long she'd been fighting to get back to New Guinea, back to Daniel and the place she loved. But was it worth it? Daniel, yes, but the home she once knew wasn't something to be proud of. She'd loved her life in Salamaua, the sense of adventure it had instilled in her, but if it wasn't going to be the sort of place that was accepting, inclusive and kind, then was it really somewhere she wanted to be? She'd never cared for the rules that governed her mother, the society of women so busy with impressing one another that they lost all sense of empathy. Was that why she always felt the need to point out Daniel's heritage? To make these people see there was more to him than his skin colour? She hadn't realised she'd been doing it, but she could see now how belittling it was. Daniel was right. She didn't know what it was like. Daniel was a local. He was a Niuginian. That was more than enough.

# 42

## Daniel

Daniel kicked the jeep's tyre with the toe of his boot. He was tired of being angry, but didn't know how to quell the anger that festered inside. It wasn't fair to hold the world's prejudices against Amelia. She was only trying to help; even if she couldn't see her own bias, her intention was there. And yet, still, he couldn't let it go.

An image of Silas flashed through his mind. Always able to see the good in people when others couldn't. To rise above the hate and let it go. Daniel didn't know how he did it. Maybe because he saw the ways Papuans and Niuginians could also be prejudiced, with century-old tribal warfare coursing through their blood. And while it may not have been about the colour of their skin, they were still blinded by their differences in language and culture. Prejudices were everywhere.

Amelia emerged from the club, a sullen look she usually reserved for her mother across her face. He'd waited so long for this, and now here he was stuffing it up. She stopped at the bonnet and shifted on her feet.

"I'm sorry," she said. "You're right. I make too much of your Scottish heritage. And I don't know what it's like, not the way you do. I shouldn't pretend that I do. Being a woman has its frustrations, but I'll never know what it's like to be looked at differently because of the colour of my skin."

"Meels," Evelyn interrupted, her gaze on the sky.

Daniel hadn't noticed Evelyn. She hated these sorts of things and he wondered what she was doing there.

But Amelia ignored her, pressing on. "We're the same in many other ways—"

"You're wrong," Daniel said, the realisation of why Evelyn was there dawning on him. She'd been sent, by someone else – someone who didn't approve. They'd always be watching. Always be judging. He'd never be able to escape. "We've never been the same, Meels."

"But—"

"But nothing! We're not the same!" He grabbed her arm and held it against his own, the pale skin of her freckly forearm much fairer against his own. "You'll always be white and I'll always be black ... or ... or a version of black, whatever I am. But either way, it'll never be acceptable. It's as simple as that."

"It doesn't have to be."

"But it is! You have no idea what it's like"—his voice hitched—"and even though you try to understand me, you're still one of them."

"No, I'm not. I'm not like them, Daniel. Never have been."

He looked down, torn between love and anger. "I don't know what you want me to say."

The silence between them lingered, the roar of the Officers' Club much louder without any words to drown it out, until Amelia finally said, "Is that why you didn't write to me? Because you didn't think we should be together?"

He looked up to see her eyes clouded in tears, and his heart shrank.

"I turned myself inside out trying to find out what happened to you," she said. "It killed me not knowing whether you were dead or alive. I didn't deserve that! No matter how we left things, I deserved to know you were okay."

"I didn't write to you because it was easier that way."

"Easier?"

"Yeah, easier. Remember what you said to me after we left Salamaua?"

"I was wrong. I shouldn't have let my father get in my head, shouldn't have cared what everyone thinks."

He baulked. "Do you really think your parents won't get in your head again? Won't do whatever it takes to stop us being together?"

"I don't care what my parents think!"

"That's the difference between us. I do. I want to be accepted for who I am, and I'll never have that with your family."

"You're willing to give up on us because my parents won't accept you?"

He looked away, refusing to let his own tears escape. He couldn't believe he was doing this again, and yet he couldn't stop himself.

Amelia rushed forward and grabbed his hand. "We don't need them! Evelyn has helped me to see that we can live on our own terms, away from the confines of society, of everyone else. Right, Ev? Evelyn! Tell him! Tell him what we spoke about!"

Amelia searched for Evelyn, who was standing a few feet away, eyes glued on the full moon, not moving, not speaking. An eerie silence fell between them, as if the world had been swallowed, until Evelyn's voice rang through the night.

"We have to go. Now! The Japs are coming!"

# 43

# Amelia

The loud chattering of bombers swooped through the harbour and triggered the scream of the red alert. Amelia froze and stared at the clouded sky, wondering how many planes were up there, how many were coming for them this time.

But Daniel's voice was calling in the distance. "Come on!" he yelled through all the noise. He pushed her inside the jeep, before racing around to the driver's seat and revving the engine to life. Dust engulfed them as he veered onto the road, pushing through the officers who were scrambling out of the club.

*Where's Evelyn?*

Amelia whipped her head around. She exhaled when she discovered her sister sitting in the back. Evelyn leaned forward between the seats. "We … we need to get back to the hospital. There'll be casualties," she said, voice quick.

The taste of bile lurched up Amelia's throat. *How many people have to die?* But she didn't have time to dwell – a high-pitched whistle, followed by the whomp! whomp! of bombs exploding assaulted her ears. Large circles of water whooshed out of the bay, the salty spray of the ocean raining down, a torrent of water washing over them as more and more bombs fell, huge explosions of fire lighting the night. She gripped the seat as Daniel navigated through the chaos, his grip firm against the gear stick. She placed her hand on top of his, the shake in her hand easing as he wove his fingers around hers. Then came the rattle of the ack-acks, and relief flooded her as the anti-aircraft guns fired back at the Japanese bombers. Amelia looked to the sky and squealed. The Allied Bostons and Beaufighters had begun pursuit.

The planes were weaving in and out of the clouds, the moon lighting their way as they chased down the Japanese bombers. She imagined being up there – how exhilarating it'd be – then an explosion lit up the sky and one of the Bostons came spiralling down. A scream surged from her lungs ... another life lost. The other planes continued their chase, Amelia's heart racing as she watched the intricate race, the way the pilots carved through the clouds, tumbling and looping to avoid being hit.

One of the Japanese bombers swooped into the bay, and the crack of bullets thudded around them. Dirt sprayed up, pebbles clinking against the windscreen while the stink of cordite swirled in the air. Daniel swerved off the road, propelling them through an empty field while Amelia cowered and covered her head with her arms. She wanted to crawl inside herself and disappear, like a turtle ... until a hand rested on her back, beckoning her out of her shell.

"It's alright," Evelyn said as she pulled Amelia up. "They're ... they're gone." But Amelia heard the wobble in Evelyn's voice, the uncertainty that laced each word. And yet Evelyn was still that pillar of comfort. She reached behind for Evelyn's hand and gripped it fiercely, trying to be supportive in return.

Amelia steadied her breath as the jeep bounced along the dark field, refusing to let go of Evelyn. She looked at Daniel, trying to make out his profile – the tight square line of his jaw, the stubble that shadowed his still-gaunt cheeks. Would she ever see those dimples again? She was so tired of fighting, so tired of it all. But this was only the beginning. They had to keep trying, had to be willing.

Letting go of Evelyn, she reached for his hand again – when a *THUD!* shook the earth so forcefully that she was catapulted forward, and her grip on Daniel, on Evelyn, on everything she knew, was ripped apart.

# 44

# Daniel

Daniel's ears rang as the taste of dirt penetrated his mouth. He couldn't move and wondered if he was dead. But his head was pounding like a kundu drum, a dull reminder he was alive. He pushed himself up and sputtered through the blinding smoke, searching frantically for Amelia and Evelyn – when he fell upon her, a limp body devoid of life. His Amelia ... gone.

He screamed her name, pulling her to his chest, willing her to come back to him, that last conversation on repeat in his head. He'd been such a fool, yet again stymied by his own lack of self-belief. She loved him. He loved her. That was all that mattered. His throat burned as the tears poured down his cheeks, body rocking back and forth as he held her tightly.

"I'm sorry," he said, chest hiccupping. "I'm so, so sorry. I didn't mean it."

She lay perfectly still.

"Please," he whispered, stroking the soft strands of hair that'd been tangled with dirt. "Please, don't go. Not again. Please don't leave me."

No breath escaped her lungs.

"I'll do better. I'll try harder. I won't get so angry. I promise. We'll find a way, our own way. We'll make it work. No matter what."

Nothing, except the beating of Daniel's own broken heart, until ... Amelia's chest hitched into a cough.

She was alive.

He held her tightly, tears flowing.

She blinked, eyes clouded as if she was in a dream – and then she looked at her hand. She stared at it blankly, as if it shouldn't be there, as if something was missing. She pushed Daniel away, shot up, whipping her head around, searching ahead and then behind, skimming the field, knees buckling, forcing her back to the ground. But she wouldn't give up, she crawled through the grass, desperately searching for something ... someone. Daniel followed her, relief and fear surging through his head, when Amelia stopped and stared at what was left of the jeep.

She screamed. Evelyn's name rang through the night.

The Japanese were gone, but the remnants of the devastation they'd caused were captured in Amelia's cries of sorrow, the agony of her loss piercing Daniel's heart. Evelyn was dead.

# 45

# Amelia

The blinding overhead fluorescent lights pierced Amelia's pupils and a persistent beeping noise prickled her ears. Her mouth was dry, sticky with a faint taste of phlegm that was threatening to expel itself at any moment. She tried to push herself up, but it seemed as if her body was glued to the bed, all her strength gone. Her head spun. Where was she? The astringent smell of disinfectant and the sight of her mother sleeping in the corner confirmed her suspicion. She was in hospital. In Australia. Except she couldn't remember how she got there.

She looked to her mother, searching for answers. She'd aged considerably in the year since Amelia had seen her last, with deep creases etched around her mouth and her skin pale and leathery. Amelia opened her mouth to call out to her, but nothing surfaced. And that's when it came back to her – the fight with Daniel, the air raid, the bombs ... Evelyn.

She swallowed, the searing pain like glass scraping her throat. Her sister was dead. A bomb had hit them and ripped the back of the jeep from its front, propelling Daniel and Amelia forward as it devoured Evelyn in its wake. That final moment with Daniel – the way he'd cradled her when he discovered she was alive, and the overwhelming relief that flooded her body in return. A moment of hope up until she realised who was missing, then the desperation that seized control as they searched for Evelyn in the wreckage, and the tremor that shook her body when they found her. The earth had been split open, sweeping away everything she loved. Daniel had tried to calm her, to hold her again, but the shock was so disorientating that she must've fallen into a state of unconsciousness, her evacuation to Australia wiped from her memory.

It was her fault – Evelyn had been there to chaperone Amelia and Daniel. If they hadn't gone out, hadn't put *their* needs first, then Evelyn would still be alive. It was all for nothing anyway, she thought, as that last conversation with Daniel came back. And now she was in Australia with no hope of making things right. She closed her eyes, the sadness so consuming she'd prefer to fade away. Her sweet sister would be nothing more than a memory now … a memory that rested in the hollowness of Amelia's chest. The realisation was too painful too fathom, the emptiness so encumbering that she forced herself back into a blissful state of unconsciousness where no memories could exist.

* * *

"Amelia," her mother said. Amelia opened her eyes and stared blankly. Her mother was hovering next to her bedside. "How … how do you feel?" she added, a slight wobble to her voice.

Amelia exhaled. It hurt to breath. "Water," she managed to say in a voice she hardly recognised.

Her mother took a cup from the bedside table and pressed the straw to Amelia's mouth. She savoured the simple pleasure of cool liquid coursing down her throat – something Evelyn would never do again. Something Amelia wished she didn't have to either. If she were lucky, whatever had put her in the hospital would become fatal, except she wasn't sure if her parents could weather the loss of two children. But why should she have to live her life for them? That was one of the last things Evelyn had said to her; their last conversation was seared into her mind.

Amelia's chin trembled, the thought of putting Evelyn's death into words too irrevocable, too final.

"It's okay," her mother whispered. "She's in a better place."

Amelia looked at the ceiling, her throat burning. She hated when people said that. How did they know where Evelyn was, where she'd gone to, and if it was any better than here? She met her mother's gaze. "Is she?"

Her mother looked away, her own sadness threatening to spill over. Amelia told herself to be nice, and lifted her fingertips in search of her mother's hand. She flinched under Amelia's touch. Even grief couldn't soften her heart.

* * *

"Hello, lass," her father said. She turned to see him entering the room, holding a bouquet of daisies, face beaming in a warm smile. He laid the flowers on the bedside table and kissed her forehead. "How're you feeling today?"

"The same," she said in soft voice, still finding it hard to find the words to shake off her shock.

He took a seat on the edge of her bed. "You'll be better in no time, even back flying if you want." Amelia didn't reply, staring at her father's face instead. He'd made a decent recovery after his evacuation last year; his cheeks were rosy and plump under his speckled beard, while his eyes were no longer shadowed, though she could see a freshly formed sadness resting behind.

"Thought you'd like to know I received a letter from Daniel," he added. Amelia's stomach rolled, a wave of nausea rising. "I think he wanted to explain what happened, how things came to pass."

She looked away. "I told you what happened," she forced herself to say.

"Aye. But he wanted to offer his own explanation ... how he forced you out that night, insisted on going to the Officers' Club, how you two got into a blue ..."

Her chest tightened.

"He says he's at the PIB camp. Waiting to be deployed back to the front for their next campaign." A fresh surge of nausea surfaced at the thought of Daniel going back to the front. "He also wrote a letter for you." Her father handed her an envelope, still sealed. "Go on. Read it."

Amelia swallowed. "Since when have you become so supportive of Daniel? He told me the things you said to him on the Black Cat."

He took off his glasses and wiped the lenses. "Why do you think Silas was in the PIB with Daniel, when he should've gone back to his village like the rest of the Kanakas?"

Amelia flinched. "Do you have to use that word?"

"What word?"

"Kanaka."

He waved her away. "That's what they are. As I was saying, Silas joined the PIB because I asked him to ... so he could look after Daniel."

"But ... but you never said—"

"I didn't need to. It wasn't your concern."

"Don't you think I would've liked to know?" Amelia pushed herself further up the bed, a sudden heat radiating through her body. "You sending Silas actually shows that you care, that Daniel means something to you!"

"Daniel does mean something to me. He's my best mate's son, and regardless of where or who he was born to, that means something." He cleared his throat, taking his time, before adding, "But I didn't want to encourage you. A relationship with Daniel is not what we had planned."

Amelia threw her hands up. "See—"

"Let me finish, lass," he said in a firm voice. He inhaled as if to cool the fire that burned inside. "Your mother and I can't help the way we feel. It's how we were raised and what we know. Living in New Guinea has opened my eyes to a lot of things, and I like to think I've been more tolerant over the years because of it, even more so after this war, after losing—" his voice hitched, causing Amelia's own throat to burn.

"I know I can't stop you from doing what you want to do," he continued. "I could see *that* when you were a wee lass, when you insisted on learning everything you could about my planes, and later on demanded that I teach to you fly." He smiled even though his eyes were wet. He wiped them with a finger before reaching for Amelia's hand. "And I know I can't stop you from loving Daniel. Not without the risk of losing you forever, and you can be certain I won't be able to bear the loss of another daughter."

Amelia's chin trembled. She didn't know whether to laugh or cry, both relief and trepidation coursing through her veins. She decided to laugh, the absurdity of the situation so bewildering that when her father reached forward and wrapped his arms around her, she didn't protest. The tears spilled out as she buried her face into his chest, inhaling the familiar scent of her childhood. She was overwhelmed by the fact that the only reason she had her father's approval was that Evelyn was dead. It took losing Evelyn for her to win Daniel. And yet she was unnerved that her father was still openly prejudiced and justifying it by blaming the way he was raised. Would it really be fair to Daniel to have to spend his life tolerating that?

* * *

"Absolutely not," Amelia heard her mother say outside of her hospital room. She leaned forward, ears prickling. "There is no chance in hell that I'll allow my daughter to marry a native!"

Amelia stiffened. *Marry?* Had Daniel said something about marriage in his letter to her father?

"Goddammit, Ruth," her father replied, the words clipped. "You must understand the consequences of not allowing Amelia to follow her own path. You know how wilful she is, how determined she'll be to be with him! We must allow it or risk losing her for good!"

"Then so be it!"

"You're a stubborn old lass and I won't have it," he yelled, causing Amelia to snicker through her sadness.

"And I won't have my daughter tarnishing our family name!"

"Oh, Christ, woman! What do I care about my name? I live as far away from my birthplace as possible—"

"What would people think?"

Amelia could imagine her mother's expression, the way she would be raising her hand to her chest.

"You need to stop caring so much about what people think ..."

But Amelia was interrupted by the arrival of Sofia, her younger sister looking as glamorous as ever in a green-and-yellow tartan utility dress and wide-brimmed straw hat. She took one look at Amelia and threw herself at her.

"Oh, Meels," she managed to say between sobs. "I'm so happy you're alive."

Amelia stiffened; affection from Sofia was unusual. She hesitantly patted her back in return and managed to say, "It should be Evelyn."

Sofia offered a small smile, as if she agreed. "Did you hear Mum and Dad out there?" she asked.

Amelia stared out the window. "Mum hasn't changed."

"Hmm … well, never mind," Sofia replied nonchalantly. "It's not like you can get back to New Guinea anyway. Who knows when this war will end? Might as well get on with life down here." Amelia turned back and watched how casually Sofia spoke. She pressed a hand to Amelia's arm as her eyes expanded. "Do you know how many eligible men are floating around Sydney? American men, no less! You'd pick one up in no time. I've got three on the go at the moment, trying to decide which one I want. It really has to do with where I'd prefer to live in the States. I always saw myself somewhere like New York or San Fran, but I think I'd be better suited to the country—"

"Do you ever shut up?" Amelia cut her off.

Sofia jerked her head back. "Don't be so rude! I'm trying to tell you about my life—"

"Well, to be honest, Sofia, I don't care," Amelia replied, matching Sofia's earlier casual tone. She pinched the bridge of her nose, and added, "I'm tired, my head is killing me and I'm trying to deal with the fact that I'm stuck in a family that is so far up its own arse, I don't think they'll ever make it out."

"Then leave!" Sofia shouted. "Go! Back to New Guinea or wherever the hell makes you happy. We don't want you!" She stormed out of the room, heels clicking on lino floors the last thing Amelia heard.

"Gladly," she whispered, wondering how she could make that happen.

* * *

She stared at the letter, the compulsion to open it hard to resist. Her hands shook as she tore the seal.

March 31, 1943

Dearest Amelia,

Where do I start? Perhaps sorry is a good place. I'm sorry for everything that has come to pass. I'm sorry for letting you walk away from me at Salamaua. I'm sorry for not writing to you, for not letting you know I was okay. I'm sorry for being so angry that night. And I'm truly sorry for what happened to Evelyn. It was my fault we were there, my fault we were arguing. I can't imagine how you must be feeling. I keep thinking of what you would feel if it was me who died. Heartache? Sorrow? Relief? Disappointment?

I'm disappointed in myself for not fighting for us, for letting you go so easily, for not ensuring that at the very least, you know how much I love you. I don't know why I didn't fight harder for our love when I'm so willing to fight in this war. Perhaps I only have so much fight in me, and I must fight for my place before I can fight for anything else. But I realise now that you are the only thing worth fighting for, and that I can't give up whenever it gets hard. You know I'm no good with words, but I'm determined to change that. I promise to keep writing, to fight for our love.

All my love,

Daniel.

Amelia exhaled, tears splotching the paper. Daniel had always struggled with his place in the world, but she'd never understood the full toll it took on him. His putting it into words seemed to quantify the heartache. Her heart yearned for him. It wasn't fair. It wasn't fair of her, either, to pretend that colour didn't matter. It did matter. It would always matter to some, and while things might be shifting, it'd still be a long road until they were living in a more tolerant world. Could the two of them survive it? She'd told him so many times she was willing to try, but maybe words weren't enough. Did he need more from Amelia to help him trust that things would be different? A gesture, an act of faith? Evelyn had told her to go, to give up her former life. She thought of Tiger Lil, of how she always played by her own rules, and what she had to sacrifice to live the life she wanted. Could Amelia do the same?

Her body relaxed as she opened herself to the idea, mind slowing as if it was finally surfacing from the swarming seas.

But the shrill voice of her mother quickly stymied that. "Amelia, dear ..."

Amelia sighed.

"The doctor thinks you'll be ready to come home soon," her mother said. "He thinks a few more weeks of bed rest and you'll be right. Your room's all ready, and I've organised a tea with the New Guinea Club ladies next week at home. A little something to slowly introduce you back into society—"

"No."

"We can pencil tea in for next month, though I do believe Lady McNicoll will be away then, and I really did want you to speak with her—"

"I won't be speaking to anyone."

"Pardon?" Her mother pressed her lips together.

Amelia's muscles tightened as she readied herself for the fight. "I won't be going home with you."

Her mother felt her forehead. "The doctor's wrong. You're clearly not well."

"I'm perfectly fine, Mum. Or I will be once I figure things out."

"And what things are those?"

"How I'm going to live my life, free from all of you."

"Don't be ridiculous, Amelia. You've suffered a major injury, a major loss—" Her voice broke and she took a moment to steady it. "You need to be around family."

"Daniel's my family."

"Daniel's in New Guinea, about to be sent back to the front. Let's not waste our energy trying to change something we have no control over. Come home, and when things are better, when we're in a better position with the war, we can discuss it."

"No."

"Honestly, dear, you're not thinking straight. I'll suggest to the doctor you stay longer—"

Amelia sat up, heat flushing through her body. "I'm thinking perfectly clearly, Mother, and what I know is I want nothing more to do with you."

"Amelia!" her father's voice boomed, causing Amelia to tense. She glanced over her mother's shoulder to see him walking into the room. "Don't speak so callously to your mother."

The tension spread to Amelia's stomach as she considered what she was about to do. She loved her father, her mother too ... in a way. She loved several things about them – the sacrifices they'd made to build a life in New Guinea, their dedication to their children, their home, each other – but she could no longer pretend that their take on the world didn't matter, that their prejudices were okay.

She inhaled, looking to her mother first. "For too long I've sat back and watched as you look down on others, judging them based on preconceived notions on what you believe to be acceptable. And that might be 'what you know'"—she glanced at her father—"but it's up to you to change that, to evolve and grow, which you, Mum"—she flicked her eyes back at her mother—"clearly have no interest in doing. I'm done. I'm done pretending that it's okay. That the terrible things you say about black people, the terrible things we do as a society are okay – because they're *not* and never will be!"

"You have some nerve, lass!" her father spat out. "I've done a lot for New Guinea, for its people. Raised half of Morobe out of poverty, given them jobs and security, introduced them to a standard of living they'd never dreamed possible—"

"By paying them one tenth of what you'd pay a white man?" Amelia cut him off.

"That's economics!" he roared.

"George," her mother said, words clipped. "Let's all calm down. There's no use getting fired up when we're still grieving. We'll take some time and reassess—"

"Take all the time you need, Mum, but my decision is made." Her voice was even, the tension releasing. "When this war is over, when it's safe to return, I will be going back to New Guinea. Alone. I don't know what the future holds, but I'm willing to risk it all for him. On the chance of a life with the person I love. I'm sorry it has come to this, that I have to give up one for the other, that you have to lose another daughter"—she swallowed—"but you give me no choice."

"Meely, lass, I told you that we accept you being with Daniel. That it's okay."

Her mother opened her mouth, but her father shot her a look that told her to keep it shut.

"And what I'm telling you, Dad, is that I don't need – nor do I want – your approval. From here on out, I'm freeing myself of that burden." Amelia leaned against the bed, a sudden lightness taking hold.

"We can discuss it later," he said as he turned to leave, shoulders slumped. She watched him walk away.

"Goodbye, Dad." Her voice was quiet, barely above a whisper. She stared at the door for ages, knowing that would be the last time she'd see him.

"Amelia," her mother said, forcing Amelia to shift her gaze. Her lips were pursed and eyes hard. Amelia took it all in, the features she'd come to loathe over the years, trying to see through them. But her hardened nature was fixed in place … until, briefly, her mother reached out a trembling hand.

Amelia flinched, giving her mother enough time to regain her composure and pull away.

"Goodbye, dear," she said in such a way that Amelia knew they'd be the last words Amelia ever heard from her.

"Goodbye, Mum," she replied coolly, confident in her decision.

# Epilogue

*April 1946*

Amelia leaned against the rail of the ship, the salty air kissing her cheeks. The bow sliced through the calm waters of the Huon Gulf as the sun rose above the Rawlinson Range. A trickle of sweat dripped from her brow; she'd have to get used to the wet, sticky heat again. A pod of dolphins leapt out of the glassy sea. She laughed – a full body laugh that helped to settle her churning stomach – and hoped it was sign: how some things never lose their magic.

The towering peaks of the Herzog and Saruwaged ranges that lined the Markham Valley remained lush and verdant, exactly as they were when Amelia last saw them. She shuddered to think of Daniel climbing those ranges – some twelve thousand feet – when the Allies chased the Japanese out of Salamaua and Lae, before advancing further north to Finschhafen and Madang. He'd written about it over the past three years; his letters had arrived every week as promised. She wrote back, first informing him of the falling-out with her parents, then how she'd secured a position with the RAAF's air evacuation unit stationed at Morotai.

His latest letter had informed Amelia that he'd been discharged from the PIB, or the Pacific Islands Regiment as they were now called, and was returning to Lae. He wanted to start an airline and had bought a small plane with some gold he'd found when he was on the Lakekamu. When he asked if she'd consider coming back, Amelia did everything she could to seek approval from the Australian Government to return to New Guinea and had secured a passage on the *Ormiston* – the first ship carrying the civilians who'd been allowed back to the territories. She'd written to tell him of her arrival date, but there hadn't been time to wait for a reply. She didn't know if he'd be there to greet her when the ship docked. But it didn't matter; she was getting what she wanted after all these years, and while she didn't know what was ahead, she was determined to make a life back in New Guinea – her own life, on her own terms.

As the ship pulled into Voco Point, she leaned even further over the rail, joining the other women as they searched the faces of the men who were there to meet them. These men were mostly discharged Australian soldiers who had gone straight back to Lae after the war ended, straight back to the place they all held dear to their hearts. She'd been polite to the women on their journey up, several of them being former acquaintances of her mother, but left it at that, wary of falling back into old habits. The women burst into tears as they spotted their husbands, running into their arms as they disembarked. Amelia waited for the crowds to clear, for the husbands to sweep their wives and families away to what was left of their former lives, before she slowly stepped onto the gangway, single case in hand. She paused to look out across Voco Point, towards Lunaman Hill and beyond, at what was left of Lae.

The detritus of the Japanese occupation littered the foreshores, and further out, directly opposite the airstrip, the bow of a Japanese freighter rose out of the sea at an acute angle. On land, the Cecil Hotel, the houses that once sat beneath the hill and the family house she once called home had been swallowed by the sunken craters that were now scattered about, the buildings replaced with makeshift tents and marquees that'd serviced the Army. Lae was a dilapidated version of its former self, the ruins of war devastating. She'd heard the stories – and couldn't even imagine how she'd feel when she got to Salamaua, having been told the town had been flattened out of recognition – but to see it in real life, to witness the utter fall of her former world was shocking. Her old life really was gone.

Amelia suddenly felt faint. She steadied herself on the rail of the gangway, breathing in the warm air. The familiar scent of frangipani floated in the breeze. She smiled. Lae was still there. Underneath the rubble its natural beauty prevailed. Everything else could be rebuilt. She smoothed down the front of her khaki trousers, lifted her chin and walked the length of the jetty, heart accelerating.

She took a final look at the men who lingered, searching for a single face, that last remaining connection to her past, the familiarity she refused to give up. Her shoulders slumped and chest constricted when she couldn't find it – until, out of the corner of the eye, she saw a glimpse of the dimpled cheeks that'd stolen her heart, the boyish grin that'd forever be hers.

She'd finally made it home.

*Em Tasol*

# Author's Notes

When I set out to write this book, my intention was to create a story that celebrates Papua New Guinea. It is a uniquely beautiful and richly diverse country that I have come to call home, and a place that many Australians have a connection to. But as I delved into the research, I soon learned that PNG has a dark colonial past, a past that still lingers today. As the story began to take shape, I realised I couldn't do it justice without considering Australia's part in its history. That soon became the focus of the story, a story that I believe is worth knowing.

Language is significant. The words we choose to use can shape a narrative. Good or bad, they hold meaning. The derogatory language used throughout the book was commonplace in the 1930s and 40s. Many of the quotes said by George and Tom were taken from real speech from the time. I also wanted to highlight the behaviours towards Papuans and Niuginians at the time. Many of Tom, George and Ruth's behaviours were taken from real-life anecdotes I'd gathered in my research. It was shocking to learn that Australians and Europeans would rather hit the local carriers than give them clothes or blankets to keep them warm. I also wanted to note that whilst "pikinini" may be derogatory in other parts of the world, the word does not hold such meaning in PNG. Sensitivity readers encouraged me to use it.

Whilst most of my characters are fictional, there are a few real-life people who are worth noting. Kevin Parer was a pilot who lived in New Guinea during the 1930s. He was the cousin of the famous war-time photographer Damien Parer and brother to Ray Parer, a pioneer of aviation in New Guinea during the 1920s. He was the first Australian to be killed by the Japanese Imperial Army. Kevin flew many of the evacuation flights for the women and children in December 1941. It was on January 21, 1942, upon returning from an evacuation flight, that he landed at Salamaua. Japanese Zeros and Bettys arrived shortly after, and he was killed instantly by a cannon shell.

Ernie Clarke, the other pilot who was at Salamaua, tried to save Kevin and was shot by the Japanese. He was evacuated up the coast with the injured and sick men. The diaries of Robert Melrose, the district administrator who accompanied the men, indicated that Clarke's wounds had become infected, and he became very sick as they awaited uplift from Kokoda.

Tiger Lil was another real person who had made a bit of a name for herself in the Territory. Known as Lilian Barclay Millar, she was considered the uncrowned Queen of Salamaua, a strong, non-conformist woman known for being sexually liberated. According to Jan Roberts's book, *Voices from a Lost World,* she was the only white woman not invited to a tea party at Salamaua. And as I recreated in the opening chapter, she showed up anyway.

Amelia and Evelyn's trek up the Morobean coast was taken from the real-life accounts of the sick and injured men who were forced to evacuate from Salamaua after the town and aerodrome were destroyed. There was one woman left at Salamaua, Sister Esther Stockland, who accompanied and cared for the men. It was her role that inspired me to send Amelia and Evelyn on this quest. The twenty-eight able-bodied civilian men remaining at Salamaua were also forced to trek up the Black Cat to Wau, and inspired me to recreate this event through George and Daniel's trek.

Miss Mavis Parkinson and Sister May Hayman from Buna are real-life missionaries who remained in Buna after civilians were evacuated. The speech Miss Parkinson quotes from the Anglican Bishop Philip Strong was real and inspired many missionaries to remain in Papua and New Guinea.

The Orokaiva man, Ambogi, who Amelia speaks to as they are trekking to Kokoda was a real person, and the person responsible for betraying Miss Parkinson and Sister Hayman to the Japanese. The words he says to Amelia are what he actually said to Australian forces after the women were killed in late 1942.

Captain Alan Hooper led 'B' Coy (Company) of the Papuan Infantry Battalion, and was respected and admired by his men. His autobiography,

*Love War & Letters* provided a colourful insight into the PIB and the ways in which locals were treated during the war.

As with most historical fiction, I used my creative licence to ensure the story flowed logically. Most of the white women and children were evacuated from New Guinea in December 1941. It wasn't until a month later that the Japanese attacked Salamaua and Lae. For the purpose of pace and timing, I made these events happen concurrently. The coast watcher's house that Amelia and Daniel spent the night in wasn't built until March 1942, after a coast watcher had been assigned and the Japanese had invaded.

My research was extensive, but I'd like to acknowledge a few of my primary sources. Historian Hank Nelson's works were imperative to my understanding of colonial New Guinea, including his many journal articles and ABC radio series *Taim Bilong Masta*. Various books helped me understand the time and place better, such as *A Bastard of a Place* by Peter Brune, *Kokoda* by Peter FitzSimons, *Hell's Battlefield* by Phillip Bradley, *The Bulldog Track* by Peter Phelps, *Fear Drive My Feet* by Peter Ryan, *The New Guinea Volunteer Rifles* by Ian Downs, and *Voices from a Lost World* by Jan Roberts. The Australian War Memorial and Trove were also essential to understand the events that took place and the language used at the time.

Whilst I grew up in the Pacific, I am a white woman who has never experienced racism. It is because of my privilege that I have been able to write this book. I do have an understanding of what it's like not to belong, and it was through this knowledge, and other observations of living in PNG, that I felt I could write from Daniel's point of view. It was important the emotional impact of his struggle was conveyed, and a story like his was heard. I have engaged sensitivity readers from Papua New Guinea to ensure his voice was accurately portrayed; however, if I have unwittingly caused any offence, then I apologise.

# Acknowledgments

Thank you to my sensitivity readers, Theola, Ron, Tina and Lynne. Your insight of your people, cultures and languages have been essential in shaping this story. Thank you to my mentors Kathryn Heyman and Cathie Tasker for your expertise, as well as writers Kim Kelly, Michelle Hamadache, Sarah Clutton and June Yu Steward for reviewing the novel in advance, and Ann Antrobus for proofreading.

A big shout-out to my book club gals – Danielle, Tiff, Lynne, Carolyn, Helen, Renate, Isabel, Mikal, Belinda and Gemma. I love our get-togethers and thought-provoking debates. It was a historical novel we read in our early days that formed my love of the genre and inspired me to write. I hope you enjoy my book.

To all the self-published authors out there … I see you. Rejection isn't easy, but your stories matter and deserved to be read. Don't give up.

For my editor, Jane Smith. I loved working with you and learning from your insightful expertise. And thank you to Nada Backovic for designing a beautiful cover and being patient with my multiple changes.

Finally, thank you to my family. My mother for always encouraging me, and my late father for inspiring me to strive for a better world. Martina … you are the glue that holds our family together. My three beautiful kids for always keeping me on my toes … I love you more than you'll ever know, and my husband for always believing in me. Without you, I couldn't do any of this.

If you enjoyed *A Dangerous Land*, please leave a review. They make all the difference for self-published authors. And if you would like to keep up to date with my next book, *A Forgotten Land*, visit my website www.marisajonesbooks.com.

# About the Author

Born and raised in Hawaii, with her late teens and twenties spent in Australia, Marisa loves travelling and can often be found wandering the edges of the globe. She currently lives between Lae, Papua New Guinea and Brisbane, Australia with her family. Marisa draws inspiration from the Pacific, bringing its varied cultures and history to life through words. Prior to fiction writing, she worked as a freelance writer for magazines such as *House & Garden, International Traveller, Yoga Journal, Aniko Press* and Air Niugini's inflight magazine, *Paradise*. She has a Master of Creative Writing from Macquarie University.

**You can connect with me on:**

- https://marisajonesbooks.com
- https://twitter.com/mkjoneswriter
- https://www.facebook.com/profile.php?id=100089492937466
- https://www.instagram.com/mkjoneswriter

Made in the USA
Columbia, SC
25 March 2024